She grabbed his arm to make the point she twisted it till the elbow must have strained. Then she pushed him on the nearest kitchen stool. 'Look, you're fitter and stronger than me. You could break me in half if you wanted to. But my timing's sharp. It has to be because I'm small. Now, think about what I said and see if my timing doesn't make sense in this job, too.' She turned and left the room, closing the door quietly behind her.

About the author

Judith Cutler was born and bred in the Midlands, and revels in using her birthplace, with its rich cultural life, as a background for her novels. After a long stint as an English lecturer at a run-down college of further education, Judith, a prize-winning short story writer, has taught Creative Writing at Birmingham University, has run occasional writing courses elsewhere (from a maximum security prison to an idyllic Greek island) and ministered to needy colleagues in her role as Secretary of the Crime Writers' Association.

JUDITH CUTLER

Hidden Power

NEW ENGLISH LIBRARY
Hodder & Stoughton

First published in Great Britain in 2002 by Hodder and Stoughton
A division of Hodder Headline

1 3 5 7 9 10 8 6 4 2

A CIP catalogue record for this title is available from the
British Library

ISBN 0 340 82069 1

Typeset in Plantin Light by Palimpsest Book Production Limited,
Polmont, Stirlingshire

Printed and bound in Great Britain by
Clays Ltd, St Ives plc

Hodder and Stoughton
A division of Hodder Headline
338 Euston Road
London NW1 3BH

To the memory of my dear friend, Edwina Van Boolen

Thanks, Keith Bassett, for your bottomless fund
of CID anecdotes.

I

'Congratulations on your promotion. You'll make a great inspector, Kate.' DI Sue Rowley beamed, shaking Kate's hand in an embarrassed official way.

Kate returned the shake: after all, she was still technically Detective Sergeant Kate Power and Sue was her line manager. But Sue wasn't usually that sort of manager.

Then Sue grinned more widely and threw her arms around her in a sisterly hug. 'And I'm sure it won't be long before they find a vacancy for you. In the meantime, congratulations, and welcome back to Steelhouse Lane.'

'Thanks. It's good to be back,' Kate said.

It was, in most respects. Colin Soper, her best mate, was already brewing tea back in the office. And she had this kind-hearted woman as her immediate boss. Perhaps the hug had been more motherly than sisterly. After all, Sue was in her mid-forties, and specialised, in her spare time, in urging her not always willing children through the educational system. Because she herself couldn't afford to let work haemorrhage into free time, she protected her team from overlong hours. The corollary was that they were expected to give maximum effort between eight and six.

'It's a pity that promotion means you'll have to leave CID and have a spell in uniform. You're a good detective. I'd have thought Fraud could have used you while Lizzie's off sick.'

Kate shook her head firmly. 'They need an experienced officer in charge there – I was never doing more than feeling my way.'

Sue collapsed into her chair, laughing. 'Don't you think that's what we all do? Every day of the week? Anyway, it's good to know that Lizzie's breast lump was benign. A little bird tells me she'd never have gone to the hospital if it hadn't been for you.' She pushed fingers through already disorganised hair, then smoothed it back. 'Funny time to have your attack of stress – when they've found there's nothing wrong with you.'

'Lizzie could have stressed for England, Sue. Lump or no lump. The worry about that just finished her off.'

Sue looked at her shrewdly. 'It's a lesson to us all: we need more than work in our lives. How's your tennis? Or have you packed up?' She looked sideways at the rain dashing against the window.

'They've got a couple of strategic buckets to catch drips from the roof: but the chief advantage of an indoor centre is that you can play even when there's snow on the ground. Which, for all it's only just September, there may well be if it gets any colder.'

'You know poor Graham Harvey's on his annual leave?'

Kate nodded. Fatima had mentioned it that morning, almost as casually as if she thought Kate would simply want to know about their DCI's whereabouts. True, Graham was their superior in the hierarchy. But everyone in the office suspected that Graham was more than just Kate's boss.

'He's clicked for a rotten couple of weeks, hasn't he?' Sue continued. 'Imagine, walking in the Lake District in weather like this.'

'Not my idea of pleasure,' Kate agreed. But she'd rather Graham were on a mountain getting soaked to the skin each day than sitting in the comparative comfort of his office just down the corridor. The only snag she could see in her return here was that they'd have to meet again, even work together, under the gaze of all those office eyes, and pretend that they were friends, not lovers.

Ex-lovers. Kate had delivered the coup de grace when she realised that their relationship was making Graham as unhappy as it was making her – if for different reasons. She had hated the futile waits by the phone, the furtive meetings, his glances at the clock even during the stolen moments in bed. He – well, he was a member of a particularly unforgiving Christian sect: his conscience was tormented by the knowledge that he was sinning, and a conviction that while God might forgive, the other members of the congregation certainly wouldn't. He'd talked vaguely about separating from his wife, and about starting divorce proceedings. But as far as she knew he was still living in his quiet house in the quiet suburb. Fragments of long-past A level English texts popped into her memory: who was it that was *living and partly living*? Who lived a life *of quiet desperation*? The answer to both was Graham. But she knew he could never break free, much as she would have liked to help him. She could have taken on Graham's wife, but didn't stand a chance against his version of God.

Meanwhile, let him walk in the rain and enjoy it so much he delayed his return. Perhaps he could even catch a chill, or sprain an ankle . . .

Sue was looking at her with a mixture of curiosity and compassion. 'It really is over between you two, isn't it?'

Kate nodded.

'And – well, you know you can't sneeze in this job without everyone knowing you've got flu – there's a bit of a rumour—'

'About me and Rod Neville. We're friends, Sue.'

'Close friends?'

'As it happens, yes. And there's no need to smile like that.'

Sue laughed. 'I don't need to when *you* smile like that! If you're not in love with him now, you—'

'Give me a break. He's a charming, attractive man, and I really enjoy his company, but – well, he's a superintendent, going far, I'd guess, and I'm a sergeant—'

'Inspector.'

'OK, an inspector. But I don't want people to think I'm sleeping my way to the top.'

'They will, anyway. You've no idea how many times I'm supposed to have dropped my knickers to get this desk. At least you're not in one of Rod's Murder Investigation Teams any more. And he's in Lloyd House ensconced behind a big desk while you're safely tucked away here in Steelhouse Lane nick.'

'But everyone still knows and gossips,' Kate grumbled.

'Don't you like a bit of gossip too, or are you in Goody Two Shoes mode? Come on, Kate. Lighten up.' Sue stood and stretched. 'Actually, what would worry me most is not the difference in rank but the age difference. I know he's well preserved, but he's nearer my age than yours.'

'I don't see a problem.'

'You will if you stick together like Derby and Joan. He'll be an old man when you're middle-aged. And you're likely to be a widow a long time.'

'Did you choose your husband on the grounds your ages were compatible? Oh, Sue!'

'Funnily enough, he's eighteen months younger than me. OK. I've got a lunchtime meeting with Them Upstairs – the latest Home Office initiative. What about you?'

'I'm off with Colin Roper: he needs a new going-to-court suit and I said I'd help him choose. Maybe the rain's easing a bit . . .'

It might have been, but by the time Colin had chosen his suit, it was pelting down again, and he and Kate were battling across the pedestrianised New Street sharing his regrettable but efficient golf-umbrella. She'd tucked her arm firmly into his, and was holding down her raincoat to protect her skirt.

'Excuse me!'

They had to stop. A young man, his hair plastered to his head where the wind had blown back his cagoule hood, was accosting them, flourishing a clipboard slipped into a plastic bag.

'Can I ask you just three questions? It's a travel survey. No catches, I promise you,' he added. 'And we enter you in a prize draw. Just to say thank you. Only three questions!'

'Do you have to do a quota before you're allowed to knock off for the day?' Colin asked.

The young man – he probably wasn't more than seventeen – nodded miserably.

'OK,' said Kate. 'Fire away.'

The questions were simple enough. How many times had she been abroad that year? Where? And if she could choose a perfect holiday destination, where would it be? Oh, and could she give her home telephone number – just in case, the boy added with a wry grin.

'And when do they let us know – if we win?' Kate laughed.

But the boy was fighting another squall and didn't hear.

'Guatemala!' Colin yelled as he hung up his raincoat and stowed the streaming umbrella in a waste bin. 'Come on, Kate, what possessed you to say you wanted to go to Guatemala?'

Sue popped her head round the door. 'Got any tea? God, I hate working lunches.' She stepped inside and felt the kettle, flicking the switch on the handle to bring it to the boil again. As she dropped a tea-bag into the last clean mug, she asked, 'What was that about Guatemala, Colin?'

'According to Kate, it's where she wants to spend her next holiday.'

'Oh, I had to say *something*. This poor kid stopped us in the street, Sue. Absolutely soaked to the skin. But he couldn't go home until he'd inveigled a certain number of punters into answering some silly questions.'

'Consumer research,' Colin explained. 'And just to sugar the pill you got entered in a prize draw for a holiday.'

Sue looked alert. 'What's the prize?'

'I didn't even ask,' Kate admitted. 'Waste of breath.'

'Well, let me know if you win,' Sue said, seriously enough to make them raise their eyebrows to each other as soon as she'd left the room.

That evening Colin propped himself up against Kate's kitchen doorjamb. 'Fancy you cooking!' he chortled.

'I've always cooked. Well,' she conceded, 'from time to time.'

'So what's prompted this sudden rush of domesticity to the head?' he enquired, hauling himself upright to top up their wine glasses.

She shrugged. 'You have a lovely kitchen like this: you ought to cook in it,' she said.

'Nothing to do with Rod Neville, then? It isn't that he doesn't want to be seen eating with you in public?'

'Why shouldn't we be seen together in public? We do lots of things in public! Damn!' As she tipped the pasta into the pan, a few drops of water splashed on to her forearm. She licked the place, and rubbed it vigorously.

'So I hear. Art exhibitions. Antiques fairs. Not your sort of thing, I'd have thought, Kate. I'd have seen you at soccer matches, or running or—'

'It may have escaped your notice that it's still supposed to be summer and that they play soccer in the winter.'

'The season started weeks ago.'

She stuck out her tongue. 'And the medics have officially forbidden running.'

'All the same . . . Shall I chop this parsley for you?' He picked up the knife and started work.

'Hell, I'd forgotten all about that. So much for me being an expert cook, eh?'

'You can choose a good wine, for all that. Or is that down to Rod, too?'

She blushed, and, furious with herself, blushed all the more deeply. 'He doesn't like cheap stuff,' she admitted. 'But then, there's no reason why someone on my salary with no mortgage should drink cheap wine.' She raised her glass in a toast. 'Thanks, Aunt Cassie, for the house.'

Colin drank. 'How is the old lady?'

'She's pretty well got over a head cold. But she won't let on that she's better. Oh, Colin, she's getting more and more self-absorbed. This pain; that ache; her bowels; her bladder.'

'But you still go up and see her practically every day.'

'Of course I do. Though it's no more than every other day,

sometimes less than that. We're family. And she's outlived most of her friends, and she's had rows with those still alive. You know what a tongue she's got. Plus, I owe her: I know I didn't enjoy living here while the place was being done up, but I've no complaints now. And I wouldn't have had it if she hadn't been so generous.'

'True. Is that the only reason you go and see her? Gratitude?'

She sensed he was asking another question, but answered, 'I suppose it is. I used to love her dearly, but each time I go up she seems less and less Aunt Cassie and more and more some miserable stranger. There's nothing to talk about. She used to be such a game old bird, too.' The saucepan boiled over. She snatched it off the gas ring, which she had to relight. 'That'll teach me! Never mind, only salt water – could be worse.'

Kate had laid the table in her dining room – the table Rod had helped her choose, though she didn't intend to bring that to Colin's notice. As she carried the bowls of pasta and salad through, she put them on two layers of mats: she didn't want any harm to come to the lovely glossy table. Imagine having something from George II's time in your very own front room. She could hardly believe it. Of course, Rod had pointed out that it was a little early for the chairs she'd bought at a different antiques fair, but both table and chairs were so simple and quietly elegant she didn't mind. She didn't even mind that one of the table feet had been badly restored, or that someone long ago had spilt ink on one leaf. All she knew was that for two centuries women's hands had rubbed it with love and beeswax, and that she was going to continue the tradition.

Colin deposited the wineglasses on coasters with equal care. 'Nice bit of wood,' he said, as Kate returned with the plates. 'Rod chose it, did he?'

'He watched me sign the cheque. And he shoved it into the back of his mother's people carrier.'

'His mother! You've met his mother! Oooh,' he continued, camp as they come, 'things are getting serious, aren't they!'

'Like they were when I met your mum and dad?'

'Hardly! OK, that's something I wanted to tell you this evening. I told them last weekend. About me and Bruno. And how I was gay.'

She took his hand and squeezed it. 'How did they take it?'

'As well as could be expected, as they say. Dad went all gruff, but he clapped me on the shoulder as he went off to the boozer and said he wished me well. And Mum had a little weep but said it was because she was happy for me. She's suspected all along, she says, and she's just happy I've met a nice boy.'

It all sounded a bit too easy, didn't it, for a working class Black Country family? A lot too easy. But until he admitted otherwise, she must take his account at face value. 'So am I. And I'm glad you've come out. What about work?'

'I've told Sue Rowley.'

Who, as Kate was aware, already knew. As did most of her colleagues, Rod and Graham included. Not through her, it had to be said. Other people had intuitions too: there seemed a general consensus that provided Colin didn't make a big deal over his sexuality, they wouldn't either.

'But can you imagine Graham Harvey's reaction?' Colin continued.

Kate frowned. 'No. Should I?'

'His sort of Christianity isn't big on forgiveness, Kate. Not as big as it is on Sin. And if you're a right-wing Christian, being a homosexual is an abomination in the sight of the Lord,' he concluded, in a fair impression of Ian Paisley. 'He may suspect, poor man, but he mustn't know, or that poor overworked conscience of his may force him to do something.'

Kate knew her smile was pale and inadequate. 'I think you're misjudging him,' she said carefully.

'You haven't been and bloody blabbed?'

'Not my secret to tell, Colin. But people aren't fools. And they join CID because they're good at detecting things.'

'Sorry.'

She passed the Parmesan.

'Are you getting over him yet?' Colin asked at last, scooping salad on to his plate.

'What do you mean, "over him"?'

He looked her straight in the eye. 'Surely you know the word on the street is that you took up with Rod Neville to throw sand in people's eyes because you were actually fucking with Graham.'

'And do you believe the word on the street?'

'No. Because I think you're too honest to treat either bloke that way. But I do think you might go with Rod to take your mind off Graham.'

'We always got on. OK, he was keener than me. But he's a good man. He knows the score.'

'Are you –?' He raised an eyebrow delicately.

'Sleeping together? We did at one point but it didn't work out. He thought I was too much of a maverick.'

'You!'

She couldn't work out whether or not he was being ironic. 'I'd disobeyed a direct order.'

'And then there was Graham . . . You do like a complicated life, don't you? Why don't you fall in love with an ordinary straightforward guy for a change?'

'Why indeed!'

'Poor old Kate. Anyway, I think I was the only one to notice the expression of relief on your face when Fatima dropped out that Graham was on leave. You didn't know, I gather.'

'I haven't been in touch with him for ages,' she said repressively. Then, reaching for the wine and filling both glasses, she added, 'Whatever there was between us is over, Colin. Over.'

He dabbed a spot of wine from the polished wood. 'Poor bastard. The only chance he has of a bit of joy in his life and he can't take it. The dear old Seventh Commandment. And the poor bugger's still going to be in a spot when he comes back – remember that bit when Christ says it's as bad

to look at a woman with lust in your heart as it is to sleep
with her?'

She nodded, biting her lip. Poor Graham.

'You were on to a loser from the start, sweetheart. Remember
when Princess Di said three in a marriage was a bit crowded?
Well, Graham doesn't just have a wife; he's got the Almighty
checking him out. He might leave his wife, though in my
experience men tend not to. But he'd never give up God.'

'That was more or less what he said. What am I going to do
when he comes back to work?' It was so good not having to
pretend: why on earth had she fended Colin off earlier? After
all, she'd trust him with her life.

'Let's hope your inspector's posting comes through
fast. Otherwise you're going to have to act fit to win
an Oscar. And while you may be able to, I doubt if he can.
Now, did I see some scrumptious Ben and Jerry's in your
freezer?'

Kate was loading the dishwasher when the phone rang. At a
nod from her, Colin answered.

'You're joking!' he said after a couple of minutes. 'Really?
My goodness! Let me just tell Kate!' He put his hand over the
mouthpiece and shouted, 'We've won that prize draw! That
holiday thing.'

'I don't believe it!' Nor did she. They'd completed the
questionnaire only a few hours ago, for goodness' sake. Surely
it would take longer than this. Did she smell a scam of some
sort?

'Well, we have! Just repeat those options again,' he continued,
for Kate's benefit, presumably, his voice getting increasingly
dubious. 'A week's holiday anywhere in the world . . . Or a
fortnight in Europe . . . Or a weekend in the UK. And we
can choose.' Then he said positively, 'Yes: sure. We'll be there.
Now, you'll be writing to confirm all this, I hope. Yes. Kate did
the questionnaire, so send it to her.' He dictated the address,
stumbling only over the postcode.

When he put down the phone, Kate had already slipped the chiller sleeve round a bottle of bubbly. OK, scam it may be, but she and Colin had more personal things to celebrate. And why not do it in style?

2

'Of course winning a holiday's great news: but I don't want you to tell anyone else in the squad – preferably anyone else full-stop,' Sue Rowley told Kate and Colin the following morning. 'I want to have a word with someone in Trading Standards. And someone else,' she added thoughtfully, moving the photo of her children a fraction nearer the middle of her desk.

They exchanged a glance. 'Lips sealed, Gaffer,' Colin said.

'But only for a couple of days,' Sue conceded. 'Nice little prize like that—'

Kate put in, '*If* it's genuine!'

'– you deserve a celebration. Preferably one that involves taking the rest of the squad to the pub.'

'You too, Gaffer?' Kate grinned.

'You bet your life. Or your holiday – wherever it is. Meanwhile, if you don't mind, it's business as usual. I take it you two would like to be paired up again. Unless you'd rather take Selby under your wing, Kate?'

'Selby! What the hell's he doing back here?'

Selby had been one of the most unpleasant officers it had ever been Kate's misfortune to meet. He was a racial and sexual bully, and had only escaped disciplinary action by going sick on the grounds of stress.

'Nothing yet, thank God. But he's running out of sick leave, I'd say. I've told Personnel there's no room for him back in my squad, of course.'

'But we've got a couple of unfilled vacancies,' Colin observed, adding, in his best Black Country accent, 'so that cock probably won't fight.'

'So I'll find another that will. Provided Graham Harvey'll back me.'

'I don't think there was much love lost between them,' Kate said. She couldn't not talk about him, after all.

'But he's not terribly hot on equal opportunities stuff, is he, for all the courses he's been on? If a man and a woman tell him different stories, he'll automatically believe the man's. All God's fault, if you ask me, for creating Adam first.'

Kate raised an eyebrow. She'd had a bit of that treatment herself, before she and Graham had become lovers, of course. And while they were lovers, come to think of it. But she'd thought it was simply because Graham was trying to deny his feelings and ended up being extra hard on her. For Sue Rowley to say it implied that she too had suffered – not a good thing at the hands of your immediate boss. And it could mean trouble for Graham: Sue wasn't the sort of woman to take prejudice lying down.

'Anyway, I'll fend off Personnel as long as I can. If you have any thoughts you'd care to put on paper, Kate, I'll pass them on. Right. Now, have you got plenty to do, Kate, or do you want me to find you something special? No. Forget that. You may well have something special coming up.'

Kate opened her mouth, but shut it again.

'Just go and sort out the Beach Boy's in-tray, will you?'

'Just a bloke who dressed rather more snappily than most,' Colin explained as they walked back down the corridor. 'And had the sort of perma-tan you only get after hours under the sunlamp and pecs to die for because he worked out and a peachy little bum and hands he got on half the females in Steelhouse Lane.'

'But he doesn't seem to have been here more than five minutes.'

'Apparently the camera *luuurrves* him: he's gone to the press office so next time there's a crime crisis there he'll be on all the region's TV screens, teeth a-gleam and pecs a-twitch. I should imagine he'll improve our clear-up rate by fifty-one per cent.'

'Fifty-one per cent?'

'All the women phoning in.'

'Ah. Pity they had to choose a man: I hoped Fatima would get a job like that. She'd do it so well, and it wouldn't half improve our multi-racial image.'

'She didn't want to. Said she wanted to prove herself at the grassroots level first. Now, why aren't we supposed to talk about our trip round the world?' At least he'd dropped his voice to conspiratorial level.

'We'll speculate at lunchtime. Now, lead me to the Beach Boy's in-tray.'

Three days later, Kate and Colin spread on Sue Rowley's desk the letter that had arrived that morning. As Kate had feared, it didn't come from a consumer research organisation, but from a firm calling itself Sophisticasun. They'd already had a good wince at the name.

'Mr and Mrs Power, eh?' Sue chortled. 'Nice to know you're a new man, Colin, taking your wife's name. Anyway, what does it say?'

'Well, the week anywhere in the world, all expenses paid, doesn't seem much of an option: we go where and when they send us. At three days' notice. Or there's the free fortnight in Europe – but you have to pay the airfares. Or there's a completely free weekend – at a location of your choice in the UK.'

'*Your* choice? They're letting you choose something?'

'Well, the options are limited. Here you are – the Lakes, the Highlands, Cromer—'

'I didn't know anyone went to Cromer, these days,' Colin interjected.

'Devon, Kent, mid-Wales . . .'

'So what's the snag there? There's bound to be one.'

'Well, you have to arrive between six and nine on a Friday. And leave by ten on a Monday. And you have to choose by return of post.'

'I take it you can fax the answer? That gives us a bit longer. Anything else?'

'We have to go together to a presentation on Saturday morning.

And a presentation at whichever location we fetch up at. Oh, and we fill in this questionnaire about our income and so on.' Kate put it on Sue's desk.

Sue adjusted her reading glasses. 'They seem very keen on your living together, too. But not your marital status.'

'Thank goodness for tiny mercies,' Colin said.

'OK. You haven't mentioned this to anyone?'

Kate shook her head. 'Too busy with the Beach Boy's work.'

'Well, keep it under your hats a little longer. And don't book anywhere for a celebratory lunch. You may be getting sandwiches in here.'

Colin gave his campest smile. 'So long as we don't have to pay for them!'

They were in Sue's room hardly long enough to eat them, let alone pay for them.

Passing over paper napkins as if dealing cards, Sue announced, 'You go to the presentation on Saturday morning. You are the perfect live-in lover, Colin, and Kate thinks the sun shines out of your arse. All lovey-dovey. You smile at each other and at the organisers, and you go along as if you're really keen on what they have to offer.'

'Which is probably a time-share?' Kate suggested.

'Yes. And you'll tell them how keen you are on sun and sand and tennis and golf and all the other things that make people buy time-shares. Only one thing: you won't be going round the world and you won't be paying to fly to Europe. You'll be going for a weekend in Devon, just as soon as you can get there.'

'Not Devon! My Gran lives in Devon.'

'I daresay Kate has an uncle in Cromer. We all have our crosses to bear, Colin, one of which is that you'll find yourself tangling with the M5 just when it's at its nastiest: 4.30 on a Friday evening.'

'Gee, thanks, Gaffer.'

'Anything we should know about this?'

'At this stage, Kate, no.'

'Which means there is, but you can't tell us,' Colin said.

Sue sighed, massively. 'Just go along on Saturday and do everything everyone else is doing. Except at this stage you won't sign on any dotted lines. Tell them you'll see what's on offer in Devon, and make your decision then. Lovey-dovey, remember.'

'Lovey-dovey it is, Gaffer.' Colin executed a peerless curtsy.

'And best bib and tucker, too.'

Saturday morning saw Kate and Colin setting out from Kings Heath – they'd decided that it was easier for him to spend the night in Kate's spare room. Best of mates they might be, but breakfast had proved they were far from compatible. Kate was showered, dressed and made-up before Colin stirred. He looked distinctly seedy when he crawled down for black coffee and dry toast.

'It's your own fault,' Kate informed him, without sympathy. 'Coming in at four in the morning. You're too old.'

He winced as she plonked the coffee mug down. 'Who said anything about four in the morning?'

'My alarm clock did when I looked at it. It's an old house, remember, Colin, and every floorboard creaks if you so much as look at it.'

He hung his head in contrition. 'Did I keep you awake long?'

She shook her head, smiling. But she did rather wonder what he'd taken to keep him active so late into the night, and to drive him so often to the loo. It had been well after five before she'd slept again. But she wouldn't let him know that.

'We've got time for you to shave and shower before we go.'

He groaned. 'Bath?'

'The heating and the water are on a combi system – so it takes forever to fill a whole bath. But the shower's fierce – it'll really wake you up.'

Kate took the M40 as far as the turning for Oxford, and then followed Colin's directions to what was coyly described as a modern village. She left her car – it was notably the smallest – in a car park tucked discreetly to the rear. Access to the complex was via a keypad door, currently wedged open by a cast-iron shoe-scraper.

'Did you ever go to Butlin's or whatever when you were a kid?' Colin asked.

'No. I usually had my holidays with Aunt Cassie. She might have been a working-class Brummie, but she didn't go for working-class Brummie holidays. Her lover must have put his hand in his pocket for more foreign ice creams for me than he'd ever bargained for. Good job he was stinking bloody rich! What about you?'

'Porthmadog. Every wet summer without fail. Mind you, we had some laughs. I won a talent competition once. Impersonating Liberace.' He paused and looked around. 'Hang on; this doesn't look like Redcoat territory. You wouldn't have to rise and shine here.'

'If you did you'd be summoned by some very hi-tech sound system, I should think.'

Built round a courtyard, in reclaimed bricks, was a pseudo-country, but extremely neat collection of apartments, some with balconies. As if on cue, the sun came out, watery at first, then definitely warm. The raindrops on the pots of petunias and fuchsias shone like diamonds. There were private terraces, cut off from intruders by low, decorative walls. The clear implication was that the type of person who might take undue advantage of their proximity to other people would not be encouraged to purchase property here, be it for as little as one week a year.

It's OK, sweetheart, you look the bizz,' Colin whispered.

'So do you,' she responded, less truthfully.

'Don't worry: I'm sure they'll offer us coffee. I'll have mine black. Thing is, Bruno just seems to keep going.'

'And how old is he?'

'What's that got to do with it?'

'It depends how old *you* are.'

'Which as my little wifey you're supposed to know. But you're right. He's got youth on his side.' Colin sighed. 'How long before a bloke can take HRT?'

★　　★　　★

There was indeed coffee, accompanied by an assortment of pastries and croissants, offered by a woman a couple of years older than Kate who smiled at Colin as if determined to show off her orthodontic work. Were she not here in her professional capacity, the teeth said, she'd be available.

He smiled back, a finely tuned smile telling her that but for his commitment to monogamy he'd be available too. Kate, amused by the bluffs and double bluffs, opted for fruit juice: supermarket freshly squeezed. The napkins were starched linen. Small enough sprats, true, but they'd perhaps lure the wealthy mackerel. Kate and Colin's bibs and tuckers might have been their best, but for diamonds and good watches they were simply outclassed. They were ready to sit down, when two or three couples arrived late enough to cause a frisson of irritation to cross their host's forehead. For there was a host. Genial enough to be a quiz-show compere, his spruceness suggesting ex-army, he introduced himself as Harry, and then the woman in charge of refreshments as Amanda. From nowhere emerged a startlingly handsome man, darkly glamorous enough to have had some Mediterranean or African-Caribbean blood in his veins. Labelled Gregorie, he gleamed with self-confidence and good grooming, if unusual spelling. Whatever game it was playing, this organisation was fielding fine-looking players.

After the presentation – a slick slide-and-sound show of developments all over the world, the first couple to sign up were invited to open their prize on the spot: six bottles of champagne. Everyone clapped enthusiastically, Kate and Colin included. But they'd all been given envelopes guaranteed to contain a voucher for some prize or other. Would people who didn't sign up be treated with equal generosity? And how would they know who was likely to sign, who not? Possibly Guatemala had given a clue as to her seriousness: yet Kate had still had this invitation, had still won some sort of prize. She touched the envelope, wishing she were sitting at the back and could slide an unobtrusive finger under the flap.

Those who'd prevaricated were taken on a tour of the complex, almost as if as an afterthought. Clearly there'd be another attempt on their willpower later. Kate was glad she'd resisted: she'd never seen such well-planned accommodation as this, making the most of available space and light without ever seeming cluttered or contrived. Yes, she was impressed by the baby-sized bathroom and kiddie-kitchen: holiday accommodation this certainly was, but if she had equipment like that at home – if in a slightly larger form – she'd be as happy as she was with her own new fittings. The colour schemes were as tastefully unobtrusive as in a good hotel: after all, striking individuality might offend one inhabitant as much as it pleased another. And no one would be here more than a fortnight a year, presumably.

Back to the main hall and the next part of the entertainment . . . and the discovery that she'd won a bottle of ready-made Buck's Fizz.

It was obviously the job of Gregorie to fix on Kate, charming her as if his life depended on it. And the sad thing was, he wouldn't be able to accommodate her and Colin in Devon.

'Oh, what a shame! He was hoping to see his grandmother!' Kate sighed.

'They're short of apartments because they're refurbishing the site,' he explained, swiftly enough for Kate to feel he might be lying. 'We like to maintain standards. But all the other options are open to you – how would you feel about our development near Barmouth? Or Hornsea?'

Kate shook her head regretfully. 'It's a matter of logistics, you see. We're not supposed to finish work till five-fifteen on Fridays, and . . .'

'Your boss won't let you off a teeny bit early?' Gregorie smiled winsomely.

'Colin's might – but mine's a tough woman.'

'Oh, that's awful.' He ran a concerned finger down an impeccable jaw. 'Of course, some establishments might be able to deal with a slightly later arrival. Let me just check my file.' It was true he made a show of opening it and running a beautifully manicured index finger down an index. But Kate was sure he had the answer anyway. 'I can offer you a late arrival facility at Allonby – or again near Hythe.'

'M6 or M25?' Colin mused. 'Oh, let's go for Hythe, shall we, sweetheart? It can be remarkably cold up in the Lake District in the autumn. When do we go?'

'I'll have to check date availability,' Gregorie told them. 'Bear with me one second.'

He relinquished his file, and flipped open a mobile phone, turning a shoulder discreetly and managing to drift away so that they couldn't overhear his conversation. But he soon returned, with a beatific smile. He might have arranged the treat especially for Kate.

'As it happens we do have site availability next weekend. But there is one problem. I'm afraid that that village is also in the process of upgrading. The apartment you're allocated may not be up to the standards you see here.'

'No problem,' Colin said. 'I assume the facilities . . . ?'

Back to the file. 'Golf; tennis; sea bathing. You might even want to dash across to France – Eurostar stops at Ashford, or you can go through the Channel Tunnel . . . Get some real champagne,' he added, as if the Buck's Fizz were a cause for personal shame.

'Kent! You're going to bloody *Kent!*'

Monday morning found Kate and Colin closeted once more with Sue, whose hair looked as if she'd spent the weekend tearing it: history homework, perhaps, for which she always found more enthusiasm than her children.

'The problem is, Gaffer,' Kate said, 'that they're currently refurbishing the Devon village. No vacancies.'

'What a surprise.' Sue leaned back in her chair, one arm across her chest, the other pulling her cheeks towards her chin, exaggerating the worry lines. 'So how do we get you to Devon, eh?'

'What's so special about Devon, Gaffer? My Gran apart,' Colin asked.

'I wish I could tell you. Whatever it is is causing interest at the highest level. Meanwhile, do you intend to nip down to the sunny south this weekend?'

'Why not? Might as well watch the rain there as anywhere.'

'It's a long way down for thirty-six hours of weather watching. If you're not going to Devon, I'm afraid you'll have to be back at your desks at the usual time on Monday. Sorry.'

'Hang on, Gaffer,' Kate said. 'This is part of some sort of enquiry – that's obvious. So doesn't sniffing round Kent constitute part of that enquiry?'

Sue produced an impish smile. 'When I was a teenager, I used to go to chapel – regular as clockwork, because that was what people did in my part of Wales.'

'You don't have any accent,' Colin observed.

'I know you like flaunting yours, but some of us prefer to be discreet about our origins. Anyway, back in the valley there was a joke going round that this really devout young couple, saving themselves till their wedding night, found they wouldn't arrive at their honeymoon hotel till the Sabbath. So they asked their minister if they were allowed to consummate their marriage on a Sunday. He and the Elders watched and prayed –' Sue's accent emerged from hiding and exposed its full glory – 'and at last were vouchsafed an answer. "It's all right to have sex," the minister told the couple, "so long as you don't *enjoy* it."'

Tickled by a side of Sue quite new to her as much as by the joke, Kate grinned broadly. 'So we can come back on the Monday morning provided we have a really miserable time? Which precludes trips to France?'

'I rather think it does. Unless you pay your own way.'

'Not that it would have been easy to fit it in,' Colin put in. 'They want us to go to another presentation as part of the deal. Sunday morning. Starting, God help us, at ten.'

Sue nodded. 'OK. Spend as much of the weekend as you can on site. Talk to the other guests. Go to that presentation and pick up as much as you can without actually signing anything. Just a word of warning.' She leaned forward conspiratorially. 'The M25,' she said. 'Don't try to get on it before seven in the evening, or, coming back, before ten in the morning. My bloke's on the road a lot, remember.' She touched the side of her nose.

'Which means we should work late here on Friday to compensate for not getting back till lunchtime on Monday,' Colin said sourly, looking down the corridor to check that no one could overhear. 'And no bloody France.'

'And a weekend for you with no bloody Bruno,' Kate observed.

'And a weekend for you with no bloody Rod. About whom you've kept distinctly quiet.'

'I told you, he's been on a course.'

'Which ends?'

'This Friday, as it happens.'

'But you haven't said anything! Why did you agree to go to bloody Kent? Or even bloody Devon?'

'We agreed: work must always come first.' Hell, she sounded so pompous! 'After all, we're not even properly together . . .'

Fatima emerged from the ladies' loo, shaking her hands dry.

'Let's talk about this over lunch,' Colin said. 'I've got the glimmer of an idea.'

'So,' agreed Kate, 'have I. A bit more than a glimmer.'

'Phone. Kate! Phone!' Fatima was calling, trying to suppress a snigger.

Blushing, Kate reached for the handset. It had been like that all morning. Her head was low down over the files, maybe, but her brain was engaged with the much more urgent problem of Rod, who, for all their fine words about professionalism, would be as disappointed as she was that they couldn't have some sort of reunion – even just as friends, which they still were. Just friends. Just about. There was no doubt he wanted to return to a sexual relationship, and her body insisted that there was nothing wrong at all with bonking a handsome man with a gorgeous body. But her head still had doubts, and her heart still felt as if a cold fist clutched it every time she thought of Graham. Forget Graham. Think Rod.

* * *

Sue slapped her thighs with amusement. 'I wondered how soon you'd be back with that idea. Poor Colin, a lowly DC, rejected for a Det. Supt. Well, a detective superintendent must be a good detective. In theory. But my caveats about your working hours still apply. And when you tell him about the assignment, remind him it's all top secret.'

'Ma'am.' Kate opened the door.

'And I shall want a written report. Very soon.'

'Ma'am.' She closed the door again. 'This is serious, isn't it?'

'Very. Now, remember what I said about enjoying it!'

3

'I thought,' said Rod Neville, retrieving their cases – predictably he'd insisted on carrying both – from the path in front of the door marked Reception, 'that you'd told me this firm ran a tight ship.'

Kate nodded gloomily. 'But it looks as if this particular vessel's leaky.' She rapped the door again with the edge of a coin, but to no avail. 'OK. We drive the best part of five hours in vile conditions and now there's no one to let us in. What next?'

'Shall we go and find an hotel and bill the organisation? Or even West Midlands Police?'

'Yes! If you dare,' she added with a grin.

It was obvious he didn't – quite.

So she had to say something to save his face. 'Shame, isn't it? I'm supposed to be working, aren't I? And you're supposed to be a substitute for DC Colin Roper, aka Mr Power. And I'm sure *he* wouldn't suggest bunking off duty.' She stuck her tongue out. 'Hell, there must be a way of getting in.'

'If you're truly determined – and if you're sure Mr Power would have been equally determined – then I suggest we try the bar over there. It smells as if they offer food, too. Even if I would hardly anticipate it being a centre of gastronomic excellence.'

He picked up the cases and let Kate lead the way to what modestly – but perhaps accurately – described itself as a social club. Anything further from the sophistication of the Oxford set-up would have been hard to imagine. The décor, the menu, the games machine: nothing seemed to have happened since the seventies. But the equally tired-looking woman behind the bar managed a smile in response to Rod's and as soon as she'd heard his problem fished under her counter for their key, pointing vaguely over her shoulder when asked for directions to their unit. She also looked pointedly at her watch.

'What time do you finish serving food?' Kate asked.

'Five minutes. So if you want anything . . .' But it was Rod she was smiling at, the half ogle, half fuck-me eye flutter that Kate was used to seeing him evoke in older women. His height, his build, well-cut casual clothes: he was decidedly easy on the eye, especially when he removed his mandatory work-place frown, replacing it with a charming boyish grin that took ten years off him. Bother Sue and her worries.

The rain, recently a heavy drizzle, suddenly swirled against the window. Whatever the nearby towns offered, this place was warm and dry, and, come to look at it, fairly clean. Fish and chips and bitter for two seemed as good as anything. And certainly better than plunging back on to unknown roads in the hope of anything else.

Their fellow diners – no, in fact everyone else was simply drinking – were equally far from the Oxford set. The women seemed to favour the sort of stretch slacks with elasticated waists that Aunt Cassie used to wear before she became, as she put it, properly old. She'd usually gone for a smart navy; most of these ladies sported a sad dun, matching their menfolk's polyester cavalry twill. Shoes were dully sensible. There were even one or two transparent folding plastic rain hoods drying on the tables. Rainmates, that's what Cassie called them.

Rod seated her as if they were at the Ritz, retrieved packets of sauce and other condiments, and, at last sitting opposite her, raised his glass.

Kate toasted him in return. She could trace the thought circling round his head: he'd better not be so transparent when dealing with criminals. But perhaps she could only see the wheels turning because the same thought was making her temples chug. How would they deal with the sex part of the weekend? He'd wanted to know what the apartment offered by way of bedrooms as soon as she'd suggested the weekend: deadpan, she'd reported that there were two. In the car journey – and the M25 section seemed interminable – they'd talked about everything and anything, from the course he'd been on to her garden. Everything except sex. Interestingly, he really did seem to know nothing about what she'd taken to calling their assignment, and demanded a detailed update.

'This'll take all of fifty seconds! Sue's terribly gnomic about the whole thing. I even have to swear you to secrecy.'

'I swear. I wonder if . . . ?'

'You do know something!'

'There's a lot of rumours about drugs factories on the Moor. But nothing to connect them as far as I know with holiday camps. Well, we'll just have to do as we're told and keep our eyes and ears open. I'll take my cue from you,' he'd added.

No doubt he'd take his cue from her about sex, too. Well, was their relationship back on or not? Her body firmly switched her head off.

It was evident that, new licensing laws notwithstanding, this bar closed at ten thirty. Draining their glasses, they complimented the barmaid on the food, and set off for their apartment, trailing along walkways that seemed to go everywhere except where they were wanted. At last, shoes awash and hair streaming, they found it – in the only corner with no security lights.

Eventually they stopped laughing. Rod had sprinted back to the bar for change for the meter, returning wetter than ever to find Kate sitting in total darkness swathed in the sheet she'd used as a towel.

'No light, no heat, no towels, nothing in the fridge: this isn't the sort of weekend break I'd had in mind,' she admitted, passing him another sheet, which he applied to his hair.

No longer dripping, at least, he fed the meter. The place looked slightly worse in the rosy glow cast by a forty-watt bulb inexplicably shrouded in a crimson shade, but at least they could conjure warmth from a space heater. He towelled his hair again, but stripped off only his jacket before disappearing into the kitchen. Returning clutching two mugs, he said, 'What a good job I brought the sort of bottle that doesn't require an opener . . . Where did you put my case, by the way?' he added, not quite meeting her eye.

She responded with another paroxysm. 'In the master bedroom!' she managed at last, pointing. She gave him thirty seconds before following.

'God Almighty,' he exploded, taking in the chaste single beds with sheets drawn as tightly as in a hospital. 'And what's the other one like?'

'That's where I got these sheets. Bunk beds!' she howled. 'And Toy Story curtains.' She collapsed on the nearest bed, only to watch him fish a champagne bottle from his bag and head purposefully back to the living room. Drawn by a series of soft grunts, she followed. He was unfolding the sofa to discover a bed.

At last they were driven by the vicious sofa bed mattress to seek what Rod had started to call the nuns' dormitory. Perhaps it was better that way. To have wonderful sex with someone didn't imply the same sort of commitment as going to sleep in his arms, she told herself. In any case, after a vicious journey on top of a heavy week at work, sleep was undoubtedly called for. So why couldn't she settle?

She lay on her back, eyes wide open, getting used to the sounds of the place. It might not be the city, but it wasn't quiet out here. There was a dull roar: it took her a few moments to work out that it was the sea. And nearer to the complex there was the tear and groan of trees. Rod had already fallen asleep, not snoring, but making gentle popping noises as his lips relaxed in the outward breath. She turned, enjoying the sight of his profile outlined against the thin curtains: even if their security light was out of action, the complex was still well lit.

So why couldn't she sleep? She felt watched, that was why.

Uneasy enough to swathe herself in the sheet she'd worn before, she slipped silently out of bed and padded to the window, ready to yell at a Peeping Tom. No one. Gathering up her toga, she decided to use the bathroom – there was all that champagne to get rid of, after all. But she didn't switch on any lights, relying on memory and touch when the ambient light let her down. Back in the bedroom, she was in bed and about to snuggle under the blankets when something caught her eye. A tiny, tiny pinprick gleamed in the angle between the wall and the ceiling, up in the far corner. All hope of sleep fled. It couldn't be – Christ, it might be a surveillance camera. It might just be. What if they'd made love in here? Thank God for the convent beds. Until she'd worked out what was going on, she'd better pretend she'd noticed nothing – fall asleep, dream, move round in her sleep. No one watching must suspect she was anything other than a relaxed holidaymaker.

Well, she told herself, feign sleep. And feign it well. For she'd better be awake in the morning before Rod, hadn't she? Because she knew exactly how Rod liked celebrating a new day.

A root around the kitchen produced half a dozen catering tea-bags and some plastic pots of coffee whitener. While the kettle boiled, she retired to the bathroom to get dressed, not because she was embarrassed to be naked in front of Rod, but because she was still mortally suspicious of the dark little hole in the corner of the bedroom.

As she carried his mug through, she stood looking at him, tidy in the little bed as if entombed. She took in the errant hair that gave his left eyebrow a quizzical tilt, and a stray lash cast adrift on his cheek. She wanted to kiss it away. The mug clattered slightly as she put it down, but not enough to wake him. So she flung back the curtains. By daylight, despite what looked like sea mist hovering over it, the complex looked as potentially attractive as the Oxford one – terraced apartments built round a central quadrangle.

The light woke Rod, who emerged from his cocoon stretching and registering her fully clothed state compared to his naked one. Her back to the camera – if that was what it was – she touched a finger to her lips.

He stared.

Pointing to the living room, she mouthed, 'In there.'

But he dressed before he emerged, puzzled, hurt looking, even a mite angry. Perhaps he hadn't noticed the tea. She slipped back to get it. She also retrieved his jacket, patting the pocket to check his keys were there.

'Breakfast out, this morning,' she said brightly. After all, there might be listening devices. 'In the absence of any supplies. There must be a decent café in Hythe. Soon as you've shaved.'

'Kate—'

'Tell you what, while you do that I'll go and see if I can buy a paper.'

At last he seemed to be twigging that she was trying to tell him something. 'Maybe I'll skip the shave. Until we've eaten.' As he let her into his car, he asked, 'Can you tell me what's going on? Have I upset or offended you in some way?'

Before fastening her seat belt she leaned across to kiss him, very chastely, on the cheek. 'Not at all. The reverse, I'd say.'

'So why all this frost?'

'I'll tell you once we're off the complex. Just smile in a cousinly way and drive.'

'*Cousinly!*' He started the car and set off gently down the speed-ramped drive. 'Don't see any tennis courts, Kate.'

'And I don't see me doing any sea bathing. This bears remarkably little resemblance to the Oxford complex Colin and I lusted after.'

'Perhaps they'll explain why at the presentation tomorrow,' Rod observed, turning the car on to the Hythe Road. 'And perhaps you'll explain the cloak and dagger stuff.'

'Now we're away from the thought police, of course I can. There's a lay-by over there – do you want to pull in?'

He managed to infuse irony even into his parking.

'How does the idea of surveillance cameras grab you?' she asked, without preamble.

'Surveillance cameras? Where, for God's sake?'

'In the main bedroom. I think. There's a tiny black dot in the corner, over by the window. In the angle between the wall and the ceiling. I wasn't sure what it might be, and I'm afraid I may have over-reacted. But I could scarcely stand on the dressing table to investigate.'

'A fish-eye version of your face in close-up would certainly disconcert whoever has to check the film. If it is a camera, of course. Tell me, why on earth should they put surveillance cameras in a place like that?'

She turned more fully to him, raising an amused eyebrow. 'Let's hope they don't have one in the sitting room. It wasn't very cousinly behaviour, was it?'

'What's all this about cousins? Perhaps I shall think better after a coffee.' He rubbed his hands over his face, and grimaced. 'Perhaps I should have shaved.'

She rubbed the back of a finger over his cheek. 'You'll certainly have to if you want to indulge in any more uncousinly behaviour. The thing is, Rod, some members of this organisation have already seen Colin and me as Mr and Mrs Perfect.'

'Kate, you sound paranoid to me.'

'I am. But if they care enough to install cameras—'

'*If* they care enough to install cameras.'

'Then they might well check up on whether the people at the Oxford presentation match the people coming here. That's all.'

'And what would happen if they did and they found us wanting?'

'I'm sure there's something nasty in the small print. And Sue wanted us here as Joe and Josephine Public to sniff around surreptitiously, not draw attention to our presence by being exposed as frauds ourselves.'

'Is she expecting to find fraud here?'

'She expected us to find something. That's why I've got Monday morning free. She wasn't precise. Perhaps even she didn't know what I was to look for. No, I'm sure she did. Just not telling.'

Rod took her hand. 'Have you found anything of interest yet?'

'Oh, yes. But not the sort of thing I'd want to report to Sue.'

'How about we put it about that we've met some friends –

relatives, maybe – and are going to stay the night with them. Prize or no prize, we deserve something . . . less Spartan.'

She had an idea from the warmth of his voice that he'd been intending to say something else. But she answered lightly, 'Why not? So long as we're back for the ten o'clock presentation. The only thing is—'

'We must case the joint first,' he said, dropping into a creaky American accent. 'Though how we see if it really is a camera I don't know,' he continued in his usual voice. 'Wave at it: see if it waves back maybe. Now, breakfast.'

'If anywhere's open yet: I've only just realised it's not yet eight.'

'Eight! So why—'

'Because I couldn't quite trust either of us to behave in a cousinly way, not after last night, not if we stayed in bed. I certainly couldn't trust me.'

He swooped on her, emerging from a decidedly incestuous kiss to say, 'I'd say you were a very good judge of character, Sergeant Power. Come on: there must be some greasy spoon somewhere that does early breakfasts for workmen. God,' he added, surveying the lowering skies and windswept marshes, 'there must be some other reason you chose Hythe.'

Replete, and armed with the *Guardian* and *The Times*, as if ready to make a day of it in their apartment, they parked and, finding Reception showing signs of life, popped in to announce their presence. They were greeted by a bored sixteen-year-old with a pierced navel.

'Tennis? No. No, I don't think so. And there's certainly no swimming pool. I mean, you wouldn't want to swim in this weather, would you?'

'Indoors?'

'Closed for refurbishment. There's a gym, but there's a sur-charge for that. Is that your car over there?' she asked, alert for the first time. 'You're supposed to park in your designated space.'

'What other facilities are on offer here?' Rod asked quietly.

The girl's expression returned to its previous blank. 'Facilities? Well, there's the shop – that's eleven till three – and the club.'

Rod gripped Kate's wrist: she could feel the suppressed laughter. 'And when does that open?'

'Twelve till two. Six till ten-thirty.'

'But what do people do while they're staying here?' he asked mildly.

'There's sailing. And they go to France. Or there's a big shopping centre in Ashford, ever so good.' Her eyes sparkled. 'The Outlet. Junction Ten of the motorway. It's a big egg-shaped place and you park in the middle.'

Kate could tell from the way his fingers were exploring her wrist that Rod wasn't enthralled by the prospect of a day's shopping. She moved hers to caress his palm.

'What now?' she asked when they'd eased themselves out – with remarkably little effort.

'I think the mist's lifting. I'm not sure about the delights of Folkestone or Dover, but I've always wanted to go to Rye: Henry James once lived there. And E. H. Benson. And Radclyffe Hall.'

She dug in her memory. 'The lesbian writer?'

'That's right. Then there's Hastings and Battle – we could go all 1066 and walk the site. If the weather improves. And soon, Sergeant Power, we'll find a nice hotel and check in for tonight. As for night things, I fancy we shan't need much, and what we do need – damn it, we can smuggle out in your tennis bag.'

4

Sunshare deemed it necessary for two representatives to talk to Kate. They met in a room above the social club, which, though newly painted, was far from ideal: it had little space for more than the four of them, the flip chart, the slide projector and a screen. Kate and Rod had decided to come clean (-ish) about their official relationship. 'Rod's my cousin,' Kate said blithely. 'I'm afraid Colin's been brewing flu all week, and it came on in all its glory on Thursday night. So rather than cancel, I asked Rod – he's got friends down here.' Which might explain their absence last night – had anyone noticed it, of course.

Sebastian (tall and dark and very slim) and Veronica (short and blonde and very tanned) had not been pleased, that was evident, but Kate doubted whether anything would have pleased Sebastian, who, from the disapproving angle of his nose and mouth, might have been the snobbish butler to a particularly aristocratic house. He showed them to their seats, managing at last to smile – though condescendingly – as he passed them folders. 'For your perusal,' he explained. 'You'll find a complete set of our company's sites, together with information about travel – nearest airports and so on.' For a man in his twenties, he managed pomposity very well.

Veronica, although much the same age, was a keeny-beany, teeth agleam with her passion for selling. She did the presentation, a close copy of the one Kate had already endured but to which Rod came mercifully fresh. He asked a variety of intelligent questions with far more enthusiasm than Kate and Colin had mustered between them on the first encounter. But he wasn't asking just any questions: he was asking questions which demonstrated conclusively to both the sales people and Kate that time-share simply didn't make sense for someone with her life. When she went abroad, she wanted (he told them, Kate included) cities to provide her with the galleries and concert halls without which her holiday could not be complete. Because she liked to drink, but was totally abstemious when driving, she wanted to find a cluster of top-flight restaurants within walking distance. Sunshare's complexes might be beautifully designed and equipped – though he dryly admitted that he for one found their present apartment wanting – but they were all off the beaten track, and though their sporting facilities might be beyond compare, they were not offering the Prado or the Louvre, were they?

There was no answer to that, of course, so Veronica came in with a diversionary tactic: an escorted tour round the refurbished apartments. Kate, always a sucker for looking at other people's lives – perhaps in a previous existence she'd been a fly on a wall – swiftly accepted. Rod made a decent show of reluctance, but eventually conceded that he might as well come too, since there wasn't anything else to do. This was the first time this morning that he'd sounded anything other than reasonable and the first time Kate had ever heard him sound like a sulky teenager.

'Kate told me there'd be swimming and tennis and goodness knows what. All we've got is an underheated apartment with a hole in the bedroom ceiling.'

What the hell—? But Kate knew better than to shoot a look at him.

'A hole?' Sebastian was shocked out of his oleaginous pride in the organisation.

'Hmm. A hole. Not very big, I grant you, but distinctly a hole. Anyway, if we've got to look at someone else's pads, so be it. Let's get moving.'

Sebastian smiled, but not with amusement. 'I must remind you that one of the conditions of this holiday is that you spend two hours in our company.'

'Is it? Is it in the small print where they tell us to bring towels and food? Oh, and toilet rolls?'

As if trying to calm a tantrum, Kate said, 'We can get some on the site shop.'

'*Complex*, Mrs Power. And I'm afraid you'll find it opens from ten till eleven on Sundays.'

Rod pulled a face. 'Why don't you just hang on here while I nip out? I'll only be five minutes.'

Kate found she dared not contemplate the idea of the fastidious Rod carrying out this tour clutching a packet of loo rolls. But he didn't have to, in the event: it was already eleven ten.

Even Rod managed to admire the refurbished units, which turned out to be almost identical to those in the Oxfordshire complex. Perhaps it was his unfeigned pleasure that led Veronica to retrieve from a cupboard concealing a cistern a soft pink loo roll, which she surreptitiously slipped him as they left the second apartment. Kate was convinced that Veronica would have called it quits at that point – it was eleven forty – but Sebastian herded them back once more to the little room over the social club, and embarked or what could only be described as the harangue of one who, his own Sunday morning spoiled, was determined to ruin everyone else's too. He touched on the convenience of the sites, the excellence of the communications, the fine sporting facilities, and contrived to insinuate that they were fools not to have accepted at the first time of asking. Neither responded to his provocation.

Veronica gathered up her files, waiting in vain for Sebastian to collapse the screen and unplug the projector. At last, she put down the files and did the other jobs herself, refraining from indicating by so much as a twitch of a muscle that she thought her colleague a pain.

'This hole,' Sebastian asked suddenly. 'Where is it?'

Rod responded with a smile epitomising polite calm. 'In the bedroom ceiling. The master bedroom.'

Master bedroom! Kate snorted silently. *As opposed to the bunk bedroom, no doubt.*

'And which apartment are you in?'

Rod smiled again. 'The one in the far corner where the lamp doesn't work. Tell me, Sebastian: Kate raved about the Oxford complex. She was within a whisker of signing up. Why do you put a potential purchaser in such a dump?'

'A dump?' Sebastian repeated in apparent disbelief.

'Compared to the ones we've just seen, yes, our place is definitely a dump. And not much cop *per se.*'

Kate kept her face straight, something she did not find easy during Rod's occasional forays into Latin.

'Was it something I said?' Kate asked. 'Or the size of my car?'

'What on earth do you mean?' Sebastian demanded, hauteur a-twitch.

'I just wondered if you used external factors like a car to assess someone's spending power. And if it seemed a tad on the low side, you'd assume they were just going for a freebie, and not treat them seriously.'

'I assure you that all our clients are assured of the same warm welcome and serious consideration.' Sebastian realised too late the clumsiness he'd been harried into. And entirely missed the irony.

'The problem is,' Veronica said quickly, 'that if we put guests such as yourselves into the newly up-graded apartments, we wouldn't be able to show other clients round. Would we?'

'But if we hadn't been so put off by the poor quality of what was offered us,' Kate objected, 'we might have been more receptive to your sales patter.'

Sebastian snorted. 'It seems to me that your mind was made up from the start. At least your cousin's was.'

Veronica coughed.

Sebastian flushed, recalled to the seemly. 'Well,' he said, stretching a beam almost to but not as far as his eyes, 'I'm sorry we weren't able to suit you. But please enjoy the rest of your weekend.' He gave a half-bow, and was gone.

However embarrassed she might have been, Veronica smiled peaceably: 'We know we score with about one in seven. You're obviously just number six.'

'You're not just on commission, then?' Kate asked.

'Basic plus commission. And we get to go and check out overseas apartments, when they're vacant. That's a real bonus. Sebastian's new to the team,' she added, as if that excused everything.

'So I gathered,' Kate said dryly. 'The Oxford team were professionalism itself. As you have been. How did you get your job, by the way? It seems a nice idea, combining sales with travel.'

'Through the trade press,' Veronica said. 'You need the appropriate background,' she added, not encouragingly.

'Which is?'

'Oh, the travel industry. Were you thinking of applying? What do you do?' She was distinctly more animated.

Kate smiled. 'Just a civil servant.'

'And your cousin?' Now Veronica's smile might have been an attempt to mimic her colleague's. But surely there was more steel behind it.

'Oh, even more boring. Local government. Desk bound. That was why it was such a treat to be able to get away.' Rod had evidently decided to charm. 'Though we were disappointed when we learned there was no tennis: it was listed on the letter you sent confirming the details.'

Veronica grimaced. 'Our receptionist should have phoned through to Hythe for you: we have an arrangement with the local club. And you wouldn't get much in the way of swimming, would you? I'm so sorry the weekend's not the success we all hoped for. But I'll sort out that hole, and hope the remainder of your stay is enjoyable.'

They stopped long enough to drop the Sunshare folders in the apartment before bunking off for lunch in a pub on the coast road.

Rod turned to her. 'So?'

'So at least the surveillance camera will see someone else's ugly mug peering into it. I suppose they'll dot it with filler.'

'Do you propose to hang around to find out if they do?' He ran a finger along the inside of her wrist.

She made her head reply, 'You know, I think I do. Not for long. But – I'm sorry—'

'So am I.' He kissed her fingers delicately. 'But I understand. The job's addictive, isn't it?'

'You should know. Oh, thank goodness we've got that hotel reservation for tonight. There's no way I'd swap that for incarceration in the nuns' dormitory.'

The finger stroked again. 'I'm glad.' His voice changed. 'I can't see what we have to lose by going back to have another sniff around. We haven't exactly insinuated ourselves into conversation with any of the other guests yet, have we? And I think we should. If we can find any. They'll all be out in pubs like this.'

'Not necessarily. After all, they *own* their apartments, for part of the year at least. They'll know about taking food and towels and loo rolls. I bet we'll find several couples to talk to.'

'Oh what excuse? You can't just barge into their post-prandial bliss, shoving your warrant card under their noses and demanding information.'

'I can if I've run out of toilet paper: watch me!'

Rod's features expressed extreme distaste: his eyes twinkled.

'Woman's work, this: I'm not asking you to do it! And it can be milk or sugar we're out of, if you find that less aesthetically distressing. Anyway, you can get stuck into those posh sales files and I'll chat up the happy campers.'

'And what time do you fancy abandoning ship and heading off for that nice king-size bed?'

In two minutes. 'As soon as I'm ready to file my report, Superintendent.'

It took three attempts to find anyone at home, though Kate suspected that other front doors concealed couples unwilling, for whatever reason, to respond to her knock. At last, though, clutching an empty jug – Rod's sensibilities had prevailed – she found a friendly smile on the face of a middle-aged woman who took in the problem at a glance and invited her in. She shut the door swiftly against an increasingly vicious wind.

'You moving in down here?' she asked over her shoulder, as she padded through to the kitchenette. She'd managed to cook what smelt like roast beef in the tiny oven.

'No. Just down here for the weekend,' Kate said. 'I was tempted though – very nice, aren't they?'

'You must be in one of them tarted-up ones, then. I mean, look up there.' She pointed to a damp patch green and grey with mould just over the kitchen window.

'Ooh, that looks nasty,' Kate agreed. OK, if the woman had a Cockney accent, she'd better slip into the London twang she'd acquired during her time with the Met. 'Have you complained?'

'Have I complained! I've complained till I'm blue in the face. Where does it get me? Nowhere, that's where. You know what I think?' the woman said, filling the kettle and switching it on. 'Cup of tea? I always have one this time of the afternoon.'

'Love one,' Kate grinned, consigning Rod to his chilly fate a little longer. But she mustn't forget the milk she'd come for. 'Mrs – er?'

'Ooh, I'm Madge. Everyone calls me Madge. Called me Madge even before everyone called everyone else by their Christian names. Only you're not supposed to call them Christian names any more, are you? First names. Family names. That's what my daughter says.'

Time to interrupt. 'Well, I'm Kate: first name or Christian name – choose your pick.'

'That's a nice old-fashioned name. Go on, sit yourself down. Biscuit? No? From round here, are you?'

'Croydon. But I work in Birmingham, now.' She tweaked the conversation abruptly. 'Have you had this place long?'

'Ooh, ages. I won this premium bond, see – must be twenty years ago – and thought a time-share would be a nice invest-ment. And my old man – that's him you can hear snoring – he says, "Madge, the south coast's the nearest I want to be to the Continent, thank you very much," so we come down here.

Usually click for a nice bit of weather – your Indian summer, like. Don't know what's gone wrong this last couple of years. Global warming, they call it, don't they? Only it seems to me to be getting colder and wetter. Listen to it now.'

Kate listened, and thought of the double-glazed room she'd be occupying later. 'You like it enough to come down the same week every year?'

'Well, it was real lovely when it was new. As posh in its way as those places they're doing up. But that's the trouble, see: it isn't new any more and they won't spend on the maintenance we all have to pay. If you ask me, that's their game: they want us to sell back to them cheaply so they can do them up and sell again at the top of the market. But you should talk to some of the others. We've just got damp: they've got bad drains, and worse. Trouble is, you can put up with things for a week, can't you? And you don't get the chance to band up with everyone else.'

'Hmm. Divide and rule.'

'Anyhow, my old man reckons they should call in the environmental, that's what.'

'That bad, is it?'

'And they don't do anything. That's what gets me. That patch was there two years ago. Not so big and not so brightly coloured,' Madge reflected. 'But my old mum always used to say, "A stitch in time, Madge, you remember that. A stitch in time!"'

'Quite right. We've got this hole in our bedroom ceiling: we told them about it, of course. I wonder if they'll do anything about it?'

'How long are you down for?'

'Just this weekend. We won it.'

'Won! Ah, you fell for their old three-question trick, did you? They say that's the way they pull the punters in. And are you going to buy?'

Kate shook her head. 'Might have done if they'd put us in one of the new apartments. But imagine, a hole in your bedroom ceiling!'

'What sort of a hole?'

'Just a little one in the corner.'

'In the corner? Well, I'll be blowed: Dad was saying he'd seen a hole. Now, where would that be? Finished your tea? Well, pop your head round the bedroom door and see if it's in the same place.'

Kate got to her feet but demurred: 'But your husband's asleep—'

'Well, nothing'll wake him, not with his Sunday lunch and a couple of pints in his belly. You come on.' Madge led the way.

Kate followed. The stertorous snores continued with no variation in pace or volume. Madge peered exaggeratedly round, but Kate, lurking behind her and hoping to be out of the camera's range, spotted it immediately.

'In the corner. Up there,' she whispered.

'What, that thing that looks like some spider curled up? Fancy Dad spotting that. And fancy having two just the same.'

'Just fancy,' Kate agreed.

Rod was in the living room when she returned, huddling pointedly over the electric fire and reading a police folder he returned in his briefcase.

'Any joy?' He eyed the milk. 'I think our last quid's about to run out, so I don't think there'll be any call for that.'

She swilled it straight down the sink. 'Let's talk as we head for the car. Though I suppose we should wait a decent interval in case Madge spots us going.'

'Madge? Ah, the milk lady.'

'The same.'

'We can sneak round the back. If we leave the nuns' dorm curtains drawn, she'll think we've retired to bed.'

'Like her snoring husband, sleeping off his Yorkshire pud.'

'Quite. OK, got everything?' As before, he seized both cases.

She looked round – even, in a way that would have made Aunt Cassie proud, under the beds and in the wardrobes. 'Yes, I think so. What about those sales folders?'

He smiled. 'I've got something to report, too. No, Kate – after you!'

So she gave him a heavily edited account of her dealings with Madge. 'And you? Come on, Rod: you've got a very silly grin on your face.'

'That's merely in anticipation of this evening. But maybe you'll find it interesting that not only is the hole – as you predicted – covered with Polyfilla, but the folders they gave us have disappeared too.'

'But why?'

'Perhaps the charming guy who looked like a Florentine princeling thought we were unworthy of them. Or perhaps my observation about the hole scared him a little and he wanted to make sure there was no evidence.'

'I wondered why you were as open as that.'

He kissed her lavishly. 'I was open because all I could think about was – nothing to do with police work and I wasn't concentrating.'

'So what were you thinking about?' she teased. It must have been the same thing that was dominating her thoughts.

'I'll show you when we get to our hotel.'

5

Kate had never before had the luxury of typing up a report while being driven up the M25, but, then, she had never before had the luxury of being stuck unmoving on it for an hour and seven minutes. According to the car radio, there was a problem on the slip road to the M3. Rod hummed along to Radio Three while she used his laptop.

'Sue said it was best not to try to get on the M25 before ten,' Kate reminded him apologetically.

'We weren't on it till ten. We may not be off it till ten – tonight, that is. We should have brought iron rations and that pink loo roll.'

'There's water in my tennis bag,' she volunteered. 'And some chocolate. I could scramble over and get them out.'

'What are you waiting for? Scramble away!'

As if on cue, the moment she unclipped the seat belt, the traffic started to move.

'Shame,' she said. 'It would have been nice to stay here another hour, just us, cocooned from the world.'

'Back already, Kate?' Sue asked sarcastically, looking at her watch.

Since it showed after three, Kate could scarcely blame her. 'Awful traffic, Gaffer.' She thought it tactful not to mention a leisurely lunch with tender conversations in a pub off the M40. It was the sort of village, Rod had said, holding her hand, that he wouldn't mind living in one day.

'We heard. Nasty pile-up. We should be glad we're not in Traffic, and Motorway Traffic in particular. Just let me have your thoughts on paper – shall we say this time tomorrow?'

What on earth was going on here? Sue, wanting stuff in writing and at such short notice? 'No problem. Earlier if I can make it.' She'd been on the brink of offering to download it on the spot, to make up for her lateness. But she remembered the dictum of never apologising and never explaining. She'd simply get it on Sue's desk at eight the following morning and graciously accept whatever Brownie points Sue chose to dish out.

Tuesday, the report safely delivered, saw her back in what passed in CID for routine. Lunch, in contrast to Monday's, had been a sandwich eaten on the hoof. She'd just left a meeting with a probation officer when her phone rang. She was to join a hurriedly set-up surveillance from the top floor of a run-down college with an unsurpassed view of a scrap yard reputed to be dealing in counterfeit BMW parts. But she'd hardly settled her elbows on the windowsill and focused the binoculars when her phone rang. Sue. A replacement was on her way. Kate must return to the city centre, but not to Steelhouse Lane. She was to report to the Assistant Chief Constable's (Crime) office in Lloyd House, the headquarters of West Midlands Police, as soon as she could. The ACC? Lloyd House?

The crawl back was almost as protracted as the M25 trip. But there was no Rod beside her.

Sue wasn't audibly tapping her nails on the central table when Kate finally arrived, but the ACC (Crime) was. No doubt he'd have preferred to give a better impression of the efficiency of his force to the third person present. Kate recognised her immediately, but wasn't sure how she'd react to a friendly smile.

Soon after her arrival in Birmingham, Kate had been despatched to Devon to liaise in a case of possible child abduction in a little seaside town. The Detective Chief Inspector down there – a formidable woman out to prove that there was no need to retire at fifty, or sixty, or even seventy – was a stickler for protocol. In others, at least. But, though she always expected to be addressed as 'Ma'am', she'd taken an intermittent shine to Kate, possibly because, an unexpected overnight guest in the DCI's cottage,

Kate had proved adept at washing up. Kate could still see the tottering heaps of food-encrusted crockery and saucepans she'd boiled umpteen kettles to clean. And now DCI Earnshaw was up in Birmingham, getting to her feet with the dignity of Victoria R rising from a plinth.

She shoved out a comradely paw. 'Nice to see you again, Power. They got rid of the stupid sod who sent you on that wild-goose chase down to Dawlish, I hear. And so I should hope. Complete waste of space.'

Kate hoped her smile of agreement might appear to the ACC more like acquiescence.

Earnshaw sat down, smacking her palms together and grinning. 'Now, Power, how soon can you pack your bag?'

Kate felt her face pale. Leave Rod, now?

'Assuming, of course, you want to,' Sue added, swiftly. 'You do have a choice in this.'

How much choice did an ambitious young officer ever have? Even one rapidly falling in love?

'Sit down, Sergeant Power,' the ACC said firmly, with an avuncular smile. 'This is the situation. The Devon and Cornwall people need someone to go undercover. Fast. In a Sophisticasun complex.'

'Dawlish, again. Or nearby, at least—' Earnshaw interrupted him.

The ACC continued, 'They want a bright, experienced officer—'

'From a different force, of course. So I said I wanted you,' Earnshaw said. 'Just the woman, I said. I came up by train so you can drive me down this evening and I'll explain as we go.'

To her fury, Kate started to blush: the way she'd meant to spend this evening was very different.

'Oh, got other plans, have you?'

Kate smiled as coolly as she could. 'None that can't be altered if you need me. But I would like to know what the job you have in mind entails.'

The ACC said, 'That seems not unreasonable. And seems not

unreasonable for DI Rowley to make her observations, too, since she is already short of officers. Meanwhile, I think we should ask for tea and coffee.' He pressed a button on his phone.

Sue nodded approval. Perhaps sympathy. But she sounded a note of caution. 'I've—' Then she smiled warmly. 'I've already told the ACC how speedily you got that report on my desk. Well done, Kate.'

'Thanks, Ma'am.'

Sue acknowledged the formal response with the flicker of an eyebrow.

Rod, hair still damp from the shower, uncorked a bottle of rioja. He was wearing a silk dressing gown that he'd produced from his briefcase. He'd just tucked a toothbrush and some Sensodyne toothpaste into the tooth glass with Kate's. He was making a statement. What a pity she had to ask a question.

Each time she tried to frame it she failed. Her mouth just wouldn't say the words. It wanted to say silly, affectionate, tender things, the things lovers always say. She wanted to touch and hold him, just as every time he passed her his hand accidentally or otherwise brushed against her. At last, when she'd placed the steaks and salad on the dining-room table, she forced the words out. 'How would you feel if I was sent undercover?'

The shock and anxiety in his eyes belied the cool way he submitted the wine to his inspection before he spoke. Yes, his hands were shaking. 'That depends on a number of factors. Where and why? And – more importantly – if you want to go.' He made a great show of dressing the salad and tossing it.

'This sounds like a re-run of this afternoon's meeting. Something's up in a holiday complex in Devon. Another Sophisticasun. I'm to go in as a cleaner.'

'That's absurd! Middle management, more like.'

'They don't have a vacancy for a middle manager. They want nice clean loos. And a pair of eyes and ears.'

'On the alert for what?'

'They're so bloody vague. They wouldn't send in the cavalry for a few more surveillance cameras, surely.'

He shook his head. 'I'll try to winkle more out of Sue. I don't want you put at unnecessary risk.' That sounded good. 'And don't forget, some of the Sophisticasun people would know you if they saw you again. I'm not sure I'm happy about this – purely from a professional point of view,' he added, his eyes telling her what he thought of it from a personal one.

'Earnshaw wants me to start tomorrow,' she said eventually, failing to keep her voice light and business-like. She swallowed a sob.

He responded by peering round in an exaggerated hunt. 'So where is Earnshaw? In your spare room?'

'Sue Rowley guessed I had company this evening: she took her off my hands.'

'Which implies she'll be returning her to them tomorrow. So your decision's made.' His voice was tight, sharp.

'On the contrary. I said I wished to discuss it with you – no, I didn't mention you by name – before I made any decision at all.' She reached to clasp his hand.

Retaining hers, he said slowly, 'We agreed, when we became – friends – not to let our relationship get in the way of work.'

'Nor work in the way of our relationship.' Oh, that was what mattered. She could reach for the phone and tell Sue now.

'It needn't.' He gave a sudden, positive smile. 'How long do they want you in Devon? And would you be working round the clock seven days a week?'

'Depends on the shifts in whatever job I get. I suppose we ought to be pleased that our weekend's activities slotted a piece into someone's jigsaw.' She withdrew her hands to break bread, which she found she didn't want to eat anyway.

'I'm glad our activities fitted a far more important pair of pieces together.' He toasted her, but left his food untouched too. 'Cleaning! Not even clerical work.' He shook his head.

'Maybe if I'm good they'll let me try selling apartments. Even fitting up little surveillance cameras.'

'But what are they hoping you'll find?' It was a rhetorical question.

'Drugs? Fraud?'

'Those wouldn't explain the surveillance cameras.'

'Whatever it is has got Important People like ACC's interested.'

'Which sounds big-time, not small-time. And that means you're up against dangerous people. Oh, Kate.'

'I know that. Which is why I haven't made up my mind yet.'

'What would you have done a year ago?'

She said with simple truth, 'Jumped at the chance and hoped I'd be killed. But' – she dropped her eyes shyly then raised them to his – 'I wouldn't want you to go through a quarter of what I went through when I lost Robin. And I wouldn't want to die without knowing what could have happened between us.'

'You're very quiet, Power,' Earnshaw observed, wrestling with her seatbelt after a comfort-break at Michaelwood Services. 'On the juice last night?'

'No more than usual, Ma'am.'

No need to tell her about the heady rioja and headier emotion. In the end both her and Rod's brains had agreed that she couldn't throw up the chance Devon offered. What their hearts and bodies felt was entirely another matter. She had an idea that Rod might be as unwilling for her to take risks as she suddenly was to take them. She also suspected that he'd make use of his rank to bully their Devon and Cornwall colleagues into giving him more information than they would want to about the back-up they intended for her. And – as they'd affirmed over their breakfast toast – it wasn't as if Dawlish were off the map. In fact, it was only a few miles off the M5, and he could be down within three hours if his free time chanced to fit in with hers. 'Which I'll try to ensure it will,' he'd promised.

Though they both knew that a sudden death on his patch could render the promise void, they'd pretended to be comforted by it.

Then there was Aunt Cassie, who they'd made time to see after their supper. She'd put her head down and wept at the thought of not seeing Kate ever again.

'It's only a matter of weeks,' Kate had insisted, kneeling beside her, clutching the liver-spotted hands and wiping tears. The old lady, always so proud of her appearance, was beginning to sprout coarse hairs about her lips. Though she'd rather do the service herself, Kate must ask the care assistant to attend to them.

'Weeks? When you're my age you don't have any weeks to spare!'

Rod had stepped forward to put his arm round Cassie's shoulders. 'I'll come and give you news of her as soon as I have it myself,' he promised. 'And if there's no news I'll come anyway.'

'What about that other chap? Will he come too? Because I haven't seen hide or hair of him for a while.'

Oh, dear. But she'd told Rod about Graham's visits to Cassie, made when he was supposed to be seeing his mother-in-law. 'Graham's on holiday, Cassie. But I'm sure he'll look in when he gets back.'

'Holiday? But Mrs Nelmes is still here.'

Kate's stomach sank. Cassie was beginning to lose it, wasn't she? Not quickly, not obviously, most of the time. But there was just the odd slip of logic – Rod would refer to it easily as a *non sequitur* – to betray her.

'Yes. His mother-in-law stayed here. She didn't want to go on holiday with them—'

'That's all you know about it. She'd got her bag packed. But they left her behind.'

It sounded as if Graham had his own problems with elderly women and their memories. Poor Graham. But the weakness of her sympathy surprised her. All she could think was that Rod cared enough about her to visit her great-aunt.

'You got PMT or something?' Earnshaw demanded. 'Because you've been driving like an amateur. Are you insured for other drivers?'

'Fully comprehensive, Ma'am.' Kate fished the keys from the ignition and walked round to the passenger door, expecting to hold it open for Earnshaw. But the older woman had other ideas – she'd already hitched herself over the gearlever and handbrake and was adjusting the seat. Kate surrendered her keys. Was the gesture symbolic? She hated being driven by other people, putting herself in their hands. But she was about to put her whole life into Earnshaw's care. Maybe if she drove well it would be a comforting omen.

'So if I give you some idea of the set-up, we'll fill you in on the detail later,' Earnshaw said. 'Jesus, look at that pillock over there – mobile and fags and trying to drive. Serve him right it I pulled him over. And what does that stupid cow . . . ?'

'So it was a case of too much bed, not enough sleep, eh, Power?' Earnshaw chortled as she pulled into Taunton Deane Services. 'Need a pee; that's the trouble with getting older – can't trust the bladder.'

Kate followed her to the loos. Was Earnshaw right – she'd just needed a nap? Certainly she felt much better. What little of Earnshaw's driving she'd seen before her eyes closed had convinced her that she was in the hands of an expert, and that the woman's eyes missed nothing. In fact it was her continuous commentary on the faults and foibles of other road users that had lulled Kate into a defensive doze. The trouble was, she'd probably missed important briefing material. Still, no doubt it would be repeated.

'That's better. And now we'll have a cuppa and a bite of elevenses. At the tax payers' expense, Power – we don't have to shell out these prices. All that for two coffees and two Danish!' She grabbed the receipt and pressed it into Kate's purse. Then she narrowed her eyes like a mariner scanning the sky and headed for a table in an alcove, already occupied by a couple of men, one Kate's age, one Earnshaw's.

'Nice kisses all round,' Earnshaw ordered. 'Mother and daughter-in-law being reunited with a couple of husbands. I shall be glad when the hairdresser's got hold of you, and you've got more appropriate clothes. Don't pull that sort of face. Young Sue Whatsit tells me you've got a bloke who'd like to have you back in one piece, and since he's a rank above me, I'm doing what she says and getting you thoroughly disguised. OK?'

'OK, Ma'am.'

'Better make that Ma for a bit. Now, your father-in-law here is Superintendent Knowles, who's co-ordinating this for the Devon and Cornwall Constabulary, and your husband's Craig – er – Knowles, a sergeant like yourself. It's Craig with whom you'll have everyday contact. In fact you'll be living with him for a while. So where's the ring, Craig?'

Craig produced a battered specimen, holding it up for her inspection and then pointing to one area, as if he'd been having it repaired. She slipped it on. It was on the loose side, but she rather preferred it that way. 'I've kept my own surname, then?'

'You're that sort of woman. Stroppy,' Craig said.

She might as well behave that way. 'Hang on: you're supposed to be our parents but you're still active police officers. Does that make sense? Shouldn't we be orphans or something?'

There was a silence Rod would have described as satisfactory. Jesus, it seemed as if they hadn't thought of such an elementary precaution. Here was she, about to give up all her life – her friends, relations and lover – to become someone else, and they hadn't sorted something as basic as that. If mistakes were made, it would be she and this Craig who would pay for them.

Earnshaw was extra gruff – with guilt, Kate hoped. 'You'll go back with Craig. Your dad and I'll take your car and lose it. You're sure there's nothing to identify you in your luggage? No photos or anything?'

That was the hardest part. She dug in her bag for her organiser. 'Keep this safe for me, Ma.' She attempted Rod's ironic tone. They'd know she was angry, but wouldn't be able to fault her professionalism. 'All my life's in there. Driving licence, warrant card, donor card. And all my phone numbers – I deleted them from my mobile.'

Her 'father' patted her affectionately on the shoulder as Earnshaw stowed the diary in her own case. 'You'll do. You toddle off with young Craig, now. He'll tell you everything you still need to know.'

She hoped so, but there was something about the set of his mouth that told her she couldn't guarantee it. What if she pulled out now? She still could. She could report to her Birmingham superiors that Devon and Cornwall hadn't got their act together. But there was this pulse of adrenaline telling her she was starting an interesting case. She shut her mouth on her protest.

'Have a good time,' Knowles added more loudly. 'But remember, don't do anything mother and I wouldn't do!'

'As if I would,' she said equally loudly, dotting kisses on their surprised foreheads.

6

Currently sporting a mousy wig with blonde highlights until she could get her hair unrecognisably restyled, Kate was now reincarnated as Kate Potter, aged thirty-one, unemployed, and living with her common law husband Craig. He was officially an odd-job man who made most of his no doubt undeclared income tidying gardens for pensioners. They'd just moved, it seemed, into a house in one of the many new estates circling Newton Abbot: half the homes were still being built, and the roads mere tracks. The bonus was that no one knew anyone, of course.

According to Craig, Kate Potter had had a variety of jobs, ranging from work in an old people's home – true, of course, in Kate Power's case – to being a dinner lady. She'd done phone-sales and data inputting, but had had to give that up as a result of RSI.

'What about my paper qualifications?' Kate asked, watching Craig fill the kettle with far too much water. Rod had been punctilious about never using more than enough.

'What about them?'

'Well, I need to know why I've got such a funny work pattern – some people stuff, some unskilled, some skilled.'

'I'd say you're a bit on the feckless side, to be honest, Kate. You got – let's think – five or six GCSEs.'

Needled despite herself, she said, 'So I'm not stupid. I presume I managed to keep the certificates safe, just in case an employer needs to see them.'

'Of course. And you started a couple of computer courses, but your elbow meant you had to give up. It's better now, to all intents and purposes. If admin work involves keyboard skills, you can do it. But you have to take regular breaks – right?'

'During which time I keep my eyes and ears open.' Kate looked around the bright little kitchen. For a starter home it wasn't bad, but it wasn't what she was used to, and Craig, though probably likeable enough when you got to know him, wasn't Rod. She sipped the tea Craig had passed – he'd sloshed in so much full-cream milk it was miserably lukewarm – and tried to suppress a sigh.

If he heard it, Craig ignored it. 'Thing is, you've got to be flexible. Whatever vacancy Sophisticasun ask the agency to fill, you've got to be able to do it. It's just a huge slice of luck that they recruit this way.'

'Presumably it's a way of cutting costs. But, as you say, convenient. And we've got a mole in the agency?'

'Right. She's useless. But even I don't know who it is.'

'Bloody hell! Are you sure we're not in the wrong movie? Shouldn't we be in a James Bond or something?'

'Maybe we are.'

'In which case I'd have thought I'd need much longer to pick up this new identity. Not to mention sorting out whether I've got parents. It'll be easy to make slips.'

Craig stirred three sugars into his tea and sat beside her at the breakfast bar. 'I thought you were supposed to be a fucking pro.'

'I am. You are too, I daresay. But our gaffers are behaving like a pair of amateurs,' she insisted.

'You keep your tongue off them. They're good officers.'

'Perhaps they haven't handled undercover work before.'

'They'll be fine. If we are. You, more particularly. You've been briefed.'

Brief was the word. 'Yes, but—'

'There you are then. So no more fucking carping remarks. OK?'

'But Earnshaw said—'

'Are you deaf?'

So this wasn't the moment to confess she'd slept through some of Earnshaw's monologue. She'd try a different tack. 'Does the agency debrief people leaving Sophisticasun?'

'No. Why should it? It's there to find them other work, of course. But it was the speed of turnover that alerted our contact.'

'OK.' She managed to convert another sigh into a yawn and a stretch. 'I suppose that nice little fridge doesn't run to the ingredients for lunch?'

'That's one of the things we need to do. A supermarket shop. And a visit to a garden centre. You're a bit town-pale, you see, and we reckoned you'd probably turn your hand to the garden.'

'You're supposed to be the jobbing gardener.'

'Quite. When did you last know a builder with a decent house, or a plumber whose taps didn't drip? OK? So am I going to get out and soil my hands in my own garden? I think not.'

Kate shrugged off his patronising sneer. 'Point taken. It'll be a nice way of keeping fit, too. I take it Kate Potter won't be playing tennis or using the gym.'

'She might play tennis in the park, but not with the sort of fancy racquet I'd guess you use. Unless she got one second-hand, or off the back of a lorry. We're not on sergeants' incomes any more, Power. I'll show you our bank statements after we've grabbed ourselves some food. But I daresay I could afford a pub lunch, so long as we have something cheap. We'll go to Teignmouth. There's some nice pubs in the old docks area.' He looked at her critically. 'Shouldn't you get that wig on straight?'

'Let's put a hairdresser's on the agenda too.'

Perhaps it was easier to become someone else when you were younger. To shed the habits of speech and posture and dress and tastes in food and music you'd acquired over the years. To say goodbye to loved ones for indefinite periods. To stop being yourself . . . Kate couldn't remember feeling this disorientated the time she'd started work in the old people's home. On the contrary, she'd sailed in, improvising if necessary, like a kid in a Wendy House. No cares, no responsibilities – just a bright girl being nice to old ladies. Now she felt unbearably tense.

Craig was driving. She wasn't sure if the M reg. Escort would have been his natural choice, but thought it better not to ask. He must have upgraded the sound-system, which now sported a CD player.

'Ministry of Sound,' he said, slipping in a CD. 'House OK for you?'

Ah, the music, not the place. As it happened, it wasn't. The combination of the heavy beat and the in-car air freshener (pungent pine) was tightening her temples until she was ready to scream. Especially when he drummed offbeat on the steering wheel and half-sang the odd phrase. Instead, she fished a couple of aspirin caplets from her bag and managed to swallow them without water. Roll on the pub and lunch. Meanwhile, she must take her mind off her headache, and the thwack of the badly adjusted windscreen wipers – which might have been left off for all the good they did – by asking questions. Next journey, after all, he'd probably while away the time by asking her questions about her fictitious life. If he were a pro he would.

'What about my accent, Craig? Not very Devon, is it?'

'I told you: you're originally from Birmingham. That's where you've just come back from. We had a tiff, you see, and my mum went to fetch you down.'

'Why Birmingham? Not Leicester or London?'

'Because, you've got a fucking Brummie accent.'

'I never have!'

'Bloody have.'

'Oh, my God. I shall have to sort that out—'

'But not while you're down here. You stayed with friends in – hang on, is there somewhere called Kings Norton? Right?'

'What sort of friends? Apart from close enough to stay with if we've had a spat. And why didn't you come up for me?'

'Working: that's what the rows have been about. My not pulling my weight. This is Teignmouth, by the way.' He turned down a steep hill through what on a drier, sunnier day might have been a pretty seaside town. He pulled into a parking slot on a sodden sea front, the fairy lights and attractive gardens looking as off-key as Christmas decorations in January. After feeding a space-age parking meter, he led the way through increasingly narrow streets to what was obviously an old part of the town.

'Some nice pubs down here,' he said. 'Choose any of them.'

She was about to turn into the first when she stopped. 'That's the sea down there! But I thought you parked by the sea.'

'I did. By the sea. That there's river – the Teign estuary – and the harbour. They used to build ships down here but where the yard was they've put up posh flats. See? Come on. I wouldn't recommend the cider in here: it goes to the legs before you can say *pissed*.' They stepped inside the bar, small, cosy, with a real fire at the far side. 'Over in that corner – you get the table and I'll get the drinks. What'll you have?'

She must have been tired. 'White wine, please,' she said without thinking.

He turned back, stabbing her chest. 'None of your fancy stuff down here, my girl. You're not in Kings Bloody Norton now. Lager? Coke?'

He was quite right, of course.

'Sorry, Craig. It's what my friend Caz always has and I've got a taste for it. But I've got such a bad head I could fancy – I'll just have water.' She sat, without waiting for a reply. She had a feeling that she and Craig would do tetchy couple very well.

She looked at him as he waited at the bar. His head was unusually round, and his cropped hair didn't improve it. He'd obviously got his share of sun earlier in the year, and was tanned wherever you could see – including, as he leaned forward to talk to the barman, his builder's cleavage. Nothing if not authentic. He had the right build, too: very solid, compact. Not much above five eight or nine.

As if aware of her scrutiny, he turned round and smiled, ambiguously. God, what if he got the idea she fancied him?

Picking up their glasses and a couple of packets of crisps, he came back over. As he sat down he raised an eyebrow.

Yes. Bad mistake. And a woman wouldn't have inspected her man like that either. She'd have known how he looked, fastened, after an absence like this, on the parts she loved the most. Rod, now: she'd be looking with tenderness at the way his hair curled softly, vulnerably, into the nape of his neck.

Craig sat on the bench but leaned heavily against the back of her chair. 'Penny for them.' He clinked his glass against hers.

'Cheers. Thanks.'

'I said, "Penny for them".'

'If you must know I was thinking about this chap I met in Birmingham,' she said, loud enough for anyone to hear. 'Though what my thoughts have got to do with you I'm sure I don't know.'

'That sort of thought's my business all right!' Yes, he was good at this.

'I daresay you met other girls while – while I was away!'

'What if I did? It was you walked out, not me.' He looked up. 'Ah, here's our food.'

Kate wasn't sure when she'd last eaten burger and chips. Certainly not since she'd been with Rod, either as a friend or now as a lover. For one thing, he was getting to the age where cholesterol mattered – it hadn't taken a colleague's untimely death to remind them of that; for another, he just didn't seem to be the sort of man to want to munch his way through a burger and bun. No, he wasn't finicky, certainly not effeminate. It was just that – yes, come to think of it, Rod had the neatest table manners of any man she'd ever met.

'Why didn't you ask what I wanted?'

'You always have burger and chips.' Craig looked genuinely affronted.

'Well, in Birmingham I had other things. And liked them better. And lost half a stone,' she retorted. 'So next time, if you wouldn't mind just asking—'

'There won't bloody well be a next time if you carry on like this! Just shut up and get on with it.'

She decided they'd done enough to establish themselves as unhappy – should anyone be interested, of course. The burger was surprisingly good and the chips excellent. But if she didn't want that mythical half stone to make a genuine appearance, she'd have to be firm about choosing for herself. She'd also make sure she was in charge of the shopping trolley when they did their supermarket run.

The rain had given way to pallid autumnal sun when they came out. She headed straight to the estuary end of the road and breathed in the smell of childhood holidays – the early holidays spent with her parents, as opposed to the later ones when Aunt Cassie insisted on taking her. Diesel; seaweed; salt. Then there was the slap of rigging – was it called the shrouds? – on all those little boats. Across the estuary – the tide must be high, since a cargo ship was picking her way, low in the water, out to sea – was another town, more a village, climbing up a huge red cliff.

'Good to be back, is it?' Craig asked, pointedly.

'Funny thing: I think I have come back. I'm sure I've been here before,' she replied, her voice very low. 'When I was very tiny. Four or five. Isn't there a ferryboat – a little bucket of a boat? Black and white?'

For the first time he looked at her with real respect. For a feat of memory! Not for the decision to give up her real life. Her happy life. She realised with a sudden glow that since she and Rod had been together, she'd been happy. For the first time in years. But Craig was talking.

'If you come along here – these used to be proper fishermen's cottages, but you can see they're all poncy weekenders' places now – you can see where the ferry sails from.'

It was chugging towards them as they arrived.

'Don't even think of asking if we can go across on it,' he continued. 'We haven't the money, and it's too bloody touristy. Shaldon's not Kate Potter's sort of place, either. Very few shops, and some very posh houses.'

'Isn't there some sort of tunnel through the cliff? And a little zoo?'

'Right. Back home –'

Home? The sight of Rod in her kitchen ripped through her. That was home.

'– there's videos, slides, picture postcards – you name it. And maps. You have to memorise things you haven't even seen. You should do well with them.'

'Fine.' Yes, she'd always had a good visual memory – could read Ordnance Survey maps too, thanks to a martinet of a geography teacher, who'd dinned contours and spot-heights into them till they could all read them like books. Thank you, Miss Firth. You never knew to what use the skill might be put, did you?

'I suppose I could take you along to Dawlish – show you a bit more of the coast.'

'That'd be useful. It's a nice day for a quiet drive, too.' She meant it as a straight observation.

'No need to be sarky.'

'It *is* a nice day – now. Look at it! Perfect for September. There's even steam coming off the street.' She thought of Madge and her desire for an Indian summer, and her resentments against Sophisticasun. Well, she must get stuck into this for the sake of Madge – and all the other Madges no longer getting value for money.

Surly, whether in response to her naïve pleasure or simply in role, Craig strode off back down one of the narrow streets. She dawdled, looking around her, trying to fix buildings in her mind. Then she stopped dead. A tablet on one of the tiny houses told her that Keats had stayed there. In 1818 – only a couple of years before his death. She'd remembered crying at school when she'd learned what a short life he had. God, the discipline and organisation of school seemed a long way away. She could have done with that comfort now: especially a bell ringing to tell her she could go home.

'Now what?' Craig demanded, stomping irritably back to join her.

She'd better lie. Any moment now the sniping of their roles could be for real. In any case, Kate Potter wouldn't be worrying about Keats. 'I was wondering about that hairdresser.'

'Yes?'

'There'd be some in Exeter, I suppose.'

'Bloody hell, there are hairdressers everywhere, woman. We're not looking for a top salon here.'

He was right. Forget the good cut that she tried to make part of her monthly routine. She must keep thinking on her feet. 'I'd have thought a big anonymous place with a brisk turnover of clients, wouldn't you? Not a salon in a small town like this where you'd be remembered. Or am I getting paranoid? Besides, I shall need cheap clothes: I can't wear jeans forever.'

'Cheap?'

'As you said, cops earn more than the Kate Potters of this world. I need bottom of the range chain stores.'

Craig looked at her anxiously. 'You won't need me, not if you're crawling round the shops.'

'You could always advise me on colour and style,' she suggested, tongue in cheek.

'Not bloody likely.' He didn't seem to have noticed he was being teased. 'OK. You can go into Exeter in the morning.'

She bit back an angry retort: she hadn't been asking his permission.

Apparently he didn't have her forbearance. 'In the meantime, you'd better make sure the wind doesn't take that wig.'

Craig drove her along a coast road with impressive views of a seriously choppy sea.

'Is that the railway there?' She pointed down to their right.

'The main line. It runs right along the coast here. We're dropping into Dawlish now, and then it's Dawlish Warren – lots of caravans and chalets. And it's just inland from the next little place, Cockwood, that you'll find the Sophisticasun development.'

Cockwood was a scattering of cottages and a tiny but idyllic harbour, picturesque as a jigsaw puzzle scene. Presumably some of the little boats bobbing in the breeze belonged to Sophisticasun owners.

'Nothing but a couple of pubs,' Craig observed disparagingly. 'And the railway line.'

'Is there a bus? I mean,' she added, as he manoeuvred round badly parked cars, 'a regular service? Good enough to get me here from Newton Abbot? Or a train?' As if on cue an HST roared along the line.

He snorted. 'Plenty of trains, but they don't stop at every hole in the hedge. And believe me, Starcross, your nearest station is just a hole.'

'Bus?'

'Every couple of hours. When it decides to run.'

'I'll have to get a bike then.' Surely that was unanswerable.

'A bike on these hills? You've got to be joking! Maybe a motor scooter or a tiny fart-and-bang motorbike. That's what I'd go for. But you'd need a licence.'

'Passed my test when I was seventeen. Not that I've ridden one for years.'

'Something you never forget, riding a bike. I'll have a word with Earnshaw when I see her.'

So he got to see Earnshaw and she didn't? She turned her head sharply enough to betray her disquiet.

'I do her garden, don't I? My dear old mum's. Part of the set-up.'

So he had Earnshaw's ear on a regular basis. But such a bloody unnecessary risk. Should anyone ask, of course. She hated this punching at shadows. As for her contacts with the others – well, she wasn't about to ask this man. She'd better just shut up and get on with things.

But that didn't extend to sharing his bed.

'Get real, Craig. Nice try, but—'

'But we've only got curtains up at the one bedroom window.'

'Then you can sleep without curtains.'

'Me sleep without curtains! What about you, if you're so awkward?'

She sat down on the stairs. 'Craig, I suppose we have to quarrel for the sake of our neighbours. But I really think we've done enough for tonight. Let's just call a truce – a nice audible one if you want – and then behave like the professionals we are. Where are the curtains for the spare room?'

'In the airing cupboard,' he mumbled.

'Hang them, then.' She'd had quite a day. Their drive had culminated in an acrimonious trolley-push round Tesco's. Since then she'd read and re-read her new life, and been questioned on it. Then there'd been six hours of maps and photos and questions about maps and photos interspersed with questions about Kate Potter. Now she was too knackered to do any more. 'I fancy some camomile tea. Want some?'

He leaned towards her, as if to prod the chest of some rookie constable. 'Truce? You want training, that's what, Power. Kate Potter drink fucking herbal tea? You're off your head.'

She mustn't engage. 'Let's just say it's something she picked up in Birmingham. Like I picked up the camomile tea-bags in Tesco. If Craig Knowles doesn't like herbal tea, then he can drink what he bloody does like. So long as he gets it himself.'

'You're sure you're all right, Kate?' Rod persisted, the concern in his voice warming her heart. Thank God for mobile phones. Though even they would be out of bounds when she got really stuck into role.

She tried to be more positive. If she smiled, the smile would come out in her voice, wouldn't it? 'It's just jet-lag. And before you say I haven't flown anywhere, you should have seen Earnshaw's driving. And there's no doubt that Teignmouth is in a different time-zone from Brum.'

'It's not far off the motorway, though. Would you fancy a visit from your cousin this weekend?'

This time the smile was unforced. 'Rod, I'd like that more than anything in the world.'

'So would he.'

She was still smiling when she went to sleep with the mobile phone tucked under her pillow.

The weekend, and Rod. Kate was sure that it was only the thought of seeing him that had kept her going through the hours of preparation. She only wished her superiors had thought things through as well as she and – yes, she had to hand it to him – Craig were doing. Nothing had quite prepared her for the prosaic little phone call telling her that she'd be starting work the following week at Sophisticasun, and that she should go in to the agency to sign all sorts of forms and disclaimers. But once she'd signed, and been given her instructions, she felt better than she had since she'd arrived. And there was Rod. Only another seventeen hours to go.

Did the secrecy they'd have to maintain add a frisson? Possibly. But being with him in the same room wouldn't, surely feel like imprisonment, not if it were for the whole weekend.

Earnshaw had decreed that Craig and Kate should leave as if for a weekend together. Although he was eating into his own free time, Craig dawdled so much setting out that Rod, despite his hundred and eighty mile drive, had reached the meeting place in Plymouth half an hour before they had.

'Why on earth did they have to land you with such a gorilla?' Rod demanded, the preliminaries once over. He'd booked in at a suitably anonymous hotel, one of a chain, under his own name. Kate had been happy – if embarrassed – for it to be assumed that she was his married cipher.

'God knows.' She watched with pleasure as he padded, still naked, over to the kettle and returned with cups of English breakfast tea. 'The story is supposed be that although we've bought a nice new home – goodness knows how we pay the mortgage on our combined pittances! – the relationship isn't very good, and I'm happy to work hours of overtime as much to keep out of his way as for the money. Which is how it's turning out to be.'

'Whose idea was the hair?' He ruffled it, but with some amusement.

'These streaks? All the rage, I'm told. I don't think I can blame him for it. Someone had provided me with a wig, so I had to imitate that. More or less. And less, it has to be said, rather than more. Anyway, it'll grow out.' And though her Birmingham hairdresser would blench at both colour and cut, he'd be able to remedy the depredations of Tammy, the soi-disant stylist.

'And you start work – not that I'm sure you haven't been working your socks off preparing and rehearsing – on Monday?'

'Yes. Getting out of the house should improve the atmosphere. And I'll carry on with the garden.' She explained.

'You're good at gardens. Will you advise me when you come home?'

Home: it was the caress of the word that made her heart leap.

'It's so anonymous. Yours – you've already set your stamp on your house – and your garden too. It feels more like home than my place has ever done. Though perhaps it's because you're there. Would you – would you bring your toothbrush over to my bathroom to see if it makes any difference?'

'"I'm a blue toothbrush, You're a pink toothbrush . . ."' she sang, cornily.

And the rest of the weekend passed in a glorious blur of silliness and sex and affection and – yes, it was love, wasn't it? The L word. The feeling of ease and comfort she'd once had with Robin, though he was such a different man. Never with Graham. She'd always felt she had to gain his approval. As if he were some reliable, responsible father, the sort she'd never had. It was time to let him go: they were better off without each other.

Until five o'clock on Monday morning, she could count herself a very lucky woman.

And even though it had hurt horribly to bid him goodbye – they'd risked the change-over at Exeter Services this time – his promise that he'd be with her the following weekend would keep her going this week. Of course, there was always the caveat that work must come first – his or hers. But if the gods had been unkind enough to pull them apart during the week, perhaps they'd smile on them at weekends. Meanwhile, there was his smile to remember – and his touch, his taste, and his smell.

So this was her first day cleaning the lavatories and other public areas in the Sophisticasun Cockwood complex. There'd been no one to meet her, just an overall and keys handed over by a night-time security guard going off duty. The list of instructions was crumpled into the overall pocket.

A quick look round as she'd walked into the complex – she'd taken a long route, on the excuse, had anyone asked, that she wasn't sure of her way – hadn't suggested any of the building works that had been supposed to keep potential purchasers away, but perhaps all the work was internal, and the builders and decorators arrived when builders and decorators got around to it. Or a round tuit, as one of her acquaintances had called it, saying, come to think of it, that you could buy round tuits in the South-West. She must keep an eye open for one of those, too. A silly present for Rod.

Nothing at all suspicious. Nothing to raise a single hair on the back of the neck. It'd be more scary helping kids across the road in Kings Heath. She couldn't get into the apartments, so she wouldn't be able to check on whether they too had little surveillance cameras.

So on to the lavatories.

It didn't need Gary Vernon, the complex manager – how many meanings might that have, varying with the way it was stressed? – to tell her that her predecessor had been a disappointment. Kate believed in clean lavatories with the absolute faith her Irish ancestors might have had in the Sacred Heart. How they'd come to do a volte-face and become Protestants – indeed, fully-fledged Baptists

– she didn't know. Perhaps she could research her ancestry when she retired. In the meantime, as she filled in a chit requesting new (and plentiful) supplies of bleach and other cleaning fluids, she felt a certain sour pleasure in a job well done.

Next job: dusting and vacuuming the manager's office.

'Shouldn't you have done this first? Before I started work?' Vernon asked irritably, pushing at fair, wispy hair that would soon give up trying to cover his pate. At least he hadn't gone for close-shaven brutalism, which wouldn't have suited his rather gentle face. She put him in his late thirties.

'Sorry, Mr Vernon. But I didn't know where the keys were kept. And I could get on and do the other stuff so I did.'

'Good girl. Well, I usually take a stroll round about this time to check that everything's OK – I suppose I could do that now. Now, I'll leave the voice-mail activated, and the fax switched on. So don't worry about trying to answer anything.'

'Thank you, Mr Vernon. Goodness! When was this place last given a thorough going over?' She ran a finger over a shelf in a gesture that Aunt Cassie would have applauded. 'And those poor plants –'

Today she wouldn't even attempt to look at files, though he'd obligingly left the computer running. As she ran her long-handled duster round, she realised it was a good thing she hadn't. Lurking behind a cobweb was a little black lens. She stared straight into it, giving it an extra tickle with the duster for good measure. Christ! What a good job she'd done nothing untoward. A punctilious wipe down of the filing cabinets and cupboards showed they were filthy and fitted with far from standard locks. It looked as if she was thoroughly stymied. But on the principle that she had to do something that might push things forward, without alerting any watcher, she scraped together a hazy plan. Attacking the fax machine with the duster, she mimed getting the fabric stuck. Anyone seeing her would have approved of her determination to wrest it free. In doing so, she removed a considerable length of fax paper. If he needed to replace it and couldn't, she would leap to the rescue and so impress him with her skills he'd ask her about her background and move her on to clerical work. Well, it was a nice fantasy. Meanwhile, today – and for several other days – she would simply demonstrate, to him and to the little eye, what a good worker she was. To her annoyance, the first thing she had to do was empty the vacuum cleaner, a procedure that took longer than it should have done because there was no instruction manual and the diagrams on the machine might well have defeated a rocket scientist.

'Still here?' Vernon demanded tetchily when he came back. Despite a healthy outdoor complexion, he nurtured his reputation as an overworked middle manager by hunching his shoulders and carrying a file wherever he went.

'The vac was full: that's why your carpet looked scruffy. Trouble is, I'm almost up to today's hours. Looks as if I'll have to leave it till tomorrow.'

He looked harassed. 'I've got a meeting in here later. You couldn't put in a bit longer? Do less another day?'

She pulled a face. 'They said at the agency I mustn't do that. I mean, I'm willing to oblige, but you have to fill in proper time-sheets and things.' As he well knew. For Sophisticasun's records and the agency's.

He tutted with irritation. 'I have a budget to keep to.'

He'd only been trying to screw extra hours from someone on no more than the legal minimum wage. The mean bastard!

'Oh, dear. Thing is, Mr Vernon, like you said, the girl before me let things slip a bit. If you want things brought up to standard . . .' She gave him a sudden smile, the one that released her dimples. *You'll find a way*, the dimples said.

To her amazement he blushed. 'Look, just do your best for today: I'll sort out extra hours for later in the week. If I can.'

She looked with touching regret at the dust. 'If you can sort it out, I'll have another go tomorrow. That'll be best, won't it?' Not only best for his organisation, but also best for her plans. 'And then we'll see how we get on. Right, Mr Vernon – give me just two minutes with this vac, and I'll be out of your hair.'

That done, she trundled her vac and trolley round the rest of the place. Even in this building there was a mixture of the new and prestigious and the older and distinctly tatty, so perhaps Gregorie had been telling the truth. The manager's was the only office to be smart, despite its patina of dust. Some of the other offices – the catering manager's, for instance – were so ill-lit and badly organised she was amazed no one had reminded management of minimum health and safety standards for the workplace. But she was here not to raise a dust, merely to clean it up. She worked with a will, but it soon became apparent that to make any real impression she would have to work far more hours than she was contracted to do. Perhaps this explained the brisk turnover of her predecessors, and there was nothing sinister at all.

So why was everyone taking the whole business so seriously? OK, patchily seriously. Silly question, with that little lens in the corner of the manager's office. Innocent businesses didn't usually run to those. Interestingly, none of the other offices seemed to have them. What about sound bugging? She'd have to get one of them organised, as soon as she could.

The morning's hours completed, she returned to her little motorbike. While it was hardly a transport of delight, she'd become quite attached to it since it had arrived on Thursday. She'd already spent hours pootling round the steep-sided lanes, learning all the routes to the complex, which lay between a separate caravan park – yes, run by a different firm, absolutely legitimate according to Craig – and Cockwood village. At first she'd confined herself to learning the twists and turns while the visibility was good. Now she was happy to explore even in the mist that hung cold and damp over the coast. She wanted to know it like a native: better than a native. She couldn't believe it could happen, but one melodramatic scenario was that one day she'd have to make her escape on the bike, maybe in the dark. She would be prepared.

And she wouldn't be trapped in the house with Craig while she was preparing herself. It was hard to tell how much of his truculence was an act, how much his real personality. She rather feared it was the latter, that he was a far from new man still expecting a woman to play a natural second fiddle and be grateful for any crusts of kindness. The brief time he'd been in Rod's company had been interesting to say the least, the hostility between the two men almost palpable.

The mist had lifted by mid-day. She was getting hungry and ought in any case to report back to base. Base meant Craig, of course, unless he'd found some sort of work. So though she headed back to Newton Abbot, she chose the coast road from Teignmouth so she could stop off at a big garden centre. She was supposed to prettify the garden on the grounds of getting exercise and putting colour in her cheeks, and apparently their budget would stretch to buying what she needed that wasn't already in Craig's kit. When she found an arrangement of ready-planted pots she was tempted, and when she found one small enough to fit in a pannier she couldn't resist it. For balance she bought two. They would go by the front door, cheering the grass patch – she could hardly call it a lawn – with colour from the pansies and golden-green thuja. Though she bought for Craig's plot, in her mind's eye she saw Rod's.

The following morning saw her maintaining her standards in the lavatories, and arriving at Gary Vernon's office once again while he was still in it.

'Sorry, Mr Vernon. Still no key. And I'm afraid if I'm to make any impression on this I shall be more than the seven minutes I'm allowed. Did you sort out the extra hours, by the way?'

'I must admit,' he began, tipping his chair back and making his hands into an irritating, headmasterly steeple, 'that at first I was reluctant. But after I saw your work in the facilities – well, I shall certainly do my best for you.'

'Thank you, Mr Vernon. Now, I don't have to worry about answering anything, do I?'

He checked. 'Voice-mail on. Fax on. OK? No problems.'

'Thanks. I'll get on then, shall I?'

As soon as he'd gone, she put the vac down, as casually as

she could, against the door, and, under cover of dusting his desk, removed more paper from the fax. The work of seconds. There. And then on to the rest of the room.

'I'd really love to get those windows clean,' she said confidingly when Vernon returned. 'And I know I won't have time for that. But I have thought of something. So long as we don't tell the agency.'

He jerked back his head in suspicion.

'It's just that when I've cleaned the swimming-pool area, I've noticed there's no one around. I suppose I couldn't swap an hour on those windows for a bit of a swim? When it wouldn't offend anyone?'

He relaxed. 'There's hardly anyone here to offend,' he admitted, 'after this weather. Have you ever seen so much rain? And now this mist. No wonder people don't want to come down.'

'But haven't they already paid for their week in advance? It seems such a waste . . . I mean, if you've booked to go to your holiday camp you'd want—'

Vernon waved an admonitory finger. 'Holiday camp! Uttering those words is a sacking offence! This is a holiday complex. People own properties here for a week or so a year. So the complex doesn't have to be seething with people for the apartments to be occupied. Sometimes people will rent them out to friends. Or they could swap them for one year with people in another complex. Sometimes they'll come for just two or three days of their seven.'

'If I'd got somewhere like this I'd want to get my money's worth.' A comment that applied equally to both Kates.

'Anyway, having a half-empty complex'll make life easier for you this Friday, of course. And on Saturday.'

'Saturday?' she repeated, hoping her dismay didn't show.

'Yes, of course. Changeover day. Or perhaps the agency puts in someone else at the weekend.'

Kate nodded. 'That'll be the answer.' She didn't add it was probably an attempt on someone's part to evade employment law support for part-time workers. 'Do you and all the admin. staff have to be here Saturdays, too?'

'It's our busiest day.'

So when did he take time off? But she wouldn't ask yet.

'Especially,' Vernon continued, 'when we have punters coming down to see how they like our facilities.'

So why had Gregorie put them off? 'Punters?'

'We need to sell on properties to new purchasers.'

'Oh, I thought people rented them or something.'

'They buy them,' he said firmly.

'Ah! Time-share!'

He shook his head. 'We prefer not to call it that. We prefer to call it joint ownership. You can't have seen any of the apartments, yet, of course. I'll have to arrange that for you.'

Yes!

'Oh, I'd love to see them. So long as you don't try selling me anything. We're up to here' – she raised her hand an inch or so over her head – 'with our mortgage. And bad weather means people don't want their gardens done. Can't have them done, really, whatever Craig says. He reckons they're just being awkward, of course.'

'Craig's your husband?'

She leaned forward as if sharing a secret. 'That's what I call him. And – well, I know I wear his ring. But you know how it is with men these days.'

'Not me, Kate, I assure you. My wife and I – we've got our tenth anniversary next month.'

'Well done! That's really cause for celebration these days.' She beamed. 'Goodness me, look at the time. Right, Mr Vernon: I'd best carry on, if it's all the same to you.'

'Of course. And I'll think about that swimming. I personally can't see any objection, but if people have paid for something, they don't always like sharing.'

She nodded glumly. She might have asked to swim when there was no one around: what she really wanted to do was bump into as many people as she could when she wasn't decked out in her cleaner's uniform.

'Leave it with me,' he said.

The conversation clearly at an end, she pottered off and threw herself with a will at the carpet of the bar. She rather thought wiping the tables was the province of the bar staff. At least, it would have to be today, if she was going to finish anything like on time. And for the wages someone like her was getting, she was damned if she was going to work unpaid overtime. Not without a swim to compensate.

8

'What do you mean, you're not going to change shifts to get on this weekend lark?' Craig demanded, slamming the tea towel he'd not got round to using on to the breakfast bar.

'Precisely that,' Kate said firmly, wringing out the J-cloth and hanging it over the mixer-tap to dry. 'Not this weekend, anyway. It's too early. Vernon's marked me down as a goody-two-shoes: I don't want to be promoted to plaster saint. Not yet. In any case—'

'I suppose your toffee-nosed boss is coming down for another poke, is he? That's the way you got promotion, is it? Funny: the word on the street is you were shagging some other boss—'

She slammed down her rubber gloves and turned on him. 'That's enough, Craig. We have to work together. Unfortunately for me it means we have to live together. But I don't have to take that crap from you or anyone else.'

'Too close to the truth, was it?'

'I don't suppose you'd know the truth if it poked you in the eye. My relationship with Superintendent Neville is that I'm a sergeant.'

'But not for long . . .'

'No. People on the accelerated promotion scheme don't hang around that long.' It was the first time she'd ever been glad to be fast-tracked. 'I take up a posting as inspector as soon as there's a suitable slot. And my relationship with Rod the person is none of your business.'

'It is if you'd rather spend the weekend fucking than doing what you're paid to do.'

'Currently the complex pays me to work seven till twelve five days a week. I've wangled a couple of extra hours. I've got permission to use the swimming pool, which means contact with the residents. Hasn't it penetrated into what you call a brain that if I suddenly turn up on Saturdays as well it'll look bloody suspicious? Jesus Christ, call yourself a detective!'

'Don't you take that tone with me. I'm fucking good at my job.'

'And you notice I don't tell you how to do it. I treat you as a professional. Have the courtesy to treat me the same.'

Most of the argument so far had been conducted in fierce undervoices, lest the detail of their quarrel carry to their neighbours. Now Craig audibly changed gear.

'*Have the courtesy! Have the fucking courtesy!* Who d'you think you are? Lady Muck? Get out before I throw you out.'

'You try it, Craig. Just you try it. You'll be out of your job quicker than I can say cop.' She grabbed his arm to stop him hitting her. To make the point she twisted it till the elbow joint must have screamed. Then she pushed him on to the nearest kitchen stool. 'Look, you're fitter and stronger than me. You could break me in half if you wanted to. But my timing's sharp. It has to be because I'm small. Now, think about what I said and see if my timing doesn't make sense in this job, too.' She turned and left the room, closing the door quietly behind her.

The following morning, she risked it. As soon as Vernon left the office, she nipped behind his desk to dust it. And to look at the computer. Nothing but a screensaver, of course. A casual dab with the duster brought back the original screen. A memo. Dare she scroll down? Printing was out of the question with that eye on her.

The door opened. Jesus Christ! Thank God for plan A.

'Tell you what, Mr Vernon,' she said, pointing. 'Your fax paper's a funny colour. Pink streaks on it. Doesn't that mean you're running out?'

'Surely not – yes, well spotted. I'd better fit a new roll.' He unlocked a cupboard, which proved to contain stationery, and, clutching a roll, strode authoritatively back to the machine, which he then stared at blankly.

'Shouldn't your PA do that for you?' Kate asked. She was fairly sure that he had no more than the part-time services of a temp from the agency that employed her, but a little judicious flattery rarely came amiss. And her hands were shaking too much to offer to try, herself, at the moment.

'As and when she manages to get in. Hell!' He stared at the machine much as Craig would no doubt stare at their washing machine, unused, so far, except for Kate's things.

Kate cleared her throat. 'D'you want me to see? – I mean, they say two heads are better than one.'

As soon as he stepped aside, she could see what had to be done: with luck it would take several minutes to slide the slippery paper through the tiny gap.

'There. You have to slide it in there, somehow.' She must let him try, and boost his ego with a bit of admiration if he managed it. If he didn't, then she too could waste a few moments. The hands would soon be steady.

No prizes for him, after four or five attempts. Nor for her, until, inspired, she folded the sheet to a point, as they mysteriously did with loo rolls in the sort of hotels Rod favoured. Immediate success.

'Well, I'm blowed,' he said, obligingly.

'Me too. Nasty fiddly thing. You'd think they'd design something that takes five seconds, not five minutes.'

'My God, has it taken that long? Oh, Kate, I'm so sorry. It must have thrown your schedule right out.'

Not as much as being found accessing his computer would have done. And she'd managed to turn a nasty moment into a chance of brownie points. 'I'll just have to rush round a bit. But I don't like skimping, Mr Vernon. I don't want you getting complaints about me. Or the agency. I really need this job.'

He looked at her under his blond eyebrows. 'Things still bad at home?'

She nodded, looking away as if to stop him seeing tears. 'Still, as my gran used to say, what can't be cured must be endured. Best get on, Mr Vernon.' She switched on the machine and attacked his carpet with vigour. She'd let him settle down before the next move, so she started on the corridor outside. After a few moments, she tapped his door, popping her head round immediately. 'I forgot your bin, Mr Vernon. Seeing as I'm running late, can I pop it in the ordinary waste or does it need to go for shredding?'

The shredding pile was something she still hadn't managed to check. Next week, maybe she could risk offering to deal with it.

Vernon hesitated. 'Oh, general rubbish. Or is there—? No, it'll be OK, just this once.'

She'd always wondered why cleaning ladies wore capacious overalls: as she stuffed a couple of memos marked CONFIDENTIAL into her pocket, she realised why.

The trouble was, when, on her way back to Newton Abbot, she fished them out of her pocket and smoothed them out, she couldn't work out why anyone had bothered with the warning in the first place. As far as she could see, all she held in her hand was information about a new office plant supplier – quite justified, if the state of the present droopy specimens was anything to go by – and an invitation to join a neighbour for a drink. But since she wasn't likely to have been sent undercover simply to detect neighbourly hospitality, she folded it again and replaced it with the other in an inner pocket. At least she would have something to discuss with Craig.

There was no sign of him or the Escort when she got back: perhaps he was out pursuing what Rod had called his undercover avocation. With luck, some hard physical work should tap some of his testosterone and improve his health and temper. She was just rinsing salad for an early lunch when her mobile rang. Only three people had her number: Earnshaw, Craig and – oh, please let it be – Rod.

'Well?' It was Earnshaw.

'I've got a couple of memos that might make more sense—'

'I didn't mean that. I'm sure you're doing your work thoroughly. But what about this business with Craig?'

Alarm bells rang. 'What business?'

'You tell me.'

'I think he's been taking his role a bit seriously.'

'How?'

'Well, we're not supposed to be your ideal couple: the neighbours are supposed to here us yelling, aren't they?'

'Can you keep on working together?'

'Do I have a choice?'

'It's not so much you as him. And he says he can work better on his own – he'll try and get a maintenance contract for the grounds.'

Heart leaping at the chance of giving up and going home, she heard her mouth say, 'Trying to get isn't the same as actually working in the boss's office.' Damn her mouth.

'Or as filching the odd memo. OK. I'll bollock him, shall I?'

'What for?'

'Have you eaten yet?'

'Not yet.'

'Where? Somewhere halfway?'

'Not close to Sophisticasun, though.'

'OK. Any ideas?'

'Jack's Patch.'

'Eh?'

'It's a garden centre. They do nice lunches. And it's full of ladies treating their daughters. Even if most of the mothers are twice your age.' She gave directions. Although it was much nearer Newton than Exeter, the way Earnshaw drove and the rate her little bike phutted along, they'd probably arrive together.

As it was, she set off straightaway to give herself enough time to ramble round the outside section of the centre. Mentally she selected plants not for the Newton Abbot garden, but for Rod's: height, year-round colour – yes, she could soon have had it looking good. But daydreaming when she was supposed to be meeting her current boss for lunch wasn't a good idea. She walked briskly back to the covered area, past birthday card and pot pourri sections, till she fetched up in the little café. She bought herself a fresh orange juice and settled at a table from which she could see everyone who came in. She was given a certain amount of cover by a collection of half-abstract, half-representational metal sculptures of birds. Their labels said they were made in Zimbabwe, from recycled scrap metal. A particularly fine pheasant, slightly over life-size, had caught her eye – it would look wonderful on Rod's lawn – when she spotted DCI Earnshaw, looking as if she'd just emerged from the autumn pruning session of a particularly dense hedge.

The two women were well into their flans and salad. Once Kate had reported the surveillance camera and fancy locks, they'd talked about what in normal circumstances both would normally probably have stigmatised as girly things – Kate's hairdo, for instance, and her new clothes, which Earnshaw had considered looked too smart. 'Trouble is, when you're as slender as you are, even cheap nasty stuff looks good. Next time, go to a charity shop.'

Kate pulled a face. 'Wearing someone else's skin's one thing; wearing someone else's clothes is another.'

'Never knew you were a snob, Kate. How about some uncomfortable shoes?' Earnshaw pointed downwards with her knife.

'Uncomfortable shoes?' Kate peered at her trainers.

'Yes. So you don't walk so well. Old dodge. Surprised you don't know it.'

'I'll try anything. But maybe I don't need to do much more: they seem to believe in me at Sophisticasun as I am.'

'What's this about you refusing to work this weekend?'

Kate laid down her knife and fork, very carefully. 'That's what Craig says, is it? Bastard.'

'He may well be. But he's angry.'

'He should try listening when I'm briefing him. The cleaning work is divided between a number of workers. I'm their weekday woman for the admin and common areas. The only one.'

'What about the flats?'

'The punters clean them themselves during the week – if they want to. Other contract workers give them a proper clean during the weekend changeover. I'm busy making myself invaluable, but I don't want to push suspiciously hard.' She finished the water she'd had with her meal. Just now, she'd rather be on strong coffee.

'And you think getting on to the weekend roster would do that?'

'Always assuming I could, of course! We're talking about an agency being fair to its clients here – both the employers and the employees. We can't expect them to sling perfectly good workers back on to the dole just because Kate Potter fancies doing more hours than she's entitled to. There's another issue too: the sales team.' She reminded her of the problem.

Earnshaw shook her head. 'They wouldn't associate you now with the smart young woman I'm sure you were at their presentations. Even if they came across you, which they're unlikely to. No, no one notices cleaners.'

She pulled a face. 'I think the Hythe two would – you tend to remember people you don't like. Anyway, next week – as I told Craig – I shall approach the agency and ask if there's more work there. Or better still I'll get the manager at Sophisticasun to approach them.'

'What if Vernon wants a spot of the old quid pro quo?'

'He prides himself on being a family man.'

'Often the worst.'

So how many times might Earnshaw have been propositioned? She was just about the most asexual woman Kate had ever come across. 'Craig isn't serious about trying to get a job at the complex, is he? Because I wouldn't want him treading on my toes.'

'Well,' Earnshaw equivocated, scrunching her napkin, 'he's a dab hand when it comes to gardening.'

'You mean you've said yes?' She felt her grip tightening on the tumbler.

'I didn't say that. But there's a feeling that two might work better than one.'

'Gaffer: I've painted a nice little scenario for Gary Vernon, the boss. I need plenty of hours because the bloke I'm with has over-extended us on the mortgage. If the said bloke suddenly turns up on site with a nice fat contract, that blows my story out of the water. And maybe me with it. These people are pros, remember, even if we don't know exactly what they're professional at. Innocent employers wouldn't scan their employees' moves or go to such lengths to prevent anyone getting into a cupboard. I dread to think what their computer accessing system's like. Honestly, there's no way you should even consider the idea.'

'OK.' Earnshaw fished out her purse. 'Coffee? Of course,' she said, heaving herself to her feet, 'it would be good to have back-up on site – if there were any trouble.'

But Kate wasn't halfway convinced. 'If he goes in, Ma'am, I come out. I quit.'

'You're supposed to be doing a job, Kate.'

'Then let me do it. My way.'

'Craig's just as experienced as you. A sergeant, like you.'

'And a young man with a bob on himself. We can't afford to let ego get in the way.'

'You mean, not *his* ego.'

'If you like. I don't need this, Ma'am. Any of it. I'm under cover with a fraction of the time I should have had to prepare myself.'

'I briefed you. It was Craig's job to fill you in on the details: are you saying—?'

A chance to land him in it properly! Kate took a deep breath. 'All I'm saying is that I've got a house and garden crying out for me back in Brum. I've got an inspector's posting coming through any day. You want Craig to do the job – he can do it. Fine by me. Absolutely fine. I can go home.'

Earnshaw regarded her steadily. 'That's your last word, Kate?'

Kate held her gaze. 'My last word.'

9

Time to turn for home, then. The thought made her sick. She pulled herself together: that place in Newton Abbot wasn't home, of course, not within any definition of the term that she knew. It was merely a house she'd stay in just as long as she was doing this job. If it was shared by another officer she didn't like, and whose competence she seriously doubted, that was too bad. She was a professional, and professionals dealt with problems. But not necessarily by leaping on underpowered motorbikes and heading off into the hills.

And yet, why not? The sun was warm, the sky blue and almost cloud-free. The main road from Newton Abbot to the west called. Why not go to some of the touristy places she was supposed to know intimately? Buckfastleigh, for instance? But a couple of close-ish calls with Euro-monster lorries on the A38 convinced her that a trunk road was not the place for her, so she turned off at Ashburton, heading roughly for another tourist mecca, Widecombe-in-the-Moor. This time the road was crammed with coaches, which were worse than fast lorries. The best thing was to plunge on to a maze of tiny roads. Even without the Dartmoor speed limit, for which she thanked the powers-that-be, no one could hope to do more than twenty or thirty along these. There were vertical as well as horizontal bends, and some had worn so deep between the steep-sided banks she might almost have been riding through tunnels. But the tunnels always led upwards. She was heading, whether she liked it or not, for the moor.

Kate scanned the horizon. So this was Dartmoor. This was where they sent the worst cons. Except they wouldn't send them to a lovely area like this. She was on the elbow of some river, the grass in front of her showing all the signs of family picnics throughout the summer. There was even the tiniest of beaches – a patch of river-washed shingle at least. As she took off her helmet and shook her hair loose, combing it with her fingers just as if anyone might see and care, a couple of cars drew up. Eight elderly people got out, making much of erecting chairs and tables and making tea. The pretty wildness was immediately a domestic idyll. She consulted the OS map. This must be Hexworthy. So Princeton must be – yes, over there, just a few miles to the north-west. And maybe the moor wouldn't be so golden and lovely if you were an inmate on the run. You might have to pick your way through the sort of mist that had swirled round her on her early-morning journeys – thicker, more disorientating, because it wouldn't be just sea mist. It would be swirling low cloud, soaking to the skin, chilling to the bone. And the map told her that while the area between Hexworthy and the prison might be bleak, at least there were signs on the map of habitation. The section of the moors to the north of the jail would be far more intimidating – acres of exposed land, without even lanes to pick up and follow. What was it like to be so far from the next house?

Well, she told herself, folding the map, she wouldn't be finding out today. Or any day, probably – you could only walk that sort of terrain, and even then, to judge by the number of red-marked danger areas, you might find yourself being casually shot at by the Army.

Where next?

Home, she told herself ironically.

She locked the bike in the garage, remembering to heave it as close as possible to the rear wall so Craig could park his Escort. Which meant, it dawned on her slowly, that he wasn't back yet. Great. She pulled off her helmet and stowed it. A stretch reminded her how stiff she was – it was one thing to be fit, but another to use the muscles that cleaning used. How about a cup of some of that herbal tea and a long hot aromatherapy bath? She double-checked she'd bolted the bathroom door.

The bath was uncomfortably short even for someone of Kate's height, but she could submerge parts of herself in rotation while she lay and thought.

How would Earnshaw deal with the situation? She hadn't liked Kate's forthright rejection of Craig's suggestion: that was clear. But she wouldn't have liked it any more if Kate had been mealy-mouthed about it – rather less, probably. The trouble was, Earnshaw, formidable as she was, was only part of a team, and not the most senior member, either. How Chief Superintendent Knowles would feel about her threatened insurrection she'd no idea. It would largely depend on how Earnshaw reported it, no doubt.

What also mattered was how the hierarchy reported their decision to Craig. And when. And where she was at the time. Despite the steam still fugging the bathroom, she shivered as she dried herself. She might be sure of back-up in a professional emergency, but there was no friend to chew things over with. Not even a girlfriend to meet at the pub. She'd never lacked for companionship when she'd been at the old folk's home – part of the job had been to mix with the other carers as much as she could. But now she had no one but Craig, who was, of course, the problem. The bastard, going behind her back like that! That was better: a little righteous anger to counter his assumptions that he was boss, both in the job and in the house. There must be some straight talking tonight.

What irked her as much as anything was how the others were treating him. He had access to Earnshaw on a regular basis, while she waited at the end of the phone. He also hinted, though he'd never said outright, that he knew the purpose of their operation. Which, of course, she still didn't. Why hadn't they briefed her? Yes, she could get angry with them, too. But not until she'd gone and bought some food.

*   *   *

'You just don't get it, do you?' Craig exploded. 'Bloody prawn stir-fry!'

She touched her lips. 'Tell me what we're supposed to be arguing about this time, will you? If I'm to give a public performance, I need the script first.'

'What the fuck—?' But his voice died as she pointed slowly and exaggeratedly towards the party wall.

'Do you not like stir-fry?' she asked very quietly. 'Because I don't think you told me you didn't.'

'Little slags like fucking Kate Potter don't do poncy stir-fries, you silly bitch. Oh,' he continued, 'your high and mighty fast-track cop might, but not a working-class—'

'Keep your voice down, for goodness' sake. For your information I trailed round Tesco watching what other people put in their baskets. No – listen! Women on my sort of income don't go for the cheap nourishing stews that sustained my great-aunt: they go along the shelves looking for reduced items. Here: ready-prepared vegetables with stir-fry sauce – reduced by eighty pence. Chilled prawns, not to be refrozen, reduced by a pound. Frozen peas and young onions and coriander for the rice. What anyone would have bought. And – in case you're worried about not getting enough good old-fashioned British cholesterol – here's some end-dated Eccles cakes for pud.' She threw the packet on to the table, all the angrier because she knew in her heart he was right. She should have bought a ready-made stir-fry and left the coriander on the shelf. She hadn't even mentioned the ginger . . . Shit. 'Well?'

'Well what?'

'Well, what are you moaning about, for a start? Or how about, *Well, I'm sorry I flew into a silly paddy*?'

'Don't you take that tone with me!'

'What tone do you want me to take?'

'As if – as if—' He slammed his hand hard on the kitchen bar. The knives on the chopping board juddered; one fell off.

She poured a couple of glasses of the wine she'd bought. Yes, that had been an extravagance. But there was nothing in her contract anywhere that she knew of that said she had to go teetotal. And it was the sort of wine she'd bought before Rod had come on the scene.

'In here,' she said, heading into the living room. She turned on the radio, to give them some cover, in the unlikely event that their neighbour, so intrigued by the lack of shouting, might press a glass to the party wall. Then she sat down, in one of the easy chairs, not on the sofa. A cosy chat might be on the agenda, but not too cosy. 'Isn't it time we talked properly, Craig? This unhappy-relationship scenario seems to be going too far. We're supposed to be colleagues, supporting each other.'

'If you're talking about me taking on Sophisticasun's gardening contract . . .'

'We could talk about that if you like. It would have been nice if we'd talked about it before you took the idea to Earnshaw. Then you could have explained the pros, as you saw them, and I could have told you what I saw as cons.' When she got no response, she added, more roughly, 'Neither of us is playing solo, here, Craig. It's Jack and Jill time. You fall, I come tumbling after. And vice versa.'

'I don't like leggy tarts who sleep their way to the top and then come lording it over me! Fancy accent! Fancy clothes! Fancy fucking food!'

'Accent – Brummie: you said so. Clothes – I've yet to hear that Matalan's haute couture. Food – we've already spoken about this. OK, you were prejudiced against me from the start. And that stopped you telling me what I need to know: what I'm looking for, up at Sophisticasun.' OK, it had stopped her asking him, but in her anger she wasn't going to mark herself down for inaccuracy. 'All I know is stuff about my past, and a bit about your present.'

'You know all you need to know.'

'Wrong on two scores. I need to know the entire purpose of the operation. Earnshaw clearly assumes I know all about it and there's no way I was going to drop you in the shit by telling her you hadn't filled me in, chapter and verse.' Or to admit she'd slept her way through important discourse. No, attack was the best means of defence. 'Secondly, if I know what makes you tick, then I can work out if I can trust you – and I'm talking about trusting you with my life, Craig, because that's what playing big-time involves.' Rod would have raised lovely, darling elegant eyebrows heavenwards at the rash of clichés.

Craig didn't. 'Why does Earnshaw want to keep me off the Sophisticasun contract if it isn't something you've said?'

'Because it doesn't fit, I suppose, with the scenario of us being at each other's throats. You'd hardly want to come and work at my place if you were playing away from home.'

He jabbed the air. 'But I've got this idea for getting in . . .'

'Get this into your head, Craig: I *am* in. Five days a week. Maybe, if I think it's safe, at weekends. Under the steady gaze of a surveillance camera, remember.'

'If *you* think it's safe!' He rolled his eyes.

She must keep calm. 'I've already been to two other Sophisticasun sites as a potential buyer, don't forget: it'd look a bit weird if one of the sales staff who work at weekends recognised me. In fact, I'd say it'd blow the whole operation.' She sipped at her glass, then drained it. Not the quality Rod would consider worth savouring. A bit thin.

'Fucking hell, why didn't you tell them that before?' Craig jumped up, towering over her. 'I tell you, you're just not professional!'

'Sit down and listen. You heard me say it yourself. At the service station. Didn't you? No, hang on – while you're on your feet, why not bring in the rest of this?'

'What did your last slave die of?'

'Was I going to cook tea for one or for two? For Christ's sake, Craig, what is it with you?'

He slunk off, returning with the bottle, topping up his glass as he walked. He parked the bottle by his chair as he sat down. She stuck out a hand for it. She wasn't going to kneel to him, no way. After a moment's hesitation, he grasped the neck and swung it so she could just reach, if she stretched. Her hand remained where it was. If the battle of Chenin Blanc were in progress, she would win.

He swung the bottle again. It was a good job it was half-empty. Still it came short of her hand. At last, sighing hugely, he inched his haunches far enough forward for the next swing just to reach her. She could chalk up victory in that skirmish: now she had to win the battle and eventually the war.

She would start off with what seemed a concession. 'They've obviously kept you in the dark too – about how I got involved. I won' – she hooked her fingers into quotation marks – 'a holiday with Sophisticasun, and my boss told me to go along with what was obviously some ploy to make me buy something. So I turned up first at their complex near Oxford and again at one near Hythe. All this was part of some investigation Sue – that's my boss – knew about. When I put in my report, Earnshaw was on to it before you could say knife and had "invited" me down here.'

'Why you?'

She shrugged. 'They wanted someone from a different area. I got a conviction last time I was undercover. They haven't sorted out my first posting as inspector. I'd been to two sites. QED.'

'QED? What? Is that Greek or something? Us country bumpkins don't know Greek.'

'How's your maths?' she shot at him.

He frowned. 'I got my GCSE.'

'Including geometry? All that stuff about working out angles and stuff? In that case you know as well as I do what QED means. "This is what was to be proved."' So she couldn't hear Rod's voice pronouncing the Latin, she topped up her glass. 'Do you want to finish this off?' She leaned forward so he could take the bottle.

He pulled a face. 'It isn't very—'

'You're right – it's a bit thin.' Her face matched his. 'Trying to keep in role, see – buying cheap stuff.'

He managed a snort, which might have been reluctant laughter.

'So that's why I'm here,' she concluded. 'What about you?'

10

So why was Craig on his feet, looking at his watch and peering round the net curtains at the road.

'What's up?' Kate scrambled to join him.

He dropped the curtain. 'Jumpy, aren't you? What are you expecting?'

'Not so much what, as who.' Except she knew she was being illogical: she'd done nothing yet to arouse anyone's suspicions.

'Lover Boy from Brum?' he jeered.

Hell, she'd asked for that. 'Clever, clever. When it was you who was looking out? Did you hear something?'

He put his hands on his hips and turned slowly. 'Do I need to hear something to have a gander out of the window? I don't think so. Silly bitch: if you're as skittish as this, you shouldn't be in the team. Fucking hell, you don't even know what's worrying you, but you're sweating cobblers.'

She was, but wouldn't give him the satisfaction of hearing her admit it or give so much as a nervous, apologetic giggle. 'So why,' she asked, picking up the glasses and the bottle, 'this sudden interest in the street? Or our neighbours, or whatever? Or did you have a sudden attack of aesthetic distress because the curtain was hanging badly?' *Aesthetic distress* – Rod would enjoy that. Without waiting for an answer, she swept into the kitchen. Yes, he'd had the better of her in that encounter. But she still had to find out what he was up to, so she slung the empty bottle into an empty carrier – sooner or later she could take it to a bottle bank – and returned to the fray.

Or would have done if Craig hadn't been halfway through the front door.

'Where the hell—?'

'Going out with me mate, aren't I?'

'Mate? We're not supposed to be seeing our mates. Not from this house.'

'Nosey, aren't you?' He pressed her nose in what an outsider might have seen as an affectionate rebuke. The pain drew reflex tears, despite herself. He went halfway down the path, then came back to pat her cheek, again with force, not tenderness. 'Just so's you don't go whining off to Earnshaw, it's a new mate. Met him at a builders' merchant's a few days back. OK, your ladyship?' Another slap, and he was gone. Trying to stay in role – what would Kate Potter do? Ask him when he wanted his meal? She couldn't stoop to that. Wave dismally? Slam the door? Or simply droop miserably, holding her face, before trailing slowly indoors? She drooped.

The stupid thing was, she didn't know what to do about his dinner. He wasn't the man to come back and cook his half for himself, not with the skinful she expected him to have on board when he returned. And she wasn't going to get up in the small hours and cook it for him, no matter how touchingly wifely that might seem.

She could cook the lot, and put his share between two plates, so he could microwave it. That seemed the best option. By the time she'd started to worry what would happen if he didn't eat it then, about the waste if it were thrown away or the danger of attracting scavengers if she slung it on their infant compost heap, she knew she was cracking. Cheap wine or PMS? On the grounds he'd drunk more than half the bottle, she did what would at least have made Aunt Cassie cackle: she got her bike out and headed for the twenty-four-hour Tesco.

Fortunately – for she meant to buy decent, Rod-worthy wine – she'd only got as far as the confectionery aisle when a familiar voice hailed her. Which – given the breadth of her acquaintance in Devon – rather limited the field.

'Hello there, Kate: didn't recognise you at first,' Gary Vernon told her. As he pushed his trolley towards her, he was orbited by two school-uniformed children who might have been his clones, with their fine blond hair and ruddy cheeks. And their receding chins. The girl was about eight, her brother a couple of years younger.

Kate rather expected them to descend like locusts on the chocolate, but they held back, looking at their father, till he grinned. 'OK. A pound's worth each. You've been very good.' The look he gave Kate was sheepish. 'Parents' evening – and they both got excellent reports. So I've promised them a real treat the next weekend I get free. In the meantime,' he added, watching as they argued the merits of chocolate versus sweets, his eyes naked with love for them, 'I don't think this'll hurt them. Ah, here's your mum!' he added, more loudly.

Dressed like her husband in a suit meant to impress, Mrs Vernon was a neatly built woman a year or so older than Kate. She walked with a slight limp, and seemed glad to rest her hand on the trolley handle – certainly there was nothing possessive about her gesture.

'This is Kate, one of the cleaning team at Sophisticasun,' Vernon said. 'Kate, my wife, Julie.'

Julie smiled, exposing tired lines already meshing under her eyes, and put out a hand to shake Kate's. A decent woman, to shake hands with a cleaner; and a firm handshake, too. Kate smiled, allowing her dimples an airing for once.

'I've heard about you.' Julie's voice was surprisingly strong.

'All good, I hope,' Kate said, adding a slightly flustered giggle to compensate for the swiftness of the response.

'All very good. And you've worked wonders in Gary's office. I've often wanted to take the Hoover to it myself. Well done.'

'Thank you.' Kate Potter looked at her feet before managing another smile. Kate Power told her to turn the compliment to the kids. 'Mr Ver – your husband – was saying about your children doing well at school. Wish I'd worked harder,' she added, as the children came within earshot. 'You only get these chances once, don't you?'

'What did you want to be?' asked the girl. 'That you couldn't be, I mean?'

'Oh, something a bit better than a cleaner. A nurse, something like that.'

The girl looked at her with something like scorn. 'Why not a doctor? My teacher says girls can do anything!'

'I'm sure your teacher's right,' Kate sighed, 'so long as you get your exams and that.' At times like this she hated the sloppy vocabulary, the lapse into Brummie. She wanted to take this eight-year-old and talk woman to woman to her. 'Best be getting on, if you don't mind, Mr Vernon. Mrs Vernon. Early start, you know.' She reached for a smaller bar of chocolate than her original target, and trundled off. Before she bought any more wine, she must watch them safely through the checkout. As she peered at cheap offers on tinned beans and breakfast cereals, her path kept coinciding with theirs. From time to time they'd exchange half-embarrassed smiles. There were still no squabbles. The kids might be pushing the trolley but they made sure it went in straight lines and the girl kept flashing glances at her mother. They seemed anxious looks, too – as if there were something wrong. The limp? The tiredness? As they reached the checkout queue, Vernon hefted the boy on to his shoulders, as if he were three, not six or seven. The last thing Kate heard, as she made for the drinks, was all four voices raised in laughter.

Her nightly phone conversation with Rod over – this one had been distressingly short – Kate went to bed. She'd left Craig a note telling him his meal was in the fridge, and had taken the wine and the chocolate up with her, concealing the former in the bottom of her tiny built-in wardrobe. She would feed it into the common supply at intervals, provided, of course, that Craig showed some sign of reciprocating.

Empathy didn't seem to be his strong suit, however. Or even, what she'd have been happy with, common courtesy. She'd been deeply asleep when he at last came in, apparently trying to make as much noise as possible. OK: that was unfair. But he certainly made no obvious effort to be quiet. Apart from moving round a great deal, and using the bathroom a couple of times, shutting the door firmly, and audibly bolting it on each occasion, he must have devised a method of removing his shoes which involved dropping them: Kate heard the separate thuds.

By now she was so enraged she doubted whether she'd ever sleep. At home she'd have reached for one of her favourite books. The only reading matter here was a pile of magazines: *Hello!* and *OK!* Well, she supposed that Kate Potter would be interested in the lives of soap-stars, so she set to to memorise as much as she could of someone or other's tacky wedding. The trouble was, the following morning she couldn't remember whose.

She was always up and off before Craig surfaced – according to their preparatory notes, that had been a cause of dissension. Kate Potter had always accused him of lying in bed when he should have been off drumming up work. But this morning she was relieved not to see him. She'd had so little sleep she couldn't trust herself not to fan the flames of their previous evening's dispute by yelling at him. She might – to use Rod's word – remonstrate with Craig, when neither was quite so touchy. And he'd be touchy all right, if his regular flushings of the loo were any indication of the amount of booze he'd sunk.

But not as touchy as Kate would be if ever he parked his Escort again so awkwardly that she couldn't get her motorbike out – at least not without risking both sets of paint. After three or four attempts she knew she'd have to move the car. Was he careless enough to leave the keys in the ignition? No. They'd be in his pocket, presumably. She ran upstairs, intending a quiet burglary. But his bedroom door was locked.

Five minutes later, she was about to wield the pickaxe he used in his gardening work. But just as she lifted it, she heard him mutter. This time she'd simply bang on the door using the shaft. And yell, as she'd not stopped yelling.

The door opened. He was naked. 'What the fuck do you want?'

She glanced at his early-morning hard-on. 'Not that, anyway. Your car keys. You've parked so I can't move my bike.'

''Course you fucking can.'

'I'm already late for work. Move your car. Now.'

'What, like this?'

'Don't see why not. Shift your arse, man. I'm late for work. Can't afford to be late for work, can I?' she added, as he started to hunt for his keys. 'For Christ's sake, hurry up!' She joined in the search, shaking the jeans and trousers he'd left in a heap on the floor. Nothing.

'My things!'

'Your keys!'

'Don't worry – I'll move your fucking bike for you.' Grabbing a towel, he groped his way slowly down the stairs. She followed: she could check the living room and kitchen as she went. It was best to ignore the swearing coming from the garage, not to mention the ominous scrape of metal on metal.

She found the keys down the side of the sofa. And he'd manhandled the bike on to the path.

She'd talk to him about the damaged fairing later. At the moment the priority was work.

Gary Vernon looked at his watch as she came in.

'I know. I'm really, really sorry,' she said, before he could speak. 'Bloody Craig, wasn't it – he parked so I couldn't get at my bike. I'll make sure I do all my hours, don't worry. Oh, Mr Vernon: it won't happen again.'

'I hope you won't. But it sounds as if it isn't up to you. You're a good worker, Kate, but we need dependable people here.'

What had happened to the kindly family man of yesterday evening?

'I'll leave my bike on the drive or somewhere. Honest, Mr Vernon – I really need this work and I'm giving it my best shot.'

'What if the bike gets stolen?' he asked pettishly.

'The sort of chain I use?' No, that sounded too Kate Power. 'And I'll get another. Or I'll nick Craig's car.'

Vernon dropped his voice. 'Are you? – I mean, that sounds . . . Kate, sit down a moment. Does he – does he hit you?'

She remained standing, but shook her head, eyes filling at the sympathy, no, real kindness, on his face. 'Not yet. I'll go back to Brum if he does. My friend in Kings Norton. She says she'll get me a job at her place. But – well, I'm here now, Mr Vernon, and I'd better get on,' she concluded awkwardly. 'Tell you what, if you'd rather, I could leave your office for now, and come back later. Whatever's most convenient.' Did she dare ask about the stuff to be shredded? On the whole, not. She'd re-establish herself by working more than the half-hour she was late – goodness knew she had no reason to dash back to Newton Abbot. Then perhaps tomorrow she'd press a bit harder. At least while she was pushing the cleaner backwards and forwards over the carpet in the bar she could ponder her next move with regard to Craig: to grass him up or not to grass him up?

'See you back here later,' he said, nodding dismissal. Then he picked up what looked like the morning's mail. Damn, if only she could have hung back: she might have seen something, anything.

There was nothing to see when she came back to his office, either. He was still at his desk, attacking the computer keyboard as if it were a personal enemy. Then he transferred his attentions to the mouse, some pallid ginger Tom avenging a psychological defeat.

She made herself finish the vacuuming before she asked, 'You got a problem there, Mr Vernon?'

'The screen's got all these funny marks on it – it must be a virus or something! God, now what? You don't know anything about computers, do you?'

She inched across. 'I did start this course . . . Then I got a bad wrist: that thing that some doctors say exists and other say doesn't exist. Teeno something. It existed in my wrist, all right.'

'Computer course? I didn't realise you'd got qualifications.'

'Oh, yes. Not as many as I'd like, like I was saying to your little girl. But I got enough GCSE's to get on this college course. Only

I had to drop out, and the wrist means I can't do inputting and jobs like that.'

'So what are you doing cleaning?'

'It's a job, isn't it? And sometimes I get other casual work. But I can't pick fruit or flowers because of my wrist, see.' By now she could see the screen. 'Oh, Mr Vernon – you know what you've been and done. No, it's nothing to worry about. You just clicked on this little box down here, see? Where it says, "Outline View". All you have to do is click on one of the other little boxes down there: "Normal View" – that's how it looks then. Or "Print Layout View" – which isn't all that much different. Which do you want?' As she pushed the mouse she contrived to bring the top of the document into view. Hmph. A memo about health and safety: surely the wretched man had something more exciting to write about than that? And couldn't he write it in better English, for goodness' sake? 'The thing I always like was up here,' she said, clicking on the ABC icon. 'All those red and green lines under the words – it explains why they're there. See: it's telling you your sentence is too long or something. And it wants you to write it this way.'

Vernon gaped at her as if she were pulling rabbits from the screen.

'Oh, it's not rocket science, just what they told me at college,' she said.

'Can you – can you type?'

Yes! 'Only for a bit. In case this thing comes back to my wrist. Honestly, it's like red hot needles stabbing in to you.' She rubbed her right wrist as if in painful recollection. 'Now, I'll put that poor fern in a bowl of water in the loo – it'll turn its poor toes up if I don't – and then come and do your bins. OK?'

'Fine. Thanks, Kate. You've done a great morning's work.'

'You won't have to tell them at the agency – about me being late?'

'Not this time.'

★   ★   ★

'Poor little thing,' she cooed to the fern. 'You really need repotting, don't you? See if this nice drink'll help, just for now.' Under her breath she added, 'Funny that he didn't say not to bother – the plant suppliers should be dealing with you and your mates, like they said in that memo.'

This morning she had no time to make more than a random grab of paper destined for the shredder, folding it as flat as she could and stuffing it in her overall. She returned both bins with a cheery smile. 'Just got to bring that fern back, Mr Vernon, then I'll be off.'

'You haven't brought your swim things then?'

'You mean you've fixed it for me? Oh, aren't you nice! If you weren't a family man I'd kiss you!'

'If I weren't a family man you could,' he said, laughing. 'Yes, you can swim any time after work, so long as you promise to sort out this bloody thing next time it throws a wobbly.'

Kate bowled home the long way round – right up the Exe estuary, aiming to find the A380 just outside Exeter. But she got diverted. She'd never been to Topsham, had she? Why not go now, while the sun was shining and she felt good about herself and her morning's work? She found a parking slot in the main street, and wandered along enjoying the mixture of small shops and tempting restaurants: now, this would be a place to bring Rod, if it weren't so close to base. Look at that delicatessen, now! At the far end of the road she came to the river. How about lunch at that pub? No, not a very Kate Pottery thing to do. Nor, perhaps, was homing into the warehouse the other side of the car park: but being with Rod had given her a taste for antiques and she knew she couldn't resist three floors of them. In the event, she bought nothing, and felt curiously flat. Yes, it must be PMS. She always wanted to treat herself, as if buying things re-established a fading identity.

So to discover she'd parked right outside a charity shop was a wonderful surprise. At first she'd thought it was just a dress agency, but it seemed it was supporting the local hospice. Flexing her Kate Potter credit card, with its pitifully low limit, she sailed in.

11

When Kate got back from Topsham, Craig was back in bed, and, judging by his regular snores, sound asleep. What the hell did he think he was playing at, getting back in the small hours and needing to lie in till after midday? No need to ask what the smell was. Kate knew it all too well: cannabis. They'd agreed a no-cigarettes rule for the house, and here he was, not just smoking but smoking a particularly pungent type of pot.

Shaking out the clothes she'd bought, she felt a pang of guilt herself. Yes, she'd obeyed Earnshaw's injunction to buy clothes from charity shops, but Earnshaw hadn't meant her to buy a Yarell skirt, even if it was now cheaper that its new Matalan equivalent. But those colours – not to mention the cut! No, she couldn't have left it there. What she could do was shove it back in its bag and get Rod to take it back to Birmingham for her when he went back after their promised weekend together. Better still she could wear it this weekend while he was here. And putting it with her other clothes was better than trying to hide it, which would only draw attention to it. Out of the bag it came again, to be smoothed lovingly as she hung it in the tiny wardrobe. And then she reached for the scissors. It didn't need its label, did it? That would be much better cut into slivers and flushed down the loo. Except Craig wouldn't recognise Yarell anyway. What was happening to her brain? It must be the amount of Craig's ganja still left in the atmosphere.

Lunch? Well, that was easily dealt with. Last night's stir-fry would fill the bill nicely. She trotted downstairs to find it half-eaten on the kitchen table, a spliff stubbed out in the middle of the remains. The stupid bastard! Talk about leaving the evidence in full view!

'Well?' she greeted him icily when he at last came downstairs.

'Well what?'

She pointed.

'Shit!' He picked up the fag end, and crushed it into the sink.

Great. 'It'd be better flushed down the loo, I'd have thought,' she said.

He retrieved the by now soggy mess and sloped off.

She waited. There was nothing to be gained by laying into him as she wanted – not until whatever he'd put into his bloodstream was completely out again. Then they might have a rational conversation. Meanwhile, she had to eat, and there was some salad left in the fridge. Enough for two? Who the hell cared! As for his portion of stir-fry, that had better join the fag end in the sewerage system.

The afternoon was fine enough for her to continue her explorations of Dartmoor. First she went to Tesco, where she bought tights and, planning another attack on Vernon's computer, a special anti-static duster for TVs and computers. She also picked up fifty pounds in cash. Then she headed out again. This time she picked her way north on the A382: an A road, this steep and narrow? The Midlands road network must have spoiled her. At last, needing a loo, she pulled into a car park in Moretonhampstead. Whether it was the wind or the light, up here it felt quite autumnal. Perhaps she should turn round and go straight back. But she might as well see the place first, even buy something from one of the village shops. That was what she and Craig ought to be doing: buying local, not diving into Tesco for every last morsel. Except that was what Kates and Craigs did. Today, though, she'd pick up local cheese and a couple of bunches of wallflowers ready for planting. And then a sign to a second-hand bookshop summoned her: almost anything would be better than those gossip magazines. What would Kate Potter buy? How about a selection of crime and romance? A couple of Mary Wesleys? Yes. More interestingly, the bookshop also doubled as a pottery outlet. She could smell wet clay, so presumably it was made on the premises. And nice stuff it was too: highly individual, but reminding her in shape and texture of the Ruskin Rod lusted after. OK, Potter wouldn't have bought it, but Power couldn't resist a vase some ten inches high, crystalline blue-mauves merging into a cream background. The potter knocked a couple of quid off for cash, too. She'd ride home extra carefully: the vase must reach the sanctuary of her wardrobe. Then she could give it to Rod this weekend.

Except she wouldn't be able to. Almost as if someone had punched her stomach, she knew he wouldn't make it. Something would crop up, if it hadn't already. He'd be stuck on a messy case.

The potter, clay still grey under his fingernails, looked at her under bushy eyebrows: 'You all right there?'

She managed a smile. 'Someone just walked over my grave.'

He nodded seriously. 'Watch yourself on the way home. People think these roads are racetracks, come rush hour.'

Rush hour? Here? But he meant the commuters zapping home from Exeter and Newton to their desirable country dwellings, didn't he? And he was right to warn her. Suddenly her bike had become invisible, its red paint merging with hedge or tarmac. Give her the M6 any day: at least she dealt with that with the full-body armour of a car.

The call she knew was due came through at ten thirty. She took it in the kitchen. A vagrant had been kicked to death in Cotteridge.

Rod sounded as upset as she felt. 'I just can't leave everything to the squad. Oh, I know technically I could, but – Oh, Kate, I'm so sorry.'

'Of course you must be there. I do understand. I promise you I do. There's next weekend. But keep in touch. Please.'

'Of course I will. I spend all day wondering when it'll be OK to call you. Kate.' The tone of his voice said far more than any words. 'And I worry about you. Undercover's never easy. I've tried to pick Sue's brain, by the way, but she's very cagey. So do take extra care. Especially with that bugger as your partner.'

She responded in kind. 'You mustn't worry about me. It's all very quiet and normal. The only espionage has involved the theft of a memo about office plants.'

'Office plants!'

'Drugs, do you think?' No, she mustn't pour out her frustrations and irritations. She must sound positive. Except it was hard to sound positive when you were telling someone how much you missed them but they mustn't shirk at their end.

Craig pretended to vomit in the waste-basket. 'God, all that bloody billing and cooing. Turns your fucking stomach.'

She should come up with some riposte. Put him in his place. But nothing came to mind. She turned to leave the room.

'Your bloke pulled the plug on this weekend? Can't blame him. God, it must be like fucking a bloody hedgehog, you're so bloody prickly. There must be fucking loads of eager beaver if you're a Super. I might try for promotion myself.'

'That'd be a good idea. A spot of study would be good for you: better than sitting on your arse smoking pot.' She shut the door quietly behind her.

'Kate!' Gary Vernon greeted her on Friday morning, as if genuinely pleased to see her. 'Any more computer tricks you could teach me?'

'Oh, I never was an expert,' she demurred, fingering the duster she'd bought. 'Not a geek. Never even finished my CLAITS course.'

'Of course: your wrist. What's the problem? You're looking a bit down.'

Was she? Hardly surprising, given the amount of sleep she'd had: her disappointment over Rod apart, Craig had seen fit to make as much noise as he could, slamming out late, slamming back in even later, and using the bathroom and bedroom doors as percussion instruments. She would tell him a half-truth. 'Shows that much, does it? Sorry, Mr Vernon, you don't want a miserable face in your office. Always leave your troubles at home, that's what my gran used to say.'

She applied herself to the windowsill.

'What's the problem?'

To think she'd once thought him a mean bastard. 'The usual: my Craig. Supposed to be going out tomorrow we were, only now he's gone and fixed something with his mates. So Cinders won't be going to the ball. If,' she added, managing a rueful grin as she moved the remaining pot plants, 'you can call a disco in Paignton a ball. Goodness, is that fern still in the loo? It'll have drowned, poor thing – I'd better get it.'

The soaking had done it good: that much was clear. She pulled off the dead foliage, popped it back in its pot, and took it back to the office. 'There. Not out of the wood yet, but we might save it. And the others: they're not so bad, are they? I suppose your budget doesn't run to some Baby-Bio or Phostrogen?'

He laughed. 'Petty cash might. Come back at the end of your stint: I'll see what I can do. If you can postpone your swim, that is?'

There was no one in Vernon's room, but the computer was still switched on. Another chance. Grabbing her duster, she clicked the mouse. More stuff about office plants. Yes!

'Kate! What the hell—!'

'Oh, you didn't half make me jump, Mr Vernon.' She flourished the anti-static cloth. 'Only I was giving your computer a bit of a clean. There. Better?' Despite her smile, she was shaking. Thank God for a bit of forethought.

He clicked irritably to clear the screen. 'Dirt or no dirt, you must wait till the computer's off. It's all confidential, woman.'

'I'm sorry. But I saw these cloths in Tesco and thought of you straightaway. And the Betterware lady says she's got special little brushes for cleaning keyboards.'

'Hmph. So long as you use your sense. Damn it, you could – you might wipe stuff if you start messing!'

Yes, she'd rattled him. She must be more careful. But that would mean standing still. And the sooner she made progress, the sooner she'd be back with Rod.

'The point is—' he started. But the phone interrupted him.

So as not to appear to be listening, and to maintain her image, she fished another cloth from her pocket, and attacked the tops of some books, taking care to put everything back in order. And to listen carefully, especially as she was almost certainly the topic of conversation. Extra weekend hours? A real bonus on so many counts: the money to pay off her credit card, time away from Newton Abbot and a chance to grab more information. But then she froze.

'After all, she'll be a familiar face,' Vernon said, as if to clinch the matter.

It took seconds for common sense to click in. The voice at the other end was a woman's: his wife's? So what was he suggesting?

'OK,' he said, terminating the call with nothing more affectionate word-wise than, 'talk to you later.' But the way his face softened confirmed it. He turned to Kate, laughing. 'You and that duster really are inseparable, aren't you? Look – am I right in thinking you're really at a loose end this weekend? Because – well, I wouldn't have asked you except – you know . . .'

'The weekend shift, Mr Vernon?'

'Oh, no. That's all dealt with by the agency. No, my wife and I were wondering if you'd consider baby-sitting our kids. She's ever so keen on music and we've been offered tickets for some concert in Exeter Cathedral. So it wouldn't be a late finish – no after midnight bonus, I'm afraid!'

'A couple or three hours would suit me grand, Mr Vernon. So long as they wouldn't mind: they're not exactly babies, are they?'

'Needs must when the devil – no, sorry. Didn't mean it like that. Like I said to my wife, they've seen you before.'

'Only in the c – the sweets aisle.' Hell, she'd nearly said *confectionery*. 'But they were nice: no doubt about that. And ever so well behaved.'

'Five quid an hour! For farting round all evening in someone's cosy little house. Bloody hell.' Craig fished a glass from the kitchen cupboard and poured himself the rest of what should have been tomorrow breakfast's fruit juice.

'Depends how vile the kids are,' Kate said, as off-hand as she could make it, adding juice to the shopping list she was scribbling on the back of an envelope.

'Suppose I came too: I could give the place a right going over while you sort the kids.'

She turned to him, arms akimbo. 'Forgotten part of the plot, have we? You're supposed to be having a night out with the lads, remember. That's why I'm free on my precious Saturday – and after you'd promised to take me to a disco and all.'

'For fuck's sake, I change my mind, don't I?'

God, was there nothing between his ears? 'And the story that we're off each other – the one I've carefully been nurturing at work? No, Craig isn't going to turn up to keep Kate company: he'd be more likely to go to the disco on his own and pick someone up.'

'You know, I just might. I just might.' Either he was a superb actor or he really thought he might make her jealous.

'Fine. So long as you remember all the story, even when you've got a headful of pot.'

'We could do three in a bed, you and whatever cunt I pick up,' he sniggered. 'After all, that bloke of yours'll be on the town himself, won't he, looking for a quick shag? Lot of talent in Brum, is there? Three in a bed himself, most likely.'

The thought of Rod propped up against a noisy bar eyeing up the talent at a disco! She suppressed a smile. And if Rod ever wanted three in a bed, she had an idea the third wouldn't be a girl from a club: it would be her, him and a good book.

'No, he wouldn't need to pick anyone up, would he? He'd find some other WPC looking for easy promotion,' he pursued. 'Do you have to do it in black stockings? Or handcuffs?' He came to stand over her, leering.

She took a pace back, but only to look him up and down. 'Don't judge others by yourself, Craig. He doesn't need silly gear to turn him on.'

'What are you implying?'

Time to exit. As she closed the kitchen door behind her, she permitted herself a loudly muttered, 'Silly little prick.' Let him take it how he would.

With all this wonderful countryside around them, why should the Vernons have chosen to live in suburbia? Oh, it was very nice, Exeter-type suburbia, but the only views were of other houses, back and front. And Exeter wasn't all that convenient for Cockwood, either: he could have got a house like this within walking distance, almost, just down the coast in Starcross. The village even boasted its own railway station, and had a ferry across to Exmouth. But no, he'd chosen to live perilously close to Exeter Crematorium. Perhaps it was to do with the location of good schools: that was what seemed to preoccupy most of her colleagues when they bought houses. Well, if – and it was a big if, still, of course – if anything ever developed between her and Rod, then maybe they should consider her house: you couldn't be much better placed in a school's catchment area than she was, just fifteen yards from Worksop Road Junior School. But she couldn't imagine Rod being torn from his present, elegant abode for the doubtful pleasures of morning and afternoon parent-induced traffic chaos.

She locked her bike, and chained it to the only vertical thing she could see – a drainpipe. Removing from her pannier her spoils from a morning rooting in charity shops in Teignmouth, she presented herself at the front door, punctual – thanks to ten minutes' bird watching out on the Exe estuary at Powderham – to the minute. Early baby-sitters must be nearly as big a pain as late ones, if you were flapping round half-dressed, half-made-up, and trying to explain where everything was.

The Vernons, at least, seemed quite ready. Mrs Vernon – Julie – was taut about the mouth when she opened the door, but relaxed into a friendly, if relieved, smile. Kate stepped into a square hall: perhaps the house was more spacious than it looked

Gary Vernon, emerging from a downstairs loo, smiled too. 'Elly? Peter? Here's Kate!' He stepped to close the front door behind her. 'Now, we've made a list of where everything is, and this is my mobile number – of course I can't have it on during the concert but I'll switch it on in the interval. Elly knows it anyway. And it's programmed into her phone. Imagine, a kid of nine having a phone . . . Anyway, I've left the answerphone on, you see.'

'Just like at work,' she agreed. 'So I can dial out – not that I'd need to, I'm sure.'

'Yes. But not take incoming calls.'

'No problem there, either. Now, what time did you expect to be back? Just so I can have a good old worry if you're late.'

'Oh, by ten. Unless we decide to go on the razzle: that's up to Julie.'

'So how will I know? If the answerphone's on?'

'Have you got a mobile?'

She shook her head. 'You could leave the machine off and I could take messages?' Or she could phone him at nine thirty, but she wasn't about to suggest that.

'No.' Surely his response was far too swift. He smiled as if to correct himself: 'You'd never hear the phone, the racket the kids can make. No, if we're not here by ten, assume you won't see us till midnight.'

He might almost have been issuing an invitation to search the place. It was one she'd be most discreet in accepting.

12

'There's never anything worth watching on TV on a Saturday night,' Elly declared. She'd make a wonderful headmistress one day. Or even a Thatcherian Prime Minister. 'Nothing but football and stuff about war.'

'That's why I brought this along,' Kate said, producing her carrier bag of cheap goodies.

Peter, who'd been messing with some collapsible car – pressed in the right places it became some fearsome robot – perked up. 'Sweets and things?'

'I thought you might have had enough sweets – didn't your dad treat you in Tesco the other day? No, this is something quite different: you may never have seen anything like it before.' She dipped in and came up with a battered flat cardboard box.

'Oh, is it magic? Like Harry Potter?'

'No. Not magic. But you might enjoy it anyway.'

Peter grabbed it.

Elly barked, 'Be careful!'

'Yes: we don't want to lose anything. And you'll need this board too. It's a game. From the days before all your games were on computer.'

'Funny writing,' Elly remarked, opening it.

'What's it say?' Peter demanded.

'"Sorry", silly!'

'What are you sorry for?'

'It's the name of the game,' Kate intervened. 'The game's called "Sorry"! What you have to do it this . . .'

The kids took only minutes to grasp the principle: all they had to do was to get all four little wooden pieces out of an oblong marked 'Start' and into another marked 'Home'. There were cards instead of dice. They were frayed and greasy with age, and hard to shuffle, but the typeface had its own charm. Soon the children (and Kate) were sliding and knocking each other's pieces off squares and sending them back to Start with noisy abandon. What Kate insisted on was what Aunt Cassie had insisted on, all those years ago: the courtesy of saying 'Sorry', however gleeful you might feel.

It was after eight when they surfaced, Kate realising that is was long past the time the children should have had their snack – pure fruit juice, and an assortment of nibbles. It was also close to Peter's bedtime. He'd never settle to sleep if he was as excited as this, blowing bubbles with his juice straw and trying to shove crisps down Elly's neck.

'Right,' Kate said carefully, 'we can have one more game – with only two men each, not four. And then a story. Or no more "Sorry" and two stories. Which is it to be?'

She'd expected bickering and got it. The carrier bag again. This time she produced another find, a book so old it must surely have been undervalued at fifty pence. It took her straight back to her childhood, right back in the earliest days. Her own copy of the book must have been lost or given away: her mother had had the instinct of generosity, but at other people's expense, especially Kate's. Old toys and books, put aside till the next day off school with a cold, simply disappeared. They might be mourned, loudly, genuinely, but they had gone, probably, given her mother's passion for the minister, to the church jumble. Kate reeled: all that from a tatty copy of *Milly-Molly-Mandy*.

Years of Sunday-school teaching meant Kate read well: this evening she gave it her all. If anyone were going to baby-sit these two in the future, it would be Kate they demanded.

It was nine before the two children were settled, and Kate switched on the television, which set out to prove that Elly's strictures were right: nothing worth watching. But wouldn't Kate Potter watch anyway? She'd hardly work her way through the *Guardian* crossword, already half-completed by someone. Mrs

Vernon? Gary hadn't struck her as a *Guardian* reader, let alone a *Guardian* crossword freak. Come on, she was a baby-sitter. For a start, she'd better stash the tumblers and snack dishes in the dishwasher. No, she wouldn't. Kate Potter would wash them meticulously by hand. Then she'd leave the living room even tidier than when she'd arrived.

And, of course, she'd check on the children from time to time. Peter was so deeply asleep she could scrape all his Lego into its box, but he stirred at the rattle of plastic on plastic. Had she woken him? She sat beside his bed, reciting nursery rhymes in the quietest voice she could manage. There. Sound asleep again.

Elly's room had been even messier than Peter's. Arms akimbo, she surveyed it, sighing at the prospect of trying to bring order to the chaos, when she realised Elly's eyes were open.

'My teacher says that girls shouldn't think they have to be cleaner than boys, or tidier, because it's all a matter of – soci . . . sterry . . . Something,' she concluded defiantly.

'Gender-stereotyping?' Kate prompted, nonetheless bundling up dirty socks and knickers and T-shirts – nearly enough for a washing-machine load. 'Or socialisation? In any case, some of the tidiest people I know are men. It's difficult for whoever does the vacuum-cleaning if a room's as untidy as this.'

It took Elly a moment to digest that. Then she sat up. 'But you must be gen-whatever you said,' she objected. 'You wouldn't be a cleaning lady otherwise.'

'How about calling me a cleaner? You can have men doing my job, too, you see.'

'You can. But Daddy says you're the best cleaning— The best cleaner he's ever had. And he says you're far too clever to be stuck in a dead job.'

Kate knew what he meant! But she must be careful not to get too much of a reputation for cleverness. That wouldn't fit Kate Potter at all. 'Dead end,' she corrected Elly gently. 'Of course I am. But I never worked at school, not properly, and then when I tried to study afterwards, my wrist got bad. When I can afford it, maybe I'll go to night-school – that's classes in the evening.'

'Does it cost a lot of money?' Elly rubbed her face: Kate ought to make her lie down and go to sleep.

'More than I've got at the moment, anyway. Now, seeing as it's girls only now, how about I read you one more bit of *Milly-Molly-Mandy*? So long as you promise to close your eyes while I'm reading it. That way you'll be able to see the mushrooms she's picking in that field . . .'

When she carried down her spoils from Elly's bedroom, Kate discovered in the utility-room a basket full of shirts ready to be ironed. Would it be over the top to start on them? Not for Kate Potter. But while she soon ran the iron to earth, she couldn't locate the ironing board, and didn't like to snoop around. *Stupid woman: that's exactly what you're supposed to be doing. Not baby-sitting, but checking these extremely desirable premises for something, anything, incriminating.* Oh yes, hunting for an ironing board would be the perfect excuse for sifting the papers on Gary Vernon's desk. At least, in Craig's eyes it would be. And Craig'd be right this time. They wouldn't have surveillance cameras in their own home, surely. She bloody well should be sifting through Vernon's things. Now was a perfect opportunity. But it was so close to ten that she'd be risking discovery.

She couldn't do it. And it wasn't fear of their early return that stopped her either. It was something much deeper.

At last, not sure whether she was angry or upset with herself, she did what she used to do when she was a student: she laid a thick towel on the kitchen table. She might as well switch on the radio. It was tuned to Classic FM, which suited her and which she could more or less justify on the grounds that Kate Potter wouldn't have the temerity to retune it. But she had it on very quietly, and kept the door open to listen for the children. It wasn't them she heard, though, but the older Vernons letting themselves in, just as she tackled the second shirt. Thank God she'd not tried to find Vernon's files.

Gary came into the kitchen first. 'Kate! What on earth are you doing?'

'Well, I didn't want the TV on in case I couldn't hear the little ones. They were ever so good: no fuss at all about bedtime.' She rested the iron on its heel and looked up at Mrs Vernon, who came in returning her smile.

'Both fast asleep. And the wonders you've worked in – Oh, Kate: you didn't have to do those.'

'Well, I found them when I was shoving stuff into your washing machine. Young Elly and her idea that being tidy is too girly!' She shook out another shirt, contriving a glance at Mrs Vernon. She looked more than tired: she looked quite ill. 'I hope those shirts are all right, Mr Vernon – I couldn't find your ironing board.'

'Julie had this brilliant idea of having one in a cupboard. You open the cupboard and out comes the ironing board, spring-loaded. Look!'

Round-eyed, Kate gasped, 'Ooh, what a lovely idea. Saves all the business of getting your fingers caught and your shins barked.'

'Until you try and put it down again. It's got a life of its own then,' Julie said. 'Many's the nail I've had sliced off. I think putting it away's man's work.' She glanced at her husband, but he was busy in another cupboard.

'I could finish these before I went, if it'd help? There's only a few more. I mean, you're back really early, and I haven't anything to rush back for.'

The Vernons looked at each other. 'So long as you let me pay for another hour,' Julie said at last. 'Oh, yes please!' Vernon had produced a corkscrew and a bottle of wine. 'What'll you have, Kate?' Julie sank down on to a chair opposite Kate, pulling her back straight with an obvious effort.

'I wouldn't want to put—'

But Gary was already pulling the cork. 'No trouble.' He produced three large glasses and sloshed red wine into them.

Kate didn't need to read the label to tell it was good: the bouquet sprang right across the table at her. 'Only a drop please, Mr Vernon. I've got to get back to Newton, haven't I? Don't want anything to go to my head!' She finished the shirt she was on before she picked up her glass. Not the moment for a Jilly Goolden sniff and savour. But she stopped before her first sip. 'Ooh, this smells nice. My friend in Birmingham, she gets me to drink white wine. I've never had anything like this.'

The others leant towards her to touch glasses. 'Cheers – and here's to many more evenings of your sitting for us!' Gary said, with a little sideways smile at his wife.

'Cheers – and thank you very much.' Kate put down her glass to fold the last shirt.

So it was a satisfactory evening all round. There was only one thing to worry her: the familiar smell now sweetening the kitchen.

Which of her kind hosts had been smoking pot?

13

Steady rain. Steady, root-reaching rain. A day for staying in. But not, for God's sake, staying in closeted with Craig. If only she were in Birmingham: on a day like this she could have found plenty to do: lunch with friends, potting bulbs up for winter, tennis at the indoor centre.

Better still, she could have spent time with Rod. After a sexy dawdle in bed and a leisurely breakfast, music on his hi-fi and the Sunday papers spread across his carpet. Well, she could nip out for the papers at least. Oh, no, she couldn't. No matter how under-educated the bright Kate Potter might be, she wouldn't buy the *Observer* or the *Independent* – the cost, apart from anything else. So the answer was: no quality Sundays.

Was the rain easing? Was it any lighter to the west?

If Rod had been working, what else would Kate Power have done in Birmingham? She herself might well have been working, of course. Whatever she'd been up to, she'd have tried to see Cassie. She sometimes resented having to visit her so regularly. But in some way the old woman gave a shape to Kate's spare time – even filled otherwise empty corners. If she could have seen her today it wouldn't have been a chore. It would have been a pleasure to sit with her and hold the knobbly, arthritic hands and remind her about Milly-Molly-Mandy's adventures. It must have been Cassie who'd read them to her. Her mother had never had time for such luxuries as reading aloud. No: she probably hadn't had time to do a lot of the things she'd have liked to do – working mothers didn't, did they? An old dear her dad might be, but he'd never been much of a husband – or much of a father, come to think of it. He could have taken some of the domestic chores, even played with the children. But he was always busy helping a mate take a gearbox out of a car or re-felt a roof.

So perhaps it'd been not Mum but Cassie who'd got rid of the book. But now its twin had come back to her. Grabbing a bowl of cereal, she padded back to her room, sitting cross-legged on the bed. She'd read as slowly as a child, savouring the little drawings of the girl with dots for eyes.

Then Craig got up, thudding across to the door, to the bathroom. Idyll over any moment now. She dressed quickly – pants and jeans on before she stripped off her dressing gown. And the quickest dive into bra and sweater she could remember.

No. It was all right. Craig was going back to bed, pulling his door closed after him so the catch made its loudest noise. That, if nothing else, would have woken a deeper sleeper than her. There was one noise she hadn't heard, though. Oh, the antisocial bastard. Couldn't even be arsed to flush the loo, could he!

She was just going to abandon Milly-Molly-Mandy in her sweet dormer windowed cottage when the house phone rang. Cursing economy – could a house be civilised with only one phone and that in the kitchen? – she legged it downstairs. Whoever it was would ring off, sure as God made little apples.

'Took your time, didn't you, Kate?' Earnshaw had evidently forgotten that she was supposed to be fond of her quasi daughter-in-law. She had also forgotten that people lay in on Sunday mornings. Not necessarily asleep. But unwilling to answer the phone. Earnshaw the DCI wouldn't have given it a second thought. But Earnshaw with an undercover son might have done. On the other hand, Kate couldn't blame her for failing to imagine Craig and her having a friendly Sunday bonk.

'Hi, Ma,' Kate said pointedly. 'Yes, I was upstairs reading.'

'Reading! Oh, well. Now, I'm treating you both to Sunday lunch. Twelve thirty. Where would you fancy?'

'Up to you, surely, Ma, if you're paying.'

'Hmph.' Earnshaw's memory must be fading fast. Or had the word 'treat' been a violation of the Trades Descriptions Act?

'Is Dad coming?'

'You bet he is.' Earnshaw's tone suggested he'd have little say in the matter. 'Luton. There's a nice pub at Luton. Wonderful steaks. Twelve thirty.'

''Bye. Love to Dad,' Kate added ironically to a silent phone.

So where was Luton? Not in Bedfordshire, that was certain. Come on, Kate. You should be able to place it instantly. Yes! Near another hamlet called Ideford between the A380 and the B3192. She flicked her fingers in irritation. The name of the pub! No, that was gone.

'Fuck off, will you? Just fuck off.' Craig withdrew to the cocoon of his duvet, hunching into it so far that his feet stick out the far end. They were not over-clean.

'I'd be delighted to. But we're due for a session with your Ma and Pa in just over an hour and I thought you might welcome the chance to shower and shave. Oh, and to flush the loo.'

'What's it to do with you?'

'Everything, since I have to share it with you. I don't want the bathroom reduced to a stinking urinal. As for the shower and shave—'

'I thought I told you – hey, shut the bloody window! And who told you to – draw the fucking curtains, you bitch?'

'Draw them yourself. Go back to your stinking pit of a bed, if you want. But if you're not parade-ground smart and ready to drive me by twelve, I shall go myself. And explain why. Got that?'

His language got even fouler. Her message had clearly been received.

She'd had to let Craig drive, of course – though she suspected it'd be her turn after lunch so that he could drink. He'd had difficulty with the tight turn into the Elizabethan Inn's car park, and had parked untidily in what were admittedly quite narrow slots. His 'parents' emerged from their car – a P reg Rover. Her heart sank. If they were being watched – and she'd no reason to believe they were, of course – they'd be found out straightaway.

Some people managed not to look like police officers when they were in mufti; others didn't. Rod – though she was probably biased – might have passed for anything, just as she hoped she would. But even in what looked like his second-best gardening clothes, Chief Superintendent Knowles might just as well have worn an arrow pointing down at his head saying 'COP'. Not even army or ex-army. 'COP'. Maybe Earnshaw looked like a fierce matron, in the days when hospitals had such things: not the new NHS incarnation, perhaps. Or just maybe the head of an old-fashioned girls' school. Not motherly, that was certain. At least Craig passed the disguise test with flying colours. He hadn't shaved, his jeans were deplorable for a man lunching with his parents: he personified a yobbish lout, scraping a dubious living that the taxman and the Job Centre knew nothing about. While Knowles brought over their drinks, his 'mother', settling herself at a square table in the bay window of the dining room, looked him up and down.

'My fault for potty training you too young,' she observed. 'Still in rebellion, I suppose. Oh, for Christ's sake, pour the stuff into a glass, not straight down your throat from the bottle!'

'You keep on like this and I'm out of here,' he snarled, grabbing Kate by the upper arm as if to drag her away too. His fingers tightened into a fierce pinch.

She shook him off, but couldn't resist catching Earnshaw's eye.

Knowles stepped forward. 'That's no way to behave. Sit down. Kate, my dear, let me get you another glass of wine. Most of that seems to have ended on the floor.'

'Thanks. The people I babysat for last night gave me some nice red,' Kate said, conversationally. 'My boss at the time-share complex,' she added, sitting down next to Earnshaw. Goodness knows why they'd chosen this place – surely the tables were too close for them to have a confidential conversation.

Her eyebrows shot up. 'He asked you to baby-sit? You must be making a good impression!'

'I'm certainly going the extra mile—'

'Short of getting on to the weekend roster!' Craig put in.

'I'd have thought baby-sitting was' – Earnshaw struggled visibly to get back into role – 'a big improvement on extra cleaning. Was it a nice house?'

Kate waited till Knowles was back from the bar before she said, 'Absolutely lovely. In Exeter. The kids kept me busy all evening, of course.'

Craig sneered, 'So you didn't—?'

'I did some ironing and I'm invited back,' Kate cut in. 'How did you get on yesterday, Craig? A good gardening day?'

'None of your fucking business.'

Knowles, very forbearing, said, 'I'd have thought it was, son. And you shouldn't swear like that in front of your mother.'

Which they all knew was rich, since, when roused, Earnshaw could have won an obscenities competition hands down.

'Didn't the poor girl see you all day?' Earnshaw demanded. 'That's not the way to get back together, is it?'

Kate averted her face. She'd have thought the more anyone saw of Craig, the less likely they were to stay together. Perhaps she shouldn't have grassed him up like that, though. Still, he should be able to think on his feet.

'Worked all morning – I was off before her ladyship deigned to get up.'

Which was a lie. But let that pass. What else had he been up to? They were supposed to let each other know – just in case. Oh, in case of nothing, so far. But they ought to be building trust. Becoming a team. Perhaps she'd been mistaken about him and his contract gardening. Perhaps she should have made more effort.

More effort for a man who bruised your arm like that?

'Then I went off with my mates to the footie – Torquay United at home. Not a bad match, as it goes. And since I knew she was off on the razzle, I had a pie and chips and watched some wide-screen telly down the pub. Any harm in any of that?'

'None, lad. Except you should be doing what the counsellor told you: communicating.'

'She buzzes off on a Saturday night, she can expect me to go out with my mates, can't she?'

'So earning good money's buzzing off on the razzle, is it?' Kate shot at him. 'Yes, I really like looking after other people's messy brats and doing the ironing for an hour's extra pay.'

'Ironing? Not like you, Kate,' Earnshaw chuckled. Yes, she was good at this, wasn't she?

'Well, I wasn't sure what time they'd be getting back, so I didn't want to get stuck into a TV programme or anything else,' Kate replied, stressing the last three words enough to give them the message. 'A good job too: they were back before ten.'

'Was it an interesting house?'

'I only saw the kids' rooms and the kitchen, really. I didn't see Mr Vernon's office. His wife says to call her Julie, and I know he's Gary. But I don't like to call him by his first name. I fancy she isn't very well. What is it people smoke pot for?' Craig shot her the swiftest of looks. 'MS, isn't it? Poor woman.'

'Or pleasure. People smoke it for pleasure, don't forget that,' Craig put in.

Trust? Well, he must have trusted her to offer her that sort of opening. Kate responded by reaching for the menu. It was a good job it was Earnshaw's treat. Or at least Devon and Cornwall Constabulary's treat. Not that the amount of information she was passing back was enough to justify the latter. Not unless the stuff rescued from the shredder was worth having. It'd be nice to know, wouldn't it?

'They say they'll want me to go and sit again,' she said.

'And if they do, I'm going too,' Craig said swiftly. 'You won't be doing the ironing for a fiver, not if I have anything to do with it?'

'Will you be doing it then, while I'm playing board games with the kids?'

'I don't see why he shouldn't go with you one day, my dear,' Knowles said.

'Things'll have to be a lot better before he does. Vernon's trying to get me extra hours, because he knows I need the money.

And the other day he was afraid Craig might be into domestic violence.'

'I'm not having you broadcast our business to every Tom, Dick—'

'If everything was right between us, I wouldn't be so desperate for extra hours, would I? I want him to trust me, so I do all his chores – including emptying the stuff for the shredder, and, with a bit of luck, using his computer.'

'Computer? That's a bit of a move for a cleaner!' Knowles objected.

'He knows about my CLAIT course – and I've had to help him out a time or two, when he's been stuck. As an expression of gratitude he says I can use the swimming pool after work. He was a bit afraid of what the apartment owners would think about it. I might take him up on the offer tomorrow.'

'Swimming!' Craig spat.

Knowles asked, 'You're hoping to talk to owners, are you, Kate?'

'I can't think why she hasn't questioned other people working on the site. I said I should—'

Kate interrupted, 'I haven't seen anyone else working on the site. I'm the only office cleaner. The clerical women are agency. I wonder if that's their policy – good old divide and rule. It'd be really good if Mrs Mole could talk to you about it. And find out why there's such a high turnover generally.'

'I'm sure Ratty or Toad will, if she doesn't,' Knowles laughed, jotting in a tiny notebook.

'It'd make playing Hunt the Thimble a hell of a lot easier. Actually, it'd help me even more to know what the thimble is.' She'd gone too far. She knew even as the words were out of her mouth she shouldn't have said them. Craig should have told her, shouldn't he? She'd just dropped him in it. She scrabbled to retrieve the situation. 'In a little more detail than I've got,' she added.

There was a distinct silence at their table. But perhaps it went unnoticed – wasn't it amazing how much noise other people could make over Sunday drinks? Knowles, flushed with anger, though whether this was at her or at Craig she couldn't tell, opened his mouth to speak but shut it as a waitress came to take their orders.

'You've seen the seafood menu? On blackboards round the wall in the bar?' she prompted. 'Oh, you should, before you choose. Go on,' she urged. 'I'll come back in five minutes.' She smiled and headed off to another table.

Craig reached for Kate's wrist. 'People like us don't eat fancy stuff, remember. You have a steak and like it.'

'Let the girl make up her own mind,' Knowles said, in the weak tone of a man not going to follow up his suggestion. 'Off you go, my love – you can tell me what I ought to try.'

Earnshaw pulled herself to her feet and set off as if only the blackboards stood between her and starvation. 'Look at that fish! And the seafood. Yes, I shall go for the chicken with prawns and grape sauce. What's this,' she added more quietly, 'about not eating fancy stuff?'

'I keep forgetting I'm C2 at best,' Kate admitted. 'And much as I'd love a seafood salad, maybe he's right. Not that they'll be checking on every morsel I order, every dress I buy. But it's all too easy to step out of role. Not just my walk' – she flashed an apologetic grin at the older woman – 'but my vocabulary, sentence structure, everything. If my boss walked in here – big if, but you never know – and saw me eating anything exotic, he might just put that eccentricity alongside all my other eccentricities and do the right sums! But I do fancy that crab and smoked salmon salad.'

'Compromise,' Earnshaw said briskly. 'In food as in everything else. Have crab as a starter and steak and chips for your main course. When we've ordered, we'll go to the ladies'. OK?'

'So what's this about not being properly briefed?' Earnshaw asked, setting the hand-drier a-roar. 'OK, I know you were half asleep when I drove you down. But Craig should have filled you in twice over. Why didn't you ask him?'

'I shouldn't have said that: he'll kill me.'

Earnshaw leant back on the washbasin. 'You seem to have got into cowed-mode already! You do it pretty well, too. Tell me, is he really as violent as he seems? Or is he just a fucking good actor?'

For answer, Kate rolled up her sleeve.

'Hmph. Anything else?'

'Let's just say, I'd prefer you not to touch my nose.'

'He's taking all this a bit too seriously, then? But not enough to tell you all you need to know?'

'To be honest, I didn't know how to ask him without him flying off the handle.'

They heard the outer door open, and Kate was already applying lipstick before the inner one admitted a smart-looking woman about Kate's age. The colour was just not quite right for Kate, and she suspected the make didn't suit her skin: her lips seemed permanently dry.

'So you see, Ma,' Kate added clearly, 'I do my best, and though he's your son and that I just don't know how much longer I'll be able to cope.'

'He touches you again, Kate, he'll have me to deal with. And Dad. He thinks as much of you as if you were our own. You know that.'

Kate looked at her feet, swallowing hard. 'Thanks, Ma. But maybe it'll be all right.'

The meal went as well as could be expected, and Kate had to admit that her steak was excellent. It would have been outstanding had it been rare, not the medium Craig insisted she always had. As it was, she enjoyed it. Fresh vegetables, good chips: yes, she'd really enjoyed it. But she ate meat so rarely these days she was so full she truly couldn't manage a sweet, despite everyone's urgings. All she did with the ice cream Craig shoved in front of her was push it around the dish. And she stuck with ordinary coffee, despite the dazzling list of liqueur coffees.

Good job. Craig thrust the car keys at her and ordered

Caribbean for himself. Was that what louts would drink? She wasn't at all sure.

'So what did you tell Earnshaw, when you were having your nice girlie chat?' Craig demanded unpleasantly, gripping her wrist as she tried to fasten her seatbelt.

'How hard it was to stay in role. That I didn't like the role. That you were overplaying your role. But they'd seen that anyway. And if you don't let go they'll be coming over to see why I'm not starting the car and heading for what is laughingly called home.'

He flung her away. 'There you go again! *What is laughingly called home.* You just listen to yourself. You're not Kate Potter, you're Kate Power, and what a miserable, snotty-nosed bitch she is.'

'And you? Are you an Oscar-winning actor or just a vicious yob? You ease up on the violence, Craig, or I'm off this case and back to Birmingham before you can say knife. And I shall put in a full written report to Knowles and my boss—'

'The one you're fucking? The one who's too busy to come down because he's fucking some other bitch ready to open her legs for promotion?'

'Shut up or get out.'

'"Shut up or get out!"' he mimicked. 'Don't you come the hoity-toity with me, Kate Power – or it'd be worth doing time just to wipe that smirk off your face.'

14

Clearly there wasn't room in the house for the two of them, not until their tempers were better under control. Kate parked in the driveway. Without speaking, she retrieved her bike from the garage, then stowed the car. At least it wasn't raining now, though the roads would be mucky. It was a shame she had to change into waterproofs and use the loo before she set off, but Craig was already flicking TV channels and took no notice.

Inland or the coast? Whichever way she went, the roads would be busy. No, she wouldn't fancy meeting Sunday drivers on some of the narrow Dartmoor roads. So how about doing something really touristy, going to Brixham and feeding the gulls? Going for local knowledge, she made what she soon realised was a mistake, taking the A3022 through Torquay and Paignton, rather than nipping round the outskirts of the town on the A380. Torquay – or was it Paignton by now? – went on for miles, a sort of Birmingham on Sea, despite the magnificent looking hotels. Did people ever pay the sort of room-rates needed to support such ostentation or did they simply hop on a plane and go to the French, as opposed to the English, Riviera? She snorted: from the average age of both drivers and pedestrians, she could see why the place had acquired another nickname – Costa Geriatrica. But here she was at last, plunging down into Brixham. Consciously virtuous, she found a slot in a multi-storey car park, and headed down to the harbour. But not to feed the gulls. There were notices everywhere forbidding it. She'd have paid to explore a modern replica of the *Golden Hind*, but a wedding party was just boarding. By now the sun was warm, and, having seen all there seemed to be of the town,

Kate looked at her OS map again. How about Berry Head? A good cliff-top breeze would blow away her residual bad temper. Not a lot of point, after all, in being in a foul mood if the object of your anger wasn't there.

As she parked, locking her wet-weather gear into a pannier, she even managed a laugh. In the Smoke and up in Brum there'd been standard police jokes about the sort of car drug dealers used: flash Audis with tinted windows were almost a stereotype. One would hardly be remarked in Brixton or Handsworth. But here, in rural Devon, on an SSSI to boot, the one in front of her eyes stuck out as if it had beacons on it. She could hardly stake it out on her Honda. More to the point, it was none of her business. All she was now was an office cleaner who was good with kids. But she jotted down the number – yes, it was a Birmingham one – before setting off briskly towards the headland, the wind gusting fiercely in her face. Catharsis: that was what this was. Another word Kate Potter wouldn't know, of course.

She still hadn't been briefed, of course. The ladies' loo was hardly the place for an up-date. Worryingly, Earnshaw hadn't made any arrangements to talk to her. If Earnshaw were to phone her, the chances were that Craig would 'forget' to pass on any message. If he dared. She had a strong feeling he'd nearly acted his way out of a job over lunch. Of course, he still had access to Earnshaw, while she didn't, so he could go and plead. No. No point in thinking about Craig and Co.

Oh, if only she'd had a kite! What a day this would have been for flying it. All around her families were fighting to control bobbing, diving, weaving shapes: there'd be some tears tonight if small hands weren't strong enough. She battled her way closer to the promontory, pausing to scan the information boards: pity they were so weather-worn they were virtually unreadable. But there was enough legible to tell her that she was in the grounds of a fort built to house Napoleonic prisoners of war. Like the prison up in Princeton. Which prime site would she have preferred to be trapped in? Well, despite the gale, despite the thunder of the ocean on the cliffs, she rather thought here. Especially if you were

let out from time to time to look at the jewel of a coastline –
rather tarnished by endless coastal strip development these days.
She pressed on, educating herself in a barn-type building with an
exhibition giving an account in words and pictures of how man
had shaped the place. And someone else had made the same
choice for being immured: an official nuclear shelter had been
sunk just behind her. She was still laughing when she emerged
to find herself staring Elly and Peter in the face. She fell into
step with them as far as their parents, fifteen yards away.

'So it *was* your little Honda,' Gary declared. 'I told you, didn't
I? What are you doing here, Kate?'

'Just having a bit of a blow,' she said. She'd had fifteen yards
to think of something plausible and this was the best she could
come up with? 'Walking off Sunday lunch, too,' she added. 'My
parents-in-law, bless them, don't think they've fed you unless
you can hardly get off the chair. And today they took us for a
pub lunch.'

'So your partner's . . . ?' Julie looked around.

'Oh, he's sleeping it off. I prefer a nice brisk walk. Always
have.'

'So you get on all right with his parents?' Gary asked.

'Oh, yes. Golden, they are. Anyway, he'll be waking up and
wondering where his tea is. Best be getting back.'

'We're just going to have a pot of tea and a scone—'

'And ice cream!'

'– *and* an ice cream! Care to join us?' Julie asked. She was
looking better than yesterday, though maybe it was just the wind
whipping colour into her cheeks.

'That's ever so kind of you. But' – she checked her watch,
wrinkling her nose – 'but I really ought to be going. Thanks all
the same.'

But as she turned, the family turned with her, one child to her
right, the other to her left.

'When are we going to play "Sorry" again?' Peter demanded.

'And have some more *Milly-Molly-Mandy*?' Elly asked.

'Oh, one of these days.' After all, it wasn't up to her, was it?

'Soon, I hope,' Julie said. 'Now, look, the café's only a step away – you really should have a cup of tea and a scone with us. Tell that man of yours where he gets off.'

Kate stared at the ground, genuinely torn. Half of her told her that the more she engaged with a man whom her superiors wanted watching, spying on, the better. The other half reminded her of the constant danger of going undercover: the growth of real friendships between the officers and those they were one day going to have to testify against in court. She'd even heard of officers falling in love with their quarry. At least that wasn't on the cards. But she liked the Vernons enough for friendship to be a distinct possibility. She braced herself. She must reject the chance of half an hour's fun with the kids in favour of staying in the role of cowed woman afraid what would happen if she were late with her man's food. She hoped the struggle showed in her face. Let it show a bit more.

'I'd better not. Really. No point in stirring things up, is there? I'm sorry,' she added to the children. 'Another day, promise. See you tomorrow, then, Mr Vernon.' And since she could hardly use his wife's first name if she didn't use his, she merely smiled awkwardly at Julie and muttered, ''Bye.'

So what was Knowles's Rover doing outside the house when she got back? She didn't know whether to be relieved or alarmed. Craig might be calm and polite in his seniors' presence, but that didn't mean he wouldn't take it out on her later. She shuddered. She could walk out tonight if she wanted, and to hell with her CV. How many women were suffering exactly the same anxieties, without her escape route?

Knowles looked up sternly when she came in. 'A bit casual about time, aren't you, Power?'

'I didn't know I had to be in time for anything, Sir.'

'I told her in the car. She was too busy sounding off to listen,' Craig obliged. 'Six, I told you, Kate. Not twenty to seven.'

'Sounding off about what?' Kate asked, wishing Earnshaw were there too.

'The usual stuff.'

'Which is?'

'Me.'

Wrong-footed, she tried to recover. 'And which aspect in particular?'

'Listen to her! She can't hack it, can she? Gets it wrong every time. Always your bloody university graduate with a plum in her mouth!'

'She is off duty, Craig.'

Craig? Compare and contrast with *Power*.

'I didn't think there was such a thing as off duty if you were under cover, Guv.'

Arse-licker! Kate said, as smoothly as she could, 'As far as I know, Sir, Craig and I didn't exchange any words at all during the drive back here. If we did, and he told me to be here, I can only apologise. Has he made you tea or coffee?'

'Coffee would be good, please.'

'Craig?'

'OK.'

She had a nasty suspicion that Knowles was the sort of man who would prefer domestic charms even in an officer tough enough to be undercover. She spread a clean tea towel on their only tray, and fished out a selection of biscuits she'd had the foresight to store in a jar marked 'Flour', arranging them prettily on a dinner plate. While they had no cups and saucers, only mugs, she made sure there was a plate to lay dirty spoons on and sugar and milk in the matching set. Oh, and individual plates for the biscuits. There. It wouldn't do any harm to make them wait even longer, while she changed her scruffy jeans and sweatshirt for more presentable versions. It would take only as long as the kettle took to boil. OK, brushing the hair and slapping on some lipstick added a couple of minutes, but all in all she thought the improvement justified the delay. The sooner she got him back into role the better, too, so the first thing she said, as she carried through the tray, was, 'Call us paranoid, Sir, but Craig and I reckon these walls are so thin we usually have music on and try to maintain our "relationship".'

'Such as it is.'

'OK, Craig. Well, Kate, your – your mother reckons you're dissatisfied with the way we've briefed you – are you making a formal complaint?'

'For goodness' sake, of course not. I'm just asking to have my darkness lightened a little. So I know exactly what I'm supposed to be looking for. So I don't miss it when I see it.'

'I told you, Kate, we're looking at money-laundering here.' Craig sounded as bored as if he'd repeated the information times beyond number.

'You what? I'd thought it was drugs! Jesus!' Her surprise was genuine. 'Money-laundering's a bit heavy for a holiday complex, isn't it? OK, lots of holiday complexes. Any idea who for?'

Knowles sighed. 'We always suspect terrorists these days, don't we, Kate?'

'So that's why Sue leapt at the chance of my taking a freebie holiday! And wanting it to be down here. Any hard evidence? Apart from that that Craig and I have failed to come up with so far?'

'Not yet. That's why we're depending so much on you.'

She nodded soberly. 'Anything else? Blackmail, drugs, the sort of thing I expected?'

'Why drugs?' It was his turn to look puzzled.

'Because of those rumours about Dartmoor being the drug-making capital of England.'

'Hmm. And why do you ask about blackmail?' Knowles demanded.

'Because of what I put in my report about the Hythe complex: at least two of the guest rooms were fitted with what looked like tiny surveillance cameras.' What the hell had gone wrong with police communication? 'And there's the one in Vernon's office, as I told – Ma.'

'What was your take on them?'

'Not just mine: one of the residents there had the same idea, though she didn't know about any cameras. Pressurising older inhabitants to sell, so their apartments could be refurbished and sold at a vastly improved price. If they didn't respond to the general lack of maintenance which was characteristic of the Hythe complex at least, then I'd guess any more interesting nocturnal activity would be used to blackmail them into selling. Except older people . . .' She tailed off.

'You'd have to talk about considerable profits to make that sort of thing worthwhile,' Knowles reflected. 'Are there any cameras in the Cockwood bedrooms?'

'She hasn't even been inside one yet!'

'No, I haven't. Because it's no business of mine to go in. I'm pushing as hard as I can, Gaffer—'

'Gaffer? Oh, you Brummies!' Knowles laughed. 'Nothing wrong with Guv down here, Kate.'

'Except I should call you Pa, shouldn't I? Craig's right. I do find it so hard to stay in role. But I seem to be convincing my boss: he and his wife offered me a Devonshire cream tea this afternoon. We met on Berry Head.'

'Berry Head? What the fuck were you doing on Berry Head?'

'Improving my local knowledge, Craig. Whenever I've got any time free I hop on the Honda and explore a bit more of the locality,' she added, for Knowles's benefit. 'I've been round the foothills of Dartmoor, that sort of thing.'

Knowles laughed. 'Not much fun on that little fart-and-bang machine. Tell you what, Kate, I'll get some of the lads to soup it up for you.' He chewed his lip.

'Trouble is, I need it to get to work. I suppose I could always take Craig's Escort.'

'No, you fucking couldn't. How would I get to work?'

'Get a lift from a mate?' Knowles suggested.

'Maybe it wouldn't take too long, Pa. I could take it in somewhere after my morning's stint and collect it again at the end of the day.'

'Somewhere like Headquarters!' Craig jeered. 'Cracking idea, Kate.'

'I'm sure there are other places where they work on police

vehicles,' she said. 'Or maybe the mechanics could come round here – you know, those service-your-car-at-home people. That'd be the sort of people Kate and Craig would use: much cheaper. And dodgier.'

'Good girl. OK, I'll get that sorted. I'll phone and tell you when, so you won't be off gallivanting round a bit more of the National Park.' Knowles looked from one to the other. 'Make sure she gets the message this time, Craig. Or I shall want to know the reason why.' He put down his coffee mug and got to his feet. 'I'd best be off. Now, er – your mother was saying she thought you were taking this role-playing too far. Perhaps it's time you were a bit nicer to each other. Can you manage that?'

'I'm sure we can, Pa. How much nicer?'

'Nice enough to get me working on site!'

Kate shook her head. 'Let's take it slowly, Craig. Vernon's sufficiently fond of me not to trust any instant changes on your part—'

'Just what the fuck have you been saying?' Craig was on his feet, standing over her.

'You don't say – you hint, you use body-language.'

'You've been saying I'm violent?'

Knowles pushed between them. 'This is what Earnshaw was worried about. And we both saw what you did to Kate in the pub, there. Let's see that arm, Kate.' He fished for his reading glasses to inspect it more closely. 'Hmm. No more of that. Or you'll be off the case and on a charge of assault. Do you hear me?' He voice was rising in crescendo: he remembered just in time. He bit back whatever he'd meant to say next. 'D'you hear me?' Now he sounded much more like an angry father.

'OK. But she asks for it!'

Kate couldn't contain herself. 'Now where did I hear those words before? In the Rape Suite?'

'And you remember, young lady,' Knowles interrupted, 'that you two are a team. You just button your lip. And you, young man, keep your fists to yourself. No violence, physical or verbal. Do you both understand? Right. Any more trouble and you'll both be up for disciplinaries.' Rather too late he dropped his voice. 'Do I make myself clear?'

15

The dutiful young couple were just waving off their wise old father when the phone rang. Kate beat Craig to it by a short head.

'I've been thinking,' Earnshaw announced, 'about this needle between you and Craig. If you can't settle it, one of you will have to move out. Not necessarily off the case. Just out of each other's hair. What do you think?'

'So long as it was part of our on-going scenario, I don't suppose either of us would object. We could have touching reconciliations from time to time, with you and Pa to referee. But I must discuss it with Craig – or, better still, why don't you ask him how he feels?' She passed the handset to Craig, but didn't withdraw from the kitchen: no reason too, since he hadn't.

'So long as it gets the stuck-up bitch out of my hair,' Craig was snarling. 'And so long as you get me into that complex too. She's obviously getting nowhere fast.' He listened a few moments before continuing truculently, 'That's what she tells you, of course. It's not how I see it. We're supposed to be partners in this and . . . Yes, but . . . Yes, Ma'am. Yes. Ma'am.' He cut the connection.

What had Earnshaw been saying to get him so angry? All those clichés about blood vessels pulsing in the neck and forehead, about fingers gripping so hard the knuckles went white: Craig showed they were true. Kate braced herself: she would have liked a good old-fashioned rolling pin. Because Craig was going to get violent. Any moment now.

But he simply turned on his heel and left in silence. She'd stay where she was. No need to make a bad situation worse. And perhaps that was how he saw it. She heard him moving round upstairs. He came back down again. He slammed the front door hard enough to set china in the kitchen a-rattle, and probably to damage the hinges on the door itself. God knew how he'd drive – yes, that was the roar of the Escort. Good job she'd left the little Honda chained up on the drive out of his way.

She dialled 1471. If Craig wasn't going to tell her what Earnshaw had said, she'd better check for herself. Number denied! Shit and shit! What the hell were her bosses playing at? Why should they communicate with only Craig? Why should she have to wait on their whim, and not him? Now whose pulses were pounding, whose knuckles white?

Except, of course, Earnshaw had called her. What was it that was making her so paranoid? For goodness' sake, she wasn't alone. She had Rod's number, after all, and even Sue's. Either would offer advice, and even support within the system. The phone lines would be red-hot tomorrow. But she didn't want to bring in reinforcements to fight her corner. Chewing her lip, she drifted upstairs: yes, she wanted to check Craig's room, to see if there was any evidence of how long he might be gone. The state he'd left his room was so dire it wasn't possible to say. Cassie would have gathered the underwear strewn across the floor and shoved it all into the washing machine. Or on to a bonfire, more likely: Cassie had a temper when roused. Kate wouldn't demean herself by doing either. Neither would she check so much as one drawer. But she'd pop her nose round the bathroom door. Filthy bugger hadn't flushed the loo, of course. But he'd taken his shaving things. And a towel.

She froze. What about her own room? No, she really was losing it. A colleague, a man on the side of right against wrong, wouldn't inflict vindictive damage on her things? A spurt of doubt speeded her steps. No. Everything seemed as she'd left it. Seemed. She sensed something wrong. She tore back the duvet: no, nothing there. But he'd been in the room: she knew it. Her clothes? The wardrobe seemed much as she'd left it. But she was sure things had been touched. She pounced on the carrier bag she'd left the vase wrapped in. Thank God, it was still in one piece. But it was vulnerable – all the more because it was evidence of how far she'd slipped from role. If only she'd put it obviously on display. Yes, she'd marked it out as special. And it was. Bought for Rod, just as the skirt was to wear for Rod. Well, there was only one place that – as far as she knew – Craig wouldn't think of looking. Gathering it to her chest and wrapping it in a couple of towels, she tiptoed downstairs, as if he were still in the house, and stowed it in the Honda's pannier.

As she did so, a car drew up at the end of the drive. Shit, was he back already? So much for the vase, then. But the person walking towards her was no other than Earnshaw.

'I thought you'd better come and have supper with me tonight, Power. Kate. We'll have to have a full-scale review of the case this week. And until we have, I'd rather we didn't provoke that young man any further. Go and pack some overnight things and hop on that bike of yours and follow me.'

Never had a week's washing up looked so attractive. At least Earnshaw had turned the water heater on this time: the first time Kate had stayed overnight with her, she'd found herself boiling kettle after kettle. But apart from that it was business as usual: a supper of hard but tasty wholemeal bread with some cheese dismissed by Earnshaw as mousetrap but actually surprisingly good, and some pears which might be ready for eating in a couple of months' time. The bed would be just as hard, the bedroom lighting as poor – and, with a bit of luck, the following morning's porridge just as creamy.

This time, however, Earnshaw came into the kitchen and held a spare tea towel while Kate wielded the dishcloth. True, she didn't use it to wipe up, but the thought was obviously there, and Kate was duly grateful. Kate didn't try to talk: Earnshaw was clearly finding the whole evening very difficult. Good on admin and organisation, weak on emotion – that was Earnshaw. Perhaps you'd had to be to scrabble up the promotion ladder in her day.

'Maybe,' the older woman began at last, 'we could have done better at the briefing stage. But we assumed that as you were billeted together, he'd update you on everything. After all, he was a local lad with all the knowledge you needed. And he'd worked undercover before. He was so convincing the arresting officer broke his nose for him. He says he likes the work: better than Traffic, he says. Doesn't like routine.'

'I'd say,' Kate said, surprising herself, 'that he's bored. After all, all he's doing at the moment is digging gardens and hobnobbing with his mates.'

'With his mates? He bloody well shouldn't be!'

'New friends, he says. That's one of the problems, Ma'am, with being undercover. You miss people you like being with.' She'd nearly slipped up and used the word 'love'. Not the best word to use to Earnshaw. 'Rod apart, and now I'm getting closer to the Vernons it'd be foolhardy for us to meet up again, I really miss my mates. Even my great aunt. I used to think visiting her was a pain, but I even miss that! It must be even worse for Craig, knowing his friends are only half an hour down the road and not being able to get to them.'

'No excuses for the violence, Kate.'

'There may be reasons, though. The scenario always was that the relationship was dodgy. Perhaps violence is the only way he can show that. And there's no doubt he's feeling resentful that I managed to get into the complex and have stopped him doing the gardening there. Maybe I was wrong . . .'

'If he turns up there now it'll look as suspicious as it would have done when he first mooted it. I don't know, Kate: this is turning out to be a right pig's breakfast.'

'Who's idea was it all?'

'Oh, them up there!' Earnshaw pointed ceilingwards. 'They want instant results, as usual. They don't understand how long it takes to do things properly – more interested in targets and budgets: you wait till you're a fully-fledged inspector – then you'll see.'

Kate recognised a red herring when it slapped her in the

face. 'Sue was definite from the outset that she wanted us down here.'

Earnshaw gave the nearest she could probably manage to a squirm. 'Well, there may well be . . .'

'I assumed' – no need to say it was Rod who had assumed – 'that we were investigating drugs distribution. We're close to Dartmoor; there's a tiny harbour on the spot and a big port at Teignmouth; there's the memos about pot plants. But Knowles was talking about money-laundering. And terrorism links.'

'If he believes that one he's been watching too much TV. No, between ourselves, I'd go for drugs distribution. But I don't like this surveillance camera business.' Meditatively she picked up a saucepan and polished it inside and out.

At last Kate prompted her, 'So why the short notice? The lack of preparation?'

'I told you, pressure from above. They're hassling us for results already.'

'So we're talking politicians, not cops, here, are we?'

'Hole in one. These people never understand . . .'

'But surely we must be investigating from other angles too! If it's that important?'

'Oh, I'm sure we are. But they're too busy brown-nosing the bloody Home Secretary and his merry men to bother to tell us.'

'Could we get another woman in, as a weekend cleaner? Using Mrs Mole's good offices?'

Putting down the saucepan with the tea towel inside it, Earnshaw leant across and tapped her lightly on the forehead. 'Anyone at home in there? We've got a perfectly good man dying to get his secateurs on their roses and we pull him and ask for another woman? Think how much it's cost to have Craig off his usual unit and pratting round here. God, I'm supposed to be his mother!'

'What sort of gardener was he?'

'I don't know a dandelion from a dahlia: no idea if he did. It always looked tidier when he'd been. I'll say that. Wasn't there some idea of him knocking your patch into shape?'

Kate tipped away another bowl of dirty washing-up water and ran fresh. Why didn't the woman wash up every other day, at least, rather than leave the whole lot for her cleaner? 'His idea was that I should do the garden, on the basis that plumbers never change their own washers. Trouble is, if it's a choice between tootling round the tourist traps and doing solitary in a sea of mud, I know which I prefer. And my excuse was I needed local knowledge.' She plunged a pile of plates under the suds, and took a tea towel, the twin of the one Earnshaw was still holding like a talisman, to the ranks of cups and saucers on the draining board. What a paradox: a tough old bird like Earnshaw and she used china so delicate it was almost translucent. And not a mug in sight, either.

'Not so much an excuse as plain common sense. Have you come across anything interesting in your travels? Coffee?' Earnshaw shook the kettle.

'Not this late, thanks. I've got to be up with the seagulls tomorrow.'

'There's no such bird. Herring gulls; black-headed gulls; black-backed gulls. And a lot of other gulls. But no seagulls. Right: I'll lock up and go on up. I'll give you a shout when I'm clear of the bathroom. No need to tiptoe around tomorrow: always sleep like the dead.'

Which didn't augur well for creamy porridge, did it? Well, a slice of that loaf would keep an army on the march for a week. But she might give the pears a miss.

She'd just plunged her hands for a last assault, this time on saucepans, when Earnshaw reappeared, sternly covered in a velour dressing gown. 'By the way, Craig'll be here at seven thirty tomorrow to lay a new path. I'll make sure he doesn't knock off at midday. But you may need to be out in the evening so he can collect his gear.'

'Thanks.'

'Goodnight, then.' Earnshaw nodded, and then dug in a capacious pocket for a mobile phone. 'Better use this if you want to phone that young man of yours.'

*   *   *

Kate lay, staring at the ceiling, telling herself that she should be the happiest woman on earth. She and Rod had become good friends; they were the sexiest of lovers; but until this evening the L word had never been mentioned. Not by either of them. And suddenly, while they were talking about plans for a fundraising barbecue on Guy Fawkes Night, of all things, Rod came straight out with it.

'I love you, Kate: you know that, don't you? Love you. And – oh, God! – the line's breaking up!'

It was, and they had wasted all those precious minutes talking trivia. She shouted back – what did it matter if Earnshaw heard? – 'I love you, Rod. Can you hear that?'

But the line was dead. She tried ten, a dozen times to reconnect, but failed. Dead battery, no doubt. That was the logical explanation.

Logic? Logic didn't operate very strongly at three in the morning. She'd lain awake for what seemed like hours. At some point she must have slept, because she registered that she was dreaming about her great aunt, Cassie, bickering with her, that was it, over swimming. At which point she'd woken, heart pounding, because she'd forgotten to pack her swimmies, and part of her ploy for getting into those apartments was to swim with the owners. And a pretty daft ploy it now seemed. How did she expect – as an employee – to be invited back into an apartment? By a stranger? However liberal Gary Vernon might be, she was sure he wouldn't like it. He'd rather she asked him point blank if she could see what the places looked like inside. After all, he'd suggested it himself.

Rod had told her he loved her. And the phone had died. So why hadn't he used a landline as soon as he could? He must have known how anxious she'd be. She couldn't try just once more, could she? At this hour of the night?

What if he was on a case? Nonsense, policemen of his rank didn't put themselves at risk. If he was working overnight at Lloyd House or wherever, the one thing you could guarantee in a police building was plenty of phones. None of it made sense!

At last she tried his landline again, ending the connection as soon as the answerphone cut in. If she redialled quickly enough she might confuse the machine and force it to ring out. She did. It did. But although she counted fifty rings, Rod still did not answer.

16

There was still no reply from either of Rod's phones at six thirty. She left brief messages. Struggling to keep calm, hating herself for losing her grip so quickly, Kate rang his direct line at Lloyd House, Birmingham's police headquarters: there was an automatic answerphone there, too. She left the sort of message that wouldn't embarrass him in front of a third person. But while she could select appropriate words, she'd less control over her voice. As for a return contact number, Earnshaw's would have to do.

Dressed, and forcing down the dense bread, she left a note for Earnshaw herself: it involved so many crossings-out she eventually simply drafted what she wanted to say and copied it out neatly, as if it were a homework assignment.

> Ma
>
> I'm very worried about my friend in Birmingham. I've left messages but had no reply. I can't take or make calls at work. Would you try the number? If you have no success, could you try the other office numbers?
>
> Thanks.
>
> PS. Wouldn't ask if I didn't think it was important.

That would have to do. She hadn't time for anything more artistic. In fact, it was a good job Earnshaw's cottage was much closer to Cockwood than the Newton house or she'd have been late.

It was a lovely still morning, the Exe silent under thick sea mist. Another time, another day she'd have pulled into a lay-by to enjoy it. Maybe later. But she'd enjoy nothing, stop nowhere, till she knew Rod was all right.

If only the work were harder – if only she had to think about it while she was doing it. But even if she'd been working on the toughest case, she wouldn't have been able to switch off the pain, sharp as toothache, in her head. Hell, she was behaving – feeling! – like a lovelorn teenager. He was working; he couldn't return the call on anything except Earnshaw's number in case he put her at risk. Logic.

At least it had been easy enough to work out her excuse for looking so rough. It was pat when Gary Vernon looked swiftly up at her as he tackled his morning's mail. 'Kate – whatever's wrong?'

'Oh, Craig – what else? He's only gone and walked out on me.'

'My God – nothing to do with us holding you up last night, I hope?'

'No. Something Ma said over the phone. His dad had had a go at him, too: I arrived in the middle of that.'

'What are you going to do?'

'Wait till he gets it into his head to come back, I suppose. If he doesn't, then we'll have to sell up. I might even go back to Birmingham – my friend reckons there's a job waiting for me there.' Which was true enough.

'How will you manage in the meantime?'

'I'll be OK. His parents are ever so good: they'll see me all right. Funny, I think that's what gets to him – them being so nice to me, and criticising him.'

'Could you do with a few extra hours, Kate? I know it's up to the agency, really. We're supposed to take whoever they send. But I'll have a word. You're the best cleaner on site by several miles. I'd love to get you on the weekend shift: one or two of the owners have been complaining about the level of cleanliness.'

'What'd it involve, Mr Vernon?' she asked cautiously, her heart pounding with excitement.

'The same early-morning start – no, I tell a lie. You'd start at nine, and have to be clear by eleven. You'd be responsible for – I'm not sure whether it's six or seven units.'

'Seven? That's a lot in three hours – if you want them done well, that is. How big are they?' *Let him show them to me! Please let him show them to me!*

Vernon looked at his watch. 'I suppose I've just got time to take you over . . . You don't mind working over to make up? I mean, it's not going to make things worse with you and Craig, is it?' He reached for his jacket.

'He's working all day. If he remembers to turn up, that is. He says he'll be coming round to the house this evening to pick up some things.'

He ushered her through the office door, locking it carefully behind him. 'You could do with making yourself scarce, then.'

'That's what Ma-in-law says.'

'Is that where he'll be staying?'

Christ. She'd nearly said he'd be staying with his father! But the myth was that he worked away from home a lot. All the same, there was a distinct plot-hole there. Any day now Knowles might find himself moving into Earnshaw's cottage!

'With one of his rotten mates, I should think. His parents'll pass on any messages. And they'll be having another go at bringing us back together.' She sighed wearily.

'But you'd rather go to Birmingham? It's a big, impersonal place for a country girl, Kate.'

An alarm bell. 'Do you know it, Mr Vernon?'

He opened the main door. The complex looked idyllic in the autumn glow. 'Quite well. I've got – I've got some business contacts up there. They do a good curry, that's one thing I'll say for Birmingham.'

'My friend says there's lots of jobs coming up there. Some new development. The Pillar Box or something,' she said doubtfully. 'And Millennium Park?'

'The Mail Box, Kate! The Pillar Box! Oh, dear! And I think you'll find it's Millennium Point.' She'd never known him laugh so easily. But he'd given something away. He knew his Birmingham. What a good job Rod had come down just the once . . .

'Are you sure you're all right? Would you rather go home?'

'Honestly, I shall be fine, Mr Vernon. Honestly. I'm much better working. And the chance of being out of the house at the weekends too, not to mention the chance of a bit extra in the wage packet . . .' she tailed off encouragingly.

They were halfway across the central courtyard, which looked distinctly out-at-elbows, the low sun highlighting a crop of dandelions.

'You know, it's a real shame Craig and I aren't speaking – because, to be honest, he'd make a much better job of this than whoever's doing it now. Look at those weeds. And the moss in the lawn.'

'Would you really want him working at the same place as you?' Vernon asked, bending to tug at a dandelion, and coming up with leaves but no root.

'Funny: I wouldn't really mind, not really,' she said, wondering why she was going to this trouble for a man she loathed, and telling herself it was her duty. To be honest, she felt guilty for reacting with such hostility earlier: a bit of lateral thinking like this could have saved everyone a lot of sweat. Except, of course, she still wouldn't have trusted Craig to stick to his job and not act as if he were an SAS sergeant on particularly active duty. 'After all, we'd be on different shifts. I'd be going home as he came in.'

Dusting the earth from his fingers, Vernon shook his head. 'The last thing we want is domestics on the site.'

Domestics? Police shorthand for domestic disturbances? How come Vernon was using the term?

'No. Of course not. Oh,' she gasped, as he let her into one of the apartments, 'isn't this nice?' It was. It was an exact replica of those near Oxford. An extremely desirable residence. 'How much would this set you back, Mr Vernon?'

Wrong question. 'It's not as straightforward as that,' he said, flushing. 'And I'm afraid the information is confidential to potential buyers.'

'And you can't say I'm one of those!' she laughed. 'Not me and Craig! Tell you what, though, Mr Vernon – it'd be a pleasure to clean a place like this. Look at that lovely little bathroom! And the kitchen! Are they all as nice as this?'

'Well, this is one that's been refurbished. They're not all quite up to this standard. But they will be in time. Maybe you'd better see what's involved with the other ones. The bedroom's through there.' But he didn't open the door to show her. Instead, he opened the front door. She waited, docile, while he locked up. He set off at a gentle pace down a path to the sort of corner she recognised from her weekend in Hythe. Here the moss wasn't confined to the grassed area – it really wasn't worth the title lawn – but covered the flagstones as well.

'Hey, isn't this a bit dangerous? It must be ever so slippery after rain!' she said.

He looked at her sharply.

'My gran always used to get me to scrape it off her back path,' she added. 'Don't know why. Like a mountain goat she was. But she had this thing about slipping and breaking her hip and dying of pneumonia.'

'And did she?'

She shook her head. 'Food poisoning. Always saved scraps and never remembered to pop them in the fridge.' That was how Cassie had described Gran's end, at least.

He nodded, but she had a sense that she'd somehow said the wrong thing. Which was interesting, wasn't it? How had an innocent remark come to irritate him like that? Best not to pursue it but to stand aside and let him unlock the nearest door.

Damp. There was a distinct smell of damp. But she mustn't sniff, or show any signs she was critical. She followed him round the place: it was no smaller than the fresh new place she'd just admired, but the use of space was nowhere near as good. The furniture was older and no doubt heavier, and there were more crevices in the kitchen and the bathroom.

Vernon laughed. 'Nothing to say? Well, isn't silence supposed to speak volumes? Don't think much of this, do you, Kate?'

'It'd take a lot longer to make it look anything like,' she said. 'Twice as long, I'd say. But that's what cleaners are for, isn't it, to make things look the best they can?'

'You're not a very good liar,' he laughed.

Aren't I? The little you know . . . But she felt a shit.

'What are the bedrooms like?' she prompted.

'This is a small family unit, so there's a double bedroom for the parents, and a bunk-bedroom for the kids.'

'But there's only one bedroom in the other place.' And why hadn't he shown it to her?

'There are different types of apartment. We're trying to move a little more . . . upmarket. And a lot of people are put off by other people's kids, apparently. So we've knocked down internal walls in the one you saw to give just one, much larger bedroom: remember? I daresay that's what'll happen to this if the owners ever decided to sell.'

'But it must take a lot of doing – to persuade, what, twenty or thirty owners they all want to upgrade or to sell back to you.'

She'd definitely said the wrong thing – or had she? He was looking at her with something strangely like approval.

'Come and see what we're trying to get rid of – I'm not terribly proud of these, I can tell you. This is the children's room – you can imagine what my Elly would say if she had to stay in it!'

'Or Peter for that matter,' she agreed, watching My Little Pony gallop across the restricted meadows of the walls.

'And back here's the adults' room. Not much luxury, is there?' He plumped down on a hard single bed.

She allowed herself a long appraising gaze round the room, as she ran a finger along the top of the wardrobe. She showed him: it came up grey. She was observed by a tiny camera.

'I can tell which you'd rather clean,' he continued. 'OK, Kate – I'll have a word with the agency, but where they roster you is up to them. Tell you what,' he added, locking up and setting back up the slope – walking quite gingerly, she noted, 'Julie's a bit low at the moment. If I can book up the odd meal, would you be happy to sit the kids?'

'Oh, I would. But' – she allowed herself to wriggle awkwardly as if embarrassed by the hint of charity – 'I . . . I can manage, you know.'

'I'm sure you can. But I know a good worker when I see one. Now, there are some senior managers coming down tomorrow—'

Where from? Hythe? Oxford? 'So you'd like me to do the conference room today, not Friday. No problems, Mr Vernon. In fact, I'll make a start now. There's no call for me to rush home, is there? – so I'll make sure it does you proud! *No reason?* She didn't want to dash back and find what was happening to Rod? 'Tell you what – are any of the bosses likely to pop into your office? Because it could do with something to brighten it up. Those plants . . . the fern's not as ill as it was, but even Baby-Bio takes a bit of time to work—'

'And, as the saying goes, miracles take a little longer.' He fished in his wallet and came out with a tenner. 'Would that be enough for another plant?'

'Plenty. Should get some cut flowers as well – they'd look nice. Unless you'd rather have them in the conference room?' Any PA worth her salt would have organised that, of course. But the woman, whoever she was, didn't seem to be much in evidence. One day she must make sure she hung around long enough to meet her.

He flashed another fiver at her. 'When will you get them?'

'Tesco opens twenty-four hours now: I could pick them up on the way in. Tell you what though – you couldn't borrow a couple of vases from Mrs Vernon?'

'Sure. Kate, you're a good girl. I know you won't let me down.'

She nodded modestly, just as if she wasn't saying, under her breath, 'I just hope one day I don't have to send you down.'

Kate forced herself to vac and dust as conscientiously as if she were Kate Potter desperate to impress and to earn extra pounds. At least now she had something else to think about besides Rod:

the visitors. Was there an attendance list anywhere? She headed back to Vernon's room, just to give it one more flash over, as she'd put it.

Just as she'd finished with the vacuum, he'd taken a phone call. Unusually he'd hunched over the phone, which she took as a sign that he'd prefer her room to her company. Grabbing both bins – his ordinary waste and paper destined to be shredded – she made a great show of scuttling silently away. Praying that the call would take a good long time, she rifled through the confidential material as quickly as she could. More about office plants? Definitely suspect. As for the rest, she fished a couple of sheets of accounts out and stowed them with the plant memos, before strolling into the office, nodding to the couple of girls languidly stirring coffee closer to their keyboards than was sensible and switching on the shredder. Hell! Something she'd missed. Something about security camera installation. Under cover of dropping a fistful, she fished it out, shoving it deep into her overall pocket. But it didn't lie flat. If she wasn't careful the bulge would betray the rest of her pilfering. Nothing for it. Grabbing her stomach as if she were unwell, she dashed to the loo. There. Everything stowed in her bra.

'You all right?' one of the girls – a redhead of about nineteen – asked as she returned.

'Tum's playing up a bit – I had this row with my bloke last night and it always goes to my stomach.'

'And mine,' Redhead sympathised.

The other woman was on her feet looking out of the window. On her way there, she could have read any of the wad of papers Kate had abandoned. Guilty as if she really had the interests of Sophisticasun at heart, Kate said, 'I shouldn't have left these lying around – you won't tell, will you?'

'Not if you don't. Pity you came back so quick: we might have read them through and found how much pay rise we were getting. Or the boss, more likely. Tell you what, tomorrow, you have another tummy ache only make it last longer.'

'Give you the chance to have a good read, you mean?' Kate giggled.

'Why not?' Window Woman asked – she'd be a couple of years older than Kate, but doing her best to look sixteen. 'Isn't as if they pay us enough to keep their secrets, is it?'

'You're full-time, are you?' Kate settled back on the edge of Redhead's desk, apparently ready for a girlie gossip.

'No. Agency, like you. But we're on long-term contracts, which means we get better security but get paid less.'

'You're joking!'

Window Woman snorted. 'I wish! No, the nicer they are to you, the meaner they're going to get. "Would you mind just doing this? Would you mind just doing that?"'

'And you're not supposed to mind doing it – or mind not getting paid for doing it,' the other woman said. 'I'm Tina, by the way, and this here's Mandy.'

'Kate.' She smiled at both of them. 'So have you been working here long?'

'About nine months. Both of us. Tell you what, we always have a cuppa about this time – you could join us!'

'Thanks. Goodness, I'd better be getting these bins back to Mr Vernon – he'll be wondering what's happened to me. But tomorrow would be grand. See you!'

Mr Vernon might still have been on the phone, but he'd clearly registered Kate's absence. He raised an eyebrow and touched his watch.

Kate mimed a bad stomach. She was wondering whether to add a little artistic extra, and mime spewing when whoever Vernon was speaking to cut the call.

'And I've got a confession to make,' Kate declared, before Vernon could draw breath. 'I had to go just when I was about to do the shredding. And I left stuff lying around till I got back. I really am sorry, when you've been so kind to me and everything.'

He got up, face thunderous – but with fear or anger she couldn't tell.

'When I got back it was all just as I'd left it, honestly. And I'm sure they wouldn't look. Mandy and Whatshername! Not if they knew they shouldn't.'

He snorted. 'What planet are you on, Kate? It's only secret stuff people would want to read. If you told them it was ordinary office waste they wouldn't bother!'

She wrung her hands. 'But they said I'd come back so quick they couldn't have – and it's true, Mr Vernon, they hadn't moved from their desks.' Let him think it anyway. 'In any case, they said the only thing that would have interested them would have been if it was news about their pay rises.'

'Tch! Well, you were right to tell me, I suppose. But don't do it again, for God's sake, Kate. I mean, we're part of a big operation here. Confidential information in the wrong hands could cost the organisation millions.'

Kate stared, open-mouthed, open-eyed.

'Oh, in share values, things like that,' he said, offhand.

'You mean there was stuff in your bin that was that important? My God!' She covered her mouth, peering at him with frightened eyes.

'Well, not this morning, perhaps,' he admitted. 'But it only goes to show, Kate.'

'I'm really, really sorry.' She might have been on the point of tears.

'Well, it wasn't the best of days for you yesterday, not by the sound of it. So I'm not surprised your stomach let you down. Let's just forget all about it. So long as it doesn't happen again. Tell you what!' His voice changed to boyish enthusiasm. 'I've just seen this mini-shredder in this catalogue. So cheap it could come out of petty cash. Now, what if I ordered one for this office?'

Well, it could mean one of three things. His PA might shred stuff, she herself might shred it; or, being a man, Vernon might want to play with his new toy himself. Kate smiled. 'It'd certainly add ten minutes to my cleaning time each day,' she said, beaming.

Rod. She'd had enough to chew on to push her worries about him to the back of her mind. But now they flooded back. Earnshaw should have been in touch with him by now, surely. But she mustn't allow herself to phone and check. Not yet. If you chased after good news it would change to bad: that was what Cassie would say. So she made herself stroll down to the site shop. Milk; bread. She or Earnshaw could always use those. With luck she might run into punters. Or would it be better luck to speak to whoever ran the place?

The shop was tucked away in a prefabricated building towards the less appealing end of the site. It'd almost certainly be on Sophisticasun's hit list. But the door opened with a cheerful two-tone electronic beep on to what looked at first glance like an old-fashioned village store. There was no post office counter, however, and a closer inspection showed the shelves were far from full – just a token front row of tins or packets, with nothing behind. The vegetables were compost heap material. Not surprisingly she was the only customer.

She picked up milk and sugar and a packet of cheese. She might even buy a Kate Potterish magazine. Yes, she'd always liked *Bella*, turning immediately to the recipes and then the stories. OK, it was the previous week's, but she wasn't buying it for the latest news from the Middle East, was she?

The middle-aged man behind the counter smiled at her wanly, and responded to her cheery greeting with a thread of a voice. Flu or his normal state? He looked as if some weeks ago someone had rubbed him out and not bothered to colour him in again.

She felt over large, over bright. Lowering her voice to match his, she produced a much shyer smile, and handed over her booty.

He told her the total. She mustn't let her eyes widen. She'd have paid less than half that at Tesco. But she handed over a folded fiver without comment. Then she ventured, as if embarrassed, 'I suppose you don't do staff discount, do you?'

'Work here, do you?'

'A cleaner.'

'Ah, well you'll be agency, like. I'm afraid it's only full-time staff who get discount,' he whispered.

She shrugged. 'No offence, I hope.' She let him count her change into her palm. Feeling that Kate Potter might well allow herself to be miffed (all that hard-earned money wasted, for goodness' sake!) she cast a disparaging look about the place. 'Not much a of a turnover here.'

He shook his head sadly. 'People mainly bring their own. But we're due for an up-grade as part of the refurbishment scheme.'

'So is this shop yours or theirs?'

'Oh, I'm just the manager. I'm really looking forward to the new establishment. It won't be the same as this of course.' He sounded regretful.

'What'll be different?'

'Oh, the stock. We'll be dealing in videos – and DVDs, of course. And applying for a wines and spirits licence. And there'll be a hair and beauty salon, too – but I shall have nothing to do with those.'

'When will all this be happening?'

His laugh sounded offended. 'Proper Little Miss Nosey, aren't you?'

She let her mouth droop. 'Sorry. It's just nice to talk to someone else here. I mean, Mr Vernon's very nice, very nice indeed, but he's my boss, and you can't have a natter with your boss, can you?'

'Hmm.'

Was he mollified?

'And the girls in the office are a bit – well, I suppose they're very busy.'

He looked at his watch. 'As a matter of fact, I'm just expecting a delivery. So if that's all?' He handed her her purchases in a carrier bag made of the thinnest polythene she'd ever seen. Would it get to the bike before splitting? Not trusting it, she carried it like a favourite cat, pressing it to her chest and supporting it underneath.

She'd just stowed the contents in her panniers when she heard the rumble of a heavy vehicle. Expecting it to be the shop delivery, she barely glanced up. Bread? Potatoes? No. Office Gardens. Hell.

All that work on Vernon's plants and they were to be replaced. Or was it foliage for the conference room? In which case, why all that business about her buying flowers for Mrs Vernon's vases?

And why, instead of heading for the admin block, was the van heading for the furthest corner of the grounds? Abandoning the bike again, she followed, walking as if she were entitled to be there. There weren't any punters to stop her, but there, where the road dropped down to some greenhouses that had seen better days, were Gary Vernon, clutching a clipboard, and the shop manager. She pulled back behind a lollypop shaped evergreen. Though he was walking purposefully he seemed to be stopping every twenty or thirty yards to look around him. There was no more cover between her and the glasshouses. Should she risk following him with some specious excuse? Or was discretion the better part of valour, given that her carelessness had already irritated him, and her questioning annoyed the shop manager? On the whole, she thought a tactical withdrawal the best move. Waiting till they were engrossed in conversation and apparently checking items on Vernon's board, she slipped as quietly as she could back to her bike. At least she had the number of the van and the name on the side. No, she wouldn't have access to the police computer herself, but her colleagues would. They'd even have a homely *Yellow Pages* to see if Office Gardens was a bona-fide firm. Yes, she'd done her bit, hadn't she?

It was almost twelve before Kate could pull into the nearest lay-by and check for phone messages. Nothing. Earnshaw? She'd risk phoning her. And got an immediate invitation to leave a message. Hell. No point in hanging around worrying, not when she could be getting closer to Earnshaw's cottage and worrying there.

Except that that was where Craig would be working. All day. She could have done without seeing him. It would be nice, colleague to colleague, to tell him that she'd been softening up Vernon on his behalf, but he'd see it as a sign of weakness on her part, no doubt about that.

A phone box provided a solution. Pulling over, she dialled and jammed money in as fast as her fumbling fingers could manage. Earnshaw's answerphone.

OK. What about Earnshaw's official police number? It was safe enough to use that from a call box.

Earnshaw picked up the receiver first ring.

'It's Kate—'

She got one sentence before Earnshaw cut the connection: 'Get yourself into the Cathedral coffee shop – now.'

17

Scenarios shuffled and collapsed in Kate's imagination as if she were shaking a kaleidoscope. Not pretty patterns, either, any of them. Mustn't look at them. Any of them.

The bloody Honda was no more use than a pushbike, not up hills – if only she'd got a firm time from Knowles for its upgrade. But if – what if –? Perhaps she wouldn't be staying. If there was anything wrong with Rod she'd throw the whole job— No! There mustn't be anything wrong with Rod. But a man who'd just used the L word wouldn't stay silent like this without good reason. A stake-out – no, Rod was too senior an officer to be involved at that level. Illness. That was what she feared most, after a mate's death last year. But Rod looked after his heart: a healthy diet, lots of exercise. Stress: that was the downside. Stress came with the rank. Especially with pressure from all directions to find the callous killers of a harmless old man. Most of all from inside yourself, if you were as conscientious as Rod. And pressure caused not just heart attacks but strokes. What if he'd had a stroke? Paralysis. Losing his speech. Incontinence. How would he cope with that? How would she cope, working and coming home to look after him? But he was young enough to recover. Look at that writer – full-time literary editor of one of the quality Sundays. He was OK. But what about the Frenchman, who'd only been able to communicate with one eyelid? Oh, God – not that, not for Rod: he'd rather be dead. Anyone would.

It might not be illness at all. What if he'd interrupted a burglar? Not in the course of duty. Someone breaking into his own home. A simple break-in. Or a revenge attack. Making enemies of violent men came with the territory too.

For God's sake, Kate: get a grip. He's doing what you've been doing – working. He's good at his job. He keeps fit. He's simply too busy to phone. And he'll be wary about contacting you at all anyway.

The traffic slowed to about five miles an hour. Now what? Swearing like a trooper, no, like Earnshaw, she realised they'd caught up with a huge hay-wagon. It was loaded so high it was brushing the trees that overhung the road, leaving a trail of leaves and twigs and, of course, hay. Or was it straw? Whatever it was, it was part of an unsafe load, and if she could have caught up with the driver she'd have had him at the nearest weighbridge before he could say harvest. Fat chance of catching anything except cold on this bloody bike.

She'd have known if anything had happened to him. Anything really bad. Surely she'd have known. She'd known the instant Robin died. There'd been no need for the superintendent in charge of the failed raid to trail into her A and E cubicle and try to break the news through the masses of painkiller they were flooding into her. No need. But then, she'd known Robin for such a long time: they'd been friends, the closest of friends, before they'd become lovers. She'd even known when Graham had been involved in a motorway pile-up. So, no: nothing could have happened to Rod. OK, she was stupidly near to screaming with worry and fear. But it was worry and fear for someone still alive. She'd have gone on oath.

The outskirts of Exeter: this was where the Honda would shine. She nipped sharply in and out of the near-stationary traffic. So she'd always deplored it when bikes had done it to her. Tough. Close season for good manners. Kate's at least.

There were usually parking spaces in the multi-storey on the river side of the ring road. OK, it wasn't the nearest car park to the Cathedral, but Craig had insisted that this was the best option – after all, it was easy enough to leg it over the pedestrian bridge, across one road and then into the Close. She'd just have to trust Craig's judgement.

The Cathedral greeted her abruptly: far from being a haven of peace, it was crawling with hard-hatted men setting up a stage and sound system. She had to weave and dodge – were all the natives of Exeter old or infirm? – down to the refectory. And there was Earnshaw, stolid, impregnable, wading through a slice of what looked like carrot cake.

'Get yourself a coffee and come and sit down.' It wasn't just the tone of voice that said she'd reveal nothing until Kate had carried out orders; her whole body insisted.

But Kate was shaking so much by the time she'd brought her tray over to the communal table Earnshaw had commandeered, that she had to go back for paper serviettes to mop the milk she'd slopped.

'Craig's put in an official complaint against you. That's just for starters.'

Kate sat straighter. 'Just at the moment I don't give a flying fuck about Craig. The only things I'm worrying about are passing on information I picked up this morning and Rod—'

'You girls and love. You've got a bloody job to do. You and your bloody private life—'

'What's the news of Rod?'

'I don't – I really don't – know what you're making such a sodding song and dance about.'

'Is he all right?'

'As far as I know.'

'So why didn't he answer my calls?'

'Because he'd got something more important to do, you stupid bitch. One of your mates was so badly beaten up they thought they'd lose him. So Rod – who sounds a decent officer, with his priorities right, unlike some I could mention – spends the night at the hospital with the man's family. And in hospitals, you may recall, you can't use mobile phones. Does that suit your ladyship? Because I'm telling you, Power, any more of your amateur dramatics and you're off my team. And probably off this man Rod's visiting list, too, if he's got any sense. All these hysterics. For God's sake!'

'You don't want an update then? Jesus, I – the loo.' This time her stomach upset was for real. And the queue was full of old ladies gossiping and 'after-you-ing' and taking forever once they'd reached a cubicle. And the lavatory pan Kate eventually knelt before hadn't flushed properly. She vomited till there was nothing left but bile. So this was what they meant by sick with worry.

At last she was able to tidy herself up. She might as well take off the cleaner's overall: she could roll it up and stuff it in her bag. And even if she were off the case, she'd better retrieve from her bra the documents she'd filched.

If only Earnshaw hadn't seen them as a peace offering.

'Humph. So you did do some work this morning.' She stowed them grudgingly in her bag.

She mustn't rise to the bait. 'Now, when I told Vernon I'd left stuff unshredded while I threw up – yes, same problem at work – he nearly shat himself. If certain information got into the wrong hands, he said, it could cost the organisation millions. He's talking about getting his own personal shredder: you never know, he may even let me use it.'

Earnshaw nodded an approximation of approval.

'Vernon was so sorry for my wan face this morning he promised to try to get me on the Saturday roster. He showed me round a couple of the apartments: before and after refurbishment.'

'Any surveillance cameras?'

'In the older one: I didn't see the bedroom in the posh one.'

'Maybe you will. OK?'

'At one point, I said that whoever was supposed to be maintaining the grounds was doing a pretty crap job and even Craig would be better. Vernon said he didn't want any domestics on his patch, which interested me.'

'Don't see why it should: the residents wouldn't like to see you and Craig yelling blue murder at each other.'

'Ah. But, as I told him, they wouldn't because we'd be working at different times. No, Ma'am, what interested me was the word he used. "Domestic." It's a bit of our lingo, surely.'

Earnshaw fixed her with a hard stare. 'OK. I'll get it checked out. Not that the computers have suggested a police background

– and I can assure your ladyship we have been doing our home-work too.'

Again she kept her cool. 'And he may want me to baby-sit a bit more often. Now he knows Craig's walked out on me. And there's something that may be interesting about office plants.'

'That's what one of those memos was about.'

'Right. Anyway, this morning I popped into the shop and then saw this delivery . . .' She gave a full account, ending with the van's details.

If she expected half a brownie point, she didn't get one.

'You're setting up contacts like this and you think of walking out on the job? You're off your head, girl. Women like me have had to bust our flaming guts to get where we are. You swan in here, all lady muck, tell us you're not happy because lover-boy back home didn't phone: I didn't fight and crawl my way up through the ranks for the likes of you!'

'The other thing,' Kate continued, as if Earnshaw hadn't spo-ken, 'is that there's a flaw in your and Knowles's domestic arrangements. Why doesn't your husband of all these years live with you? A bit hypocritical of you two to be telling Craig and me to sort ourselves out if you two have split up: isn't it?'

'Fuck. But surely—'

'Vernon gives the impression he really likes me: he's worried when he thinks Craig may be violent towards me. He's worried I may be hard up. He doesn't live far from you, and I'd say he's the sort of man who might want to come and talk to you about what should be done.'

'Sounds a decent man. What a pity he's a criminal dealing with drugs and laundering terrorists' money. At least, the people he works for. I'd suspect him as well – the drugs side.'

Kate dug in her bag. 'I also got this number someone might want to check. A car out on Berry Head. It stuck out like a sore thumb. You know, the sort of classy, tarted-up Audi that drug dealers use?' But perhaps Exeter dealers were more discreet than Brummie ones. She added, 'Tinted windows, alloys, more sound than's decent? That sort of car. The same time as the Vernons were taking their kids to fly their kites.'

'No one would be that stupid.' All the same Earnshaw wrote down the number.

'Or careless. Or arrogant. That's what I thought. Then I started to wonder . . . After all, the people in Brum – yes, it's a West Midlands reg – have to get their stuff from somewhere. As I said, a small boat could use Cockwood. It'd be nice to get some surveillance cameras of our own set up there. And I'm sure our colleagues are keeping an eye on suspicious activities on Dartmoor – perhaps that could be stepped up.'

'Hmm. Dartmoor's not your average park, you know. In the north, you'll have to walk two or three miles from your front door to the road. I'm talking remote, here, Kate. Really remote. So with the best will in the world, we can't check to see that every greenhouse crop isn't cannabis, every barn isn't a lab. Tell you what, you keep your eyes open when you go swanning round on that bike of yours. And forget the tourist traps. Head north. That's an order.'

'Ma'am.'

'Tell you what, I'll get hold of a camera for you. Use it.'

'Ma'am.' Kate stared at the congealed mess that had once been coffee. If she tried to touch it she'd gag again. 'Can I get you another? I—'

'You sit down.' Earnshaw eyed her closely. 'You're still looking pretty green. Must have been something you ate, yesterday. That crab, maybe.'

'I'd forgotten that.'

'Can be dodgy, crab. You want to watch it.' Earnshaw hauled herself to her feet and strode off to intimidate the women on the counter.

So it was all right to be physically ill, was it? Well, of course it was. Better than what Cassie would have called 'nerves' and Earnshaw, with an ironic twist to her voice, 'stress'. That was the police for you.

But Earnshaw was back, plonking a fresh tray in front of her.

'Shouldn't be drinking coffee with a bad stomach: you should know better than that. Milk should be all right. And they tell me these scones are home-made.'

The problem, they both agreed, was what Kate should do for the rest of the day. Not to mention the evening, when Craig would be round for his gear. As long as the sun shone, Kate wanted to be out and about, and Dartmoor was now an even more desirable target.

But Earnshaw was now doing a fair impression of a mother hen trying to stop its duckling taking to the water: 'I don't want you putting yourself at risk, not with that bad stomach.'

'I shall be fine. As for this evening, I'll take myself to the pictures or something. Don't worry, I shan't stir things up any more.'

'Let's look at that arm of yours,' Earnshaw said. 'Go on, roll your sleeve up. Tut. He shouldn't be doing things like that. What do you think of these courses they keep trying to send us on: anger management, that sort of thing?'

Resolutely not gasping, Kate asked, 'Isn't there a proverb about horses and water? I'm sure Craig needs some sort of help. Was he properly debriefed after his last assignment? Post traumatic stress can do all sorts of things to people.'

'You mean he got frightened and upset then and that's why he's a vicious young bastard now? Don't give me that psychobabble, Kate. Right: nearly lunch time. A baked potato shouldn't hurt you. I'll have one myself while you're at it. Tuna and mayo. I've got a call to make.'

Earnshaw was just contemplating a luscious looking apple and blackberry crumble and lamenting that Kate shouldn't really risk it, when a phone sounded. It was clear to everyone else in the refectory that it was Earnshaw's: eventually the penny dropped, and, cursing that the pudding would soon be cold, she excavated in her bag and came up flourishing the offending phone, which had continued to play 'Für Elise' with unabated enthusiasm.

'Yes,' she bellowed, remembering not to give her name or rank.

'Excellent. I'll tell her now.' But she demolished another couple of spoons of crumble before she said, 'Two things. If you go for a walk round the shops and come back here for coffee at – say three – you'll find a carrot-head of a man with a camera for you. Foolproof. Oh, and some binoculars.'

'There's this conference tomorrow. Any chance of Carrot-head coming up with some bugs?'

'I'll see what I can do. And then there's your bike. The mechanic'll be round four thirtyish. He'll stay as long as it takes. So you won't be on your own this evening. Off you go, then. And mind how you go.'

18

In mufti, the mechanic might just have passed for a pretty but vacuous dentist's receptionist. In overalls, the message was so clear that even Craig might have got it. The lip-piercing reinforced the general idea. She introduced herself as Ned, a name that defeated Kate till she realised it might be a variant of Edwina, not Ned's sort of name at all. For the rest of the afternoon and early evening, Kate kept Ned supplied with coffee and biscuits, which she consumed having wiped only the excess of oil from her fingers.

Kate hadn't given much thought to how much work the upgrade would involve: she'd vaguely thought of a couple of different valves or whatever. But it seemed that suspension and braking systems were involved too. She wilted under Ned's scorn and withdrew to pither with the binoculars and especially the new camera: the bugs would come through the following day. As Earnshaw had said, the camera was pretty foolproof. But not, she suspected, unsophisticated. No, it wasn't digital: no point in having a photographic record if the computer could change it at will. An SLR: compact, light – yes, it fitted well into the hands. In a separate bag were several spare films. Robin would have approved. He'd always had a camera in his hand: his kids must have been the most photographed children in the western world. Well, he'd missed them when he'd moved in with her. She shivered. She'd forgotten how much she'd missed them. Not to mention missing him, going round with an ache so physical it could double her up. Not since Graham. And now Rod.

She straightened. There was work to do in the back garden. A nice bit of physical work. That should stop her thinking. But as she pulled weeds, still growing vigorously despite the lateness of the season, she started to agonise about Rod again. Should she phone him to apologise? She was quite sure that however Earnshaw had phrased any enquiries after his health, her tone had conveyed much the same message as the one she'd fired at Kate. Love was something that might occur, if at all, out of working hours. And since CID didn't have such formalised things as working hours, love had no place in CID. If anywhere in the Force. No, Earnshaw would never consider the police a service: for her and the other Earnshaws of this world it would always be the Force.

Or should she wait for Rod to make contact? She had to, didn't she? How would he do it? She no longer had Earnshaw's phone at her disposal. And she couldn't risk any other sort of call, except from a payphone. However sure she might be that Vernon liked and trusted her, she knew better than to suppose that his employers did. Their security vetting was likely to be as stringent as any legitimate commercial organisation's. Well, it was a legitimate commercial organisation. Possibly. In which case it wouldn't bother with people as low down the food chain as her.

Except throughout the assumption had been made that they would. It had to be. Just in case.

Just in case, they were souping up her bike. Just in case, they were making her live this silly life. Never again. Never. She had to be in control. She had to be herself.

'Oy! Kate! Are you deaf?' It was Ned. 'They've been ringing and hollering!'

Kate hammered round to the front, to be greeted by a bunch of flowers. Not huge. Not excessive. Lovely, all the same.

No need to ask who'd sent them. The card declared: *From your mates old and new at the Hare and Hounds. Sorry you've been feeling rough. Come up and see us again soon as you can. Love 'n' hugs.*

She beamed; she grinned; she laughed aloud in delight. Rod would have enjoyed the last phrase: *love 'n' hugs,* indeed.

All she lacked, of course, was a vase to put them in. Except she'd never quite got round to retrieving the precious one for Rod from her pannier, for all she'd meant to leave it safe at Earnshaw's. She really was losing it, wasn't she?

Ned sniffed audibly at the contents of the pannier: vases were clearly not her thing. But she managed a grin: 'They flowers have put a bit of a smile on your face,' she observed. Weird: a soft Devon burr coming from someone cultivating such hardness. 'Tell you what, this is nearly ready for you. The boss says I've got to stay till Craig's been and gone, but all the same I've got to road test this. While I'm doing it, shall I pop into the chippie?'

'Great!'

'Cod and chips? Plaice and chips?'

She'd only been about to ask for what she'd have had in Birmingham: a huge portion of chicken tikka in a naan. Oh, yes – please! But poor Kate Potter was unlikely to have got hooked on such a delicacy, and maybe Kings Norton wouldn't have the wondrous chippie that Kings Heath boasted. 'Chicken, if you don't mind. Had some crab that disagreed with me yesterday. I'm off things coming out of the sea.'

Ned regarded her in disbelief. 'But everyone knows fish is best if you've got a bad tum.'

Kate shuddered. 'Thanks all the same. Chicken.'

'Any pop?'

A glass or two of good white wine might go down a treat! 'No, nothing fizzy, thanks. Let me get some cash.'

'Leave it. I'll put it on the bill. Nice round total.'

Out of overalls, Ned affected the sort of grungy gear in-your-face lesbians had worn when Kate was younger: thick soled boots, ugly trousers, a man's shirt and a severe and ill-fitting man's waistcoat. She tugged wayward hair behind her ears, and sat with her left ankle resting on her right knee. Pity she wasn't into lesbian chic: she could have looked gorgeous. She produced a couple of bottles of Stella Artois, eschewing, as Craig had done, a glass.

'Bike's going like a dream, though I says it as shouldn't,' she said. 'Handling'll be a bit different, though. You'll need to watch it.'

'Don't worry: I shall take it gently past my granny's for a bit.'

'Have you got family down here, then? Though they said you were a grockle—'

Grockle? Ah, yes: Devon for outsider. That was Kate, all right. 'Yes, I am. It's just an expression they use up my neck of the woods.' Except, of course, it wasn't. It wasn't even Brummie. She must have picked it up from Colin, a reliable source of Black Country idioms no one else used or quite understood. Oh, if only it could have been Colin watching suspiciously as she tipped the chips on to plates she'd put to warm. Yes, she missed his company deeply – as much as Rod's, if in a different way.

'You're still working with Craig, then?' Ned asked, generous with extra salt and vinegar.

How much did the woman know? Wasn't it all supposed to be top secret? 'Working?' she began.

'Wasn't the idea that you were supposed to be having rows? And then you did, a big one, good and proper. That's what he's saying, anyway.'

'Saying to whom? I thought he wasn't supposed to be seeing any of his mates.'

'Oh, no one worries about that, do they?'

'I've an idea they do.' Or bloody well should. 'That's what we were told, anyway,' she added trying not to sound like a goody-goody, but anxious to give the message that even Ned should be careful what she was saying.

'Oh, you never could tell him anything.' Message clearly not received.

Try a different tack. 'Have you known him long?'

'Not as such. His wife – ex-wife now – was in my women's group for a bit.'

Did they still have women's groups? But Kate must not get diverted by that. 'Wife? I didn't know he was married.'

'Well, you wouldn't expect him to talk about it, not to you. Loathed you on sight, apparently. Which we took to mean he fancies you.'

'Eh? What's the logic behind that?' Kate hacked at some

chicken. Her favourite Kings Heath chippie wouldn't have allowed such undernourished, overcooked meat to cross its counter. Elbows on table, she did the obvious thing: she picked it up and gnawed at it. On the other hand, the chips were so good she suspected they might have been cooked in dripping.

'Well, you know . . . Anyway, he and this Helen got married ever so young. Real childhood sweetheart stuff,' Ned sneered. She shoved the remains of her fish to one side and concentrated on her chips, which she picked up one at a time at ferocious speed.

'And then?'

'Well, one thing young Helen can do is spend money. She got them into debt, then she fancied going to college, so they got deeper in debt. And police pay being so crap, things got worse.'

Police pay crap? That was the first Kate knew about it. Of course, in London, with property prices so crazy, it didn't buy much. But then, neither did teachers' or nurses' pay. And surely by Devon standards, where the average wage was so far below the national average, and unemployment so much higher, a detective sergeant's pay was pretty good.

'Are you in the police yourself?' Kate enquired, twisting the drumstick from the thigh.

'No. Just attached to them. You know, like civilian in-putters. Only I work on cars and bikes.'

And almost certainly wasn't earning much in comparison with Kate or Craig. Which implied someone had been whingeing.

'So they broke up because of her debts?'

'That's what he says. She says different, of course. She says he – well, her version's a bit different.' And, judging by the way she opened the second bottle of Stella, it was this version Ned was longing to tell, as much as Kate was longing to hear it. 'Well, he hit her, of course. Not much, certainly not as badly as I've seen people hit. You know, in the group. But enough to bruise her a bit.'

'In places where people couldn't see?' For a moment Kate was tempted to roll up her sleeve, but she resisted. Those who needed to know knew. And she had no special reason to confide in Ned.

'How did you know that?'

'Some of my mates work in a Domestic Violence unit – God, some of the tales they tell make your stomach heave.'

'I don't think Craig's that bad. Though she said he got much worse later. Apparently they moved him out of CID at one point. Helen seemed to think that was a bad thing.'

Now was not the moment for Kate to get on her high horse about police disciplinary policies. She merely nodded.

'They moved him to a different force, too. He was in Traffic for a bit. Up in Bristol. And this is the bit Helen worried about. End of the month time, when it's touch and go till the next pay packet, he always comes up flush. Gives her a bunch of notes. He'd never done anything like it before, not when he was in CID.'

'Bunches of notes?'

'Yes. Great wads. When she asked how he'd got hold of them, he'd either laugh or clock her one, depending on his mood.'

'Did she ever find out where it came from?'

'She reckons he took bribes from motorists he'd threatened to nick. Big ones.'

'Jesus Christ!'

'She reckons he didn't so much take as ask.'

'Bloody hell. But there was never any evidence?'

'You cops and your evidence! She couldn't grass up her own husband, could she? Marriage!' She mimed a spit. 'Imagine being married to Craig, for God's sake.'

'It's bad enough living with him.'

'You don't fuck him?'

Was this a general question or had he boasted that they shared a bed? 'God, no! Strictly separate bedrooms, whatever he says.' She must maintain the comradely grin, but make it more puzzled. 'Hang on: how much do you know about this set-up? Like I said, isn't it all supposed to be top secret? Do you mean Knowles—?'

'Knowles gave me the order. But I knew about it anyway from Craig.'

'Fucking big mouth! No, Ned, not you. It's Craig. We're

supposed to be sworn to absolute secrecy. That's why I was so cagey earlier.'

'You mean, it's life and death and that?'

'I'm not saying it is. But it could be.'

'So why's he telling all his mates? And saying he'll give you a right good seeing to before you go back to Brum?'

Kate tried to keep her voice amused, not outraged. 'Is he now! We'll see about that!'

'If he tries tonight,' Ned snorted, 'I reckon I will, too.'

'But you're not in the police – why should you take any risks?'

'Haven't you ever heard of girl power, up there in Birmingham? Part of this here women's group, aren't I?'

'So your help is purely unofficial?'

''Course it is. But Craig knows me well enough not to try anything on. Unless you want a WPC? You'd be entitled, wouldn't you?'

Kate got up, and tipped the remains on the plates into one of the chip bags. 'The fewer people that know about this the better. I'd much rather have your support than anyone else Knowles might care to bring in.'

Ned rubbed her fingers on her jeans and tipped back her chair. 'Something's really pissed you off, hasn't it?'

Kate faced her, arms akimbo. 'Of course something has. But not you. Look, Ned, when I was undercover before, my police mates thought I'd gone on a course; so did my family and friends. I had one contact only in the police. My part in the operation was kept so quiet that when I got hauled in for questioning as a possible witness, I maintained my role even then. Now Craig seems to be telling all and sundry, and even Knowles seems to be blabbing. The only one keeping schtum is me; the only one kept away from family and friends is me; the only one at risk is me. And the risk is all the greater if other people know.'

'Well, I'm not blabbing. And I'm just staying here to keep you company because Knowles asked me to. He didn't say why. And I didn't tell him I knew Craig.'

'Thanks, Ned. Honestly, it's not you I'm getting at. Honestly.'

'Well, if you want to get at Craig, here's your moment. Reckon that's his car now.' She cocked her head to one side, for all the world like a scruffy starling casing a lawn for leatherjackets.

To Kate it was just any car, but she'd take Ned's word for it. 'OK, then. He comes and collects his gear. And then what? You know more than I do!'

'I stay and change the locks, of course.' She laughed. ''Course I specialise in cars and bikes. But I can turn my hand to most things. Back at Tech they called it "multi-skilling".'

The front door opened; to her relief – despite Ned's comforting presence – she heard two male voices. It was clear the men were coming to the kitchen first. One step and she could see both Craig's face and Ned's. Time to intuit a bit of truth-telling – or otherwise.

'What the fuck are you doing here?' Craig demanded, but looking at Ned, not her.

'Souping up Kate's bike, of course. Any problems with that?' Ned's body language said loud and clear that there better hadn't be. 'Who's your friend, anyway?'

A good question. A thinnish man with ginger hair and overlarge ears. Kate rather thought he might be the man Craig had gone out with, the night of their first row. Not a police mate, then. Was that good or bad?

Craig pressed a fingertip against Ned's nose. 'None of your business. Nor yours, before you start!' he flung at Kate.

'It probably is, but so long as he's here to help you move your stuff, we needn't make an issue of it,' she said, keeping her voice as steady as possible. Should she insist on accompanying him upstairs? It would be confrontational: the last thing she wanted was further violence. But she didn't trust him to confine his activities to his own room, or to what little was his in the bathroom. Perhaps she'd give him four or five minutes, and then follow him upstairs, sitting quietly in her own room till he'd gone.

The men were hardly out of the room, however, when the phone rang. 'Hello? Kate Potter here.'

'Kate? This is Julie Vernon. I just wanted to make sure you

were all right. Gary said your partner was coming round tonight. I was wondering – I know we hardly know each other – but would you like me to come round so you don't have to deal with him on your own?'

'Oh, Julie. That's ever so kind. But I've got a mate here, thanks. She's keeping an eye on things.' As she spoke, she pointed at the ceiling, willing Ned to go upstairs in her stead. But Ned didn't seem to be into that sort of communication.

'Good. But you must be careful Kate, very, very careful. Keep out of his way. Don't try to argue. Just let him—'

Just let me keep an eye on him! Just get off the line! Why the hell hadn't she used the mobile, then at least I could have talked and maintained a presence. Kate pointed again, frantically.

'– now, if you don't feel secure where you are – and from what Gary tells me, he's a young man capable of violence – you could always stay here. Or – yes, Gary's saying something – you could borrow one of the empty apartments: no one would know, would they?'

'It's ever so kind of you – er, Julie. But I'm sure I'll be all right. Thing is, he's here now, and he'd hate it if he thought we were talking about him. And I don't want to make things worse, do I?' Oh, to be Kate Power, capable of cutting a phone call as and when required. But the Kate Potters of this world couldn't do that. She'd better try. 'In fact, I can hear him yelling for me now. I'd better go. But I'm really grateful.'

'No need to be. Now, just be careful – understand?'

'I will be. Thank you ever so much.' And Kate managed it at last: 'I really had better go.'

'What was all that about?' Ned demanded.

'I was hoping you'd go and keep an eye on them,' Kate replied, wilfully misunderstanding. 'I don't want Craig to take what isn't his.' And she headed up the stairs as fast as she could. And as quietly. But even as she reached her room, Craig barged out of his, prepared to use his bag as a battering ram. His mate had one equally large.

'That's it, then,' Craig managed.

She pointed to the bedroom floor. Socks, pants, odd scraps of paper.

'What about that lot?'

'What about it?'

'You tell me. Are you leaving it there?'

'Why not?'

'OK, then. So long as you're not going to run out of things.'

'None of your business if I do.'

'True. So long as you expect to see them in exactly the same place when you come back.'

'They better bloody had be. Or in the airing cupboard.'

Kate shut his bedroom door, shaking her head and folding her arms across her chest. 'No, I shouldn't think they'll be there. OK, then, Craig. See you when I see you, I suppose.'

He started down the stairs, but turned to face her. 'Women like you,' he said, lunging towards her, 'deserve all they get. Just you remember that.'

That was a threat, if ever she'd heard one. How would he get back at her? Policemen had been known to plot revenges in the locker rooms – strange mixtures of the crude and sophisticated. He was planning something: she could feel it in her bones.

But at least he'd spoken in front of two witnesses. Except – bugger it – Ned was nowhere to be seen. She looked over Craig's shoulder at his mate, who dropped his eyes as if already guilty.

'OK,' she said. 'See you, then. See you –?' She paused, looking questioningly at Big Ears.

'Macker,' he might have said.

'See you, Macker.' She tried for lightness. 'You keep an eye on him for me, will you?' Just as if she were a loving but misunderstood girlfriend.

When they'd gone – a good job the paint wasn't theirs to worry about, the way he slung his bag around – she found Ned watching TV. The flowers and vase were safe on the table beside her.

'Did you hear all that?' Kate demanded.

'Some, I suppose. Didn't get noisy, like, so I didn't come up.

I would have done,' she added defensively, her eyes still glued to the screen.

'OK. Thanks.' Ned wasn't a bodyguard, after all. Nor did she know she was supposed to be a witness. She left her where she was, and went off to tidy the kitchen and fix a coffee.

Then she obeyed her instinct – she ran upstairs to her room. No, all the drawers were as she'd left them. No problems there. But there was something wrong. Wardrobe OK. So what had he done?

At last she pulled back the duvet. Ah! The bastard had come up with one of the oldest tricks in the police merry-jape book – a fake turd in the bed.

It didn't take her long to realise it was entirely genuine.

19

K ate couldn't fault Ned's response: 'Shit!'
Then Ned asked, 'Has it messed the mattress and everything?'

Kate had been too busy with rubber gloves and loos and disinfectant to think about that. She checked: no, the under-sheet had a telltale patch, but not the mattress itself. More disinfectant. A full load for the machine, since the duvet cover had been soiled too. Not the duvet itself, though. So she had an efficient domesticated evening with clean bed linen while Ned was equally efficient with the front and back door locks.

'There, try these,' Ned suggested, handing over new keys. 'OK? Then give me your old ones. Don't tell Knowles, but I can get a good price for second-hand locks and keys – people don't ask to see receipts when I fix things for them. I'll get Craig's off him when I see him.'

She'd done a good job: there was no need to get officiously law-abiding with her. Kate handed them over.

'He's not going to be a happy bunny when he finds he's locked out,' Ned continued. 'Wonder what he'll think of doing then?'

'The usual response would be a load of manure or a load of ready-mix concrete. Dumped on the drive.'

'Manure'd be OK. Useful for that patch you've got at the back.'

'By the ton? Quite. But it's a bit obvious, that. And it might well get him into the manure himself. So would concrete, because this house is presumably rented to the police, who'd have to make good any damage. It might even belong to them. No, the art of revenge is to send something people would be ashamed to snitch

about. Because that's the whole ethos of the police service –
you don't grass up your mates, no matter how badly they've
treated you.'

'You mean you won't tell them about him crapping in your
bed? Jesus Christ, I would!'

'It doesn't do to get a reputation for bleating: "real" cops can
deal with everything, because if you don't it shows you've no
sense of humour.'

'And being a woman, you're not supposed to have one of
those, are you? So it's heads they win, tails you lose? Bastards.'
Ned tugged her fingers through her hair, apparently listening
to the chug of the washing machine. 'Tell you what,' she said
at last, 'there'll be some of my mates down the pub: why don't
you come along? OK, we're mostly gay, but you won't mind
that, will you?'

'My best mate's gay,' Kate said. If Colin had been here she'd
have put her head on his shoulder and wept.

'Right, let's be off then. I'll see you back – at least there'll be
two of us to deal with any manure.'

As if she had no cares in the world – and perhaps she hadn't,
apart from a load of washing it would take forever, on a misty
day like this, to dry – Kate packed the camera and binoculars.
OK, they were supposed to be for snapping suspicious sites on
Dartmoor. But there might just be the chance of photographing
the complex with the visitors strolling around. Or not. Safety
first, Kate.

As she pulled up by the admin block and locked her bike –
yes, she'd found it considerably more interesting to handle –
she almost rubbed her hands in anticipation. While there was a
distinct minus about the conference, there was a plus side too:
she should have a safe opportunity to rifle through the papers
destined for the shredder. Meanwhile, the place must gleam: she
owed that to Gary Vernon. So she arrived early and worked with a
will. Whether it was the booze she'd sunk with Ned and her mates
or the simple fact that she could lock herself undisturbed in the

house, she'd slept the sleep of the just and felt ready to vacuum and polish the whole of Devon if necessary. And then she could have a matey cup of tea with the women in the office.

The parts of the place that were her responsibility shone. The loos were pleasant to use. And she was well up to speed. Until the vac decided to play up: changing the dust bag, even though it was the second time she'd done the task, took valuable minutes. They'd be here any moment now.

And then it hit her. What if she *were* recognised? She'd worried herself silly yesterday, probably embarrassing Rod. And what she should have been thinking about was being seen. OK, the chances were that Knowles and Earnshaw were right – no one would look at a cleaning woman, and if they did, wouldn't relate her to the sleek specimen Kate had presented to the world before. All the same, the best dodge was to retire to the store cupboard till they were all safely ensconced in the conference room. She had an unexpected bonus: the cupboard shared a wall with the conference room. She could hear Tina and Mandy's voices as they laid out pads and pencils. They sounded as excited as if the visit were something to do with them. Then there was a murmur of men's voices, and one woman's – only one, as far as she could make out. Was there any point in lurking as long as she could, in the hope of picking up information? No. No matter how hard she pressed her ear against the wall, she could hear nothing distinct – pity those listening devices weren't to hand yet. When they were, she might even be able to put one in Vernon's office. Why had no one asked her to already? Come to think of it, why had she been too dozy to ask? These rush jobs. The best surveillance involved thorough preparation.

Right: everyone seemed to be in place. Now all she had to do was return with her gear to Vernon's office. She could have another look for the delegates' list. He might even have left one on his desk. She'd carry a duster: if any latecomers turned up, face averted she could busy herself polishing any handy window or door. No need. Now: that list. But Vernon's desk was bare. His confidential basket was pristine. Shit. How about a delve into his computer files? What, with the machine switched off, and not the remotest idea of the password? And the little camera keeping its eye on everything she did? Get real, Kate. Better to drift along and talk to Mandy and Tina. They might even have a list, though how she could ask she didn't know.

There was no doubt that while the cat was away, they were playing. Mandy had some new nail varnish, of which Tina strongly disapproved.

'What do you think, Kate?' Mandy demanded.

'Well, my mum would have had a fit if she'd thought I was wearing anything like that for work. But clubbing – it'd be great for that.'

Both women seemed satisfied. Kate picked up the bottle and stirred, enjoying the movement of whatever iridescent substance made it glitter. The kettle boiled.

'Better take them their coffee, then. Hey, give us a hand, will you, Kate?'

Not bloody likely. Just in case.

'What? Dressed like this?' She picked at her overall. 'And sweat – I must smell like a rugby player's jock strap.'

'Go on – don't be mean. No one'll notice.'

If she argued any more it would be obvious. 'All right.' But she wouldn't. Apparently screwing up the nail-varnish bottle, she managed to drop it, spilling a spot on to the carpet. 'Oh, God – look what I've done! I'll buy you some more, Mandy – or pay—'

'You've got it all over the carpet!' Tina shrieked.

Yes, a drop at least a millimetre in diameter. 'I've got some acetone in the cupboard'll sort it. You two go on. I'll fix this!' God Almighty, the second this was mopped, she'd be out of there.

The others returned.

She knelt back on her heels. 'There. You'd never notice!'

Tina sniffed. 'Looks like you'll have to clean the rest of the carpet. I'd no idea it was so dirty.'

Kate looked at her watch. 'OK. In their time I will. How much was it, Mandy? Least I can do is pay you.' And not flinch when she heard the price. Come to think of it, she didn't believe it: didn't Christian Dior sometimes hand out little bottles like this as part of their give-away packs? She was being milked, shamelessly – of a morning's wages. So much for the solidarity of the working classes. So much for asking for a list of delegates.

Despite everything, she wished she'd helped with the coffee. What about offering to collect the empty cups? Surely no one would register her. But if Vernon were in a good mood he might just thank her in front of the others. And her risk would be for what? Nothing a bug couldn't pick up better. Look, the mist was lifting nicely. Maybe the washing would dry after all. Meanwhile, she might as well obey orders. It was just the day for a ride round north Dartmoor.

No messing about this time. Straight up the A382 to Moreton-hampstead: the bike happily devoured the gradients. Further north to South Zeal and Sticklepath – she loved the sound of the places – or into that labyrinth of roads leading from the B3212 towards Chagford? That seemed more promising. The roads were narrow, some of them so steep-sided it was like being in a tunnel. Most had tracks leading off them, wilting fingerposts indicating farms. But she must take care. It wasn't just the bike's new power she'd be testing, it was its brakes, too, as the lanes plunged down towards a river. She consulted her OS map. The Teign? The river giving Teignmouth its name? Yes, its tributary streams, at least: right up on the moor, according to the map, was a ruin called Teignhead Farm. If she'd gone south and walked through the forest surrounding the reservoir, she'd have been able to see it. But ruined farms weren't on the agenda today.

The villages she picked her way through were so small she thought she'd have more chance of finding a pub serving food in Chagford itself. Even that was little more than a couple of streets and a church. A high street. And there was what looked like a coaching inn: the Globe. A level memories told her it shared a name with an Elizabethan theatre. She bought herself a healthy sandwich and a pot of tea: much as she fancied some local cider, she had her licence to worry about. And her neck.

The sun was now quite bright. She could pretend to be a tourist. Tourists could stop en route and photograph anything – well, anything vaguely photogenic. There might be something Intelligence could work on. So any remote farmhouse, any hidden barn was fair game. If anyone did happen to remark on her activities, then she could always say she was preparing a book on Devon domestic architecture: the camera might not be up in the Hasselblad range, but the zoom lens was far from innocent – whoever had organised this knew their cameras. Robin would have been pleased.

So she nipped round a maze of lanes, stopping wherever there was a view. She developed a routine. Stop; stare; binoculars; camera. Many places deserved photographs, they were so picturesque: centuries old, with heavy thatch. Some were simply pug-ugly. Some had greenhouses; most had barns. Once she was interrupted by a woman on an old black cycle who invited her in to tea. Once she had to leg it back to the bike to escape the attentions of a bored but snappy sheepdog.

The afternoon was drawing in. Back to the A382, then. But she missed a turn and found herself heading west, towards a glorious view with a Technicolor sunset. OK, nothing sinister for the experts to look at here – just a beautiful postcardy scene. The sort of picture Aunt Cassie had favoured for thousand piece jigsaws. She pulled over, peered and took a couple of shots. An excited whir from the camera told her she'd finished the film. She might as well call it quits and give up. But Robin had always dinned into her that she must change the film at once: you never knew when you needed a camera. Stowing the binoculars in the pannier, she fossicked around for a film. Funny, she'd managed to go through life for a couple of years or more without using a camera. Perhaps the abstinence had been part of her mourning. Now she had one in her hands again, she wanted to point and shoot as much as Robin had always – sometimes irritatingly – done. She obeyed the instructions echoing round her head in his voice, tucking the used film back in her pannier and loading the new. It went in like a dream, the motor humming away as it wound it right through – it was the same sort of safety feature Robin's had had, to save you wasting film if you accidentally opened the camera. Anyway, it sounded convincing enough – almost like the motor-drives professionals used at press conferences.

Then, seeing a feather of smoke coming from the valley at her feet, she thought she might try for one more shot. Leaving the bike where it was, she set off on foot. Training brought her back to chain it to a road sign: Gradient One in Four. The place was so remote they hadn't got round to the new signs giving gradients in percentages. There. Though whatever criminal activities there might be here, she didn't imagine vehicle theft would be one of them.

She'd only gone forty yards, framing with her hands the way Robin used to the aspects she might want to photograph, when a four-wheel drive came up the hill at her. No, not towards her. Straight at her. No. She was being paranoid. There wasn't much road, and – hell! Yes, it was *at*. She jumped backwards, grateful for a bramble for cushioning her fall. Leathers could cope with brambles.

'Get off my land.' The driver was yelling at her even before he'd opened his door. No, he didn't want a discussion about rights of way. Not the way his door came between her and the open road. 'What are you doing here?' Even if she'd been trespassing, which she was fairly sure she wasn't, he was unnaturally angry. Big men like him, faces coarse-veined and eyes bulging, got as angry as that at their own risk. But he wouldn't want a lecture on the importance for middle-aged men of keeping down their blood-pressure.

She tried the open-eyed, literal truth. 'Taking pictures of this lovely view.' Her gesture took in the rise of the moors, the colours of the heather and the few trees, the breadth of sky. 'I've never seen anything quite like it,' she added, allowing a Brummie whine to burgeon.

'Well, you won't see anything like it again. Get off my land.'

Now was not the moment to point out that she couldn't, not until he'd moved. 'I didn't know I was trespassing or anything. I'm ever so sorry.' She tried her best beam.

The treacle-brown eyes did not respond.

'I didn't know it was private – hey, are you some pop star or something? 'Cos I don't recognise—'

'Shut the fuck up and get out.' He eased the door back, but then stepped closer. 'How many photos did you take?'

'Just – hang on, what are you doing?'

He'd grabbed the strap holding it round her neck and was tugging it. 'Just making sure—'

'Please – please! My husband gave me that before he died!' Though the accent might be feigned, her agitation wasn't. Christ, what if it was a brand new model? Something to check when she got back.

'Pity he didn't tell you to be more careful where you used it.'

'Look, mate, I've told you I'm sorry. Just let me go!' With her training, she could tip him over, no doubt about that. But she'd have to make a run for it, and the bloody bike was chained. 'Please!'

He yanked, sharply, hurting her neck. The quality they had gone in for, her neck would break before the strap. 'Give it here.'

'Please! He was killed – please! Can't I just give you the film? Though it's got all this afternoon's pictures on it. Oh, God!' She managed a convincing sob.

'We'll see. Hand it over!'

He meant the camera, but she'd play daft. Tipping the camera, she found the little catch at the bottom, and, giving him one more pleading look, put her thumb to it. He stuck out an implacable hand. As the cassette slipped out, he grabbed and pulled hard. Staring her hard in the face, he tore the full length of celluloid from the cassette, crumpled it, and shoved it deep into his trousers pocket. At least he was convinced he had destroyed a whole used film. 'Now fuck off. And if I see you again it'll be more than the film you lose. Pretty little face like yours – that barbed wire wouldn't do it a lot of good, would it?'

Since he was still holding the car door, she ducked back round the back of the car, and ran up the hill. Not a Kate Power sprint: the ineffective arm-flapping run of a scared Kate Potter. And she practically embraced the bike.

He hadn't finished, of course. He tailed her, right back to Chagford, so close to her rear wheel she was constantly afraid of being shunted down the long, steep hill. The extra oomph Ned had given her was useless here: it wasn't acceleration she needed, but brakes and stability. It was only as they reached the outskirts that he backed off, turning left for the moors again. As for her, she was content to pick up the B3206. Content? Bloody relieved. Any pursuit was real police stuff, not for Kate Potter on a fart-and-bang, no matter how deceptive. She'd find a payphone in Moretonhampstead and have a word with Ma Earnshaw.

Earnshaw scanned with distaste the bedclothes draped all over the radiators: the sun had done its best, but the mist had returned to Newton earlier than to Dartmoor, and had seeped into everything. Kate didn't apologise: if she did, she knew Earnshaw would make her explain.

She'd spent enough time talking anyway. Earnshaw had listened attentively, making occasional notes but not interrupting.

'Of course,' she said at last, 'you might just have come across a bad-tempered old sod with a hell of a hangover.'

'I might indeed. But I thought you should know that someone got a very close look at my face and then my bike.'

'You hadn't got your skid-lid on?'

Kate shook her head. 'I'd taken it off to take the photos.'

'You'd better let me have the film he didn't get at. I don't suppose it'll be much use, but it might give the clever boys some clue about where this farm is.'

Kate handed it over. 'I can do better than that. I've got the

grid reference here. You know, for the Ordnance Survey map.'
She wrote it down. 'The trouble is, checking up on someone in
that sort of terrain isn't like doing it in Birmingham. A bloke
sitting in a car's no great shakes in a city: out in the wilds a
stray cyclist would be news.'

'Not to mention a stray motorcyclist. What are we going to
do about that bike of yours? I'd like to get you kitted out with
a new one now it's been seen, but you obviously need it to
get to work, and they might notice any changes we made to
the plate.'

'Quite. And Gary Vernon would know I couldn't afford a
new one.'

'I'm not happy about your keeping it, all the same. Leave it to
me: I'll think of something. As for the listening devices, they're
asking if we can justify the expense. You've given us nothing in
the way of hard evidence, yet, Kate: lots of hints and promises,
but nothing I can wave at Them Upstairs and say, give us some
fucking money.'

'Like Bob Geldof at Live Aid.' Earnshaw didn't bite. 'But I've
got the car and van numbers, the memos about office plants,
the news that the office and the older apartments are fitted with
surveillance cameras – is none of that hard evidence? What do
they want me to do? Barge into the conference room and take
their photos?'

'OK. I'll tell them I want the bugs tonight. Are you sure you
daren't risk a proper shuftie yourself?'

Kate spread her hands. 'I suppose I could take the coffee
in – but it's such a big risk for such a small gain. Tell me,
Ma'am, this mole of ours. Shouldn't she have warned us about
this conference?'

'Mole's far too grand a word, in my humble opinion. Between
ourselves, Power, it's just a drinking mate of someone upstairs
who thought the brisk turnover of staff was worth worrying about.'

'But the office women have been there for ages . . . Are we
going through all these hoops because of someone's hunch?'

Earnshaw looked her straight in the eye. 'What's the police, Power, without hunches?'

'Point taken. More coffee, Ma'am?'

'No, thanks. Better get rid of what you've already given me before I go. Just the one loo, upstairs?'

'That's right. Opposite the bedrooms.'

Kate picked up the mugs and wandered into the kitchen, putting them into the sink and filling them with water. Suddenly she felt very tired. But not too tired to respond to Earnshaw's bellow. She took the stairs two at a time.

'City slicker I may not be. But I'm not as green as I am cabbage-looking,' Earnshaw announced. 'And I can tell the smell of cannabis when it crawls across a carpet at me. Open your bedroom door, Power.'

Kate obeyed. If it hadn't been for Ned and her new locks, she wouldn't have felt so confident.

Earnshaw stepped inside and sniffed. 'All right: nothing in there. Craig's.'

'He's not here to see what you're doing, Ma'am.'

Earnshaw shrugged and opened Craig's door. 'Jesus God, there's enough bloody pot here to give a sniffer-dog hay fever.' She might have taken in the unwashed pants and socks, but it was on Kate she rounded: 'What are you doing, letting this go on?' Her voice softer, she added, 'I don't mean you had to go round with a fire extinguisher every time he lit up. But you should have told us.'

'You didn't catch the smell on his clothing?'

Earnshaw surveyed the chaos again. 'And you didn't tell us. Or about this – this shit heap.' She swung round, arms akimbo, 'And what else didn't you tell us? Come on, Kate: we need to know.' Her glare was replaced by an amused smile. 'You may be able to act your way through life at Cockwood, but I can tell you're hiding something. What is it?'

Kate sensed rather than heard a movement downstairs. She spoke loudly, clearly. 'Look, Ma'am: why should I hide anything from you? Craig and I have had our ups and downs, but apart from his preferring a pig-sty for a room, there's nothing I can complain of.'

'I suppose you'll tell me the truth in your own good time.' There was the unmistakable clunk of a door shutting. Earnshaw gripped Kate's arm. 'Who the hell's that?'

20

'Craig! How the hell did you get in?' In her moment of fear, Earnshaw had probably given Kate bruises to match those Craig had inflicted at the weekend. But her voice came out as its usual truculent self.

'Through the front door. You hadn't locked it. Tut, tut. Evening, Ma.' He teetered on the verge of insolence, then inched further to the edge: 'Kate been complaining about my bedroom floor, has she?'

'Kate? *I've* been complaining that she didn't tell me you were a bloody pothead. Kate: you've got bin-liners? Go and fetch one, there's a good girl: Craig will need it for this lot.' Earnshaw touched a pair of pants with the tip of her toe. 'Maybe two. There's stuff here that should go straight into the bin.' She pointed at a couple of fast-food containers.

From Craig's glare as she headed for the stairs, Kate knew he'd picked up the same message: she was to make herself scarce while Earnshaw wound herself up into bollocking mode. So, besides finding the bin-liners, she washed up and folded the bedclothes so the radiator aired a different damp patch. At last she deemed it safe to go up. Which face was the more murderous? Earnshaw's, probably, but only by a whisker.

'*She* won't split: *you* won't admit whatever crappy little trick you've played. What a bloody pair. OK, Craig: I want that bedroom immaculate – the way my training sergeant liked things. And when it is, you can come down and make us all a coffee and we can discuss what's going to happen next. Oh, and when I say "immaculate" I mean "immaculate" – I presume this place runs to dusters and a vacuum cleaner?'

Kate avoided Craig's eye. Damn it, who'd have thought Earnshaw possessed such domestic leanings? Not Kate for sure, not when she thought about all that washing up.

'Under the stairs, Ma'am,' she said, deadpan.

'Well, I'm sure the noise of the vac won't interrupt our little talk, Kate. Nice strong coffee, young man, and plenty of milk. Osteoporosis,' she added darkly, leading the way down the stairs and heading for the sitting room, where she sank into an armchair. 'And knowing all that,' she continued, as if in the same breath, 'you're prepared to give him a chance to work alongside you at the complex? You're off your head, Kate. Why the fuck didn't you tell us? Since when are police officers supposed to kipper themselves brainless with bloody cannabis? As a matter of interest, what else is he on?'

Kate found it hard not to flinch. Rude and eccentric she might be, but what was certain was that Earnshaw was a copper's copper. In an interview room, she'd be able to fry a villain at twenty paces. 'I've no idea, Ma'am. If he is at all, that is.'

'You must have wondered.' *And if not, why not* was the subtext.

'I'd have thought cannabis tended to relax people, slow them down,' Kate reflected, as if it were an academic question. 'Perhaps a small minority are affected differently. The Drug Squad should be able to help—'

'That's right: sit round theorising while we should be deciding what to do next.'

'With respect, Ma'am, any discussion about that must involve Craig himself. It seems to me you've done the right thing pulling him out of here – we're obviously never going to be bosom buddies. But—'

'But by the same token, we've removed your protection. Having him here as back-up was part of the plan.'

Another part that had never been spelt out. One really thorough briefing could have spared so much trouble. But Kate nodded sagely. At the moment she needed Earnshaw's total support.

'Would you have him back?' There was a pleading note in Earnshaw's voice that made her sound very much like the mother she was supposed to be.

'Depends whether he'd want to come. But we'd have to have a fresh set of house rules – impartially imposed, maybe – and both have to keep to them.'

'Humph.'

The phone rang. She set off to the kitchen: even in her current touchy mood, Earnshaw could hardly object. Whether she did or not, she tailed after Kate to listen-in.

'Kate? This is Julie Vernon here. How are you after all your trials and tribulations?'

'Fine, thanks, Julie. My mother-in-law's here with me – she came to see fair play when Craig collected more of his stuff. His floor was remarkably like Elly's.'

Earnshaw frowned, interrogatively. Kate winked back.

'Tell him to clean it, then!' Julie laughed.

'It's Ma-in-law's job to tell him that.'

Another woman-to-woman laugh. 'Now, I wonder if we could ask the most enormous favour. This conference of Gary's – we thought it'd be over tomorrow. But it seems some really bigwig wants to address the troops tomorrow evening, and that means me putting on my best bib and tucker and joining them. So we were wondering – could we ask you to look after Tom and Elly? Usual rates, of course.'

'That'd be great. Yes, I'd love to.'

'We were wondering if you'd want to stay over. We've no idea what time all this will finish, and I know you have to be up and about early to get to work on time.'

Kate thought hard and fast. 'I'd love to. But I don't want to wake everyone when I go off. And no matter how hard I'd try to start the bike quietly, there's no way people could sleep through it. So – thanks for the offer – but I honestly think I'd be better coming home. Doesn't take long, late at night. Or, better still, I could even stay with my parents-in-law. It'd take World War Three to wake them. Hang on, I'll ask Ma-in-law. She's just here.'

She raised her eyebrows: Earnshaw nodded. 'There, that's settled. What time do you need me?'

'Seven?'

'Seven it is. And thanks, Julie, for thinking of me. It's very kind.' She cut the connection. Before she could even speak to Earnshaw, Craig yelled from the doorway, 'You get the chance to stay the night and you turn it down? Jesus God! I tell you, she's off her head, Guv.'

'What can I achieve staying the night that I can't achieve in an evening? If I were staying over they'd expect to find me tucked up with my teddy bear when they got back, not prowling round in street clothes. Not that they'll find me prowling at all, please God. They'll find me doing the ironing or the washing up.'

'So you won't be—?'

'I shall do my best. But it has to be a discreet best, for God's sake. What if one of the children found me peering into Daddy's safe, or accessing his computer? What if *they* came home early and found me at it?'

Earnshaw scratched her cheek. 'Seems to me the answer's halfway. I can see you don't want to be caught out, but it's time to move a bit more quickly, Kate. Softly, softly's fine, provided the monkey's going to hang around to get caught.'

'And you've had some indication that it isn't? I really need to know these things, Ma'am.'

Earnshaw shifted. 'None so far. But like I said, Them Upstairs keep pointing out how expensive this operation is. I don't see any coffee, Craig.'

Craig clearly wished to tell her to get it herself.

Kate led the way into the living room.

'I have to say this, Ma'am – I feel that making friends of these people is morally wrong. Working in the complex is fine. Baby-sitting – well,' she rocked her hand, 'that's getting dodgy. But sleeping over and spying on people – if you insist on my doing it, I shall play it straight.'

'Will you indeed? Come on, Power, you're a police officer, not a fucking philosopher. Oh, shit!' Earnshaw clapped a hand over her mouth, rolling her eyes for all the world like a guilty schoolgirl.

Kate said dryly, 'Quite. You have to be ultra-careful, don't you? Cheap shoes, cheap clothes, hair you hate. Living with people you'd cross the road to avoid. That's what being undercover is. And it only takes one move, one word, out of order and you've messed up the whole lot.' She paused for breath. Her voice had risen too.

Craig came in, two mugs clamped in his left hand, one in his right. He plonked them on the coffee table. 'What a fucking song and dance. It's a fucking job, isn't it? No need for all these fucking dramatics.'

Kate picked up one of the coffees, taking a deep breath. Somehow she had to get through to both Earnshaw and Craig. It was time to take a risk. 'Well, some jobs are easier than others. Last time I got to deal with incontinent old ladies. What about you, Craig?'

He picked up a mug and wandered to the window. 'Vice.'

Earnshaw opened her mouth, but Kate silenced her with a quick gesture. 'Down here?'

'Plymouth. Oh, you people from the Met think tough stuff stops at Watford. But I tell you, you want to try it down there. Rougher than a bear's arse. Kids involved, too.'

'How long were you down there?'

'Long enough. Then they put me back in fucking uniform up in Bristol.'

'We've borrowed him same as we've borrowed you,' Earnshaw put in.

'Talk about culture shock,' Kate prompted.

'Yeah. But it's all part of the job, isn't it?'

'Suppose so. Incontinence pads, paedophiles, raids that go wrong and kill your partner. All part of the job.' She kept her voice at its driest.

The silence deepened with the dusk. Craig stared through the window at whatever demons beset him; Kate saw hers in the dregs of her coffee: a dead lover, dead hopes. Except that one hope burned, however grey the mood. Rod. She managed to brace her shoulders and look up, ready to smile at Earnshaw. But it seemed that she had her own ghosts: Kate had never seen her look so old or vulnerable.

She might have to take another risk. She'd certainly put herself in Craig's hands if she did. 'I got this phobia,' she said. 'Maggots. The sort that eat up bodies. So badly that when someone sent me maggots through the post I had to see a shrink.'

Craig didn't move. 'Waste of time. All this counselling and stuff. If a kid falls over and cuts its knee it's supposed to need counselling. And you do, if you see it.'

'You take me fishing and see if it's a waste of time.' Kate laughed. 'I haven't got to the point where I can warm maggots in my mouth, but I can watch while you do.'

Earnshaw pulled herself together, the effort palpable. 'Wouldn't be a bad idea if you did go fishing together. Or did something together. Give a bit of authenticity—'

'"To an otherwise bald and unconvincing narrative",' Kate concluded for her, surprising herself with a memory of school Gilbert and Sullivan. 'Oh, we've been very good on the verisimilitude when it comes to the antipathy and hostility stuff—'

'For Christ's sake! You swallowed a fucking dictionary? She's like this all the fucking time, Guv.'

'And you're like a kid whining to his mother,' Earnshaw snapped.

'Which is what he's supposed to be,' Kate observed, quietly. 'OK, I do have difficulty staying in role when I'm with you people. But I do my best when I'm with people who only know me as Kate Potter. You know the line – I may be under-educated but I'd still have been bright enough to get CLAIT if only I hadn't had RSI. Well, that's what the Vernons are happy with. The more immediate problem seems to be how far I push. And if I'm the one doing it, surely I have to be the one to decide. And before you say anything, Craig, I've managed to persuade Vernon that you'd maintain his grounds better than whoever does it now. He's not happy with the thought of us having marital bust-ups in public, but I pointed out that we wouldn't be at the complex at the same time. So he may buy it. Give me a little more time—'

'You've had bloody weeks!'

'But I'm quite sure he wouldn't buy the idea of your coming round to his house while I'm baby-sitting. I wouldn't, if I were a parent.'

'What if I just turned up?'

'I wouldn't let you in. In fact, if the kids were still up, I'd call the police. Whatever the parents may or may not be involved in, the kids are completely innocent and I won't have them involved in any way. Period.'

Earnshaw seemed to see the coffee for the first time. A skin had formed. She poked a thick index finger at it, but gave up. 'Get me another, will you, Craig? Or you, Kate – you've been resting your bones a long time. Off you go.'

God, she had as much tact as a rhinoceros. Nonetheless, Kate got to her feet. 'What about you, Craig?'

'All right.' Not looking at her, he thrust his half-full mug in her general direction.

'What I'm still not happy about,' Earnshaw began, as if Kate hadn't again spent five minutes longer than necessary in the kitchen, 'is this bike business.'

'Any ideas, Craig?' Kate asked conscientiously.

'I might if I knew what the fuck you were talking about.'

Kate explained.

'You can handle that thing, can you?' He sounded surprised.

'I told you. I passed my test when I was seventeen. But I could have done without being pushed down that bloody hill. I was this close to coming off. All I could see in my mirrors was his bonnet. With the wretched man's face snarling at me for good measure. Except when he was laughing.'

'Managed to ID him yet? You bloody haven't, have you?'

'Hard to know when she could have done, Craig. Or where, come to that. She can't go swanning up to the front desk and asking to see the mug shots, can she?'

'We must be able to get them on line. Or at least get the e-fit guys round to this place.' Now Craig was engaged, it was possible to see what a bright young man he must have been. Before – well, before whatever it was that turned him into his usual boorish self. He managed a bleak smile. 'We could even meet up down at the pub. That'd look as if you'd done your job well – Ma.'

21

The nicest thing about Devon – scenery and climate apart – Kate decided, must be its pubs. There was the attractive place where they'd eaten on Sunday. Now they were in a tiny place, the snug living up to its name with room for just half a dozen tables. The trouble was that it was too snug for their purpose. They could have done with a big impersonal chain pub, with everyone's attention on a wide screen soccer match, so that no one would take any notice of an earnest group in the corner, huddling over what were clearly not shots of Granny in the Costa del Sol.

Kate had no special preconceptions of what the e-fit artist might look like, but Mona Kearney wouldn't have fitted any of them. Inevitably introduced and referred to as Lisa, she looked more like a librarian than an artist, studious behind heavy-lensed spectacles. Why on earth hadn't she gone in for contact lenses, or at least those thin lenses you could get these days? To make matters worse the glasses kept slipping down her nose, so every sentence was punctuated by a quick jab from her index finger. She could have been anything between forty and fifty, with flyaway blonde hair coarsening to grey, but still worn in a teenage shoulder-length pageboy. Perhaps fifty was nearer the mark: although she was still slender, her waist was thickening, with a hook and eye pulled to danger point on her waistband.

If Kate had expected her to whisper, she was mistaken. The woman bellowed a request for vodka and tonic. Craig, frowning, lifted his eyebrows as if asking the other women for their choice. But Kate thought it might equally have been in shock. Even Earnshaw was disconcerted. Mona's resonant, 'Nice to meet you,

Kate,' told them they'd not underestimated the problem. Lisa had to be muted before she could say anything else. Another inadequate briefing, damn it.

Kate jumped in. 'Good to meet you too, Mona. But I think we should have a quick drink here and then head back home to talk over this idea of Craig's. In fact, we could send him to the offie for whatever you drink, while we go on ahead.'

'But I told my husband to meet me here,' Mona objected. 'I don't drive, you see. In any case—'

'What time will he be here?' Kate asked.

'Oh, about ten thirty.'

'In that case – my goodness, we've only got forty minutes – couldn't you phone him? Tell him to come round to our place?'

'No mobile.' She mimed a phone at her ear.

As one, Kate, Earnshaw and Craig produced theirs.

'No. Him, not me.' Still *fortissimo*.

Craig leant forward, putting her drink in front of her. 'Look, Mona, love: we're supposed to be having a nice quiet private chat, aren't we? I thought this'd be just the place, but I was wrong: it isn't. Why don't you and Kate go back to ours, soon as you've finished this, that is, and I'll hang on for your husband. Ma here'll go with you.'

Mona shook her head emphatically. 'You don't know him. He doesn't know you.'

'There must be some way I could recognise him,' Craig said, containing his anger – but surely only just.

'He's just – ordinary, like me,' Mona declared.

'Look – you're an artist. Draw a little picture.' Craig produced a scrappy bit of paper.

'Not any more. Been de-skilled, haven't I? All this computerisation.'

'OK. A rough sketch. And tell me any – er – distinguishing features.'

Despite her protestations, Mona's few lines suggested an anxious-looking man with little hair. Kate was sure she'd pick him out in a crowd, let alone a half-empty bar. Earnshaw downed her G and T as if it were water. Kate's wine might just as well have been. But at least Craig had tried. She caught his eye and raised her glass in an ironic toast. He grimaced back.

'Anything else I need to know?' he urged Mona.

'Well, he'll have Eveline with him, of course.' At last Mona sipped her drink.

Three pairs of eyes willed her to swig it. She sipped again.

'I'll stop off at the off-licence then,' Earnshaw declared. 'A supply of vodka and tonic, Mona, and wine for Kate. Craig?'

'I'll help Kate out with the wine,' he said.

If Earnshaw noticed his concession, she didn't show it. 'See you all later, then.' And she stomped off.

Mona blinked. 'Oh, I'd better polish this off then,' she told the assembled masses. And suited the deed to the words.

They managed to wait until they'd closed the front door on Mr and Mrs Kearney and Eveline before they collapsed into gales of laughter, Earnshaw leading the way.

At last, she sat on the stairs, holding her sides, while Kate brought her a glass of water. She waved it away.

'Who'd have thought,' she began, trying to lever herself up but succumbing to another paroxysm, 'that the Devon and Cornwall Constabulary would employ an Irish-born foghorn with a deaf husband? And they'd have a bloody hearing dog called Eveline? Why Eveline, for Christ's sake?'

'"Out of Joyce"? I thought that was how they talked about racehorses,' Craig said, suppressing giggles.

Kate drank the water herself and propped up the front door. 'Kearney: that's an Irish name, right? And despite those strange vowels, he sounded quite Irish. Maybe it's to do with James Joyce?'

'Well, who the fuck cares, when all is said and done?' Craig sank to his haunches at Earnshaw's feet. 'At least you got her to do a sketch of that Range Rover bastard.'

'She was amazingly accurate, too, once she got going. Poor

woman, having to shout like that all the time.' But Kate was more giggly than pitying.

'And poor bitch, having to answer to that poncy name!' Craig hooted, ambiguously.

'Oh, Craig, don't start me off again,' Earnshaw implored him. 'Just when I thought I'd be able to breathe again one day.'

Kate tried again. 'And poor bastard needing a wife to shout and a bitch to lead him around.'

'Good job it isn't the other way round!' Earnshaw howled. At last, pressing the heels of her thumbs against her eyes, she said, 'I thought she'd do something with a computer. You know, these eyes: click. This nose: click. This left ear: click. And then an extra big click to put them all together.'

'You'd end up with a bloody Picasso if you weren't careful,' Craig hooted. 'Your way, anyway. No mouth and only one ear!'

'But,' Earnshaw objected, 'we know the man's no oil-painting!'

That started them off again. Nothing especially funny. Not enough booze to make them giggly. But a mateyness Kate associated with her time at the Met. And with Colin and the Birmingham crowd.

At last Earnshaw shoved out both arms for them to haul her to her feet. 'Come on, young fellamelad. Time to let Kate get her beauty sleep. You're all right meeting Whatshername at my place tomorrow, Kate? Bringing photos that look like chummie?'

'So long as you can provide me with earplugs,' Kate agreed.

Kate hadn't bargained for Vernon's colleagues to be infesting the place for a second day, of course. But at least someone had slipped through her front door at an unconscionably early hour a couple of little bugs, one for Gary Vernon's desk, the other for the cleaner's cubby-hole. There wasn't any obvious cover for the latter – no shelves to conceal it under, not on the wall nearest the conference room, at least. Improvising, she propped the box of vacuum cleaner bags against the wall, and tucked the bug out of site on the skirting board. Then she whizzed round the conference room as if her life depended on it, chastened suddenly by the thought that it just might. There. Perfect. She even had time to add water to the flower vases before she vamoosed. Today she would spend extra time in the bar and the loos: she could always dive into a cubicle if necessary.

And it was. She was giving an extra polish to the mirror in the gents' when she heard the outer door open. She dived. To shut the door or leave her rear view on show to indicate a female presence? Door shut, she fancied. But she hummed – 'Don't cry for me, Argentina' – while she cleaned.

'If that's you, Kate, stay where you are for a bit. Avert your gaze!' Gary sounded as if he were in a good mood. So long as he didn't get round to feeling under his desk he'd stay that way.

'OK, Mr Vernon.' She made sure her voice was muffled by the loo bowl.

'So Mike's pulling out, is he?' Vernon continued, his voice more confidential.

'Silly sod. Just when he could do well for himself. Parker won't like it, either.'

Kate froze. She knew that voice. Sebastian from Hythe. There was no hope that he wouldn't recognise her – as she'd told Sue, in her experience people tended to remember people they disliked as readily as those they liked. More readily, perhaps. Watching Rod annoy him had been good fun, but not the wisest policy. OK, she looked very different from when they'd last met – the awful hair, the ugly tabard uniform, scruffy jeans and cheap shoes – and her voice sounded different. But people like her – and like Sebastian – were rarely fooled by superficial changes. They looked for eyes, mouths – and, yes, listened to voices.

The urinals flushed. Taps ran. Vernon called cheerily, 'You can come out, now, Kate.' But there was no sound of retreating footsteps.

'Well, Mr Vernon, seeing as I'm in here, I might as well make use of it, mightn't I?' she called as pertly as she could. 'See you this evening, about seven!'

'OK. Don't be late, will you? Not that you ever are. She's the sort of girl,' he added, obviously to Sebastian, 'I'd like to recruit on to a full-time contract. Hard-working, rel—' And the men had left.

Kate, still buying time, suited the deed to her earlier words. Now it might be safe to leave.

She made one more foray to Vernon's room. This time the shredding collection was much more interesting – faxes had come through for other delegates. She stuffed a hefty wad down her trousers, and grabbed some ordinary waste paper to bulk out the little she took along to the office. But here she was clearly out of favour. Girl wars! Not being spoken to because you refused to make the delegates coffee and carry it into the conference room, when they were paid – however inadequately – to do it themselves. Any temptation to offer to help this morning went out of the window. She got rid of her burden, hopped on the Honda, and looked ready to take off. But who could resist such an interesting collection of number plates? Pity she'd been too scared to do a proper job collecting them all yesterday. She jotted down as many as she could from her position astride her bike: no, she wouldn't scribble, lest they couldn't be read. Then she tore an unused page from the back of her notepad and wafted it into the air. Chasing after it – what, Kate Potter leave litter? – gave her the chance to record some more. There. Almost a complete collection. Her only regret was that there wasn't a familiar Range Rover sitting waiting to be ID'd. She'd have cleaned the number plate specially.

When she arrived at The Hollies, Kate found Mona sitting in a Peugeot out in the lane. This time she had come properly equipped, with a laptop computer to die for. There was no sign of Earnshaw: she was no doubt doing whatever Devon DCIs were supposed to do to earn their corn.

Mona was noisily reluctant to accept hospitality in Earnshaw's absence. But Kate insisted that until she'd had a caffeine fix she couldn't put her mind to anything.

'I had a look through myself,' Mona said, opening the laptop on the kitchen table and bringing up the programme. While the computer chuntered to itself, she eyed the would-be Gaudi architecture on the draining board. 'Phone point? Ah.' She plugged it in. 'I wondered if this might be the guy,' she said at last.

Kate set down the cups by an almost empty china milk jug and peered over Mona's shoulder. 'Might be. But your sketch looks much more like him than this photo does.' Pulling up a chair, she paged slowly down. 'No, none of them captures the menace of the guy. Perhaps I need to see him in my mirrors, right behind me,' she joked.

'Try it.' Mona sounded dead serious. 'Have you got a mirror? Go on, try! It might jog your memory, you never know.'

As much to humour her as anything, Kate did try. And got nothing. Then she picked up Mona's original sketch and repeated the process. 'No, this version – hey, I didn't realise: I've got his eyebrows the wrong way round. It's this side that's thicker, with all those stray curly Denis Healey hairs.'

Mona rubbed out and added in. 'I think I ought to scan this into the computer. See if we can get the e-fit to match the sketch.'

'Fine. Shall I see what Earnshaw's got in the fridge, by way of lunch?'

'But – oh, surely we can't . . . A DCI's—'

Kate laughed. 'Well, we can hardly turn up at a restaurant together – a lavatory cleaner and a police artist. On the other hand,' she added, peering into the ice-encrusted depths, 'it's a bit academic whether we raid it or not. Look – Mother Hubbard's cupboard.'

'Oh, dear. But she'll need supper tonight and breakfast tomorrow . . . I could always pop out for something.'

The doorbell rang. They froze. 'I'm sure it's OK,' Kate said, feigning more courage than she felt. 'Just put all that stuff away.'

But she noticed her hands were sweating as she went into the hall. Why on earth didn't Earnshaw have a peephole in the door? Or even an elementary chain?

'Here I am bringing you a few sarnies,' Earnshaw grumbled

indignantly, 'and I find my own door locked against me. Well, you were quite right. I'd be bloody furious if it had been open. Cheese salad, egg mayo., tuna – help yourselves.'

Kate coughed delicately. 'You seem to be out of milk, Ma'am.'

'Oh, and everything else, I should imagine. Sainsbury's night tonight. Or whenever. Oh, you'll be staying over, won't you, Kate? You could go and shop this afternoon. I'll give you a list.'

But probably no money. Well, it would have to go on Kate Potter's overstretched Visa card.

'Now,' Earnshaw declared, plumping herself down at the table, 'we've got some hard news at last. The guy who lives at that farm is officially one Kenneth Arthur Hemmings, a farmer. Not organic. In fact, the RSPCA have visited him a couple of times to talk about the state of his pigsties. Apart from that, he seems to have a clean sheet. No record of him having even speeded in sodding Scunthorpe.'

'Which would explain why he's not in Mona's files. Meanwhile, I've put the bugs in place and got something else for you.' Kate smoothed out the papers she'd purloined. 'And though I'm sure that all these belong to perfectly innocent middle managers, you might want to get these registration numbers checked out. This was the nearest I could get to a delegates' list.'

Earnshaw peered. 'Hmph. I hate these double-letter prefixes. I know they're supposed to make things easier, but I can never remember them. OK, I'll get on the blower while you finish off – where's the computer you were supposed to bring?'

Mona fished it out of the bread bin. 'Just in case it was someone else,' she said. 'At the door, I mean.'

Earnshaw nodded. 'Anything else?'

Kate said, 'As I feared, I know one of the delegates. He's a man I crossed swords with in Hythe.'

'On the run up to this? That's a bugger. Has he seen you?'

'I hid in the bog.'

'So long as you were flushed with success!'

Mona and Kate laughed obediently.

'When does he go home?'

'The conference was supposed to finish today. But they've got that beanfeast tonight, remember – the one I'm baby-sitting the Vernons' children for.'

'What if they have drinkies at the Vernons' house before they feed their faces? That could be awkward, Kate.'

She remembered the inimical eyes. 'Could blow the whole thing if he recognises me.' She didn't need to add that it would put her at risk.

'Pull out? I'll phone and say you're sick.'

'Kate Potter's very reliable.'

'Dress up,' Mona boomed.

Kate and Earnshaw jumped: they'd almost forgotten her. 'Dress up?'

'That's right. The kids would love it if they had some animal to look after them.'

'They're a bit grown up. At least the girl is.'

Earnshaw pulled a face. 'Dye your hair – well you have anyway! – and get some coloured contact lenses.'

'The kids'd notice. And say something. No, I daren't draw attention to my appearance.'

'Which is why,' Mona declared, 'My plan would work. You wouldn't draw attention to changes in yourself, just changes in your clothes. Oh, you could be something Harry Potterish.'

'Or maybe . . . Yes! If I could find the gear, I could go as a character from that book I've been reading to them. Elly would love that.' But where on earth could she get the clothes?

Earnshaw grinned. Then her face became very serious. 'Kate, you really do care for them, don't you? God, I wish we'd got you flying off overseas to check these people out.'

'What? You mean I could have chosen Kenya, not Kent? Cayman, not Cockwood? Bugger!' Nine-tenths of her was joking.

Earnshaw didn't laugh. 'Grow up. You're doing quite a good job here. Except for getting involved with possible cons. OK, finish your sarnie. Finish what you were doing with Mona. And go and get yourself some fancy dress.'

'Any chance you could get hold of a miniature camera for me, Ma'am? There might be a pocket or something I could conceal it in.'

'I thought you didn't want to get the family involved. How can you get photos without taking them?'

'I don't know that I can. But—'

'But if you're not in you can't win,' Mona concluded for her.

At last Earnshaw nodded. 'All right, I'll see what I can do. But don't take any risks. This stuff you're gathering is quite useful.'

Kate blinked at the lavish praise. 'I suppose I don't get to know what's useful about it?'

'When it comes down to it, Kate, the less you know, the less you can reveal.' Earnshaw looked her straight in the eye.

'You mean that if my cover were blown, people might try to "persuade" me to tell them what I'd found.'

'I mean precisely that. OK, Kate. Lights, camera, action for tonight. But for God's sake don't kiss the kids.'

22

The first thing Kate did when she arrived at the Vernons' house was, of course, to disobey Earnshaw's instructions. It wasn't possible not to kiss the kids, not when Elly and Peter flung open the front door and hurtled down the steps to greet her.

A rapid tour of Exeter's charity shops had produced a black wig, a candy striped school uniform dress with convenient pockets and some extra large Startrite sandals. White socks and a heavy canvas bag completed the ensemble. She managed to hack the wig into a fringe that looked rather less seventies, and with a judicious bit of eyeliner was able to ape a round-eyed look. A smear of black on her eyebrows and there she was: to the life, the eponymous heroine of the Milly-Molly-Mandy books. Well, as close to the life as someone her height and build could get.

'Oh, Kate, you're just like thingy! Mummy, Mummy, here's Kate!' Peter hugged her. He tried to peer into her bag but Kate fended him off. 'No, you wait till later,' she laughed. The book, the Sorry set, she could explain. But not the item right at the bottom of the bag, nor the small hole in one of the seams. There was no way Kate could carry it round, of course, but she'd worked out she'd leave it on Peter's bedroom windowsill, which commanded a good view of the drive. She should get a good haul: many of the cars that had been at the complex this morning were now jammed on to it, and more were littering the wide suburban road.

'Of course, you're much too tall. And I'm not sure your eyes are quite right,' Elly said, standing back and inspecting her.

'Oh, I thought you'd like it,' Kate said, feeling a real pang of disappointment. Yes, she'd ended up wanting the kids' approval as much as the disguise.

'I do, I do!' Elly, forgetting to be sophisticated, jumped up and down. 'Really!' She grabbed Kate's hand and dragged her into the house. 'Mummy! Daddy! Look at Kate! She's Milly-Molly-Mandy!' She obviously knew better than to interrupt the party: she headed straight up the stairs. Julie Vernon was waiting for them on the landing.

Her dress had probably cost Kate's annual dress allowance – Kate Power's, that is, not Kate Potter's. She'd have looked wonderful had she not been so obviously ill. It took Kate everything she could do not to gasp in horror, but she must have revealed something of what she felt, because Julie touched a finger to her lips.

'I shall be all right when I've got my war paint on.'

'You'll *look* all right,' Kate agreed grimly. 'But how will you feel?'

Julie shrugged. Then she straightened. '*You* look wonderful, of course. But – if it's not a rude question – why?' She led the way into her bedroom.

Kate had to follow. 'Because of the old book I found for Elly. This little old-fashioned girl living in a cottage in the country. She picks mushrooms in the fields for breakfast, that sort of thing.'

Julie turned sharply. 'She does *what*? Christ, Kate! We don't want them eating toadstools, for God's sake!'

Elly sighed with middle-aged asperity. 'Oh, Mummy. Of course we wouldn't. I know better and Peter would ask me first. Now, do you want me to do your eyeliner? Mummy's eyes are sometimes too blurry,' she explained to Kate.

'Which is how you spotted that mine wasn't quite right,' Kate laughed, her heart turning over at the matter-of-factness with which the child dealt with her mother's illness.

'Hmm. I could always do it for you later. We could use some of your stuff, couldn't we, Mummy? Like when we're dressing up?'

Kate thought Julie probably felt too ill to argue. She did it for her. 'Maybe. We'll see if you still want to when we've played Sorry and I've read to you. And it's school tomorrow so we must make sure we get you both into bed on time. No running rings round me like you did before. Now, shall I go and help Peter find his carpet while you help your mum?' She picked up her bag. The book and the Sorry set could go on his desk, while the bag lurked by chance by the window. She might even draw the curtains on it. All she'd have to do as the visitors left was press the little device in her right pocket. As for the device in the left pocket, she'd try to stick it somewhere in the living room to see if her colleagues could pick up anything apart from general party yacking.

'"Find his carpet"! Oh, Kate, you are funny!'

And far too like Kate Power.

'Oh, Kate: he must help – don't spoil him,' Julie begged.

Kate had never intended to. But Kate Potter would never indulge in a conspiratorial wink, so she gave what she hoped looked like an embarrassed nod, and headed off. Good: Peter's room was occupied by a predictable mound of plastic and no Peter. She set things up: the book and game on a space she contrived on his desk, the bag neatly on the sill. She drew the curtains.

She shouted for him from the top of the stairs: that was what Kate Potter would do.

Julie called wearily, 'He'll be down with the Sophisticasun people. Go on down for him.'

'Oh, I'd be embarrassed,' Kate demurred, gently. But her heart was pounding with excitement. Any moment now she could go and mingle with likely targets. Yes!

Julie appeared at her bedroom door. It was true that the make-up transformed her. 'My clever girl,' she said, bending to give Elly a squeeze. 'You'll be all right, Kate. He's probably handing out crisps. Extra pocket money,' she added darkly. 'Trouble is,' she continued, leaning hard on the banister rail, 'half the buggers down there will think you're in the Devon equivalent of a French maid's outfit. God, I hate these do's.'

Gusts of male laughter proved her point.

'So why do you have to go if it's all lads? Must be like being a bride at a stag night,' Kate said. Potter or Power? Hard to tell.

'Not quite all lads. I'm supposed to be there as company for the women. Hmph. God, they terrify me, some of them. Worse than the men. Hard as nails.'

'I'll go and find Peter,' Kate said decisively. Yes, there was the adrenaline rush – it was always the same when she was going into an action that might have results. Pity the camera was stuck in her bag. But MMM didn't wear dresses that would have concealed it. Still, the little transmitter might come up with something.

Gary Vernon was looking thoroughly miserable: worrying about Julie, no doubt. But he was being addressed – was weighed into too strong a term? – by a man in his fifties, with the sort of gloss that comes inexplicably with a lot of money. Not just the sort of good salary Rod was earning. Serious money. Some men achieved it with a suntan, but this man looked as if he could do with a bit more fresh air. It was the grooming, the haircut – how fortunate he had thick hair that went silver before it fell out – and of course the clothes. Kate hadn't met all that many rich businessmen, but she'd met more than her fair share of criminals who looked as sleek. Her nose twitched – but only metaphorically. She ducked between the guests – ah, there were two or three women there – looking ostentatiously for Peter. En route she picked up a couple of crumpled serviettes – as she bent to retrieve them and drop them on a used plate on a coffee table, she jammed the little bug underneath it. There!

When she spotted Peter, indeed politely passing nibbles, she gave no sign. Peering into the kitchen, she found Sebastian disdaining a cleavage shoved beneath his nose. He flicked not so much as a glance at her. There was no sign of the women from Oxford or Hythe, however: she felt quite pleased, as if they might be bona-fide employees simply earning a decent crust. Then she remembered Veronica's off-putting responses to her questions about a job with the firm, and Julie's description, of course. Gregorie, spruce as ever, wandered in. Now, he was a person to avoid, given the long conversation she and Colin had had with him. She grabbed a spare tray of canapés and returned to the living room. Although she seethed at the thought

of Sophisticasun putting Julie through all this effort, she smiled
with humble downcast eyes, and intercepted as many guests as
she could. Voices: she must remember the voices. And the faces
of course. But she mustn't stare, mustn't look back. Euridyce or
Lot's wife? Oh simply Kate Potter, concentrating on doing an
unfamiliar job. At last, remembering all she'd said about bedtimes,
she made a show of spotting Peter. Parking the by now almost
empty tray on the coffee table, she swooped, catching Gary's eye
as she did so.

'Goodness, Kate – what's up?'

'It's for the kids, Mr Vernon. Bit of a treat, like. You and Mrs
Vernon and your friends all dressed up – I thought the kids might
feel a bit left out, if you see what I mean. Anyway, young Peter,
are you ready to beat me hollow at "Sorry"?' She bent down to
disengage him from his crisps bowl. 'Will you be coming up to
say goodnight to them, Mr Vernon?'

Vernon checked his watch. 'I'll come up now. It's time Julie and
I led the charge. Come on, Sunshine!' he added, swinging Peter
on to his shoulders.

Kate put the crisp bowl on the tray, which she returned to the
kitchen. Another scan of the faces.

Gregorie intercepted her, smiling. 'Rather an unusual outfit for
a waitress, isn't it?'

No, though her hands broke into a sweat, she didn't think he'd
recognised her. All the same, she didn't like his smile, not at all.

'Would be if I was a waitress, like,' she said, mumbling with
embarrassment. 'But I'm just the baby-sitter—'

'Even stranger for a baby-sitter.'

'Just a bit of dressing-up. Kids love it.' She smiled, turned and
prepared to leave him to it.

'Wouldn't mind having you tuck me up in bed myself.' His
hand found her bottom.

Julie's voice cut crisply across the room. 'Kate's a family friend,
Gregorie. Up you go, dear – the kids are raring to go! We'll be
back late, remember.' Catching sight of Kate's raised eyebrow, she
added, 'Oh, you look just like my mother! OK, not too late.'

'Not so late, as my gran used to say, that you stop enjoying yourself,' Kate said, and ran upstairs. Aunt Cassie, the nearest she had to a grandmother, would never have deigned to spout such homely claptrap. But she couldn't say all the things she'd wanted to say.

Kate insisted on 'Sorry' before anything else. That way she could listen for voices outside – she didn't have long to wait for the advance guard but the stragglers seemed to take forever to be herded into their cars. Presumably the restaurant or club would be tolerant.

As for herself, she still needed to get out of Start. The children were crowing loudly at her ill luck. Hand in pocket, she was crowing silently as she clicked. The last thing she was worrying about was how many squares she had to progress.

At last the game was won and lost.

'Snack-time,' she declared. 'Then teeth. Then story. Go and decide what you want to eat, while I tidy the board away.'

'What about this floor?' Elly demanded. 'It's terrible. If we leave it like this, Mummy and Daddy could fall over when they come and kiss us goodnight.'

'And what about your floor?' Peter demanded. 'Bet it's just as bad.'

'It isn't. So there. You come and see, Kate.'

Kate's stomach clenched. If she left Peter in here there was just the remotest chance he'd pull the bag down from his windowsill. Only remote. But if she feared detection, she feared it most of all from these two. Their innocent questions would hurt as much as physical violence. 'I'll do my bit putting the board away,' she announced. 'Then we'll all help each other. Right? Now, what can we use to gather up all these bricks?'

While the children were cleaning their teeth and getting undressed, she made some silly excuse and took the bag out to the cycle, locking it in a pannier. She checked the anti-theft chain. Pulled at the padlock. God, she was getting jumpy. And all for some photos, which might not come out, of men and women who might be entirely innocent.

Popping them both into Peter's bed, she read them two chapters – they'd both been very good, as she told them, and their floors were immaculate. Peter was soon ready to sleep, and Elly not far off. But as Kate shepherded her into her own room, Elly said, 'We never did your eyes, did we? And I don't have to lie down till nine.'

'You wouldn't prefer a bit more *Milly-Molly-Mandy*?'

'No. I like making people look different. Maybe I should be a make-up artist.'

'That's not all that much better than a cleaner.'

'I don't mean selling make-up at Boots or Dingles. I meant a top-class one, working in TV or films. You even get your name on the credits.'

'So does nearly everyone these days,' Kate pointed out mildly. 'Anyway, if you want to change my eyes, go ahead. As long as you're sure your mother won't mind. But you've only got five minutes – right? And we leave the place exactly as we found it!' She followed Elly.

'Oh, better, I should think! I mean, look at it – it's a tip.'

Elly was right. She'd been too concerned with Julie to take in the mess of clothes on the bed and pile of papers on what looked like a Georgian chest of drawers.

'Mummy's always yelling at Daddy: he's got a perfectly good office next door and he's always leaving things here. And he shouldn't bring this stuff home either, she says. The place for work papers is work. It'd serve him right if we threw everything in the bin.'

'I'm sure it would. But it wouldn't get my eyes made up.'

'Here.' Elly thrust a bottle of Christian Dior cleanser at her. 'You get that off and I'll start on Mummy's clothes.' Elly grabbed a couple of coat hangers and picked up a jacket and shirt. 'No, this one's ready for the washing machine. And this one of Daddy's.'

Poor Elly: half child, half premature adult.

'If you leave them at the top of the stairs I'll take them down when I go. Now, these eyes of mine. What do we use?'

'You won't forget the washing, will you?' Elly murmured as Kate popped her into bed. 'And there's knickers and socks and things. Daddy's such a pig.'

'I don't like picking over your parents' things,' Kate said truthfully.

'But they were so pleased when you did all that ironing. And imagine coming home and finding our rooms perfect and their own like that! If you don't promise, I shall get up and do it myself.'

'And if you try blackmail, young lady, you won't find me baby-sitting for you again. Is that clear? Now, don't spoil a lovely evening by being a pain.'

By way of answer, Elly thrust out her arms. Kate hugged her. And then, of course, she kissed her.

Papers first. She'd hold a coat hanger in her hand, just in case the Vernons came back unexpectedly, but she must check those papers properly. She riffled through. Some extremely fancy ones, complete with watermarks and official looking seals. Pity she couldn't read Spanish. And some in Portuguese, equally impressive. Well, that was perhaps how Iberian lawyers preferred their paperwork to look. Dared she steal one? Here, with a pile of rumpled clothes and a duvet sliding blowsily to the floor, it felt like stealing. Furtively, she took one of each and folded them tightly into her bra. Clutching the rest, Kate tried the office door. With the excuse of putting them out of harm's way, she couldn't not. But it was locked – a Yale and a Chubb. Relieved, but irked, too, because that must mean he had something to hide, she stood on the landing, hands on hips, listening for the children and considering. OK, what would Kate Potter do? Tidy the living room, of course. It was such a mess that Kate spent twenty minutes tidying and vacuuming it before she even started on the kitchen. How did civilised people manage to be such pigs, stubbing out fags on food plates, grinding crisps and other nibbles into the carpet? What should she do about the bug? Her head told her to leave it where it was. But whatever Vernon might or might not be doing, she couldn't bear to incriminate Julie. She unstuck it and shoved it in her pocket. Whoever was listening would hear her loading the dishwasher for a start. No, she'd no qualms about using it. It was the common-sense approach the Vernons would expect. As for the washing, there wasn't quite a load, even with the garments Elly had dumped. But before she stowed them in the machine, she checked the pockets. Nothing.

Now, what about that bedroom? She rather thought Kate Potter would hang clothes up, but not put them in wardrobes. She tiptoed upstairs, listening outside the children's doors. Yes, they sounded deeply asleep. When she'd finished, she'd check again. She attacked the bedroom, looking for something, anything, that might be useful. But she made sure she had a coat hanger to hand, just in case. No, nothing in any of the drawers. What about—?

The floorboards outside creaked.

Breathing deeply, she said sharply, 'Elly? Get back to bed at once!' Silence. She scurried out on to the landing, still clutching the coat hanger.

But it wasn't Elly on the landing. It was Gregorie.

23

Don't shriek. Don't wake the children. Don't lose self-control. Don't even take a deep breath.

Above all, don't let on you know his name.

'Who are you? What do you want?' she breathed.

'Oh, you know what I want. And you don't need to know my name. Get back in there.'

'But that's Mr Vernon's room,' she said, trying to talk and act Kate Potter while all the time thinking Kate Power. Even Kate Potter would call the police if she were raped. Blow her cover? Ruin everything? Solution: mustn't get raped.

What if she did scream now? What if she woke Elly, told her to phone her parents?

What if Gregorie were so sick he'd make the child watch? Maybe rape her too? No. The children came first. She'd protect them at all costs.

So what if he did rape her? They said no one noticed a slice off a cut loaf.

No one was going to rape her. Even if she had to use Kate Power's self-defence skills.

'Didn't you hear? Get in there.'

'Shhh. The children. I told you, I've no right in there. It's Mrs Vernon's room.'

Yes, he dropped his voice. 'You said it was his. What were you doing in his room, bitch?'

'It's his and her room, stupid. That's what married couples do. They share a bedroom.' She closed the door firmly behind her. Its click was disconcertingly loud.

He snatched at her wrist. 'You know what happens to naughty schoolgirls, don't you?' he hissed.

'Shhh!'

'Don't you tell me to hush!' But he'd dropped his voice again. 'Take your knickers down and bend over.'

'Not here. The children. I don't want them woken up.'

'You'd better get downstairs, then.'

Kate obeyed. Her hands found the bug in her pocket. Back at Headquarters was all this just being recorded for future use? Or were a couple of her colleagues having kittens wondering how on earth to intervene without blowing the undercover operation?

Enough speculation. She had to get out of this. And protect the Vernons.

Spin it out. Julie looked too ill to be out late, whatever she'd said. Give her time to arrive. Give her police mates time to work something out.

'Look, Mr – Whateveryournameis – I'm a friend of Mr and Mrs Vernon. Mrs Vernon didn't like it when you goosed me. I tell them what you've been trying to do, you get the sack.' What a shame she was trying to keep quiet: she didn't sound emphatic enough.

'I might if he employed me. As it is, I employ him. And it doesn't take a genius to work out what'd happen to this family if Mr Vernon lost his job. I don't see Mrs V being able to go out and earn a decent buck, do you?' He laughed unpleasantly. 'So it's up to you, sweetie.'

'So I let you rape me, or you sack him. You absolute bastard.'

'I love it when you talk dirty. Anyway, if you let me, you consent, so it isn't rape, is it?'

So he was ready to waste time quibbling: she might be able to use that.

'Would you like a drink? There's some left,' she ventured as they reached the hall: she must have sounded like a perfect hostess, not a potential victim. Still, she was obeying every word of the textbooks – trying to establish a relationship, trying to make him see she was a human being.

'OK. Something decent. But don't try anything, mind. You do a runner, you'll suffer. And the kids.'

So why should such a dapper, handsome man resort to this? He could pull any bird he wanted, she'd have thought. And his physical attractions were usually matched by his social skills. If he could sell time share, surely he could sell himself.

She plundered the first bottle she found in the fridge. One of Rod's favourites – the bastard wasn't worth it. But she wasn't going to argue. One glass or two? Remind him you're a person. Two, then.

She put the glasses on the coffee table. Bending at the knees she poured, letting the bottle hover over the second glass. He dashed it to the carpet. It bounced, rolling towards the TV.

'Afterwards. If you're good. Bend over the table.'

A thin wail floated downstairs.

'That's Peter – I must go and check!'

'Over the table!' He undid his flies.

'I shall get the sack if I don't see to him!' She risked a sob.

He smiled. 'Vernon will get the sack if you do.'

The wails got louder.

'Look,' she pleaded, 'let me just go to him. As soon as he's settled . . . He'll wake his sister,' she added urgently.

'Ah, that cheeky little bitch. Make sure you shut him up. Fast.'

Peter's wails got steadily louder. Any moment he'd be coming down the stairs. She took them two at a time.

Elly had beaten her to it. 'You should have come! You should have come!' she screamed. 'Where were you?'

Hell, they'd have Gregorie rampaging up here if they weren't careful.

'Listen carefully, Elly.' She took the child's face and held it firmly. 'As carefully as when your mother tells you: do you understand?' She let her go.

Huge eyed, the child nodded, gripping Peter's hand. He buried his face in her shoulder, still weeping. And then, slowly, reached for Kate's hand.

'Go into your mum and dad's bedroom and phone—'

'But I've got a mobile. In case Mummy's not very well and is going to be late picking us up from school.'

'Excellent. Pop and get it. And come back here, quick as you can.'

It took her seconds.

'Good girl. Now, as soon as I leave you I want you to phone your mother and tell her there's a burglar downstairs!' She clapped her spare hand over Elly's mouth. 'Tell her very calmly and sensibly you want her to come home. Understand?'

Elly nodded. As Kate removed her hand, she said, 'But you're lying, aren't you? It's that awful husband of yours. Is he trying to hurt you?'

Kate squeezed her hand. 'Spot on. Which is why I want your parents, not the police. Now, I want you to be very, very quiet. And when I've gone, the two of you must push something heavy in front of the door. You mustn't open it till you hear your Mummy or Daddy telling you to. Not me. Mummy or Daddy, remember.' She kissed them both, and slipped away, closing the door.

Gregorie was admiring himself in a full-length mirror when she returned, so absorbed in playing with himself that he didn't notice her. Well, he could do that as long as he wanted. She slipped back to open the front door. Ajar, it might even attract Neighbourhood Watch attention.

Half of her still wanted simply to run. There'd be a sympathetic neighbour somewhere. And leave the children? No way. She must get back in there and trust to her wits.

He was still jerking himself off. Not urgently. As if he was simply giving himself maximum pleasure.

'Where the fuck are you, bitch?' he called, over his shoulder, still posing like Narcissus.

'Just coming.'

He laughed. 'So am I. Lucky bitch – come and see what you're getting.'

What planet was he on, for God's sake? Or, more to the point, what drugs?

Giggling, she sat in the furthest corner of the sofa. 'You don't need to rape anyone, surely. Gorgeous stud like you. Girls'd be falling over themselves to get at you.'

He turned. 'Come on, then, fall over!'

'Oh, it'd be ever so nice if you'd – well, you must have a lovely body, too.'

'You want to see my body? First bit of sense you've shown.' Slowly, sensually as a stripper, he undid his shirt.

'Ooh, look at those pecs. My old man, he'd die for those.'

'You married?' He paused between buttons, looking at her appraisingly.

'Well, sort of common law. That's what they call it, isn't it? But things aren't very good at the moment,' she sighed. 'That's why Mr and Mrs Vernon are being so kind to me. Plus, they needed a baby-sitter,' she added.

He finished his shirt and, swishing it across his penis, dropped it at her feet. As if automatically, she got up and folded it neatly. Jesus, what had happened to the bloody Vernons?

He pulled his trousers wide. 'There. Your old man's cock like that?'

She allowed herself to wrinkle her nose, as if it were a serious question expecting a serious answer. And, just as she put her head on one side, deep in consideration, she heard a car arrive.

By now Gregorie's trousers were round his ankles. He hadn't had the forethought to remove his shoes first.

To do him justice, he kept both his head and his hard-on when the Vernons ran into the room. 'Looks like we shall have to postpone this pleasure for another day.' A drop of semen ballooned and quivered.

Kate gathered a swaying Julie and supported her as she sank on to the sofa. Vernon was rigid – with anger? With fear?

'This gentleman was just leaving,' Kate said. Damn, much more Power than Potter. 'Weren't you?' She passed him his neatly folded shirt. 'But you'd better return Mr Vernon's key, hadn't you?' She held out an open palm, Sergeant – nearly Inspector – Power taking booty from a stupid scrote.

Gregorie fumbled in his trousers pocket. 'See you again, sister. One nice cunt you've got there.' He twirled the key into her hand and left.

Vernon was still standing open mouthed, so it was she who followed him out and locked the door. Suddenly weak, she leaned against it and burst into Potter tears.

It was Julie who got to her first.

'No. I'm all right, honestly. Oh, Julie, go and tell the children it's all over. And Mr Vernon. Please. I'll be all right. No, just go!'

Scrubbing away the tears, she returned to the living room. If only she dared take the wineglass he'd been using and get it tested for DNA. She wouldn't have been the first of Gregorie's victims, she was sure of that. The MO – nicking someone's keys and raping the baby-sitter – must be on someone's file. Then she grinned: that spot of semen must have fallen somewhere. And it had. She was mopping the floor in a very Potterish way when Vernon came back down.

'What the hell's been going on? You feed my children with some cock-and-bull story about a burglar and about your boyfriend, and all the time you're fucking with one of my colleagues. When did you arrange that?' He seemed ready to slap her. 'Get out of my house.'

That was all she needed. But while Power could take control, Potter could only wring her hands. 'It wasn't like that. No, and you know me well enough to know it wasn't. That's why I told the children to phone you! That's why I left the front door open. Oh, Mr Vernon. I love those kids. I wouldn't let anyone hurt them.'

'Something's hurt Peter all right. He's upstairs having the worst attack of asthma he's had in months! Julie's thinking of calling the doctor. Not that she doesn't need him herself. Where the fuck d'you think you're going?'

'To tell him I'm all right. That my boyfriend's gone away. And see if Mrs Vernon needs a hand getting ready for bed, poor lady.' In the doorway she turned, arms akimbo. 'Honestly, Mr Vernon, you could see she wasn't well. Why d'you have to keep her up so late?'

'Late? It's only eleven! We were on our way – that's how we got home so quickly. Not that it's anything to do with you.'

Poor, silly man. Not angry, so far as she could tell. Scared witless, that's what he was. She'd have to set him right. First things first, though. She ran up to the children.

Julie had insisted on coming downstairs, and now lay full-length on the sofa, drinking mineral water. Kate accepted not the whisky Julie had tried to press on her but a glass of the Beaune, which was as good as she'd thought it would be, and sank into an armchair nearby. Vernon was still pacing, settling occasionally on the sofa arm nearest Julie.

'Seems to me,' Kate began, 'he must have picked your pocket some time in the evening and come back here when everyone was speechifying. He'd already pinched my bum when he thought no one was looking.'

'Except I was,' Julie said.

'Thing is, I didn't know – I mean, some of the things you hear about men. Perverts. I was afraid – for Elly. And that's why I played for time. If Peter hadn't started calling for me, I don't know what I'd have done.'

Julie started, spilling some of the water: 'You mean – you'd have let him – let him—?'

'Not if I didn't have to.' She found she was crying again. Both Kates. Must be reaction. 'All I could think about was them. And they saved me, bless them.'

'You should have kicked him in the balls, Kate,' Julie said, with a flash of what she might have been.

Kate looked at her glass. Should she risk it? Why not? 'Thing is, Mr Vernon. He said if I didn't – you know – let him . . . he'd sack you. 'Cos he's your boss.'

'The bugger!'

'Only I didn't know, did I? Or I'd have clouted him about the ears good and hard.'

Vernon looked at her hard. A question was forming she didn't want him to ask, and she didn't want to answer. Why hadn't she dialled 999?

She made herself look at her watch, and haul herself to her feet. Much as she might regret leaving the Beaune – and the way she felt she could have downed the lot and asked for more – she had to get on her bike and drive through dark country lanes. Life and licence: that must be her motto.

'Best be getting back. Mother-in-law'll be getting worried. And – what's it say in that film? "Tomorrow is another day."'

Julie reached out a protesting hand. 'You won't be going in to work, surely? Gary, can't she have the day off?'

'It's not up to Mr Vernon, see. It's the agency that pays me. No work, no money. Simple as that. So, if you'll excuse me, I'd best be off. No, don't you get up.'

But Julie pulled herself upright. 'I'm going up now anyway. Get her jacket, Gary. There's a love.' She waited till he was out of the room. 'There's something you haven't told us, Kate. What is it?'

'Told you every last grim detail, honestly, Julie. And some of them' – she tried to beat back a giggle – 'were quite interesting details. Oh, the poor bugger: you coming in and finding him like that!'

'I'm just glad we didn't find him like anything else. Are you sure you don't want to stay over? You could call your parents-in-law and tell them.'

'Sure, thanks.'

'But have you far to go?'

'Just out to the Topsham road and then towards Exmouth.' Hell! She'd meant to reassure, not blab something as stupidly as that. 'There's just one thing – if you wouldn't mind? I just want to go and see the kids have settled.'

And give them one last goodnight kiss.

24

Just like a real mother-in-law Earnshaw was waiting for Kate on the doorstep. So was Knowles.

'Kate, my dear girl! Come on in and sit down.'

'Thanks, Ma'am. I just need to get the stuff out of the panniers and lock the bike.' She was clumsier than she liked. She stared at her hands as she stepped into the hall: they were shaking. 'Have you got a freezer bag? There's something here that ought to go into it. I've got a lot to report,' she added, sinking on to a kitchen chair as she produced her spoils: the camera; the bug; the tissue she'd mopped Gregorie's semen with.

'Less than you think,' Knowles said. 'They called us – we heard everything that was going on.'

'And—?' Kate prompted.

'If the Vernons hadn't returned, you'd have found a couple of friendly neighbours appearing from an unmarked car claiming to smell gas or something. We wouldn't have let . . . anything . . . happen to you, Power.' He blew his nose, as if unused to emotion. 'But I'd like to assure you that your coolness and resourcefulness have not gone unnoticed. You may be in line for a commendation if all this goes well.'

'It's not a commendation I need so much as a glass of something. I had to leave that wine behind,' she said, adding, plaintively, 'and a very good Beaune it was too.'

Earnshaw stared as if she'd asked for a slug of ambrosia.

'Come on, Leeds,' Knowles said, 'you're bound to have some whisky.'

'Fancy you remembering that,' Earnshaw chuckled, emerging from the wastes of her pantry with half-full bottles of The

Macallan and Laphroaig. 'They said I had an accent when I came down all those years ago, Kate.' As if she hadn't now!

She disappeared again, this time in the direction of her living room. She returned with six heavy crystal tumblers, which she held from the top, for all the world like a barmaid clearing a table. She plonked them down with equal disregard for what Kate suspected were heirlooms. 'I take it you prefer your water separate?'

Not sure whether it was a drinker's shibboleth, Kate agreed she did. The heavy tumbler sat graciously in her hand, the deep incisions in the crystal refracting the kitchen light bulb as if it were a chandelier.

'So the transmitter worked,' Kate said, breaking a long silence. 'I brought along this little souvenir of Gregorie, by the way.' She touched the tissue in its bag. 'I'm sure it can't be the first time he's attempted something like that. Might be worth a look for DNA matches.' God, she was so sleepy – and she'd hardly touched her whisky. 'I'm not so sure about the camera, because I couldn't set it up properly. I may have got nothing except streetlights. I did get these, though.' She fished out the crumpled documents. Rubbing her face didn't help keep her eyes open. She gave into a huge yawn and a stretch. 'I'm sorry. I've got to be up at five-thirty, remember.'

Earnshaw snorted. 'At your age we thought nothing of twelve-hour shifts and then some more on top.'

'Quite so,' Kate agreed mildly. 'I seem to have worked a seventeen-hour one. Or is it eighteen? I never was much good at maths.' She staggered as she got up. 'I'll do as I did last time, Ma'am – forage for some breakfast and slip off. Goodnight – Ma'am; Sir. Oh, what arrangements for tomorrow?'

'There's a nice pub at Cockwood as I recall. Two nice pubs, come to think of it,' Knowles reflected.

'A bit close to the complex, Sir. We don't want to blow it at this stage.'

'True. How about if you come back here? Leeds and I can meet you here or leave a message.'

*   *   *

Kate felt like leaving Earnshaw a message. *What about my break-fast?* Then she remembered that at one point yesterday Earnshaw had asked her to shop – though neither of them had mentioned it subsequently. So it was her own fault she rode into work with no more than a small black coffee in her stomach. It shouldn't matter, she told herself. But she'd eaten very early the previous evening, and had had nothing since. God, she was hungry. In fact, her stomach was rumbling audibly as she lugged the vacuum around and tackled the bar. At last she fumbled for change to feed a confectionery and crisps machine. It swallowed two fifty-pence pieces before conceding it was out of order. She found paper in the bar manager's office, and blu-tacked a warning notice to the machine, complete with time and date. OK: brownie points for an efficient worker. But her stomach was still grumbling. She might find something in the kitchen. This wasn't an area she was responsible for: you had to have proper training for food preparation areas, she gathered. But special training or no, she recognised a fridge when she saw it. Anything she could plunder? Oh, she'd make a point of leaving a note and of telling Vernon: she didn't envisage any problems there.

No bread or biscuits – well, she wouldn't expect them in a fridge. But there must be something somewhere to make a sausage butty with. The freezer? Yes. It was a big, wardrobe type affair, but not especially well stocked. What were those? Whole, ready-made burgers. Hell, all this huge expanse to cook in and the chef brought in ready-made – yes, complete with cheese, relish and bits of chopped onion. Still, no doubt they showed up on the accounts, and it certainly wasn't her job to grass anyone up if they didn't. Pity she didn't fancy a ready-made burger at seven fifty in the morning. What about – hell! – ready-made hot dogs? No, thanks. She was about to give up when she noticed something she didn't expect to find in a freezer. A polythene bag full of 35-mm film cassette holders: the black cylinders she never knew how to recycle. She knew experts advised storing unused films in a deep-freeze or fridge – but used ones? Shouldn't they be developed straightaway, not stored? And as for that package, flat and wrapped in black polythene, that looked like prints. Store prints in a freezer? She'd never heard of such a thing.

At which point she became aware of a movement behind her. As she turned, someone hit her.

Hard.

'The freezer? Why should anyone hit you while you were looking in a freezer?' Gary Vernon stood the far side of his desk, one hand poised over the phone, the other worrying a blackhead on his chin.

'Goodness knows, Mr Vernon. But they did. Good and proper.' She lifted the hair behind her right ear to show him. She hoped the bruise looked as impressive as it felt. Actually, whoever it was could have hit a lot harder – perhaps her sudden movement had helped her. And she probably hadn't been out for more than a few seconds. But she wasn't going to tell him that. She'd had half an hour with a pack of frozen peas on the lump before she'd felt like moving far or fast. Though that might have been because she was so hungry. 'I mean, why should anyone want pre-packed beef-burgers?'

'If that's what they wanted . . . You didn't see what they took, of course? Look, Kate, are you sure I shouldn't call an ambulance?'

'Actually, I might get an appointment with my doctor – mind you, the way things are, it'll be next week before I get to see him.'

'And only then because it's an emergency!' He laughed with her. 'Oh, look, sit down. Before you fall. Let me run you back to your mother-in-law's.'

'Why don't I just get your first-aider to have a look?'

'First-aider?' As if the first memo she'd seen him type wasn't one about health and safety.

'Don't you have to have one? Every place I've ever worked in had one. Just an ordinary person to look after cuts and bruises and things.'

'I'll find out who it is. But it's not an ordinary bruise, Kate. On top of last night, too.' He shook his head.

'The children – are they all right? I was so worried . . .'

'You were more worried about them last night than you were about yourself, weren't you? I shall phone the school and tell them there was a bit of bother – ask them to contact me if necessary.'

'And Mrs Vernon? Julie? Poor lady, she's got enough to worry about without—'

'Quite.' He tightened his mouth and stared at his desk. 'In our own home . . .'

Was he going to ask why she'd not called the police? Perhaps not. Was he going to call them himself now? After all, he had an attack on one of his staff to report. Almost certainly not.

'Yes, someone up there's got it in for me! A husband who socks me, your colleague who wants to rape me, and now someone who doesn't like me peering in your freezer. Well, they say things happen in threes. Perhaps it'll be my turn for the Lottery on Saturday – that'd prove my luck's turned.'

He laughed. 'You're a good kid, Kate. And ever so good with the children. You ought to do something better with your life than contract cleaning. Get yourself on a course – you could be a nursery nurse. Even a teacher.'

She laughed. 'Got to pass a lot of exams for either of those. And it's loans, not grants, these days. I dread getting into debt, Mr Vernon, and that's the honest truth. It's all very well going to university, but imagine coming out owing thousands of pounds! No, thanks.'

Vernon nodded. 'I bet a lot of people think like that. We've got an annuity for our children's university education, of course. Now look here, Kate: I want you to go off home. I'll clear it with the agency. If they try to stop your wages, I'll make sure Sophisticasun top them up. I'll check with Chef what's missing. I'll get a memo out telling everyone to be on the lookout for a prowler. Off you go.'

'Thanks.'

'And drive safely – I'm not sure you ought to be driving at

all, really. Look, if you left your bike here, I could collect you tomorrow morning and—'

Kate grinned. 'At six o'clock? No, honestly, Mr Vernon.' There was no way she wanted him turning up to find Earnshaw with or without Knowles. But then, last night – yes, she'd almost given Julie directions. At least he'd been out of the room then. And presumably her home address hadn't been paramount in their subsequent marital discussions.

She'd got halfway down the corridor when he called her back. But he said nothing until he was in his room with the door firmly shut. 'I have to ask you, Kate – I mean, I think it's very strange of you, and my bosses might not like it at all. What on earth were you doing in the kitchen in the first place? And why open the deep freeze?' His expression reminded her of the previous night's, when he'd irrationally lost his temper.

She laughed. 'Greed. Well, hunger, really. I only managed to grab a quick sarnie before I came to your place last night. And – well, to be honest – Ma-in-law's not the greatest of housekeepers. So there wasn't anything for breakfast this morning. I tried a snack machine but it wasn't working. I left a note on it, by the way.' How nice to be able to tell the truth, pure and simple. But from his expression she rather thought he'd have preferred an elaborate lie.

She took things very gently on the way back to Earnshaw's, stopping at the village store in Kenton to buy essentials. In fact, she felt so woozy, perhaps she ought to eat something now. Chocolate. Improve blood sugar levels. God, what if she blacked out now? Or worse still, while she was on her bike? Heroics were for pedestrians.

A phone box. Why not? Earnshaw could come and get her. Ned could come and collect the bike in a ute. They could sort everything out while she—

'Yes?' Earnshaw's phone was answered by a male voice.

'It's Kate. I need some help.' She gave her location.

Then came Earnshaw's muffled voice. 'Tell her we're on our way.'

We? Our? It dawned on her that Knowles's car had still been in the lane outside when she'd set out that morning. Well, he hadn't been in the living room, and she was in the only spare bedroom.

She was still chuckling when she paid for her iron ration – a freshly made apple turnover. And the romance was all her doing, too.

To celebrate, she fed her change into an air ambulance collecting box.

'You're sure you didn't lose consciousness?' the police surgeon asked, peering into Kate's eyes and prodding the bruise with what seemed unnecessary force. Earnshaw had summoned him to her cottage, much to Kate's embarrassment and no doubt the irritation of a waiting room full of people far more in need of treatment than she was.

'Only for a second or two. As soon as I realised what had happened I iced it: plenty of frozen peas in the freezer.'

'Any nausea? Any double vision?'

'I felt sick, but now my stomach's full I'm fine. Vision fine. No headache—'

'No headache?' He looked vaguely amused at catching her in a lie. 'Sure?'

'A bit of one. And I'll admit I'm sleepy. But that might be as a result of having had only three hours' sleep in the last thirty. A couple of hours' zizz and I shall be fine.'

He laughed. 'Just what I'd prescribe myself. But if you have any dizzy spells, let me know. And blackouts. Especially blackouts. And don't drive if you do.'

Kate nodded. Somehow they had to solve the problem of her Honda and the following morning's transport into work – there was no way she wouldn't go in – but that could come later. Smiling vaguely, she flapped a hand and drifted upstairs. That bed was calling. Loudly.

Above it, all the same, she caught the doctor's next words. 'And which of you will be keeping an eye on her? I don't like to leave concussion victims unsupervised.'

Earnshaw or Knowles as nanny? Well, they could sort that out too.

At least the knock on the head hadn't dislodged her ability to wake up when she wanted. One o'clock. Fine. Some lunch and then an update on all the stuff she'd got for them. She was entitled to that.

Her overall? She hadn't even stripped that off. Or her shoes! Well, she had been pretty knackered. She padded off to the bathroom. If only she had a change of clothes. That was the first thing to ask for: a lift home to get whatever she needed. A shower and hair wash would have to wait till then – in any case, the luxury of Earnshaw's drinking utensils did not extend to the bathroom, a cheerless, inhospitable room if ever there was one.

So why hadn't the sound of her movements, the flush of the loo, made someone call up to her? Why was there absolutely no sound at all from downstairs? Someone eating a sandwich? Sorting through papers? Watching the midday news?

No. Nothing.

Knowles, Earnshaw – one of them would have stayed on guard. That was one thing people in hierarchical organisations were good at: obeying orders. On impulse, she slipped not into her own room but into Earnshaw's. If only the wretched woman had a bolt on the door. As quietly as she could, she wedged a chair under the door-handle. The phone was next to the bed, of course. And a convenient wisteria clung to the cottage wall. How close it came to the window, and how freely the latter – an old-fashioned sash – would open she had no idea. Well, she'd see how technology worked first. She dialled Earnshaw's direct line.

'Yes?'

'Ma'am? Kate. There's something wrong here – I feel it in my water—'

Someone picked up the downstairs extension.

Earnshaw must have heard too. She cut the connection without a word.

OK, if whoever it was knew that Kate was up and communicating, she could risk making more noise. Just as she'd told the children the previous night, she dragged a chest of drawers across the door. Hell, what did Earnshaw keep in it? Pig iron? It was noisy and took forever – long enough for any professional burglar to escape without trace – but at last she managed it. There. She leant back against it, eyes briefly shut, catching her breath. When she opened them, it was to see the window moving gently upwards. Pushed by none other than Gregorie.

25

Kate charged, head down. What else could she do? She'd just sealed her escape route. She caught Gregorie in the stomach, just as he pushed the window up. For good measure, she slapped his fingers, as they scrabbled on the sill. They slithered free. Screaming, he dropped backwards.

Shit. For all she acted in self-defence, she'd just brought down on herself suspension and a Police Complaints Authority inquiry. And her cover would be blown.

She couldn't even use her police clout to speed the ambulance she called.

The chest seemed even heavier now she tried to drag it free from the door – valuable seconds wasted, when a man might be dying of spinal injuries.

Before she got to Gregorie, though, she found Knowles. He was slumped over Earnshaw's kitchen table, a nasty contusion at the base of his skull. But – her fingers were shaking so much it took seconds to find a pulse – he was still alive. To move him into recovery position or to leave him?

Screams from the garden gave her the answer. Gregorie was still alive, too.

Cold, phlegmatic Earnshaw was having hysterics. Near enough anyway. Kate was afraid she'd have to slap her.

'My house. My house. My – my territory,' she kept saying. So it wasn't for Knowles she was crying, not on the face of it, anyway. Not that he needed tears. The blow wasn't much more life-threatening than Kate's. But he'd been carted off to hospital, no one taking the least notice of his protestations that all he needed was a quiet sit down. Everyone was far too preoccupied with the Gregorie problem. Kate's only contribution was to provide tea for everyone and hope Earnshaw wouldn't notice how much sugar she'd had shovelled into hers.

Though he wouldn't admit it, and was unlikely to for some time, Gregorie had been extremely lucky. To be fair, the paramedics and firefighters didn't use the word 'lucky' either. Gregorie's fall had been broken by the front hedge.

It was only when the second ambulance and the fire appliance had driven off that Earnshaw had started to laugh. Kate tried to soothe her, but Earnshaw pushed her tea to one side and ploughed towards the front gate. She pointed at the new, hand-painted name. The Hollies.

'I was going to have them rooted out. But then someone pointed out you can't just cut down trees in a conservation area. Not if the trunks are more than a certain diameter. So I had this tree surgeon in to neaten them—'

'They look very spruce,' Kate agreed.

'"Spruce"! Oh, Kate. Oh, Lord!' More hoots and howls.

What on earth—? And then, 'Oh, God. I'm sorry. Oh, Ma, I can't think of anything better to break his fall, can you? Lovely, strong holly.'

'Not even berberis and firethorn!' The women collapsed into each other's arms.

Which was where Gary Vernon found them.

'I was really worried about you, Kate,' he said, over tea in Earnshaw's living room. They weren't allowed into the kitchen: a scene-of-crime team had taken over, cursing Kate's earlier tea-making activities. The SOCO in charge had condescended to make tea and pass them mugs, which suited Kate fine. However long her nap had been this morning, it didn't seem quite enough. She'd had to be prompted to make introductions, but congratulated herself mentally on referring to Earnshaw without a blink as Ma.

'I saw your Honda, you see, chained up in Kenton,' Vernon

explained, looking for somewhere to put his teaspoon. 'And someone had brought a pickup truck. I couldn't see any signs of damage, but I was afraid . . . So I thought I'd just drive round a bit – on the off-chance. And there you were.' He smiled. 'Julie'll be so relieved.'

Kate didn't believe the bit about chance. He must have phoned Julie. Well, that was what husbands and wives did.

Earnshaw got up and could be heard yelling into the kitchen. She came back armed with the biscuits Kate had bought earlier and wearing someone's wedding ring. 'It was very good of you, Mr Vernon. I'm sure Kate appreciates your interest. She's talking about coming into work tomorrow, would you believe.'

Kate was thinking fast. Should she tell Vernon about this second attack? She'd be damned if she did and damned if she didn't. To tell him might irritate Earnshaw, but to keep quiet about something he'd soon pick up on Sophisticasun's grapevine was dangerous – when he learnt, he'd wonder why she hadn't been frank with him.

'Actually, I don't think I shall bother buying a Lottery ticket for Saturday,' she said. 'Something else happened this morning. That's why the kitchen's crawling with the police. I had a visitor. Seems that colleague of yours couldn't take no for an answer. Gregorie.'

'Not Gregorie Phipps?' Vernon sprang up. To Kate's amazement he squatted at her feet, taking her hands. 'The bastard. You poor girl. Look, you must tell the police everything.'

Could she be hearing this? Was Vernon really recommending police intervention? 'About last night,' he continued. 'Tell them everything. He may say he's my boss, but if he tries to sack me – well,' he continued, now struggling to stand, 'he'll get more than he bargained for, that's all. How did he know where to find you?'

'Followed me back home last night, I suppose. And waited his chance.'

'I wondered what he was doing at the complex this morning. Kate, do you think it was he who – who bashed your head?'

'I don't know. And that's the honest truth.'

All this time Earnshaw had been very quiet, very watchful. Now she jumped in with fervour. 'Now the stupid doctor – do you know this silly girl didn't want to see a doctor, Mr Vernon? – says she can come back to work tomorrow if – big if – she rests properly today.'

'Tomorrow?' he frowned. 'Kate, that's not a good idea, surely. Especially as the agency have agreed to put you on the weekend shift. I put your point to them about inadequate hygiene in some of the older apartments and raised it with my colleagues yesterday: I really think you should take the whole weekend off, but if you insist on coming in at least you'll be paid four hours' time to do what's always been two hours' work.'

'Oh, Mr Vernon, that's really kind.'

'Since you've been with the agency such a short time you won't be getting sick pay for tomorrow, but I'll make it up out of petty cash.' He moved towards the door.

'That's really very kind,' Kate said, following him, suppressing all thoughts of employer's duty of care.

'Not at all.' He paused, uneasily. 'Kate, perhaps I was wrong. No. I don't think you should expose yourself in the courts – you know what these barristers are like at twisting the truth. I'll take action against Gregorie at Sophisticasun. He won't get away with it! I promise you.'

Kate wanted to object that being sacked would simply give the bugger more time to rape other women, but she was too busy working out Vernon's change of heart. Yes: it had been his heart that had made him offer the first advice. Then his head might have pointed out one or two dangers if she got involved in the legal system. He must be shitting himself with anxiety in case she wasn't persuadable.

'You mean these lawyers might get hooked on the idea that because Craig and I aren't married and—'

'They'd probably have a field day. And there was that school-girl's dress – you know what a judge might make of that.'

Unfortunately she knew all too well.

'You'll get her to do the right thing, won't you, Mrs Knowles? I don't know how your Craig would react, either. Some men – they don't like it when their partners get raped. They blame the woman.'

Which she also knew from professional experience.

'I'll certainly do my best,' Earnshaw grunted.

'I'm sure if anyone can, Mrs Knowles, you can,' Vernon smiled, with an irony Kate hadn't thought him capable of. 'I hope you don't mind my saying this, but if anyone had asked me, I'd have said Kate was your daughter, not – from what I've heard – that Craig was your son.'

Earnshaw put an arm round Kate's shoulders and squeezed hard. 'I've often thought as much. But I love Craig too, Mr Vernon. Don't think I don't.'

Earnshaw may have waved off Vernon with her best beam, but she was grim-faced by the time they'd got back inside. Kate suspected it wasn't just the icy wind suddenly blowing in off the river that was responsible.

'You must have told him far more than was necessary,' she said, shutting the door with a slam. 'I mean – all that crap about his finding this place by accident!'

'Probably phoned his wife,' Kate said shortly. 'I was daft last night – I more or less gave her directions.'

'And telling him you'd no idea who'd hit you. You must be off your head. Oh. Sorry.'

'I wonder how keen he really is to get the first incident sorted out . . . ? It'd be nice if I could persuade him to report it. If we could only go in and look around—'

'You mean Uniform?'

'– yes, and CID and SOCO and anyone else can get in there legitimately. It would also mean if I'm seen going into Alderson Drive, people will think it's to do with that. I'd say we might have had a very lucky break, here, Ma'am.'

'Hmph.'

Kate looked at her watch. 'Tell you what, let's see if we can pick up a late lunch and go and see – er – father-in-law. All this drama has given me an appetite. The other thing is, maybe you should contact Craig: he'll no doubt want to visit his father.'

Earnshaw looked at her, an unreadable expression on her face.

'And by now surely they'll have developed the photos and have picked something up from my bugs. Not to mention the paperwork I've been snaffling from the shredder. We could have a busy afternoon and evening, couldn't we? Perhaps it's a good job I'm not going into work tomorrow.' She was rubbing her hands with glee when she noticed Earnshaw's expression hadn't changed. 'Have I said something I shouldn't?'

'Apart from giving the impression that it's you running the whole shebang? Well, I never did expect tact and diplomacy from you, so let that rest. No. It's something else. Craig. He's gone missing, Kate.'

26

E arnshaw sat heavily on the stairs. 'Missing,' she repeated. 'Gone walkabout.'

'When?'

'We should have told you when we picked you up from Kenton, I suppose.'

'When? How long ago?' Strange: Kate was as anxious as if they'd really had a personal, not just a professional, relationship.

'Yesterday morning.'

'Funny: I thought we were all getting on rather better.'

'For "all" read "you two". Well, he left the place where he's been staying before his mates woke up and hasn't been back since. He withdrew two hundred and fifty pounds from an ATM at that big Tesco near you—'

'What time?'

'Six forty-five – a.m., before you ask. No calls from his mobile. No report of any RTA, though he seems to have taken that bloody car. No sighting, either. He hasn't used his credit or debit cards. Well, with two-fifty in cash he wouldn't need to.'

'What about earlier in the week? Had be been hoarding cash?'

'Not that we know of.' Hands on thighs, Earnshaw levered herself up. 'If you still want to eat . . .' she added accusingly.

To please Earnshaw the answer should have been no. But if she needed to think on her feet, it had to be yes. Unless this wooziness was really a result of the bang on the head . . . 'A sandwich on the hoof,' she suggested.

'I wasn't suggesting a three-course meal at the bloody Ritz. I can't work you out, Power. Half the time you're as steady as a rock; the rest you're as flaky as a packet of crisps. I've never known anyone so bloody self-centred, and that's the truth.'

'No, Ma'am.' *And don't let the old bitch see the tears in your eyes.*

Kate had a nasty feeling she was supposed to let the arguments flow over her head. She felt like a pawn argued over by so many Grand Masters. She looked around the small conference room: yes, mostly masters, if not grand. White middle-aged ones, too. Where were the young officers, and the women? Not to mention any African-Caribbean and Asian officers. How on earth would the constabulary reach those Home Office ethnicity targets? Angry as she was, however, she had to admit that these were silly, really, given the ethnicity of Devon itself.

Back to the matters in hand: plenty of them since it was a long agenda. Most of them to do with her, of course. But not with her input. Tucked away at a corner of the table, she seethed and smarted.

The item they were on now was the Gregorie business. It was embarrassing all round, of course. Firstly it had drawn vivid attention to the casual arrangement that had worried Kate originally; secondly anyone wanting to check on Kate would have a starting point; thirdly, and this seemed uppermost in some minds, Gregorie might have to lie on his stomach for a couple more days.

'What we have to hope,' a bald chief superintendent was saying – she didn't recall anyone introducing him and he had no name card in front of him – 'is that he doesn't decide to take legal action against Power. It would blow everything wide open. Most unfortunate.'

The clear implication was that Kate should have hauled him through the window and then lain still, thinking of the inconveniences to the Devon and Cornwall Police she was thus averting.

'What are the chances, do you think, of his going for compensation?' An anonymous ginger-haired superintendent, this one.

'He's within his rights. Perhaps,' Bald Chief Superintendent continued, smugly, 'our colleagues aren't so *au fait* with defusing methods in Birmingham. More confrontational.'

'Oh, you can't judge a force by a single officer,' someone put in, benignly.

'We call it a service in the West Midlands,' Kate snapped. What had happened to all the CID officers who might have understood and supported her? All bloody Uniforms in here.

Except for Earnshaw, of course, who now scowled her into silence and asked, 'So you don't think we should proceed with the case from our end?'

'Do you?' Ginger-hair, this time.

Earnshaw's striving to be fair was almost visible. 'I suppose it depends whether the DNA Power obtained matches that in any outstanding cases. By the time any of them get to court, this operation should be done and dusted.'

'Very well.' Ginger-hair's weary tone implied that the chances of a match were unlikely in the extreme.

'You don't feel that such a man ought to be brought to justice anyway?' Kate put in. 'We've all the evidence we need on tape, after all. Plus witnesses.'

'You're being very naïve, Power, if I may say so. How could you possibly break cover at this stage?'

'Is there any need? With clear evidence against him, Gregorie might even plead guilty.' A hazy thought that other people in the organisation might tell him to do just that to protect the organisation itself crept across her mind. 'And if we told Mr Vernon the police would be asking questions to see if the assault on one of his staff could be tied in with the other assaults, he might even co-operate. He seems – very kindly disposed towards me.' Even as she spoke she realised she was crazy; Gregorie would have to be charged with an offence against a specific woman, namely Katherine Elizabeth Power. And she'd forgotten Vernon's *volte-face*. His instincts had spoken first time: his position in Sophisticasun the second, no doubt.

Before anyone could point that out, Bald Head raised eyes and hands heavenwards. 'Dear me, Power: you seem to have forgotten

Rule One of undercover work: don't get involved with the scrote you're investigating.'

'With respect, Sir, to the best of my knowledge I have not yet uncovered any evidence at all to confirm that Gary Vernon himself is a scrote.' Except his clipboard and those plants. 'I know from personal experience that Gregorie Phipps is, however.' She overrode a rumble of disagreement from someone. 'I would, in fact, be very grateful if I could be informed of the nature of some of the material I've passed on to you.' She counted them off on her fingers. 'The photographs and audio material at the Vernons' premises; the papers I've saved from the shredder. The audio material from the complex; the vehicles whose registration numbers I've logged for you. But all these are secondary to two pieces of information I'd like simply as a human being: the news about Superintendent Knowles and Craig – er – Knowles. I've never known his real surname.'

There was an awkward silence.

Earnshaw filled it. 'Seems these Brummies like to run the show, too. Don't you – *Sergeant* Power? We're not all bumpkins with straw in our hair, you know.'

Kate managed not to stand up and yell. 'When I worked on a covert operation before, far fewer colleagues knew of my role, but I was always kept fully briefed,' she said quietly. 'Indeed, I knew what I was looking for. I've been creeping round in the dark, down here. And now you're surprised I want to know what's been picked up. And you're even surprised I want to know what's happening to my colleagues!' She heard her voice rising. Any moment she might burst into tears. Hell and damnation!

Fortunately at this point there was a knock on the door. From the tail of her eye Kate saw a young woman in an overall, not unlike her Sophisticasun outfit, wheel in a trolley of tea and coffee and leave. No one moved.

Despite a strong feeling that something domesticated was expected of her, she kept her eyes on the Chief Superintendent's face. OK, if she got a reputation down here for being a hard bitch, she wouldn't relish it, but the people who mattered, the people she admired and respected, would know better. Meanwhile, if the tea and coffee set like concrete in their pots, she didn't care.

Chief Superintendents weren't fools. Kate knew enough to know that while some reached their posts through Buggins' turn, most had worked hard for their promotions. And needed brains to do that work. If she could convince him of the rightness of her case, he'd carry most of the others with him. She kept eyes and chin steady.

He dropped his eyes and leafed through a file. On her, she suspected, from the occasional flick of his eyes at her.

The silence stewed like the tea.

'I expect,' began the chief superintendent, 'you'll all be glad to hear that Superintendent Knowles is expected to make a complete recovery. He'll be detained overnight for observation, however. I believe that's usual in cases of concussion. He sent, I believe, a message: that your skull was obviously thicker than his, Power.'

Kate nodded. The pain over her ear told her it was a mistake. She allowed herself a slight wince.

'You mean Power's been attacked too?' Ginger-hair, put in. 'I thought the reference to one of Vernon's staff meant—'

'A glancing blow, that's all, Sir,' Earnshaw informed him.

'All the same, she should be on sick leave too. Policy after a head injury.' But he didn't pursue it. He pulled himself to his feet, looking older than she'd realised, and headed for the trolley.

The herd followed. As did Kate.

Fed and watered, they returned to hostile-mode. But the superintendent had certainly softened them.

'As for DS Barnard – Craig Knowles, Power – we are exploring every avenue.'

'Do we have any – are we looking for someone who's alive or who's . . . ?' Kate asked.

He looked her straight in the eye. 'I have to say, both. There's been no sighting, no contact with him at all. Is there any light you might cast on this?'

Kate moistened her lips with the tea. 'As you're all no doubt aware, Detective Sergeant Barnard and I were supposed to play the roles of an unhappy couple. As I'm sure you're also aware, this hostility seemed to become real, and Superintendent Knowles and DCI Earnshaw suggested that we should be separated. I'm sure they've supplied you with details.'

Earnshaw brandished a half-eaten biscuit and spoke through the crumbs: 'Barnard seems to have played some prank on Power: but she wouldn't say what it was. He seemed to respect her a bit more after that.'

'What sort of prank?' the chief superintendent demanded:

'Locker-room stuff, sir,' Kate replied. 'We spoke very little about our previous undercover experiences. I got the impression that something had – disturbed him – during one of his assignments.'

'Are you suggesting he's gone off to find a shrink?'

'Far from it, sir. He thought counselling was a waste of time.' She raised a placatory hand. 'No, we didn't argue about it. In fact, I made an extra effort to find him work in his capacity as jobbing gardener at the Cockwood Sophisticasun. But I was just wondering if something I'd said had triggered some sort of memory. That's all.'

Both the senior officers looked uncomfortable. Did Craig's record show something? No one would say anything here, of course.

At last the chief superintendent said, 'I'll let the team searching for him know. Thanks, Power. Did I gather you're due for promotion, by the way?'

'Sir.'

'Hmm. All right, Power: that seems to be all that immediately concerns you. If you're unwell, perhaps you might wish to go off duty now?'

Not bloody likely. Even though the bruise was smarting, and her head ached viciously in a quite different place, there was no way she was leaving yet. She managed a smile. 'If you don't mind, Sir, I'd rather hear what data's come to light so far. It'll help when I go back into work on Saturday.'

'Saturday?' He frowned. It was impossible to tell from his

expression whether he thought she was over-keen or malingering.

'Both the police surgeon and Gary Vernon thought tomorrow was too soon, sir. And Mr Vernon's persuaded the agency to let me work four hours cleaning the apartments as opposed to the public areas during changeover on Saturday morning. That way I can see if they've all got surveillance cameras – and indeed, anything else of note. There's also a chance I may get to talk to some of the owners. There was a feeling at the Hythe complex that management might be letting maintenance standards slide in order to pressure people out. I wondered if that might ring any bells here.'

'I thought there was talk of your going swimming in the residents' pool,' Earnshaw put in.

'When I realised I knew some of the executives gathered there this week, I thought I might be recognised. So I abandoned the idea, till everyone went home, at least.'

'This man who assaulted you,' Earnshaw put in. 'Gregorie Phipps. You recognised him: are you sure he didn't recognise you? At any point?'

Dear God! He might just have done this morning!

Her expression must have given her away.

'You think he might?'

'Not last night. Not with the wig and funny make-up – I was dressed up as a character from a children's book, Sir,' she explained, switching her attention back to the Chief Superintendent. 'But of course this morning I wore normal make-up and my hair like this.' She lifted a strand. 'You'll be relieved to know it's not my normal cut and colour. But I wouldn't rule it out.'

Earnshaw said slowly, 'If he didn't recognise you, does it make it more or less likely that it was he who hit you? And if he recognised you when you shoved him into the holly, does it make him more or less likely to sue you?'

'If it wasn't he who assaulted Power, who else did?'

'God knows. I wouldn't rule out that Vernon man, if Kate was looking somewhere she shouldn't. After all, it wasn't a hard blow.'

'He'd have to be a bloody good actor, then – he looked aghast when I showed him what had happened.' *Unlike some of you lot here.* 'But you're right, of course. He did his best to lay the blame on to Gregorie, too, saying he'd been on the complex all morning.'

As if making a decision, the Superintendent rose too, pulling a white board towards his boss. In Kate's experience the special felt pens never worked, or were the wrong sort, eventually needing alcohol to get the pigment off the board.

'Let us review what we've found so far,' he said. The discoveries might have been his own. 'There is still nothing yet, Power, on the man in the Land Rover you encountered near Chagford. Kenneth Hemmings. The paperwork you've managed to obtain seems to have been almost exclusively about office greenery, I'm afraid . . .'

Back in Birmingham, in Sue's room, Kate would have punched the air. Here she refrained. 'In that case, Sir, may I suggest we're on to something. Office greenery? The state of their office plants is lamentable. I know. I've been trying to resuscitate one of them. I had to bring in flowers for the conference room for all those bigwigs, and Mrs Vernon provided the vases. If they had a legitimate contract with an office landscapes firm, something would have been done.' She subsided. She'd forgotten she didn't want Vernon implicated. But she had to add, didn't she, 'As a matter of fact, a consignment of office plants did arrive yesterday. Vernon was checking them in in a far corner of the Sophisticasun's grounds. I passed the details on to Chief Inspector Earnshaw.'

'If you're sure, we'll look into it again. The faxes for other executives were more interesting. We're having them translated. It seems as if they're Spanish and Portuguese legal papers. Very fancy affairs, like those originals you – er – retrieved,' he added, disparagingly. Then, for the first time, he smiled at her. 'Now, the photographs *were* interesting: we've sent mug shots down line and we're awaiting responses from our colleagues in Major Fraud, and also in Customs and Excise. Some familiar faces, there, we hope.'

'Sir – would it be possible to send them through to NCIS too – just in case there's a drugs connection?'

He made a silent note. 'What I'd like to do at some juncture is play through the recordings we made of the conference, of activities in Vernon's room and at their cocktail party. Again we've sent the information off to other parties. But after our little chat this afternoon, Power, I'd welcome your input.' He looked at his watch. 'First of all, though, gentlemen – oh, and ladies! – I suggest we adjourn to the canteen.'

Oh, and ladies! No wonder Earnshaw was such a battle-axe if she'd had to put up with that all her working life. She'd neither received sisterly loyalty, nor, clearly, been in the habit of giving it. What would she have been like with more support, more kindness?

'You know, you're beginning to look peaky,' Earnshaw observed, falling into step with her. 'For God's sake don't give up now.'

'No, Ma'am.' She must not stagger.

'If I could run some aspirins to earth, would that help? Though I've an idea you're not supposed to take them after a bang on the head. Perhaps the quack should have insisted on having it X-rayed.'

'I'm sure some aspirins will be OK.'

'Go and suck up to Them Upstairs then. I'll see what I can do. There's this DC in my squad always moaning about period pains . . .'

Sucking up was difficult, since Them Upstairs had hunched themselves round a table, unwilling to accommodate anyone else. Someone like Earnshaw would no doubt be able to elbow her way in, but not a stranger they already viewed with hostility. What was going on here? It seemed like the old bad days in the Met people had talked about.

Except as she hovered, with her tray, the ranks parted, Red Sea for Moses. A space. By the Chief Superintendent, no less. He patted the seat.

But she stayed on her feet: yes, here was old Earnshaw bustling along. 'Better wait for my "mum", Sir, if you don't mind.'

He blinked. Then coughed. 'Well, we'd better make room for

her, too, then, hadn't we? You're taking this undercover business very seriously, then?'

'Not seriously enough, I'm afraid. You didn't see a contract cleaner in front of you this afternoon, did you, Sir? You saw a rather disreputable junior officer desperately in need of a haircut. And the vocabulary, the speech patterns, were all those of an educated woman. To be really successful undercover, you need to abandon thirty years of family and education and not just live the part: you need to be it. That's why Craig's so good. If he'd been there this afternoon you'd have seen a loutish jobbing gardener almost certainly defrauding the government by claiming the dole.'

He nodded. 'So what's your take on the Craig business? Psychological crisis apart.'

'I haven't one, Sir. He made damned sure I never knew the real Craig at all. He certainly knew more about me than I did about him. And was rightly hard on me when I dropped out of role.'

'Past tense, Power? You think the worst?'

'Sir, I only know what's been said this afternoon. There must be officers much closer to him than I. There are also the friends he stayed with . . . There was one called Macker – ginger-haired with very large ears: the trouble is, I've no idea where he lived.'

'We've spoken to him. Craig was sleeping on his floor. He seems straight enough – in fact it was he who reported Craig missing.'

Kate managed a vestigial nod. 'The thing is, in many ways Craig's a good old-fashioned cop: he really hated hanging around waiting for something to happen. My slow waiting game really drove him mad.'

'But to do you justice it seems to be paying off. Especially the stuff you got at the Vernons'. I'd like to get you in there again, so you can have a real root around.'

Like a pig nosing out truffles. 'With respect, Sir, if anyone has to so that, I don't see how it can be me. Not with the relationship I have with the children. Especially after last night. Elly saved my bacon.'

'Well, of course, we did have officers ready to intervene if necessary,' he blustered.

'Of course. But all the Vernons believe that it was Elly's doing. And it was Elly I trusted. Her parents have been kind to me – yes, kind. I'd apply that equally to Gary and Julie. He even scouted round looking for me when he saw my bike being taken off on a tow-truck this morning.' Was it really only this morning? If only Earnshaw would produce those aspirins soon. 'He's put me in the way of extra work.' She grimaced. 'As for his being a good boss, I have to admit I've had far worse in my time in the service.'

'So you don't want him to be a scrote?'

She looked from him to her soup and back again. 'I hope he isn't. Because his wife's very ill. I don't know how ill. But I'd hate to see him doing a long stretch and those kids being effectively orphaned and put into care.'

'If people break the law they have to suffer.'

'Agreed. One hundred per cent. But we all know that when a man's imprisoned his whole family's punished too. That's what I'm afraid of here.'

'So, say we find he's at the heart of a drugs ring, laundering money and practising a little extortion on the side. What then?'

'Sir,' she said, helpless in the tightening vice of pain, 'you know the evidence. I don't. You'd know what the charges would be.'

'Serious, let's say. So he should be locked up and the key thrown away. What then?'

She shook her head and knew she shouldn't have. She pushed away the soup hardly tasted, although it was very good.

'You ask me, you should be in bed with Knowles,' he boomed, his laughter igniting other guffaws, which rolled around the table.

She knew she must eat. Or she'd be sick. What if she did eat and was still sick? The latter was the better option, especially with aspirins in prospect.

There was a general movement back to the conference room. Alert. She must be alert. Your country needs Lerts!

'You'd better have these,' Earnshaw said, barging over to her. 'Before you pop your clogs.'

*   *   *

The head might be pounding less, but now all she wanted to do was sleep. Pity the DC with menstrual problems hadn't gone in for something containing caffeine. Never mind. She could follow the tape, and was making what looked like intelligible notes.

The uniformed team had been joined by a knot of younger, plain-clothes people, men and women, all looking as knackered as she felt. And somewhat less happy to be there.

One, face like a tired monkey's, was saying he had two sorts of tape for them: copies of the originals and computer enhanced ones. The one recorded through the conference room wall first.

No. It was terribly muffled. Even Kate's young ears couldn't make much of it. The senior officers' faces suggested complete bafflement. And yet – and yet Kate started to pick out fragments, as if she were listening to a language she dimly remembered. This time when she jotted, it was genuine notes, not neat doodles. *Pressure*. That cropped up several times. *Persuasion*. Laughter each time that came up. And then, yes, surely, *cameras*.

At the end of the recording, everyone looked up, as if hoping for a prize at the end of a party game. Then came the enhanced version – not, to many ears there, judging by the expressions on people's faces, much better. Kate looked across at the tired monkey: he looked infinitely pleased with himself. Why, when he saw how many people were flummoxed, didn't he circulate a transcript?

'Of course,' Tired Monkey said, 'we don't know the names of most of these people. That's the problem.'

'Power? Any ideas?'

'I tried to get hold of a delegate list, Sir. But failed. Sorry. Interestingly, I hardly recognised any of the voices.'

'What about your assailant? Gregorie Phipps?'

'He's the one talking about persuasion. In connection with surveillance equipment. Now, I was convinced that cameras were in place in Sophisticasun's Hythe complex. In the old apartments, though not, as far as I could see, in the new ones.'

'So are they using the surveillance cameras in some sort of

blackmail scam?' Earnshaw put in. 'Some sort of "persuasion"?'

Kate scratched her head. 'But most of the owners are – well, let's just say they don't seem likely to indulge in blackmailable activity. I know they're now targeting young professionals as buyers, but most of the owners I've seen have been decidedly elderly.'

'All the same, it could make sense. Perhaps if Mr X took someone with him who wasn't Mrs X.'

'They were very keen to know that I was part of a stable couple,' Kate reflected. 'But I assumed that that was because they wanted two incomes.'

'It's hardly surprising they're trying to ease old inhabitants out in whatever way they can,' the chief superintendent said, 'if you look at the difference between the maintenance costs for the new and the old flats. And if you look at what they're selling the new ones for.' He in turn produced paperwork. 'Thanks to Kate Power, we have a set of proposed prices. You'll see that a one-bedroom refurbished apartment costs three times as much in maintenance charges – quite a nice profit to the company. And that the selling price – and don't forget the company gets a thirty per cent cut of any sale – is more than twice as much. Unfortunately, until we can prove some element of coercion, all we can say is that this is very sharp business management.'

Kate couldn't claim any praise. The information sheet must have been tucked into some of the papers she'd saved from the shredder. Still, it was something they had that they might not have had otherwise.

'We've also had those fancy documents translated, Sir,' Tired Monkey continued. 'Whatever language they're in, the message seems to be the same. They're agreements to sell the apartment in question to some overseas client, for a very great deal of money: two or three times what the place is worth. Even at the new prices. All the client has to do is sign them and send them off with a nice fat administration fee—'

'How much is fat?'

'Nearly a thousand pounds, Sir. Our guess is that the money disappears – into an unofficial Sophisticasun bank account –

and the sale never takes place. So, once they've been nicely softened up and are a good deal poorer, official Sophisticasun people leap in with a box of tissues and an offer of their own – considerably lower.'

'And if they won't sell, then they blackmail – or persuade them – into selling,' Kate concluded. 'I should imagine Gregorie might make a good persuader. I wonder—?'

'Yes?'

'Whether he participates in anything that could lead to blackmail. I should imagine he might be willing. Depending on the age of the other participant, of course. But it would be quite dodgy. This guy seduces a woman (presumably) and then says, we've got you on film: sell up or we show it to your husband. No, too far-fetched.' She shook her head. 'Hell. Why didn't I think of it before? The photographs! When my head was clocked this morning, I was looking in the deep-freeze. Ready-made snack . . . And what seemed to be undeveloped film and maybe some photos!'

'Seems to me, Power,' the chief superintendent said dryly, 'that you'd better go home right now and have an early night. Get into Sophisticasun first thing tomorrow and let us know if they're still there. Better still, bring a few home to "Mum" as souvenirs!'

27

Kate supposed there should have been something comforting in the sound of Earnshaw's deep and regular breathing. They were at Kate's house, since that was where her bike had been taken and because Kate sensed an unspoken reluctance on the older woman's part to stay on her own in her cottage, although the SOCO team had finished with the place. They'd not had much in the way of conversation: Kate had only managed to strip and remake Craig's bed for her before collapsing into her own and sleeping the sleep of the just until the snores from Craig's room woke her. The penalties of living in a modern house: Earnshaw's walls were so solid that not even these Vesuvian rumbles had penetrated.

In the end, Them Upstairs had decided not to send Kate into work on Friday morning. What they would send was a couple of highly trained officers claiming to be local authority food inspectors to talk to Vernon and the chef, and ask to look at the freezer. If – it was a big if – the photographic material were still there, then Them Upstairs would decide who should remove it and when. Kate saw fistfuls of short straws being thrust her way.

But she was too tired to worry even about that. Lulled at last by the rumbles, she fell deeply asleep again.

Earnshaw obviously believed in early hours, Kate's sickie notwithstanding.

'Look at the rubbish you eat,' she said, flourishing a packet of cereal. 'I bet there's more nutrition in the cardboard box than there is in that stuff. Whatever happened to decent porridge?

Or even decent bread? And what's this? Low-fat spread. Butter, that's what's best, not all this emulsifying and colouring stuff. Read the ingredients, woman. With butter you know what you're getting. Skimmed milk: for Christ's sake, it goes bad, not sour!'

Kate didn't allow herself so much as a smile behind her hand.

'And you go and do a day's work with nothing but this muck inside you. No wonder you're touchy. Now, today we're going to concentrate our efforts looking for Craig. The team looking for him will want to talk to you, I imagine. Hang on. Stay where you are.' Just like a school nit-nurse, she grabbed Kate's hair and lifted it. But the fingers she ran over the bruise were surprisingly gentle. 'Hmm. Wouldn't hurt you to compare notes with Knowles about your assailants. And we'd better get a medic to look at both your bumps. No, I'll make the coffee. What's this? Decaffeinated? All right, tea.' Which was mercifully kept in a caddy, so she couldn't tell that that was decaffeinated too.

Kate bit her lip – God, perhaps she'd put Craig through cold turkey! Perhaps caffeine-withdrawal had added to his problems. No. She put that to the back of her mind. What with his booze and his pot and God knew what else besides he was getting enough chemical stimulation.

The pot: she'd have to mention it to the investigating team. She'd bet her pension that Earnshaw hadn't. There might even be other drugs. Something else tapped at the foggy mess that passed for her mind this morning. 'Ma'am,' she began, 'did anyone ever check out the car I saw on Berry Head? If anyone did, I can't remember what the result was.'

Earnshaw frowned. 'I don't recall anything either. We'll get on to that this morning, too. Come on. It's almost eight already. Time we hit the road.'

Kate had to hand it to the Devon and Cornwall Constabulary. They might have been less than supportive of a grockle, an in-comer, but for Craig they were pulling out a lot of expensive stops, including a psychological profiler, who had been given the use of Knowles's office for the day. She was actually introduced by name: Dr Eve Stow. Dr Stow was a little older then Kate, perhaps thirty-five. But while Kate deplored her own current lack of style, this woman seemed to revel in hers. Why on earth didn't she at least wash her hair? Why had she never had her teeth straightened – or at very least scaled and polished within recent memory? And why choose to dress from charity shops when your salary surely ran to at least a working suit and shoes not down at heel? And why – why for goodness' sake – eschew the make-up that might have transformed a very plain woman with bad skin into a passable one? No, Kate wasn't impressed by Dr Stow. Not at first glance.

But she suspected she'd done her a major injustice as soon as she started to talk. Her eyes gleamed behind their pallid lashes.

'Kate, you're the one who's had, on the face of it, most to do with Craig. He has been in regular touch with DCI Earnshaw and Superintendent Knowles, of course, but people react differently to people further up the hierarchy, don't they? Especially to people with whom they're sharing a house.'

Earnshaw put in, 'He was a good cop, don't forget that.'

'I hope he still *is* a good cop,' Stow said patiently. 'But the more we know about him the quicker we should be able to find him. Don't forget you and Superintendent Knowles weren't just senior to him: you were actually pretending to be his parents. You know,' she added, chewing a ballpoint, 'I think we might do better to talk to you individually. Did someone say that Superintendent Knowles was being discharged from hospital this morning? Will he be well enough to come in here this afternoon, or shall I go out to him?'

'I'll find out,' Earnshaw said. 'No point in hanging round here, I can see. I'll be in my office. I've got work to do. I'll be wading through my in-tray if anyone wants me.' Earnshaw always stomped. This time her stomp sounded distinctly offended.

'Perhaps you should have spoken to her first,' Kate said.

'My job. My decision. OK, why don't we get a coffee and find somewhere more comfortable to sit?' She glanced bleakly at the police-issue walls. Nothing to make them human except some framed photos of cricket teams. 'Then you can tell me what it was like living with Craig Barnard.'

Stow leaned back in Knowles's chair: it seemed that space was at as great a premium here as at the West Midlands Police Headquarters building, and that there was nothing better on offer. 'Let's start with a fact. Craig set out on Wednesday with £250 in his pocket and hasn't been seen since – what does he do?'

'You tell me.'

Stow shook her head. 'I'm asking you, Kate.'

'Any other time of day I'd say he went to the pub, got nearly but not quite pissed with his mates, picked up some pot, bought something from a chippie. Now, Knowles and Earnshaw know—'

'I'll ask them what they know. Right now I'm asking you. "Pissed with his mates": police or civilian mates?'

'He'd got both. He wasn't supposed to consort with police officers, of course, not while he was undercover. That's the thing I hate most: being cut off from people you care about.' She wasn't about to weep, was she? 'But Craig kept in touch . . . Anyway, he'd certainly made some new mates recently. He went with them to see Torquay United play. Macker – he stayed with a guy called Macker. And he's still in touch with Ned – I don't think I ever knew her surname, but Knowles would be able to tell you. She's a gay motor mechanic. She touched on some problem he had in Bristol. But you don't want hearsay.'

'No. But I'll get on to that source now. Bear with me.' Stow leaned away from Kate to speak into her phone. 'Thanks for that: I'll be talking to Ned later, as you heard. OK. You and Craig. Why was there such antagonism?'

'I think we disliked each other on sight. We both have big egos. He was well briefed; I was in almost complete ignorance. He was in role from minute one. It took me time to get anywhere near mine. I studied my biog., the geography, the roads, the shops:

everything I could. But not him. I didn't even know his real name until yesterday.'

'Why did he dislike you?'

'I told you.'

'No. You said you disliked each other on sight. Why should he dislike you as soon as he laid eyes on you?'

'I suppose I looked smart and – sort of city-ish.'

'Whereas he—?'

'Looked like a country yokel. Yes, even his hair, his skin were right. Dr Stow, he *was* Craig Knowles. Never a word, a gesture, an allusion to suggest he wasn't. He played the part to perfection. No wonder I irritated him when I used language quite out of my character's repertoire. When I preferred clothes she couldn't afford. He must have seen me as some poncy amateur.'

'Was there anything about you he liked?'

'Maybe my memory. Yes. And I got the feeling that while he wouldn't have leapt around congratulating me, he was impressed that I was getting promoted quickly – when, that is, he knew I was on the accelerated promotion scheme. Before that, he assumed I was sleeping my way to the top. He got very angry about that.'

'Did you discuss that?'

Kate shook her head. 'The first weekend I was down, my – my boyfriend, partner, what have you – he came down and we spent it together. Craig – I was depending on him for a lift – deliberately made me late. And Rod and our relationship were certainly an irritation to him.'

'Did he have a relationship of his own?'

'According to Ned, there was an ex-wife. But I never asked him. There didn't seem to be—'

'Time?'

'The *right* time. Very soon we spent as much of our time apart as we could. It fitted in with the official scenario, after all.' She snorted. 'Do you know, he assumed we'd be sleeping together. He'd taken down the curtains in the spare room, and made up just one bed.'

'What did you feel about that? What did you say?'

'"In your dreams, baby." Or something like that. Hang on, Dr Stow: you seem more interested in me than in Craig. He wasn't even living in the same house as me when he went missing. I didn't drive him out or anything.'

Dr Stow might have been addressing a child. 'The more you tell me, the more I know about him. No one is blaming you or even thinking about blaming you. Just go on talking about him.'

Kate nodded. She hated this. Hated the knowledge that she might have picked something up earlier, which might have prevented this. 'OK. He resented sitting around while I was able to do things. I got into the Sophisticasun complex almost immediately; I was provided with a motorbike, which gave me independence. Though the bike was actually his idea, I think he saw it all as stealing a march on him. As if we were in competition, not co-operation. The only time he ever gave a hint that he might respect me was when I wouldn't grass on him. He – expressed his anger – about Knowles and Earnshaw kicking him out. And I wouldn't grass. Things seemed to improve after that.'

'Have you ever spoken about his anger? Or his violence against you?'

'Once when he got violent, I responded in kind. But – this is horrible – I found myself getting more and more into the role of a downtrodden wife. It was Knowles and Earnshaw who tackled him about the way he treated me.' She rolled up a sleeve to show her bruises. 'I didn't talk to him about his pot or the state of his room. I simply tried to avoid the issues.'

Dr Stow frowned. 'And you let him get away with some unpleasant act. What was it?'

Kate got to her feet. 'Do you have to know?' If she didn't spill the beans, Ned would. 'OK. He shat in my bed. He went into my room and picked all my things over and then he crapped, right in the middle of the bed.'

'And you told no one what he'd done!'

'No one except Ned, and only her because she heard me swear and came to see what was the matter.'

'And you didn't tell your bosses? Earnshaw and Knowles?' Stow squeaked with disbelief.

'In the police you don't want a reputation for grassing. People have long memories.'

'So do you plan your own revenge on Craig? Do, please, sit down.'

'Why? I'm not into that sort of thing – grass-cuttings in people's lockers or super-gluing car locks have never appealed to me. Boys' games.' Kate flushed. She sounded bloody supercilious, didn't she? She sat.

'OK. You didn't grass him up. And things seemed to improve. Tell me about that.'

'I wanted to make some effort . . . So I told him how I'd had to have therapy – handling maggots, as it happens – after my partner's death. Sexual partner as well as police partner. And he managed the occasional grin. But while I was talking, he was going through something. I'm sure of that. You see, I reckon something happened while he was undercover. Something that traumatised him. Something that's mucked him up. Post traumatic stress disorder. Isn't that what they call it?'

Stow laughed. 'They do indeed. If, and it's a big if, that's what's the matter with him, a proper debriefing—'

'I don't know whether he was debriefed or not. If he was, I bet he wasn't co-operative.'

Dr Stow said slowly, 'You've given me a picture of an angry man, full of latent and sometimes actual violence. Do you think that that anger might have turned against himself?'

'I don't know. He never seemed the suicidal type. But who does? No. Not with that £250 in his pocket.'

'So what would you say has happened to him?'

Kate looked round the room, finding only straight-backed cricketers for inspiration. 'You know, this may sound odd, but I'd say he's gone to find himself a bit of the action. On Dartmoor or even at Cockwood.' She leaned urgently forward. 'And if he has, I'm afraid something may have gone badly wrong.'

*   *   *

There was to be a lunchtime briefing for Earnshaw, Kate and Knowles, who would be discharged by midday. Meanwhile, Kate found her way to Earnshaw's room to tell her that Stow wanted her and to ask if she could use her phone and computer. 'That Birmingham car, Gaffer – sorry, Guv.'

'OK. You can have a look at some more mug-shots, too: that woman with the lungs has sent another batch down line.'

'Mona? Good. Guv – this afternoon. Is there – will I be needed?'

Earnshaw stopped in the doorway. 'If you think I can't tell when someone wants to slide off and do something they shouldn't, you can think again.' She stepped forward, inspecting Kate more closely. 'What do you want to do? Get your roots done or something? No, I'll give you that – you're not a skiver. Not usually. You know what I think? I think you were planning a little ride on that machine of yours. To Chagford, and our aggressive pig-farmer. There! Got you! No, Power. Not without back-up. And not until the medics have compared your lump with Knowles's.'

Was it concern for staff or concern for police work? Kate had better give her the benefit of the doubt. She switched on the computer and fed in the Audi's registration number. Very soon she dialled a familiar Birmingham number, to be greeted by a familiar groan.

'Sue, I wouldn't be asking this if it weren't important.'

'No need to apologise, Kate: it's just that my in-tray's over-flowing and I've just had a phone call from my son's school to say they think he's got glandular fever and would I come and collect him. I'll pass you on to Colin: he'll know some-one.'

Colin was the one she'd wanted in the first place, of course. But Kate knew her hierarchies, and Sue was usually good for a natter. Not as good as Colin, of course, who listened to Kate's account of what had been happening to her with a mixture of incredulity and anger. But after ten minutes' satisfactory sympathy, support and gossip, he had to give her the names and phone numbers she was after. Community officers all over Birmingham. If they didn't know something about black Audis with tinted windows, no one would.

28

'G ood news or bad news? The bad's that our Audi driver's name is Earle Gray. Sorry,' she added as everyone groaned, 'I've already done all the jokes with my contact in Brum. The good news is that he's alive and well, living in a block of council flats in Quinton. That's a suburb of Birmingham. He's got no conviction, as yet, because he's never been found with enough on him – cash or cannabis. But the local beat officer knows Earle's collar-size.'

'He's fingered it that often, has he?' Earnshaw grunted. 'Has he pulled him in again?'

'Not without your or Superintendent Knowles's say-so, Ma'am. Parking on Berry Head isn't a crime. But as soon as you have anything you'd like to talk to him about, Kim Bolton will go ahead. Here's his direct line.' She passed the paper across.

'Good. What did the quack say about your lump? And yours, Guv?' Earnshaw turned to Knowles.

Knowles snorted. 'There's some information easier to come by if you're dead, it seems. But since neither Kate nor I wished to oblige with post-mortem evidence, no one could say anything worth saying. Especially as Kate had the temerity to move while she was being thumped. And then to ice the bruise.'

'Nothing at all?' Earnshaw was visibly chastened.

'Not even the same blunt instrument. Seems it was your teapot, Leeds, that he used on me. Well, young Gregorie admits it. He's singing the "Hallelujah Chorus" all of a sudden. Not the song we want to hear, but there you are.'

Despite herself, Kate touched her bruise. 'The whole song, or just a bit? Does he admit hitting me, for instance?'

'Oh, according to the interviewing team, he's like one of those people who goes over the same bit of melody time and time again – drives you mad. This particular song is that he saw you in Kenton—'

'Not the Cockwood kitchen?'

'Absolutely not. Coming out of the village store. He says he fancied you straightaway and that he followed you on impulse and lost his head and he's dreadfully, dreadfully sorry. Never done it before. Ever.'

Earnshaw asked, 'Odd to have an impulse that makes him hang around while a doctor comes and goes. You'd have thought lurking in the lane might have made him a bit more rational. Are we really supposed to believe that?'

'Until someone much higher up tells us not to. You see, I reckon it's someone much further up in his organisation who's pulling his strings. When he wanted a lawyer, he didn't want someone from a nice old-established Exeter firm. Goodness me no. He's got this London lad zapping down the motorway to advise him. And although Gregorie doesn't look as if he lacks a penny or two, these top buggers don't come cheap.'

'You think someone else is footing the bill?' Kate asked.

'I think someone is telling our Gregorie what to say. And when they find out who his victim was, they'll tell him to say someone different. In the meantime, they don't want anyone rocking the organisation's boat. We've got enough to hold him on. And we've gob-swabbed him.'

'But you got his DNA from that tissue I saved.'

'Your word. We've had his dear little mouth officially deprived of a few cells and can compare them officially with any other samples from scenes of crime. Your part in this, Kate, will be kept under wraps just as long as it possibly can be.'

'What about dropping charges and releasing him – seeing where he goes?' Earnshaw suggested.

'We know where he'll go. Back to Oxford. He's got a legitimate life there: work, accommodation, everything. I can't imagine his lawyer letting him flit at this stage.'

Kate, whose head was beginning to throb again, was getting

angry. Another case of the villain being treated with kindness while the victim – hell! She wasn't a victim! Not her. To cover her sudden rush of tears, she asked, 'What did they find out at Cockwood? The lads who went out?'

'As you'd predicted, Kate. A terribly concerned Gary Vernon, wringing his hands. "Problems with food hygiene? Moi?" And nothing interesting in the freezer.'

'Shit. I suppose it'd be too risky to say I remembered seeing stuff in the freezer that shouldn't have been there and could that be a motive for socking me? No.' Kate let her head droop in apology – yet no one else had come up with anything more positive. 'And I suppose there's no news about Craig?'

Stow, who'd been so silent Kate had forgotten she was there, shook her head. 'Not yet. But I've told the team they should think about concentrating their efforts on Dartmoor: I'm sure you're all correct – he'll have gone after the Range Rover man.'

Kate opened her mouth to object but Knowles intervened stiffly, 'If you two had made more of an effort to get along then he wouldn't be missing now. Oh, I know I told you –' he nodded curtly at Stow – 'it was his fault, mostly. But when push comes to shove, it takes two to argue. But if you'd been more – less . . .'

'Funny thing, Guv: the less I stood up to him the more aggressive he got. But he certainly didn't like it when I did give him as good as he was giving. But that doesn't help us.'

Stowe said positively, 'For what it's worth, I'm sure he was directing anger outwards, not at himself.'

'In other words, he hasn't topped himself. But that doesn't get us very far: Dartmoor's a big place. Meanwhile, Kate, it seems as if the whole case is back in your hands. We need something concrete—'

'Isn't extortion enough? Putting pressure on to people to sell up? Softening them up with bogus offers?'

'This is all guesswork,' Earnshaw said, 'and all pretty small beer. But people are following up each strand, of course.'

Kate knew that tone of voice. She'd heard it often enough when bosses knew they couldn't ignore something but were damned well not going to waste their officers' valuable time prioritising it. So she tried a different tack. 'The plants?'

'None on the site any longer, of course. Vernon says there were some brought in for a special function, which was cancelled at the last minute.'

'I didn't know anything about a function.'

'You were only a cleaner.' Knowles's voice dropped to sub-zero. 'And we've got no photographs.'

'You mean they didn't come out? All those I took of the Vernons' guests—'

'Not those. The ones in the freezer,' he said, tetchy as an officer with a sore head. 'And we've no idea who's in the scam, who isn't. There may be any number of quite innocent people doing a decent day's work for a company that just happens to be bent. We want to nail the right people, Power. Get back in there tomorrow and do your job. Unless you'd rather be out on Dartmoor beating your way across acres of heather looking for the body of a dead colleague? Because that's where I'll be.' He touched his bruise.

Oh, the bastard, pressing emotional buttons. 'I presume there isn't a genuine choice, Sir? Because as a matter of fact I'd like to be too.'

Storming out of a meeting like that was never a good idea, not when you knew that the Super was in the right, you in the wrong. But it was either that or let them see her in tears. And that was just about the worst thing she could do.

Kate found a loo and locked herself in. If she'd known why she was crying it wouldn't have been so bad. It couldn't – could it? – be for the missing Craig. It couldn't be because they were asking too much of her. No, in many respects she was quite looking forward to nosing round the Cockwood apartments. It wasn't because she'd hoped for a weekend's rest: no, the quicker she tied up all the loose ends, the sooner she'd be back with Rod.

Oh, enough of this. Dousing her face in cold water, she pulled her shoulders straight and set off briskly down the corridor: she'd take a bloody bus back to Newton Abbot.

*   *   *

She soon found another reason to yearn for Brum: at least they'd got their public transport sorted there. At peak times the number fifty bus ran every four minutes. Well, neither Newton nor Exeter was quite the conurbation that Birmingham was, and of course the distances were greater. But the bus journey had been endless – would have been worse if she hadn't hitched a lift with a couple of WPCs in a patrol car. They'd promised to drop her at one of the stations, but had had to respond to an incident. So there she was, at the mercy of a bus system that took her well over an hour to get to Newton. On impulse, she did what she was quite sure Kate Potter wouldn't have done: she took a cab from Sherborne Street. Enough was enough. She couldn't face the long walk in heavy drizzle. At last she put her key in the lock. She deserved an aromatherapy bath and a decent take-away. In fact, she promised herself both. But she knew the thoughts of the evening were to keep her mind off the present. She had to go into an empty, inimical house. Once in, telling herself it was from habit but really knowing she was afraid of a repeat of yesterday, she stood straining her ears. But the only sound – loud, banal, but still enough to make her heart pound – was the phone. Well, if she were in for a bollocking, it could wait until she'd locked herself in. And picked up the post, which was a computer-addressed envelope with a Birmingham postmark. She knew of only one man to use such good quality stationery. Inside was an anonymous postcard showing the sights of the city with an X on the back. She sat on the stairs and cried over it. What a lovely man Rod was.

The phone rang on. She'd better answer. 'Yes?'

'Kate? I've been trying to get you all day.'

'Mr Vernon!'

'Where've you been?'

'Well, the doctor wanted another look at my head, didn't he? And when it's not an emergency, you have to take potluck with the appointment. And I thought I'd have a look at some shops but I gave up.'

'You sound really fed up.'

Who wouldn't be? Jesus, attempted rape, a bang on the head, another assault? Even Kate Power needed more than twenty-four hours to get over that lot. But she was Kate Potter. 'For two pins, I'd just do a flit and skip up to Birmingham. But – no, after all you've done for me, I won't let you down. I'll be there tomorrow. I'll make sure I give you proper notice and everything, honestly.'

'I'm sure you will, Kate. But let's hope it doesn't come to that. In fact – well, I wasn't phoning about that at all. I was – no, it's a real cheek, specially if you've had a hard day.'

'No, not so bad. Just a lot of time-wasting, that's all. I know the saying, "When God made time he made plenty of it". But not so much you want to spend hours staring at posters waiting your turn. And then the bloody bus back – the doc had said not to ride my bike until he'd seen me again, though he says I can now.'

'Oh dear. Are you up to . . . you see, we were wondering, Julie and I . . . We've been offered some tickets for a concert out at the university, and you know what Julie's like about music. And the kids'd really appreciate knowing you're all right.'

Kate laughed. 'Well, I'd love to see them. What time?'

'Seven. And Kate –'

'Yes?'

'No need to dress up this time. Come as you are.'

Kate stared at herself in the mirror: yes, she really would rather be out in the thin, drenching rain, falling over roots, skin torn by undergrowth, than spending a cosy evening with two lovely children. Much. She'd have to make sure this was the last time she saw them. What excuse could she find? Some infection? Evening classes? A new love in her life? She'd think of something.

Meanwhile she'd better put on some make-up and make herself respectable. Hell: no time to eat. She'd ask the Vernons if she could make herself a sandwich. She couldn't imagine them objecting. After all, she wouldn't be able to console herself on the way home with a magnificent chicken tikka in a naan from a convenient chippie.

Should she take something for the kids? Something they'd remember as a farewell present? She toyed with the idea of sweets or chocolates. No. They had plenty of those. And they weren't really connected with her. She'd simply leave the book and the game behind.

It was becoming the norm for Kate Potter to tidy up while the children fell asleep, so she didn't feel that that was prying. One glance at the Vernons' bedroom told her she should start there. Poor Julie: she hadn't looked as if she had the strength to sit through a couple of hours of a string quartet. She certainly hadn't managed to hang up her clothes and put her shoes away. Nice things, too. The sort of shirt Kate bought, and better shoes. Gary usually slung his things on to an ottoman. Only his jacket was there this evening, part of the cheapish suit he wore to work when no one important was due. Smoothing it out, Kate hung it up and stowed it in his wardrobe. It really needed pressing. If there were other ironing, she might just do it. Then she paused. Where were his shirt and trousers?

Before she went downstairs, she tried his office door again: still locked. Was she surprised? Sighing, she set off to tidy the kitchen. It didn't take long, and the ironing basket was empty. She'd check the washing machine – perhaps that needed emptying. Why were the only things in it Vernon's shirt and trousers and socks? You washed more than that in a load. And why were his shoes in the utility room, obviously waiting to be cleaned? How had a man with such a sedentary job got his feet so mucky?

He'd been checking those plants off his premises, of course. Obvious.

Why not slump in front of the TV? It was all she felt up to. But even as she eased off her shoes she thought of her colleagues searching Dartmoor for Craig. Poor bastards. In this weather.

But they weren't searching Cockwood. They would soon. And what would they find? Slowly, inexorably, Kate found herself getting to her feet and heading for the utility room.

Afraid to ask herself why she was doing it, she searched the kitchen for freezer bags, a knife and a pair of fine scissors. And Julie's rubber gloves.

With infinite care she teased out some still stained fibres from the inside of the right cuff. More from the turn-up. And then she scraped mud – ominously, there were two different colours, one horribly familiar if you'd ever seen the site of a bloody death – from the shoes.

No point in getting emotional now. She still had a brain. She'd better use it. Should she return the clothes to the machine or shake them out and leave them to dry? On the whole, the less she had to do with them the better, even if the Vernons might find her inefficiency uncharacteristic.

If they did, they were quick to excuse it. Julie, sinking down on the sofa beside her, exclaimed at her pallor, insisted on inspecting the bruise and called to Gary, still in the hall, to bring wine for all of them.

'Did you get around to eating? No, I bet Gary five pounds you wouldn't. What a good job we stopped off on the way! Gary said you'd liked the curries in Birmingham, so we got this huge take-away. Do you mind eating in the kitchen? If you get the stuff on the carpet the stain never comes off.' Gaily as she was talking, however, she could hardly stagger to her feet. Kate linked arms with her as if in a sisterly way, but in fact supporting her as best she could.

'Now, we bought a mixture of mild and hot,' Vernon said, 'since we weren't sure how used to curry you are. But first we've got poppadums and dips. Then there's starters. And only then do we get on to the curries proper . . .'

How could she eat with them, knowing what she'd tucked into her panniers? More to the point, how could she eat with a man she thought was a killer? But she had no proof. And Julie hadn't harmed anyone. If Julie had to chide her for not eating, it would draw attention to the fact that she herself was doing no more than crumble the poppadum and sip the lager, which Gary insisted went better with the meal than wine.

And the food was very good.

There must be something neutral she could talk about.

'This concert – this chamber music. I've heard music on the radio, of course, and my friend took me to something in Symphony Hall in Birmingham: she said I had to go there once. But it was all singing . . .'

'Symphony Hall! How wonderful! It's supposed to have the best acoustics in the country! I've always wanted to hear Simon Rattle conduct – or do I mean see him? Though of course he's left for Berlin . . .' As she talked, Julie seemed to brighten. She even ate quite well, though from time to time she'd look anxiously at Vernon, almost as if trying to prompt him.

He didn't take the hint, however, until they'd all passed on the selection of Indian sweets he'd laid on the table with a flourish. Coughing slightly, and looking at Julie as if both wanting to please her and hoping for support, he said, 'Kate – I know you said you felt like leaving Devon and going up to your friend in Birmingham. Well, we were hoping we could change your mind.' He poured more lager. 'Look, Kate. We know you're a wonderful worker. And we know the kids love you.'

'And I think you love them,' Julie said.

Kate nodded, looking from one to the other.

'Now . . . Look, there's some new treatment for MS coming on stream. Still experimental. But we've found this guy in the States who's prepared to put Julie on his test programme. A guinea pig, if you like.'

'Clinical trials,' Julie said. 'He says I'm ideal. Asked me all these questions via e-mail. And both my GP and my consultant are happy for me to go.'

'That's the problem, you see. The States or Australia. Not exactly half a mile down the road.'

She knew what was coming. God, please don't let them. They mustn't.

'So what we hoped –' they said together. Julie gestured Gary to finish, reaching across to take Kate's hand.

'What we both hoped was that you might give up working

for that tin-pot agency and come and work for us instead. As a full-time nanny.'

Let logic operate first. 'But they don't need a nanny. They're too old for that.'

'They need stability and love and a nice clean home to come back to. Nanny and house-keeper, I suppose.'

'But I'm not qualified. I mean, I can't cook or anything.' Jesus, how had she ever got into this?

'I've never seen you do badly at anything you've tried,' Vernon said. 'Look, it's late, and we can see that the idea's come as a bit of a surprise. Don't give us an answer now.'

Saved. For a while at least.

'Maybe we could talk about it in the morning? You will be in, won't you?'

'Of course I will. If I wake up – have you seen the time? Mind you, I'll be better off on my bike than I was this afternoon. An hour and a half it took me . . .'

29

Today she had to have a long talk with Vernon, and, given that camera in his office, not to mention the bug she herself had put in place, she had to talk to him outside, despite the rain. That meant they'd be out of range of the conference room bug, too. Kate didn't want what she was going to say to him to be overheard by anyone – certainly not recorded.

In the event, it was her cleaning work that gave her an opportunity. There was definitely a little lens glinting in the corner of the main bedrooms in the old apartments she tackled. Not only would showing them to him get him out of the office, it would open the conversation too. But not, of course, in the apartment. If she didn't want her police colleagues in on the conversation, she wanted his mates still less.

It certainly wasn't the best of mornings for a long talk in the open. The rain might have eased, but there was still a steady drizzle, and the trees and shrubs dripped dispiritingly. The leaves were mushy underfoot. Once or twice she'd been lucky to keep the bike upright, particularly on the road past Earnshaw's cottage, where she'd dropped off the soil and fabric samples. No, she hadn't woken Earnshaw. At least, she hoped not. She'd be in bad enough odour with her without that. Storming out of that meeting wouldn't have been the best way of pleasing her. And she didn't want to talk about what she was planning to do either. No, what she had to say must be strictly off the record.

As she told Gary Vernon, as they strolled across the grassed area towards the older apartments.

'What on earth do you mean, Kate?'

'I mean I'm going to ask you things you won't want to tell me, and possibly tell you things I shouldn't. Let's start with what I've just found in Apartments Twenty-three and Twenty-four, though. Mr Vernon: why are there surveillance cameras in the bedroom ceilings? No, don't try to deny it. The sooner this conversation's over the sooner we can be warm and dry.'

'I thought you wanted to talk to me about the job with the children,' he protested.

'I do. Later. But you must answer my question first.'

'"You must"! I don't have to do anything!' The pink and white cheeks flushed scarlet.

Oh, dear. She'd hoped he wouldn't bluster like this. 'Just answer it. Please,' she added as an afterthought.

'It's nothing to do with you.'

'I'm waiting,' she said, implacably.

'It's company policy.'

'Why? What sort of guests are you expecting, for goodness' sake? Terrorists?'

'How should I know? I tell you, it's company policy.'

Hell, she hadn't meant to get him on the defensive. 'I'm sorry, Gary. But if you do know, you should tell me. Trust me.'

Avoiding her eye, he shook his head.

'All right. Tell me why your office plants are in such a poor state when you've got an expensive contract to keep them healthy. I saw some memos before I shredded them, you see. And you had a huge delivery the other day. I saw you checking them. They disappeared very quickly. My theory is that it wasn't the plants that you wanted, but something else in the pots. Are we talking drugs, here?'

'Kate – you shouldn't be asking these questions. The less you know the better. For your own good, just forget everything you've seen, hand in your notice with the agency and come and work for us. Kate? You will, won't you?' He touched her shoulder.

'Let's talk about things here before I make a decision,' she said. 'You see, I think some of your colleagues are doing things they shouldn't. There's a scam for getting people out to far-flung

Sophisticasuns, isn't there? How does it work? People get stopped in the street, right, and asked a few questions. And, hey presto! They win a prize. Tell me about the prizes.'

'I don't know why you want to know this – my God, you're not Trading Standards?'

'No. Just tell me. I'm interested. Imagine I'm stopped. What if I won first prize?'

'The trip anywhere in the world? Well, if you can go at the drop of a hat, it's a real prize. All expenses paid. But it's like the old factory system. You're miles from anywhere, of course, because our complexes are in remote corners, and you want to buy some suntan lotion. The only place you can get it is the complex shop. And that only takes Sophisticasun currency. So you're paying way over the odds. But not many people take that option anyway. Who can at three days' notice?'

'Not people like you and me, anyway,' she said dryly, as if he were an honest worker.

'Precisely. But it's what makes people look at the offer. The second one's the one most people take. Anywhere in Europe for two weeks. You have to pay the airfares. But since we book everything, you can't go on a cheap flight. And we have a deal with the company we choose. And the drivers taking you from the airport. And again, people buy at our shops.'

Kate nodded. It tied up with what her colleagues had said, after all.

'The only really good deal is the free weekend in the UK, but while they say folk can go anywhere in the UK, they can't. Only a few take visitors. The rest are sold out throughout the year.'

'Sold out?'

'It's a well-run company – people like our complexes.' He spoke with genuine pride.

'I'm sure they do. But is that the only reason they're forbidden territory? Are they involved in other sorts of dodgy dealing? Money-laundering?'

'Good God, no. I suppose the transactions in complex currency abroad might just . . . But it's only a matter of a few pounds here, a few there. And there's nothing like that here, Kate. What do you take us for?'

She looked him in the eye. 'I wish I knew. I wish you were just into commercial sharp practice, but I think it's worse than that. The surveillance. The peripatetic plants. Gary, it'd be far better if you told me everything. Including,' she added, as if it were just an afterthought, 'where you buried Craig Knowles.'

Oh, God. She'd got it right. He crumpled.

'I didn't want to. I had to. A gun at my head. I had to. Kate, don't tell Julie. Please. Please don't tell Julie.' He was almost in tears.

'Did you kill him?'

'No! NO!'

'You just said you had to.'

'No. I had to bury him. I found Gregorie. It was Gregorie—'

She prayed he was telling the truth: a trip through the washing machine or not, the shirt would surrender its secrets to the forensic science team. Splatter marks. They'd show if the wearer had struck a blood-drawing blow.

'He'd hit him too hard. He was dying. I didn't even know who it was at first, but Gregorie made me go through his pockets. I wanted to phone the police – you know, saying we'd caught a burglar but things had gone wrong. But Gregorie wouldn't let— Kate, you've got to believe me. He died – very quickly. No pain.' He must at last have registered that Kate was supposed to be Craig's partner. 'This must be so dreadful for you . . . A drink? Brandy or something?'

The rain returned more viciously, lashing in sudden squalls their faces and hands.

'Show me where he's buried,' she said.

'But—'

'Now.'

'It's a long way.'

'Down by the old glasshouses? I still want to see.'

He led the way down, but not into the glasshouses. He pushed aside rhododendrons heavy with rain and eventually stopped, pointing to a mound quite unmistakable in shape. God, how amateurish: perhaps he was telling the truth.

They stared at it in silence.

'Can't we go now?' he pleaded at last.

'We have to talk. In there will do.' She pointed at the glass-house.

'It'll be so cold in there.'

Indeed, he was dithering, shaking as if possessed by a medieval ague.

'OK. Somewhere warmer. What was in the plant pots, by the way?' Catching him off guard had worked once – it was worth trying again.

'I don't know. I only do what I'm told. I count them in; then I count them out again. Like that war correspondent,' he said, looking sideways at her.

She didn't respond.

'Kate, I'm so cold.'

'Is there any apartment not bugged?'

He brightened. 'What about my office?'

'Oh, there's a camera there all right,' she said as dryly as she could. 'And a bug.' Let him think it was one of Sophisticasun's.

'What about the swimming pool?'

'What?' She stopped dead in her tracks.

'Oh, I shan't try and drown you or anything. I can't swim myself. But we'd see anyone coming . . . oh, come on, Kate.' He grabbed her hand and ran with her as if they were friends.

They could have been so easily, couldn't they? If she'd been fed into the system higher up the pecking order. If she became his housekeeper-nanny. If they'd all met at one of Julie's precious concerts.

He let her in through the glass doors, but didn't lock them behind him.

They faced each other in the foyer, full of well-lit display cabinets and dispensing machines. Energy drinks. Goggles. Floats. Confectionery. Some expensive looking towels and bikinis. And a lying police officer and a criminal desperate to tell the truth. She hoped.

'So tell me about Craig. Why did Gregorie kill him?'

'I'm sure he didn't mean to. I'm sure he just meant to lay him out cold.'

'Like he laid me out?'

Vernon stared. 'No. That wasn't him. That was Craig. And then Craig got something out of that big freezer, and made off. That's when Gregorie hit him. That's what he said, anyway.'

Kate's head was pounding again. 'Are you seriously telling me that Craig – Craig . . . is involved with all this?'

Vernon shook his head. 'I told you. He was taking something from the freezer.'

'You don't usually get killed for nicking a ready-made beef-burger.'

They managed sketchy smiles, pale images of the one they'd exchanged two days before.

'Or ready-made hot dogs.' Vernon fed money into the drinks machine. 'Coke?'

'Water, please. Thanks. So what did Craig take?'

'I've no idea. OK. But it's only a guess. You'd have to ask Gregorie.'

'I gather he's very talkative at the moment. But his memory's pretty selective. I'd like to have your theory.'

'You are going to press charges, then?' His eyes were terrified.

'Let's hear your theory. Craig. What Gregorie did was pretty serious. And you're an accessory, Gary. Let's not forget that, either.'

He lost so much colour she was afraid he was going to faint. She steered him to the receptionist's desk.

'There. Head between your knees. Deep breaths.' His hair was as fine as the children's. She kept her hand between his shoulders.

At last he nodded. 'It's OK. I'm fine now.'

'Come up slowly. And don't try and move anywhere quickly.'

'Trust you to know your first aid.' He turned baby-blue eyes on her. 'Except I can't trust you, can I? You're not Kate Potter at all. You're some sort of spy. Who are you with?'

'You make me sound like something out of James Bond! No. Much more boring. But it's not who I am or what I am that matters at the moment. And this is so off the record I shall deny every word if you even so much as hint to anyone I said it. Understand?'

'For God's sake!'

'No. For the children's sake. And Julie's. Gary, you've buried a murdered man. You're part of an organisation up to its ears in criminal activity. And you're the husband of a woman who's nearer to death than I like to think about and the father of two lovely children.' Aiming for authoritative, she fought to keep her voice steady. 'What you are going to do is come along to the police and tell them everything you know about the organisation. Fraud. Drugs. Blackmail. Craig's death. Every single last detail. You're going to turn Queen's Evidence.'

'I can't. I daren't.' He'd risen too quickly and was swaying again.

'Sit down. No use falling on this floor and cracking your skull. There's no alternative, Gary.'

For a moment they both thought of the water ten feet from them.

'No. You're not a pro. You couldn't make it look like an accident. And you blush too easily. You wouldn't last five minutes under cross-questioning. Would you?'

He shook his head, as if it were a matter for shame. Then he looked straight at her. 'Kate, I daren't talk to the police. Gregorie cracked Craig's skull as easily as if it was his breakfast egg. That's what they'll do to me if I talk. And it's not just me. It's the children. Julie.'

'Of course it is. You'd never sleep at night wondering who was going to get at them. When. How. And don't think of a quick bullet between the eyes. When the big boys get cross, Gary, they get very cross. Even with children. Which is why they've got to be sent down for a good long stretch.'

'They won't get everyone. Kate, what'll I do?'

She leant across and wiped his cheeks, slipping her arm round him. 'I told you: you turn Queen's Evidence. You've never heard of Witness Protection? If your evidence gets that lot as many years in jail as you can, you'll be spirited away and never surface again. You, Julie and the kids. That's what you've got to do.'

'So you're an undercover cop. I should have known. I had this cousin in the police . . .'

Didn't that dot an i somewhere?

'I just thought you were a really nice kid. I thought – it doesn't matter what I thought . . . All the time you were lying and cheating.'

'Lying, maybe. Never cheating. I never cheated on the kids. Or on your wife. Or on you. On a shitty organisation, maybe. What was in the freezer, Gary? I think you know.'

'I don't. I truly don't.'

'You've got to try harder than that, Gary.'

'No. Honestly. I'm too low in the organisation for that. Well, you saw. Dancing attendance on the bosses. Wheeling out Julie as hostess when she'd have been better off in bed. Dancing to their tune. You saw.'

She nodded. 'And so I'll testify. Why?'

'They found out about Julie and cannabis. God knows how.'

Perhaps there were other surveillance cameras she didn't know about yet?

'It might be all right to take it now, but it wasn't then. And I had to have a job to pay for it. Joining in was the price of keeping the job.'

She patted his shoulder. 'Who are the ones we need to send down? Especially Mr Big!'

'He was at the restaurant we went to.'

She reviewed the faces she'd seen. 'Not at your house?'

'Too lowly for him. He runs the drugs side, if that's any use. Ecstasy, mostly. He's even got an LSD lab: it looks like a barn, but it's a regular factory, I've heard.'

She saw the brutal face leering at her in her rear-view mirror as he shunted her down the long hill into Chagford. 'Up on

Dartmoor? I think I've met him. Does he grow cannabis in his greenhouse?'

'Pot? That's way beneath his notice!'

'Where do you get your pot from then?'

He managed a grim laugh. 'Funny. We get that from a bloke in Birmingham. I met him up there on a business trip. He's not a bad bloke. When he saw how ill she was, he started to bring it down when I couldn't go up there to get it.'

'Come on! Exeter. Newton. Plymouth even! There must be loads of dealers.'

'But I don't know who they are. You know, a respectable married man. And I was afraid to ask. In case it drew attention to us. Criminal offence, possession, in those days. And the company has a policy of sacking people who get into any sort of trouble, any at all, with the law. I didn't dare . . . Look, Earle's a decent guy.'

'How decent? Are you telling me he doesn't take a load of Ecstasy back with him?'

Vernon flushed. 'You don't really have to say anything about him, do you?'

'It's the big fish we're after, Gary, not the tiddlers.' She hoped it was true. She'd had enough of lying and deceit. 'Come on. We'll go and pick up Julie and the kids and take you straight to Headquarters.'

'Get them now? But Elly's got a party this afternoon. And it's Peter's Cubs' church parade tomorrow.'

She nodded. 'And school on Monday. Yes, all those nice everyday things. They'll miss all their friends, won't they? And all their toys. Gary, it'll be a terrible time for them. And for you and Julie. But what's the alternative?'

'Couldn't you just – keep quiet? You don't have to say anything! I could get some money together. If you—'

'I hope I'm not hearing that, Gary.'

He covered his face.

She tried to sound harsh. 'In any case, you've forgotten the small matter of a dead cop, Gary. You can't imagine them not finding his body. And they'll find the tiniest drop of blood on your clothes or shoes.' If they hadn't already.

'Cop? You mean—?'

'Oh, yes. He was undercover too. But forget I said that—'

'The way he treated you! Julie and I were—'

'Part of the job, Gary. Now, let's get back to you and the family. My colleagues will go to your home and pack essentials.'

He pulled himself to his feet. 'What about Julie's treatment? You can't stop her having that! It's her only hope!'

'I won't be stopping anything. Like you, I'm far too small a player for that.' Was she being ironic? 'But I'd have thought – did you mention Australia? I'd have thought if you sang sweetly enough that wasn't a bad bet. Her and the kids. You'd join them later, of course.' She thrust a tissue at him. 'Here – please!'

He mopped his eyes, blowing his nose and straightening up. He shot her a glance she couldn't read. 'No handcuffs, then?'

'On the contrary. Really matey, we'll be. The last thing we want to do is attract anyone's attention. Now what?' she demanded with as much asperity as she could manage.

He closed the door he'd started to open. Facing her, he held out the ball of tissue he'd used. 'Tell me: why do you need this as much as I do?' And he dabbed gently at her cheeks.

30

The Vernon family weren't the only ones on the move. In the late afternoon, Kate had been whisked from Newton Abbot to a safe house somewhere in Exeter. They'd produced a change of clothes and a bottle of hair dye. Well, it was something to do.

How was Craig's widow – they'd never actually divorced – passing the time? Was she grieving, forcing herself to organise a funeral? Kate knew from experience the police liked showy funerals for their own. And Craig had been one of their own far more than Kate could ever be. Poor bugger: so angry, so determined to have a bit of the action. But not, surely, so determined that he'd hit a colleague on the point of finding something. Surely he hadn't hated her that much. No, it must have been Gregorie. It would make the same m.o. for three people, after all. Would she be allowed to attend? It would make some sort of closure. God, Craig would have hated the term, dismissed it as psychobabble or worse.

Her colleagues would be in touch with her when they were ready, they said. In the meantime, there was food in the fridge, a radio and TV, and a smart laptop on which she might like to start preparing her report. There was no hurry. She could take as long as she needed. After all, she wasn't going anywhere for a bit. From time to time one of her colleagues would drop by. She must be prepared to move again at short notice if they thought it best.

She examined her prison carefully. It was an older version of the anonymous house in Newton, in a between-the-wars housing estate. Most of the houses were small semis. She was privileged to be in an equally small detached one. The bathroom had been upgraded, and so had the kitchen, not that she felt much like cooking. Not that she felt much like anything. A game of Sorry with the kids would have been about her level.

She wouldn't see the kids again. Ever.

That was something she could talk about when they started debriefing her.

God knew when that would be.

If only she could do something. Something active. Interrogating Gregorie for a start! She'd enjoy wiping the smug look off his handsome face. But she couldn't, of course. Even if she hadn't been undercover, she couldn't have done. Victims didn't question suspects. Not even to ask where they'd hidden the films and the photographs. And why, of course. Not even to ask them why it had been necessary to kill their partners.

If only it weren't so quiet. If only she could pop and tell Cassie she was all right.

There was nothing on TV – as Elly could have told her.

What would they be doing tonight, away from all their familiar things?

At least Peter had the board game, and Elly had the book – if they'd chosen to take them. They might have had more cherished books and toys. Perhaps they would remember her kindly. There was no reason for Gary and Julie to speak of her with anything other than kindness. Was there? So long as Julie got her treatment. At least Vernon should be spared a long sentence. He might not enjoy being transplanted, but it was better than the alternative, spending years in prison while his wife died untreated.

Hell, there must be something to drink somewhere.

All the same, he'd never stop looking over his shoulder for the man from Chagford, would he? Kenneth Arthur Hemmings. Such a normal name for a man whose drugs empire ran to millions – those pots had been full of high-grade LSD and Ecstasy – and who enjoyed tormenting people on the side. But the Vernons might not be grateful, any more than she was grateful at the moment. She picked up a mug and slung it as hard as she could at the kitchen wall. She felt so bloody angry.

And frustrated. Where were the photos? They hadn't found anything in Gregorie's car. Where could he have stowed them? Well, if they were anywhere in the complex they'd come to light. She could trust her colleagues to find a pin there if they'd been looking for one. But she'd bet her pension that the contents of the black bag weren't anywhere near Cockwood, any more than the Escort would be. She still didn't even know for sure what the photos were. The best she could come up with was the theory that they were the result of hours of silent surveillance on people who thought they could do what they liked in the privacy of their own apartments. A bit of S and M – something kinky while they were on holiday. But why go to the trouble of killing someone? Just for that?

No. It must be something more serious. Something much more. Cons didn't kill unless they could help it – it drew too much attention their way. As Vernon had told her when she'd left sensitive material unshredded, you couldn't make mistakes when millions of pounds were at stake.

There was a double knock at the front door. It was a signal devised so she'd know that it was Fanny, her liaison colleague, but she checked through the spyhole nonetheless. Yes, it was Fanny, beaming and twiddling her fingers in a baby-wave. At least she seemed to have brought something with her: she was flourishing a carrier bag like the Chancellor on Budget Day.

'I thought you might fancy a curry,' Fanny announced. 'And a bit of news. Oh, dear – had a bit of an accident, did we?' She flicked a shard with her toe.

A minder sounding like a geriatriac nurse was just what she bloody needed. Not that anyone would dare speak to Cassie like that.

'What news?' Kate seized the carrier and led the way into the kitchen, as if it were her territory. Yet she didn't even know where the plates were kept.

'They've found Craig's body. Where you said it was. Gregorie says it was an accident, of course.'

'Surprise, surprise. But he does admit he did it?'

Fanny looked at her, very oddly. 'Actually, no. He says Vernon did it. And that Vernon hit you. And that Craig came to your rescue and got hit himself. Only harder.'

'Craig came to my rescue?' Thank God for that. '*Vernon?* Is there any evidence?'

'It may be that something will come up at the post mortem. You know, they can sometimes tell whether the killer was left- or right-handed.' She smiled, just as if Kate were an infant with special educational needs, not a woman who numbered a Home Office pathologist among her close friends.

'And the photos?'

'He says they were Vernon's. Hard-core porn.'

'So where are they now?'

'In the Teign estuary, sharing a bag with a big brick. Gregorie says Vernon asked him to get rid of them, so he did. He parked the car on the bridge and slung them over.'

'He must have caused a wonderful traffic jam. There'll be witnesses, at least.'

'Oh yes. Witnesses that he did it. But not who told him to. And not what they were, of course.'

'They don't buy the hard-core porn story?'

'Do you?'

'I don't buy the idea of Gregorie doing anything for Vernon. He claimed that Vernon did things for him, not the other way round.'

'Well, then. I know what you city types think, but we don't all have straws in our hair, you know. In fact, I think you'll find rural police are more multi-skilled than the average city cop.' Fanny nodded the point home, sticking out a stubborn jaw. 'I might as well tell you, there's a feeling at HQ that your Mr Vernon may not be the lily-white boy you think he is.' She raised what looked horribly like a complicitous eyebrow: it said, *Women working undercover always fall for the scrote*. 'Still, the big thing is, he's prepared to sing like a cageful of canaries. We'll get a lot of other scrotes even if we do have to send him off to the Costa del Somewhere at the tax-payers' expense.'

Kate took another mug from the tree on the windowsill and hurled it at the wall.

Fanny blinked.

'Oh, sit down and eat your tea, do, while I get this lot up.' She fished under the sink for a dustpan and brush. 'That's the trouble with grand gestures. Always leave such a mess, don't they?' She started to sweep. 'Well, I hope you think it was worth it.'

Kate stared. It wasn't like her to do such things. 'I don't know,' she said 'I just don't know.'

'Well, how does it feel to have located the biggest LSD and Ecstasy factory in the south-west?' Earnshaw bustled into the hallway, thrusting at Kate a couple of thick Sunday papers from a Sainsbury's carrier.

Kate shrugged, shaking her head. The discovery had been pretty accidental, after all.

'And those lovely bonds you nicked.'

'Oh, those fancy things in the Vernons' bedroom?'

'Exactly what we were looking for. Even better than the faxed ones you got hold of. Sophisticasun were ripping off British pensioners £1000 a time. Disgusting!'

Kate nodded absently. Were they even in the same league as all those drugs? Still, the more material for the Crown Prosecution Service the better.

'How about a coffee? Oh, this isn't bad, is it? Nice and new.' Earnshaw patted the work-surface. 'Your friend Vernon is singing like a cageful of bloody canaries.'

Kate bit back a scream – couldn't they at least come up with a different cliché?

'His line is that until recently he was just a simple middle manager. He insists most of his colleagues are just that. Ordinary employees. Then his bosses discovered that his wife was using pot

and blackmailed him into working for them. Well, whatever . . .
Aren't you impressed?'

'I knew all that already, Ma'am. It's the photos I'm interested
in. Shall I – would it help if I were to talk to him again?'

Earnshaw appeared not to hear. 'He's dished dirt on a number
of the faces and voices you recorded.'

'Is it accurate dirt?'

Earnshaw touched the side of her nose. 'It looks as if it all
hangs together, anyway. Apart from the surveillance cameras.
He couldn't explain those. But they'd tie up with your theory
about blackmail. And the missing films and photos.'

'Seems such a heavy hammer to crack such a tiny nut,' Kate
said, doubtfully. 'Anything on something really big and juicy?
After all, it was some Big Guns that sent us in. You wouldn't
think they'd bother with comparatively trivial stuff like this. Not
unless it was one of them that got his or her fingers burned.'

'Oh, I shouldn't think so.'

'Well, what, then?'

Earnshaw blinked. 'Why do you ask?'

'Just interested.' But not enough to hit her head on a brick
wall any longer. 'Any news of Craig's funeral?'

'You didn't take much interest in him while he was alive! No,
I should think it highly inappropriate if you turned up. Imagine
what his wife would think.'

Easy sentiment. 'Ma'am, we've been all over this. Let's write
Craig and me off as incompatible. But he was a human being
and he's dead, and I'd have liked—'

'To pay your respects?'

Not quite. But there was no point in arguing. 'Tell me: have
they established why he was at the complex anyway? And at
that hour and in that place?'

Earnshaw blushed deeply and probably painfully. 'There was
a sense that you weren't getting things done.'

'Whose sense? Are you saying you sent him in behind my
back? Jesus! After all the stuff I'd just got for you! But that
doesn't explain why he should sock me.'

'It might have been Vernon, of course. And it wasn't very hard.'

'Only because I moved! Are you seriously telling me he was in there with your blessing with licence to knock me unconscious?'

'Well, not exactly. But we – you know, with his family, we want a – a decent front . . .'

'Oh, I bloody do know. Saint Craig. While the truth is he got fed up, decided to act the maverick, and while we were all worried sick about him nipped back to the complex to solve everything himself. Except he doesn't. He gets himself killed and fucks up a whole enquiry. Shit!' She slammed her hand on the surface. The kettle slopped. 'That's the long and short of it, isn't it?'

In a deep silence, Earnshaw laid the newspapers on the table, carefully folding the carrier bag. 'Perhaps it wouldn't hurt for you to talk to Vernon again. He did seem to like you. It'll take some arranging of course.'

Suddenly she was tired of all the cloak and dagger stuff. 'We could talk on the phone?'

In the event it was face to face at another anonymous house. The officer who let her in was armed. Perhaps she'd welcome a bit of that sort of company herself. Any sort of company, really. Her own, even enlivened by Solitaire and Free Cell on the computer, was beginning to pall.

She and Vernon hardly acknowledged each other's presence. Was he feeling tired or guilty at not having been straight with her?

'Let's go in the garden,' she said. 'The sun's trying to break through and I could do with some fresh air.'

Her armed colleague stood at the back door, scanning garden sheds and allotments for signs of hostility.

'Julie and the children?'

'Fine. Not happy but fine. They're sorting out documentation for Australia and Julie's treatment.'

'Good. I need to ask you one or two things, Gary – just to get them straight in my own mind.'

'If it's about the surveillance cameras, I've no idea – unless it was to keep an eye on us. The staff. I didn't even notice that one in my office. I suppose they may have wanted to see if the owners were doing anything to the detriment of the apartments. I'll tell you this – there was a rumour the Boss wanted some put in bathrooms. Actually in the loos. Sick, eh?'

'Sick.'

'I'm sure that's all it was, Kate. And I bet Hemmings had the photos kept in his nearest complex so he could go and take a shuftie when he felt like it. Julie loathed him. Said he was far worse than Gregorie. Is that it?' He shivered in the autumn wind.

'Not quite, actually. I wanted to ask about something someone said right at the start of my stint with you. Someone at the agency. They said your staff turnover was unusually brisk. That people wouldn't stay long. Why was that, Gary?'

He shrugged. 'I was always telling head office we needed to pay more for loyalty. The minimum wage, that's what people were getting – even skilled people. I mean, cleaners – they wouldn't expect much. But – well, I never had a proper PA all the time you were there. Remember how you sorted out my fax? Looked after my flowers? And the girls in the office were real bitches to girls who did give it a try.'

Hmm. Yes, she'd had the silent treatment. 'But there must have been something else. Jobs aren't easy to come by, down here. Not out of season. What made people leave? I mean, you expected a great deal of them – they certainly didn't have enough time to get everything done each day. But for an agency to notice . . .' She turned to him. 'Well?'

The bugger was looking shifty. No. Just puzzled. Maybe. It'd be easier to believe him.

'So it's really just a case of bad industrial relations?'

'They couldn't even get discount in the shop.'

'OK. Tell me something else. Just between the two of us, if

you like. Why should Gregorie, who claimed to be your boss, get rid of those photos at your behest? That's what he says, anyway.'

Vernon chuckled. '"Your behest!" It must have been really tough for you being Kate Potter. Well, I'd say he got rid of them because he had to.'

'But you can have a guess. And you'd know if there was anything similar at another site.'

'Your people' – he let the words sting a little – 'will have been through every deep freeze in every complex, won't they?'

'Do you reckon they'll find ready assembled burgers and hot dogs?'

'I shouldn't think they'll find anything else. As I said, the Boss . . .' He mimed a man jerking himself off.

'Why not keep them somewhere nearer his – his factory?'

'No point in taking extra risks.'

It all hung together. Almost. 'Come on, Gary: I hate leaving a case with loose ends trailing all over the place.'

He spread his hands helplessly. No. He knew nothing.

'Let's talk about Gregorie again. Why should Gregorie be so anxious to get rid of them? And lie?'

Now he did look ashamed. 'I should have let you get him arrested. He's not a nice man, Gregorie. I should have supported you better the night he attacked you. And told you to go to the police, not tried to talk you out of it. The Boss isn't the only one to take photos. Gregorie did too. And of people – one or two quite surprising people. Some women who should know better find him attractive. Well, more than attractive. Willing to – to do it with him. And he took photos while he was – while they were . . .'

'I suppose he didn't try to take photos of women workers? Shit, Gary, why didn't you support them? Why didn't they complain?'

'Blackmail. But it was only a few. The rest were just plain pissed off with their wages. And it's awkward to get to by bus. That sort of thing.'

She wanted desperately to believe him. 'In addition to these women?'

'A couple of very famous ones. Well, not famous themselves. But one – let's just say her dad's . . . He wouldn't want people to know his daughter shagged a bloke in the time-share apartment she owned. Especially in such – well, they were inventive.'

'So Craig died so the information didn't come out. Tell me, did you kill him? And clout me?'

'I'll go on oath it was Gregorie.'

She'd bet he would. 'Why didn't Gregorie want the photos saved as a bargaining tool?'

'He did. I didn't. Imagine – imagine Elly doing that and being photographed. I couldn't bear to see them. So I thought this Minister might not. I talked him out of it. Said it was too risky. Said if he got rid of them I'd keep shtum. Look, I'm freezing.'

So was Kate. She turned on her heel and left him where he stood.

'Isn't it nice when everything comes together?' Earnshaw observed, rubbing her hands with glee before wrapping the right round a tumbler of the best single malt the Exeter pub could provide. 'It makes everything worthwhile, doesn't it? Sensible judge. Sensible jury. Sensible sentences. Yes, it was all worth it, wasn't it?'

Kate sipped white wine and thought about her new inspector's uniform hanging up at home and about the supper Rod had promised to cook. She thought of children uprooted from all they knew, a woman desperate to survive and a man who claimed he'd hit no one and had disposed of foul photos. Because they reminded him of Elly. The trouble is, you see what you want to see in everything, don't you?

Elly. Peter. Julie. And Gary. Had she fallen in love with the whole family? And if she had, did that mean she'd loved Gary, too? If only for that moment by the swimming pool?

And did she believe him because she wanted to? Certainly it had transpired that when the Home Office initiated the investigation, it wasn't because anyone expected to find what the press were now calling a Drugs Baron. The Devon and Cornwall Police were still convinced that he was in much deeper than he'd ever admitted, and there was of course no proof for his assertions. Gregorie denied them flatly, but since he was likely to go down for some nine rapes and attempted rapes, he would, wouldn't he?

She answered her own questions and Earnshaw's with the same words. 'I don't know.'

An extract from the beginning of the new Kate Power novel, *POWER SHIFT*

The briefing didn't make good listening. Drew's team was down to four, out of its full complement of seven.

'But not to worry. We don't have to argue about who gets the car today.'

'*The* car?' she repeated, before remembering she should have been coolly observing and waiting for her grand moment. 'You've – *we've* only got the one?'

'Two. One's double-crewed for fast response. The other is shared between the rest of the relief for routine calls.'

She ignored the swift turn of heads. 'And car number two is?'

'In dock. Gearbox. Supposed to be under bloody warranty, but the suppliers and manufacturers are arguing the toss.'

'Haven't they ever heard of courtesy cars? I'll get on to it. Can't manage without wheels. So who's on sickie today?'

The consequent snigger took her straight back to the school-room. Ah.

'The usual suspects, ma'am.'

'Gaffer,' she corrected crisply. 'Who are?'

'WPC Kerr – she has a lot of problems, m – gaffer: women's troubles, like.' Drew's sneer was a challenge.

'WPC Kerr's pregnant, we think,' said a stout African-Caribbean WPC, probably in her forties.

'Well, that's certainly a woman thing.' Kate grinned. 'And the other officers? Men's or women's troubles?'

'PC Parker's got a bad back. Has had on and off for a year or more.'

Kate made a note: Occupational Health. 'And—'

'Master Bates,' Drew said.

'Does he now? And what else is the matter with PC Bates?'

'Bad stomach.'

'Bad regularly?'

'Judging by how often he farts, bad all the bleeding time. But he's here more often than he's away.'

'Just about,' added the WPC, sotte voce.

Another one for Occupational Health, then. 'OK. You've prioritised today's duties then, Neil? Anything you can't cover?'

'A meeting with the Chinese Elders.'

'Time?'

'Three, I think.'

'Let me know for certain, and I'll try and clear a slot in the diary. And if you've got any other stuff someone new could tackle, let me have it.'

So far, so good. There'd been a distinct frisson of what sounded like approval and she had a sense that she'd started off on the right foot – at least with those that were there. She was just heading for the outer office – the team's name for it, though the office wasn't even on the outside of the building, when she heard voices.

'I heard she got a collar on her last job. A big one.' Who was that? Not Drew. Parker? No, he was the bad back, Tims, Steve Tims.

'Yes. Undercover. Down in Devon. But she lost one of her team.' That was Drew all right.

Losing a colleague was never good news. Suddenly she was on the back foot – or would be, if she wasn't careful. Risk time. She stepped forward, saying easily, 'Don't let the Detective Superintendent in charge hear you call it my team. Craig and I were just foot soldiers.'

'But he died,' Drew said. It was a statement, not a question.

'You take risks undercover.'

'Wasn't there rumour of an official complaint against you before he died?'

She raised her eyebrows: Drew was going much too far.

Hardback published by Hodder & Stoughton, autumn 2003.

JUDITH CUTLER

Power on Her Own

A Kate Power Crime Novel

Personal tragedy cut short Kate Power's accelerated-promotion career in the Met. She's lucky, though – Birmingham CID give her a job, and chance to make a new start in the house her great-aunt has given her. Soon Kate discovers that she's trying to fix up the house from hell, with garden to match. Domestic equals professional pressure: though most of her new colleagues are helpful and supportive, some just think she's fresh female meat to harass.

Some seem to think Kate's not pulling her weight in their current case of the abduction and abuse of young boys. Then personal life starts overlapping with the investigation. Should Kate follow the conventional line of enquiry, or strike out on her own?

nel

NEW ENGLISH LIBRARY
Hodder & Stoughton

JUDITH CUTLER

Staying Power

Flying home after a brief visit to Florence, Detective Sergeant Kate Power of Birmingham CID engages in a pleasant but trivial conversation with the businessman sitting next to her. Two days later he's found hanging from a canal bridge – with Kate's business card in his pocket the only means of identification.

It looks like a clear-cut case of suicide – but Kate isn't so sure. And, as her subsequent investigations prove, the cause of Alan Grafton's death – and its consequences – are more serious than she and her colleagues could ever have imagined.

Still regarded as a newcomer in the Birmingham police force, still battling against prejudice and intimidation among the ranks, still fighting to prove that she's got what it takes, Kate is determined to stick to her guns until she finally uncovers the shocking truth.

Staying Power is the second compelling and ingeniously-crafted novel in Judith Cutler's gritty crime series, an incisive examination of the contemporary police force – and life for women within it.

nel

NEW ENGLISH LIBRARY
Hodder & Stoughton

JULIA WALLIS MARTIN

The Bird Yard

'You won't be able to put it down.' *Essentials*

When twelve-year-old Joseph Coyne goes missing and is assumed to have been abducted, Detective Superintendent Parker makes a promise to the boy's mother: *We'll get him back, alive.* It proves to be a promise that Parker cannot keep, and when another lad goes missing in similar circumstances, Parker is led to an aviary in a derelict suburb of Manchester.

The aviary seems a magical place to the young and vulnerable, and Parker is troubled, not only by the birds, which he sees as macabre, but by the presence of a boy who is besotted with the prime suspect.

With the help of a criminal psychologist who has problems of his own, Parker attempts to gather together the evidence he needs; but the killer is aware that time is running out and he plans to kill again before Parker makes his move . . .

'Martin cleverly portrays the innocent obstinacy of vulnerable young boys, propelled towards a fate they can neither imagine nor believe.' *Sunday Telegraph*

nel

NEW ENGLISH LIBRARY
Hodder & Stoughton